ODYSSEUS

THE OATH

Also by Valerio Massimo Manfredi

ALEXANDER: CHILD OF A DREAM

ALEXANDER: THE SANDS OF AMMON

ALEXANDER: THE ENDS OF THE EARTH

SPARTAN

THE LAST LEGION

HEROES
(*formerly* The Talisman of Troy)

TYRANT

THE ORACLE

EMPIRE OF DRAGONS

THE TOWER

PHARAOH

THE LOST ARMY

THE IDES OF MARCH

THE ANCIENT CURSE

VALERIO MASSIMO MANFREDI

ODYSSEUS

THE OATH

Translated from the Italian by Christine Feddersen-Manfredi

The Overlook Press
New York, NY

This hardcover edition first published in the United States in 2014 by
The Overlook Press, Peter Mayer Publishers, Inc.
141 Wooster Street
New York, NY 10012
www.overlookpress.com

For bulk and special orders, please contact sales@overlookny.com,
or write us at the above address.

First published in Great Britain in 2013 by Macmillan

First published in Italian 2012 as Il Mio Nome è Nessuno: Il Giuramento
by Arnoldo Mondadori Editore S.p.A., Milano

Library of Congress Cataloging-in-Publication Data
Manfredi, Valerio, author.
[Mio nome è nessuno: il giuramento]
Odysseus : the oath / Valerio Massimo Manfredi ; translated from the
Italian by Christine Feddersen-Manfredi.
pages cm
Summary: "The first book in an epic new series following the life and
adventures of Odysseus, Valerio Massimo Manfredi's masterful new novel
renders the extraordinary world of ancient Greece in his own unique
way"-- Provided by publisher.
ISBN 978-1-4683-0921-8 (hardback)
I. Feddersen-Manfredi, Christine, translator. II. Title.
PQ4873.A4776M6613 2014
853'.914--dc23
2014023456
Manufactured in the United States of America

10 9 8 7 6 5 4 3 2 1

ISBN 978-1-4683-0921-8

To Christine,

ἀμωμήτῳ ἀλόχῳ

This is what went on in the times
in which the chimeras' shrieks
still echoed over the mountainside,
when the centaurs ventured down to sate their thirst
in the dusky twilight.

GIOVANNI PASCOLI

Prologue

How long have I been walking? I don't remember any more, I can't count days or months. Is that the moon, the sun? I can't tell. The night star will sometimes light up the infinite fields of snow with an intensity like that of the sun, while the daytime star rises from the fog-shrouded horizon like a pale moon. The ice reflects the light like water does.

How long has it been since I've seen a man? How long since I've seen springtime, the sea, the holm oaks and myrtles that nestle between the crags of the mountainside? I have met wolves. Bears. They haven't hurt me, haven't attacked me. I haven't laid a hand on my bow and I've survived all the same. I must; so that my journey may come to an end.

The last journey.

I've learned to talk with myself. It soothes me, and keeps my mind from evaporating. I miss my bride, her arms so soft and white. I miss her warm breasts and her black, black, black eyes. I miss my son, my boy, the only child I've fathered. When I left him he was still sleeping. Children sleep so soundly. He surely hates me: he had waited so long for me.

I miss my goddess with her green eyes, her perfect lips that have never given a kiss to a god nor to a mortal. She leaves no prints even if she walks at my side. Her breath won't condense: cold, it is, like the snow. She loved me once. She would appear in disguise but I recognized her anyway, anywhere . . . Now she doesn't speak to me any more, or is it I who cannot hear her?

Are you listening to me? Listening to me, son of a small island, son of a bitter fate? You incorrigible liar . . . How often have you plunged your bare hands in the snow to wash them of blood? But you've never succeeded.

You're being watched, can you feel it? Walk, walk, journey on, on and on, as the horizon slips away, escapes you, and the land never ends. Vast, boundless, shapeless and sterile as the sea, flat as a dead calm.

And yet, although you may not believe me, I am a king.

You, a king? Don't make me laugh.

Laugh as long as you like, for I am a king. Without a kingdom, without subjects, without friends, without, without, without . . . but I am indeed a king. I carried out great endeavours, commanded a great number of ships . . . Warriors. Friends. Comrades. Dead. I'm cold. Can you hear me? I'm cold! Where are all of you? Near me, here? Beneath my feet? Under the ice? None of you can see your cold breath either. All invisible.

On, on and on. I don't remember the last time I ate.

I don't know why my fate cannot play itself out, why I can't live like most men do, in a house, with a family, eating food prepared three times a day.

Athena. Do you still love me? Am I still your favourite? Perhaps this is my madness: my mind is connected to mysteries greater than I am, mysteries that I cannot fathom. The feet that go on and on, wrapped in the hides of rabbits that I have eaten, are my only way of seeing. There is no end to their journey, save the one prophesied by the seer who one moonless night I called up from the nether world. Where are they heading? A place like any other, but I will not know until I get there. I've lost count of the days and the nights. I never kept count, actually, and I don't know how long I've been walking. I don't even know how old I am. Certainly not young any more.

A mountain.

Rising alone like an island in the middle of the sea. And there's a cave. Refuge from the wind cutting at my face, the sleet piercing my eyes.

A cave. It's warm inside, on the bottom, where the wind has no room to move.

A rabbit is here. White on white. Hard to take aim, even harder to withstand hunger. How sweet would it be to give in to exhaustion, to let myself die slowly. Death, coming for me softly. Who would ever find me here?

Raw-boned, baring starved teeth . . .

Caught. Skinned. Devoured. Me, or the rabbit. What difference does it make? Since then, bones have piled up in front of my cave. And memories in my mind. Spring will return and I will meet a man who will ask me a question that I must answer. I'll have to remember everything, then. Remember the screams and the groans, the echoes of agony. On the floor of this cave lies the oar I was carrying on my shoulder. I found it abandoned on the shore at Ithaca one morning after I had returned – wreckage from some old shipwreck. How long had it been floating on the sea? Years. I recognized it from the butterfly carved into the handle. A handle once gripped by a comrade of mine. The fourth oar on the right. Old friend, asleep now in the dark of the abyss . . . but you sent me a sign. Time to start out again.

My ship. I miss her. Curved flanks like a woman's, soft and sensual. Like my green-eyed goddess. Lying broken in pieces on the bottom of the sea. My heart weeps. Stop weeping, heart of mine! You've been through much worse. Endless misfortunes, yes. Remember, try, at least, in your sleep. Remember it all. Memories are sweet: birth, life. The future is death, the death of a hero, the death of a rabbit. No difference, that is the awful truth.

The dim light is swallowed up by the night. The wind starts racing again over the plain, sighing in the darkness, rousing the long howl of the wolves, demanding snow, snow, snow. What long nights! The night will never end. Was there ever a sun that rose over mountains mantled with whispering oaks? My sun-kissed island, silent under the full moon, fragrant with rosemary and asphodel: did you ever really exist?

And yet one day long ago a baby was born on the island, in the palace on the mountain, an only son. He did not cry, but tried to talk at once, imitating the sounds he'd heard in his mother's womb.

Me.

1

THEY CALLED ME ODYSSEUS. It was my grandfather Autolykos, king of Acarnania, who gave me that name when he arrived at the palace a month after my birth. I soon realized that other children had fathers and I did not. At night, before going to sleep, I'd ask my nurse: 'Mai, where is my father?'

'He left with other kings and warriors to find a treasure in a faraway place.'

'And when is he coming back?'

'I don't know. No one does. When you go to sea you never know when you'll be back. There are storms, pirates, rocks. Your ship can even be destroyed, but maybe you manage to swim to shore, and survive. Then you have to wait until another ship comes by to save you and that may take months, or years. If a pirate vessel should stop instead, you'll be snatched up and sold as a slave in the next port. It's a risky life that sailors lead. The sea shelters any number of terrible monsters, mysterious creatures that live in her depths and rise to the surface on moonless nights . . . but now you must sleep, my little one.'

'Why did he go to look for a treasure?'

'Because all the most powerful warriors of Achaia were going. How could he not join them? One day the singers will tell of this tale and the names of those who took part will be remembered for all eternity.'

I nodded my head as if I approved but I really couldn't understand why he had to leave. Why should you risk your life just so someone can sing about you one day and tell of how brave you'd been to leave home and risk your life?

'Why do I have to sleep with you, *mai*? Why can't I sleep with my mother?'

'Because your mother is the queen and she can't sleep with someone who wets the bed.'

'I don't wet the bed.'

'Good,' said the nurse, 'so starting tomorrow you can sleep on your own.' And that's how it went. My mother, Queen Anticlea, had me moved to a room all my own with an oak bed decorated with inlaid bone. She had a fine woollen blanket embroidered with rich purple threads brought to me.

'Why can't I sleep with you?'

'Because you're not a baby any more and you are a prince. Princes are not afraid to sleep on their own. But for a little while I'll tell Phemius to keep you company. He's a fine young man. He knows lots of beautiful stories and he'll sing them to you until you fall asleep.'

'What stories?'

'Whatever stories you like. Of how Perseus fought Medusa, of Theseus against the Minotaur and lots of others.'

'Can I ask you something?'

'Certainly,' my mother replied.

'Tonight I'd like you to tell me a story, any story you like. Something that my father has done. Tell me about when you met him for the first time.'

She smiled and sat down on my bed next to me. 'What happened was that my father invited him to a hunting party. Our kingdoms were next to each other; your father's was west, on the islands, and my father's was on the mainland. It was a way they could band together, join up against invaders. I was lucky. I could have been promised to marry a fat, bald old man! But your father Laertes was handsome and strong, and just eight years older than me. He didn't know how to ride, though. So my father taught him and gave him a horse as a gift.'

'That's all?' I asked her. I had imagined a fierce battle to free her from a monster or from a cruel tyrant who was keeping her prisoner.

'No,' she replied, 'but that's all I can tell you. One day, maybe. When you're big enough to understand.'

'I can already understand.'

'No. Not now.'

Another year passed with no news from the king, but at least now I had a teacher who knew all kinds of things and told me all about my father. Hunting adventures, booty raids, battles against pirates: much better stories than the ones my mother told me. He, the teacher, was called Mentor. He was young, with dark eyes and a black beard that made him seem older than he was. He had an answer for every question, except the only one I really cared about: 'When will my father be back?'

'So you remember your father?'

I nodded yes.

'You do? Then what colour was his hair?'

'Black.'

'Everyone has black hair on this island. What about his eyes?'

'Sharp. The colour of the sea.'

Mentor looked deep into my eyes: 'Do you really remember or are you just trying to guess?'

I didn't answer.

MY FATHER came back at the end of spring. The news reached the palace one day just before dawn and threw everyone into a real flurry. My nurse quickly had a bath prepared for the queen, then helped her to choose a gown and dress her hair. Her jewellery box was fetched so she could pick the pieces she fancied. Then nurse had me put on the long robe I wore when we had visitors, a red one with two golden bands. I liked it. I tried to catch a glimpse of myself in one of the mirrors in the women's quarters.

'Don't get dirty, don't play in the dust, don't play with the dogs . . .' nurse called after me.

'Can I wait under the portico?'

'Yes, if you don't get dirty.'

I sat down under the portico. At least from there I could watch people coming and going, like the servants who were preparing lunch for the king. The pig squealed under the knife and then they hung him by his back legs. The dogs licked the trickle of blood that was dripping onto the ground. The servants had collected most of it in jars to make blood sausage. That was one thing I didn't like at all.

Mentor arrived just then, grabbed his staff and started off down the path that led to the port. I looked around to make sure no one was watching me and took off after him, catching him up near the fountain.

'Where do you think you're going?' Mentor asked me.

'With you. To meet my father.'

'If Euriclea realizes you're not there any more she'll go crazy and then your mother will have her beaten; she's only too happy to . . .' Mentor stopped, realizing that what he was about to say wasn't meant for a six-year-old's ears.

'My mother is jealous of Euriclea the nurse, isn't she?'

Mentor couldn't believe what he'd just heard: 'Do you even know what the word "jealous" means?'

'I do know but I don't know how to explain it . . . I know, jealous is when you want something just for yourself.'

'Right you are,' replied Mentor, taking me by the hand. 'Well, come along, then. Hold your robe up with your right hand so you won't trip on it and get yourself punished.'

We started walking.

'Why do you need a staff if you are young and a fast walker?'

'To scare off the vipers: if they bite you, you're dead.'

'It isn't because you want to look wiser and more important?'

Mentor stopped short and gave me a stern look, pointing his index finger at me: 'Don't ask me any more questions that you already know the answer to.'

'I was just trying to guess,' I offered lamely.

The sun was already high when we arrived at the port. The royal ship had been sighted when it was still far from shore thanks to the standard waving at its stern. A great number of boats had gone out to escort it festively to land.

'There he is,' said Mentor, pointing a finger. 'That man with the light blue cloak and the spear in his hand is King Laertes: your father.'

When I heard those words I wriggled my hand free and started running fast down the slope in the direction of the port. I ran like the wind until I found myself standing in front of the warrior with the sky-blue cloak. Then I stopped and looked at him, panting. Eyes the colour of the sea.

He recognized me and picked me up into his arms.

'You're my father, aren't you?'

'Yes, I am your father. Do you still remember me?'

'I do. You haven't changed.'

'Well you've changed quite a lot. Listen to you: you sound like a grown-up. And what a fast runner you've become! I was watching as you came down the mountain.'

A servant brought a horse, the only one on the island, for the king. Laertes mounted and pulled me up to sit in front of him. A whole procession followed us: my father's friends, his bodyguards, the noblemen, the representatives of the people and the foremen in charge of the royal properties and livestock. As the procession advanced, people started pouring out along the path that snaked its way up to the palace. Mentor walked alongside the king's horse, a position of respect that showed how highly he was thought of, but from my new perch I was seeing him from a completely new point of view, and that really made me feel like a prince.

The celebrations went on until late, but I had to go to bed right after dusk. I stayed awake a long time because of the din; all that laughing and loud talking coming from the banquet hall kept me from falling asleep. *Raucous voices from the banquet hall . . .*

Then everything was quiet. The oil lamps cast flickering

shadows on the walls, doors were pulled open and slammed shut and bolts were drawn. Even though it was the middle of the night, I wasn't really sound asleep, I was still too excited over all the singing and shouting. I was only in a half slumber when the sound of a door opening startled me awake. I slipped out into the hall in the dark and saw a man entering the room of Euriclea, my nurse. I got closer. I could hear strange noises coming from inside and I recognized my father's voice. I understood deep down in my heart that what was happening in the room just then was not something a child could watch. I went back to bed and pulled the covers up completely over my head. My heart was beating so fast that it kept me awake a little longer but then finally it quietened and I fell asleep.

It was Mentor who woke me up the next day. Nurse must have been tired. 'It's morning! Go and wash up. We have a lot to do today and your father will be wanting to spend time with you.'

'My father slept with my mother first and then with *mai*.'

'Mind your own business. Your father is the king and can do what he likes.'

'I used to sleep with the nurse and now he does. I want to know why.'

'You'll know in time. Euriclea is his. He bought her and he can do what he pleases with her.'

I thought of the strange noises I'd heard during the night and maybe I understood.

'I know what he did.'

'Did you spy on them?'

'No. One day Eumeus, the swineherd, called me over when the boar was mounting the sow.'

'Well he deserves a good smacking for that! Go and get washed,' Mentor ordered me, pointing to the tub full of water taken from the spring that flowed from under the foundations of the palace.

I washed and then dressed myself. Mentor pointed to a boulder that overlooked the path about a hundred paces away. 'Go and sit up there and wait. Your father went hunting before dawn. He'll be coming back that way. When he sees you, he'll stop to talk.'

I obeyed and started walking up the path alone. I watched the shepherds pushing the flocks out of the fold to take them out to pasture. The dogs followed, barking. I got to the boulder and climbed on top of it, and then I turned to wave at Mentor: I'm here! But he wasn't there any more. He'd vanished.

I sat and watched the servants and farmers going about their business below me, the shepherds tending their sheep and goats. As one moment melted into the next, the sunlight seeped into all of the deepest valleys and lit up the crags that were most hidden. I started playing with some coloured stones I always kept in the pocket of my robe. I tossed them and picked them up, then tossed them out again to see if they'd fall differently. They were always different. I thought: how long would I have to keep tossing before the stones fell in exactly the same way as the time before? My whole life?

'Are you playing by yourself?' asked my father's voice behind me.

'There's no one to play with.'

'What do you expect to see when you toss your stones?'

'They predict the future.'

'And what do they say?'

'That I'll make a long journey. Like you.'

'That's easy to predict. You live on an island that seems big to you now. In a little while it will seem small to you.'

'I'll go where no one else has ever gone.' I looked into my father's sea-green eyes. 'How far have you gone?'

'To where the sea breaks up against the mountains. They are very high, and always covered with snow. The snow melts into rivers that rush and tumble to the sea. The journey is so short that the water never has time to warm up even when the sun is out, and it stays icy cold until it joins the water of the sea.'

'Is that where you found the treasure?'

'Who told you that?'

'The nurse.'

My father lowered his head. He had some white strands in his black hair.

'Yes,' he said. 'But do you want the real truth or the tale that the singers tell?'

That was hard to answer. Was I interested in the real truth? Why should I be? The truth isn't something for children. Once you tell about something, it becomes true. Like: the king of a little island departs for a great adventure. All of the most powerful warriors of Achaia are going. Could he possibly stay behind? That was the truth. But then, I started thinking that . . . for real, there were only men, goats, sheep and pigs on my island. But if someone should venture far away, really really far away, who knows what he might find: monsters? Giants? Sea serpents? Why not? The gods? Why not?

'Tell me everything,' I said. 'Father, tell me about your comrades: is it true they are the greatest heroes of Achaia?'

'They are!' he smiled. 'Hercules . . .' he opened his arms wide, 'is the strongest man on earth. When he flexes his muscles it's a fearsome sight indeed. I believe he could kill a lion with his bare hands. No one can win a fight with him. His favourite weapon is a club; he never uses weapons made of metal. But he can bring down a bull with that club. Sometimes he would pull our ship to shore all by himself, and tie the hawser to an olive tree . . . You know what? He was the one who cut down the pine tree that we made the ship out of. A trunk so gigantic that twelve men could not join hands around it! The last of its kind on Mount Pelion. Then the master carpenter crafted the vessel using his hatchet on the outside and an adz on the inside. It was Hercules who gave the ship her name: the *Argo*, because she is so swift.'

I don't remember how long we sat on that stone watching the slow movement of shadow and light on the contours of our island. I listened intently, enchanted by my father's voice, chewing on an oat stalk. The words poured from his mouth like flocks of birds from a cliff when the sun comes up. The sound was like a hunting horn when it rises in pitch. It would stay with me my whole life. *I still wake at night to 'Get up, we're going hunting!' Now that he's no longer alive* . . . Atta . . . my father . . . my king.

Who was the strongest after Hercules, then? Who was it?

2

I REALIZED THAT MY FATHER enjoyed spending time with me. He took me into the forest with him and the dogs; when I was too tired he hoisted me onto his shoulders.

'One on top of the other we're a rather tall man,' he would say, laughing. I liked watching him laugh: he bared a row of very white teeth, squeezed his eyes until they were just slits and the laughter burbled from his mouth.

'When are we going to see grandfather on the mainland?' I asked him once.

'Soon. Your mother would like to visit as well and it's been a long time since we saw him. When I was away she didn't want to leave the palace and the kingdom. Three years . . . a long time indeed.'

Every now and then I returned to my favourite thought: 'You've never told me about the treasure. What was it?'

'Ask Phemius. He's our poet, isn't he? He'll tell you a wonderful story.'

'I want the true one.'

'Are you sure? The truth isn't so interesting . . .'

'For me it is.'

'Well, then . . . There's a river that runs into the second sea. It is called the Phasis and . . . it carries gold. Glittering specks just under the surface of the water, but you can't catch them. The natives put sheepskins on the bottom where the river isn't very deep and hold them still with rocks. The gold specks get stuck in the fleece and are captured that way. Every two days they set them out to dry and then they shake them onto a linen cloth to catch the gold. Lots of it.'

'So that's why you needed such a powerful ship and the proudest warriors of Achaia?'

My father laughed again: 'Well said, little one. Who told you that?'

'Mentor. And so?'

'The place is full of fierce warriors. They hide under the sand along the banks and they jump out all at once as if the earth had just delivered them up. They let out terrible war cries and they don't seem to feel pain. How can you bring down a man who feels no pain?'

'Everyone feels pain.'

'Not them. Maybe they have a secret: a herb, they say, some kind of poison. The gold from the fleeces is kept inland, in a cave, and is guarded day and night. So that was our problem: how to find the place, take the gold, get back to the coast and set sail. What would you have done?' My father's eyes shone, catching the sun for an instant.

'I would have become friends with one of them.'

'We did something like that: our leader, Jason, the prince of Iolcus, sent gifts to the princess, then asked to be received by King Aeetes, her father. Jason is as handsome as a god and the princess fell in love with him. They would meet up in secret in the forest . . .'

I thought of the night he returned when he went into the nurse's room and what I heard. It that what falling in love was?

Then he lowered his voice, as if he were talking to himself, as if he didn't want anyone to hear: '. . . and they would make love, savagely, without saying a word.' Then my father's voice rose again: 'Until one day Jason showed her a speck of gold in the palm of his hand and, using gestures, tried to explain what he wanted. Up until then, no one had attacked us: we were camped on the beach with the ship's stern tied to an enormous olive tree and we spent our days fishing. Tunas as big as pigs would get entangled in our nets and we'd roast big pieces of them over the embers. Then one day Jason decided that the time had come. We set off at night with the girl as our guide, agile and silent as a fox! The sky was black and the clouds dropped down from the mountains almost all the way to the plain. It was like we were blind.

'We were all armed: gigantic Hercules with his club, I with my sword and bow . . . we were joined by Tydeus and Amphiaraus from Argus, by Zetes and Calais, the so-called twin sons of the north wind – blond, their eyes icy and skin cold – and by Telamon of Salamis, tall and strongly built with his hair gathered at the nape of his neck in a bronze clasp . . . along with Iphitus of Mycenae and Oileus of Locris. Castor of Sparta, the wrestler, was with us, as was his twin brother Pollux, the boxer; they were very young, no more than boys . . . then there was Peleus of Phthia, home of the Myrmidons, as well as Admetus of Pherai, Meleager of Aetolia and so many others. Fifty of us in all. Twenty warriors remained with the ship, ready to man the lines and set sail at a moment's notice. Amphiaraus stayed with them, sitting at the prow and staring into the darkness. Amphiaraus has big, dark eyes; they can delve into the mysteries of the past and the future, and his pupils dilate like a wolf's at night. His deep, unblinking eyes followed us that night: we were invisible to all except him. He knew whether we would come back or whether we would all be annihilated. He was a seer . . .

'Peirithous, the king of the Lapiths, the warrior who had battled the centaurs, stayed behind as well, close to the olive tree with his axe at the ready to cut the line as soon as we got back to the ship.'

I looked at King Laertes my father and I imagined him surging forward through the night, his sword in hand, with all the other champions: the strongest of Achaia, the mightiest of the world . . . I felt lucky. I looked at his arms, his bull's neck, his wide shoulders, and I knew I was lucky. I was his son. His only son. His story enthralled me. I would have listened to him all day and all night.

'Go on, *atta*, tell me more.'

The time had flown and the sun was high now on our right and it put sparkles in the water of the port, imprisoned by the green mountains sloping down between the light blue of the sky and the deeper blue of the sea. We sat in the shade of a fig tree, dappled by the light. The cicadas screeched. The dogs slumbered.

'A steep, precarious path led us through the forest. We crossed a rocky gully so narrow that only one man could get by at a time, and then a swampy valley covered with tall grasses. We finally arrived at the site of the cave and the girl halted us. Fifty of their warriors were standing in the darkness, leaning on their spears. Shadows among the shadows. She had to point them out to us one by one. The tips of their spears reflected a dim light, but it was enough for us to make them out in the dark. The dying embers of a campfire. At the entrance to the cave was a very tall warrior covered with snake skins. His face was dark and his hand was closed around the haft of his spear.

'Jason signalled for us to fan out into a semicircle and, at that instant, the girl shot an arrow into the nearly extinguished campfire and let out a shrill cry. The campfire blazed up with a blinding flash and lit up all the warriors on guard and the one standing at the entrance – he was covered with scales and looked like a dragon; his teeth had been filed to a point like the fangs of a beast. All at once we hurled our spears, all of us, then charged forward with our swords in hand. Jason took on the snake man and the night air rang with the din of their clashing. We fought like lions. Hercules' legendary strength prevailed in an incredible show of force; Tydeus relentlessly dealt one blow after another without stopping for breath; Telamon had run out of weapons he could throw and began hurling rocks and boulders; Castor and Pollux landed stud-heavy punches and with every clout you could hear the sickening noise of bones shattering. There I was, panting and drenched with sweat, finally satisfied that no enemies were left standing, when I saw Hercules dragging two enormous slaughtered warriors by their feet. Dead meat. Jason had even managed to defeat the dragon man; he lit a torch then and we followed the girl into the cave. It was there that we all saw a glittering fleece hanging from the branches of a petrified oak. We were inside the cave of the treasure! Jason took it from the tree.'

My father stopped but I couldn't break my open-mouthed stare. He was looking into my eyes to see the image already forming there of the treasure in the cave.

'Dozens of jars, shiny copper jars filled to the brim with gold. We sank our hands into them and sparkles flew from the mouths of the jars, twinkling like a thousand little lightning flashes . . .'

'Father,' I said, 'where is our share? Can I see it?'

He seemed not to hear my question. 'We put sticks through the handles of the jars and carried them off like that to the sea; two of us had to struggle to lift a single one.'

I realized that I felt short of breath. I was panting as if it were me carrying that weight of copper and gold. My heart was beating in my throat and at my temples.

'Before long the night resounded with an ominous rolling of drums, which soon became confused with the rumble of distant thunder. We crossed the forest, the swamp, sinking into the mud up to our knees, made our way down the steep, narrow path . . . The wild princess leading us seemed terror-stricken and was shouting out words that none of us could understand but she was certainly telling us to go faster, faster and faster, because the drums were getting closer, our enemies were almost upon us. Lightning flashed over the fog, beyond the threshold of the night, ghosts of pale light first and then the bolts of Zeus himself rent the earth and the sky, set fire to the fog . . .'

'*Atta*,' I said, 'the words coming from your mouth are magic ones, like the words that Mentor and Phemius use. Do you even remember now what really happened?'

Once again my father hadn't seemed to hear my question. The dogs lifted their snouts to sniff at something carried on the wings of the wind from far away . . .

'They were upon us all at once and the wild princess shrieked like a falcon rushing at its prey. She let her arrows fly and many hit their mark. Our assailants twisted and turned, making weird noises, but they neither screamed nor groaned; some tried to pull the arrows from their flesh. Maybe it was true that they didn't feel pain, or maybe they were accustomed to ignoring it. We fought back as best we could, but we were all nerves. All we could think of were the jars full of gold that might vanish while we fought in the dark . . .'

'*Atta*, why do people want gold?'

This time my father interrupted his story to answer me. 'I could say it's because it is the most beautiful of all metals. It's like the sun. Its colour never changes, it doesn't spoil or rust and every precious thing is made from this metal. But perhaps the reason is that since many people desire it, everyone desires it. And if everyone desires it, that must mean it is the most that any man could desire. Gold is power. The diadems of kings and the gowns of gods are made of gold.

'There was no time to lose,' he said then, picking up his story where he had left off. 'I recognized the voices of Zetes and Calais nearby and I called out to them: "Run, run like your father the wind, go and call your comrades from the ship!"

'They heard me and they raced down the path leading to the sea so fast that it didn't look as if they were touching the ground, and we began fighting our assailants in earnest, in single combat. The wild princess blazed with an energy like fire and storm, as if fatigue could not touch her limbs. She struck first with her axe and then with her dagger, and when for a moment I was near her, I saw – or smelled, I couldn't say which – that she was covered with blood. Jason, at her side, was no less of a fury, and Hercules, our bastion, was roaring like a lion as he took on a swarm of enemies, who probably could never have imagined that so much strength could spring from a single body.

'I don't know how much time passed. I do know that some of us were wounded, others died, although we continued to fight with all our might. But why had Zetes and Calais not returned? How long could it possibly take for the sons of Boreas to cover the distance that separated us from the ship and return?

'I turned to Tydeus then, and shouted: "The horn! Sound the horn, that they may hear you!"

'Tydeus began to blow into the shiny horn and soon a cry was launched in response. The sons of the wind were on their way back, bringing with them almost all of the comrades who had been guarding the *Argo*. Even Amphiaraus was with them: clad in bronze, his eyes in the night reflecting the light of the torches like those of a wolf. Our enemies fled. Exhausted as they were, they could not take on our warriors.

'We finally reached the ship as the sky began to lighten to the east. The wild princess stripped naked and washed in the sea and then climbed a rope up to the prow. We weighed anchor.'

The sun was just setting behind Mount Neritus and the shadow of the mountain already covered a quarter of the island although the night was still far off. The land wind rustled the leaves of the oaks around us. I couldn't say a word because I could not return to reality. I was still with the warriors battling in the dark, or maybe I was already on the ship, watching as the shore became distant.

'What are you thinking?' asked my father, getting to his feet and taking my hand.

'I'm thinking that's the way a man should live. Like you. You sail the sea and fight battles and win treasures.'

'Yes, maybe that's how men like us must live our lives, but today I've spent the day with you talking while we've watched the light and shadows passing over our island. This is a good way to live too.'

'So one day I will be able to sail the seas and I'll meet up with wild peoples in faraway lands . . .'

'You certainly will. But look over there . . . smoke is rising from the roof of the palace and that means dinner will be ready soon: meat and bread and good wine. The palace will one day be yours, son. And you, that day, will be king of Ithaca.'

3

MY FATHER LEFT AGAIN AND AGAIN for other exploits; he journeyed to meet other kings or princes, to establish alliances, to
punish unruly subordinates or plunder the territories of tribes living
in the north or in other places even further away.

Not everyone always came back. When the young warriors
accompanying him lost their lives, they were buried far from home.
Their parents would never have the consolation of a tomb on
which to weep for them. Other times, if there had been the time to
build a pyre, the king returned with their ashes inside an urn, a
covered jar with two handles, which he would give to the family
after paying last respects, as custom required. Others came back
wounded or maimed. My father himself often returned showing
the signs of bitter combat on his own body; days and days would
pass in idleness while he regained the strength and the blood he had
lost, like a lion that hides in the forest to lick its wounds after being
attacked by a pack of fierce mastiffs.

I was thirteen years old the day he was brought back to the
palace from his ship on a stretcher borne by four men. He was pale
as death and his chest was bound with bloodstained bandages.
When the women heard the news they pulled out their hair and
wailed as if they were grieving for a dead man. I cried too, but
I swallowed my tears so no one could hear, the way I had been
taught.

When that happened no one was allowed to go into his room,
not even my mother. Only Mentor was let in; perhaps he alone
knew how to cure him. Mentor knew how to do everything; he

surely must know which secret herbs and philtres could restore a gravely wounded man to health. The king was alive but wanted no one to see him in that condition. Once I even knocked on his door: 'Father, *atta*, can I come in?' I got no answer and didn't dare open the latch. I walked back down the corridor trying to imagine what he was doing, what he was thinking and why he hadn't answered me. Wasn't I his only son? Hadn't we spent long days together talking and dreaming up adventures, leaning against the parapet on the roof as the moon rose from the sea? Why wouldn't he let me in?

One night strange noises shook me from my sleep and I got out of bed. I climbed the steps leading to the second floor, holding the handrail in the dark, and peered down into the courtyard. A man was speaking excitedly to my father, who looked like he could barely stand; he was using two forked sticks as crutches. What had happened? Had there been an alarm? Was someone stealing our livestock? Was it pirates, perhaps, already pouring out of their ships and scattering through the countryside in search of plunder? How would we defend ourselves if the king could not bear arms and lead his men into battle?

My father returned to the palace, followed by the man who had been speaking to him. He would certainly be invited to stay. I curled up in a corner and remained there listening to the night-time sounds of the forest because I didn't feel like sleeping any more. Downstairs I could hear the swift steps of the servants preparing a room for our guest. Then I heard the sound of crutches tapping across the floor and up the steps until I finally saw the king's black shape walking slowly towards the parapet. He leaned his elbows on it and looked like he was weeping. I got up slowly and without making the slightest noise, since I was barefoot, I walked up behind him so that when he turned to go back to his room, he found me standing in front of him. He didn't speak or make a move but I could feel the deep anguish that seemed to be crushing him. It hadn't been an attack then: no pirates had landed in our well-sheltered port and no marauders were raiding the countryside. It was something much worse, something terrible.

'What did the messenger tell you, father?'

He did not answer, but began hobbling back to the steps that led downstairs. Was it that he didn't want to talk to me or that he couldn't?

Only when weariness overwhelmed me did I creep back to bed. I lay there listlessly, listening to the north wind that blew hoarsely through the oak branches.

Euriclea woke me.

'What happened, *mai*? Who was that man last night?'

'You have no business wandering around at night. You should have been sleeping. Now get up and get dressed: the sun is already up.'

I put on my clothes and went down to the big hall, where one of the servants had already lit a blazing fire. Euriclea brought me a piece of bread, hot milk and honey from the kitchen. It was a clear, cold day; from the window I could see the peaks on the mainland sprinkled with snow. '*Mai*, when are we going to see grandfather?'

'When your father decides.'

A man appeared in the hall. It had to be the messenger from the night before. His hair was unkempt and his eyes narrow as slits. The king came in next and sat down opposite him. A pleasant warmth had spread through the room. The carver roasted meat on a spit and served it with bread and fragrant herbs. When would I be allowed to eat meat at breakfast? I hated having to eat sweet stuff, as if I were a baby.

My father's head was low and he said nothing. The messenger was speaking in a quiet voice: I could only hear a few words here and there: '. . . a pool of blood . . . on the floor . . . walls . . . his wife, children . . . I'm sorry . . .' He stopped, and then: 'The sea . . . the tide.' He rose to his feet, bowed deeply and took his leave. Euriclea filled his knapsack with freshly baked bread and added a blood sausage and a small skin of wine.

I came close and sat at my father's feet. 'What happened?' I asked.

He sighed and lifted his head. His eyes were filled with tears. I'd never seen him this way.

'Hercules: do you remember him?'

'Of course I do. The giant who used a tree as a club, who was so incredibly strong. Your friend when you went seeking the golden fleece. Has he died?'

'Worse. He slaughtered his family at Mycenae, three nights ago. They found him asleep, lying in a pool of their blood. He was snoring like someone who had drunk too much pure wine, while the limbs of his wife and children were splayed all around him, slain by the sword he still held in his hand.'

My father seemed delirious himself, and the images he described came alive in my head. I wasn't seeing the big hall of our palace with the fire burning, baskets full of fruit and cheeses from the orchards and cattle stables, the dogs curled up half asleep by the hearth, but a dark room, hemmed in by forbidding walls, its floor slick with blood. I trembled at the sight and my teeth chattered like when the north wind comes bringing snow.

'How could this have happened?' my father kept saying. Tears welled under his eyelids, rolled down his cheeks.

I was terrified. So a father can kill his own child? Would King Laertes do the same to me if I made him angry? He looked up at me and he must have realized what I was thinking because he touched my cheek. 'Hercules is quick-tempered and he attacks like a lion in battle but he has a good heart, I know him well. He would never hurt a disarmed man, or anyone who could not defend himself. How could he have raised his sword against his own blood? Perhaps he's gone mad, understand? Or perhaps someone, envious of his glory, gave him a poison that made him lose his mind . . . the king of Mycenae . . . I've never liked that look in his eye, that sinister smirk on his face . . .'

'What's going to happen now?' I asked.

'I don't know. Whatever the reason for his crime, he will have to atone for it.'

'What does that mean?'

'He'll have to pay for what he's done, even if it was not his fault.'

I fell silent. The words were too heavy for my heart.

'When are we going to visit grandfather?' I don't know why those words came to my mouth. Perhaps I was trying to escape from the fear of something too enormous for me to understand. But it was only natural for a boy to want to visit his grandfather: to receive presents, listen to some good stories, not to have to think about terrible things. I knew very little about my grandfather, apart from the gossip of the servants and my nurse. I'd never seen him. It was only natural for me to be curious, to want to meet the man who was my mother's father, the king of a barren, mountainous land who lived in a palace of stone on top of a cliff.

'It's not time yet. You'll go next year when you've become a man.'

The carver removed the leftovers from the table. Euriclea set fruit, hot milk, bread and honey on a tray and brought it to the queen's quarters, making her way up the steps carved in the rock.

My father began speaking again: 'Do you know how your grandfather got his name? Autolykos means "he himself is a wolf". He's called that because he's a ruthless predator who has no consideration for anyone. He is hard and calculating; he cares nothing for rules or for respectable behaviour. He thinks nothing of breaking an oath. He lives in a steep-walled fortress, grey as iron, guarded by murderous cut-throats, on top of a cliff which is second in height only to Mount Parnassus itself, which looms behind it. He strikes fear into the hearts of all those living in a vast territory around him.'

I dropped my eyes, confused. My playmates had wise, loving grandfathers who took them out fishing on a boat or out to pasture with their flocks of sheep and loyal dogs.

'The only time he came here to visit is when you were born. Your mother placed you on his knee and he gave you your name.'

'Why him? Why not you, who are my father?'

'Because he had waited so long for you. Even though we had assured him that if a boy were born he would be the first to know, he sent us messengers constantly to ask whether a son had been born in the palace. He seemed satisfied when he saw you. He furrowed his brow and said to us: "Daughter of mine, my son-in-law: give this child the name I will tell you now. I come here today nursing hatred in my heart for many a person, men and women alike. So the boy's name shall be Odysseus.""

Tears came to my eyes when I heard that story; the name I'd been given was cursed! My father said nothing. He watched me thoughtfully. But I could tell he was feeling the same dismay that had washed over me.

'And thus it was. Once a name has crossed the threshold of the teeth, it cannot be taken back if the man pronouncing it has the child's same blood, in a direct line of descent. And this is what happened.

'But don't be afraid. It will be you, by your actions and your deeds, the strength of your arms and your mind, who will give meaning to your name. Greatness can emerge from even the most bitter destiny. If your heart is strong and fearless, if you do not tremble in the face of any challenge, be it from man or god, you will have the life you deserve.'

I nodded to show that I understood even though the brief portrait of my grandfather that my father had sketched out had devastated me. He seemed to realize this: 'In any event, before Autolykos left, setting sail on his big black ship, he turned back and said: "I'd like to invite my grandson to a hunting party."

'"Now, wanax?" I asked him.

'"When the first hairs shadow his cheeks and his upper lip.""

'How old was I when grandfather invited me?' I asked.

'Six months old. But that's how he is.'

I was even more confused. Inviting a six-month-old baby to a hunting party must mean something that I couldn't fathom. And I couldn't stop thinking that a troubled fate was written in my name.

My father read the look in my eyes: 'Even if there is a shadow in the name you bear, no omen could ever darken your path because . . . because I love you, Odysseus, my son.'

That's what he said and he hugged me tightly. I could feel the heat of the fire blazing in the hearth and the heat and smell of the big body of my father, the hero Laertes, king of Ithaca.

4

I SPENT THAT YEAR in great anticipation. When the first hairs sprouted on my cheeks and upper lip I would be a man and go to visit my grandfather Autolykos on the mainland. Euriclea explained that my grandfather had other sons who were my uncles and that they were formidable warriors as well. I had stopped thinking about the disturbing things I'd heard about my grandfather and was very curious to look him in the eye, and to meet my uncles and my grandmother as well. I dreamed about how I'd soon be entering an impregnable fortress on a rock nearly as high as Mount Parnassus and how I would explore its every corner and learn its every secret.

Mentor had told me that Parnassus was the place most beloved by the god Apollo, who lived there with the Muses. How had my grandfather dared to build his palace on a peak so high it challenged the mountain of the gods? Why had Apollo tolerated it?

As I approached manhood, my father turned me over to an instructor who would train me in the art of hunting and managing the hounds. He was a powerfully built man of about forty, greying at the temples, a native from the plains of Thessaly. His name was Damastes. He had been Jason's shield-bearer on the *Argo* expedition and in Colchis. I could barely understand a word he said, but he made his will known well enough by shouting and caning me on the back and shoulders. It took me nearly three months to learn to track deer, boar, hare and wild goats, and to begin to master the bow and the javelin. By the time summer came, there was enough hair on my upper lip and cheek to give my face a hint of a shadow.

The eve of the great day arrived in no time: my father had chosen the summer solstice. That night my mother came to my room and told me a strange story: 'Tomorrow you'll be going to see your grandfather. Well, do you remember when you were little, and you asked me how I met your father? You wanted to know more and I told you, "Not yet. I'll tell you when you are old enough to understand." Remember? Well. That time has come. There's something you need to know.'

My mother had a cold light in her eyes when she began speaking again. She said: 'I was a young girl myself when one night, as I was sleeping soundly, I was woken by strange noises coming from a room that I'd always been forbidden to enter. I'd only been sleeping by myself, in my own bed, for a bit longer than a year, and I was terrified. The noise sounded like a muffled growling or snarling, as if a big animal were trapped inside and trying to escape. I made my way down the corridor without making a sound until I realized that the door to the room was half open and that the moon's rays were streaming through. Even though I was scared to death, I felt compelled to look inside. I saw something that I'll never forget. My father was writhing on the floor like a wounded animal. The growling I had heard was coming from his own mouth. His limbs were covered with coarse hair. At that moment – maybe because he'd felt my presence – he leapt outside. I ran to the window and saw a wolf crossing the courtyard and disappearing into the forest.'

I wanted to ask her if she was certain she hadn't been dreaming but I already knew the answer: if she'd decided to tell me now it was because she thought that what she had seen was real.

'I wanted you to know. Now you decide whether you want to depart on this journey.'

'More than ever, mother,' I answered.

'Then I have something for you to give my father. There's a message inside.' Saying thus, she held out a small clay amphora. It was tiny, fitting in the palm of her hand.

'I'll give it to him from you, mother.'

She gave me a hug and a kiss and turned to go back to her bedroom.

THE NEXT DAY it was my father who woke me and walked me down to the port.

'You'll leave alone, like a man,' he told me. 'You will journey by sea and then by land, until you reach the palace of Autolykos . . .'

'He himself is a wolf,' I repeated in my heart.

'You will find your way up to the eagle's nest. You'll enter the wolf's lair.'

Everyone came to the port to see me off: my parents the king and queen, my nurse Euriclea, who was weeping and wiping her eyes with a handkerchief, Mentor, who was cross because he could not leave with me, Damastes, who gave me three javelins and girded a dagger at my waist. It was sheathed in a bronze scabbard with fine silver decorations, the work of a craftsman from Same who had presented it to the king.

'Your grandfather will surely take you hunting, which is the only pastime befitting a king or a prince,' said my father. 'He likes to hunt boar because it reminds him of a dreadful beast that was brought down by all the greatest kings and heroes of Achaia together: the boar of Calydon. A monster, he was. A gigantic, bloodthirsty specimen with enormous tusks, keen-edged as swords. He will certainly tell you the story even though he himself was not invited to the hunt . . . the only king to be excluded, I believe.'

We were waiting for the wind to turn, favourable to filling the sail and taking the ship out of the port. The sky was clear and cloudless, the sun was mirrored in the gulf as if by a polished silver plate. Oh, Ithaca . . .

'The boar was killed by Meleager of Aetolia, one of my comrades on the *Argo*,' added Damastes. 'Beware, a boar is one of the most dangerous animals on earth. It is lightning swift and when it charges it can mow down any obstacle, even a horse five times its weight. When the hounds close in, a male can easily disembowel them all with his tusks. If you hear one coming, seek cover and get ready . . . If you see it coming from a distance, use your bow: you may not kill it but you'll slow it down, and when it comes into range hurl your javelin with all your might.'

'Take care, my son,' said my father and he hugged me. I kissed my mother and she held me tight. Euriclea would not stop crying.

'Stop your weeping, *mai*, that's bad luck!'

The helmsman nodded to me as the sailors were hoisting the sail and I jumped onto the ship. My mother's eyes were moist as well but she maintained her dignity. As the ship took off from the shore she said to me: 'Remember the message I gave you for my father!'

'Of course I will!' I answered and waved goodbye to her.

My first journey.

I was leaving Ithaca for the first time. I would see the mainland approaching, feel the sea crashing against the stones on the shore and who knows what else. How small the king and the queen and all the others were becoming as we moved out into the open sea!

The wind remained in our favour and before night fell we dropped anchor in a little natural harbour.

'That's your grandfather,' said the helmsman, pointing to a man on the shore. He was grey-haired but his body was lean and muscular. He wore a raw wool robe with a leather belt and was armed with a sword and spear. Flanking him were two warriors taller than he was, with long black beards, bushy eyebrows and hairy arms. I jumped out and walked over the pebbles and then on the sand towards him.

'*Wanax*, you who possess this land,' I said, 'I am Odysseus, son of Laertes who rules over Ithaca. I've come because fifteen years ago you invited me to go hunting with you.'

'Where did you learn to talk that way, boy?' he replied. 'You sound like an old master of ceremonies. I know who you are and I've been expecting you. I'm your grandfather and that's what I want to be called. These are two of your uncles, brothers of your mother. Come now, dinner is waiting.'

We got into a chariot as the sky was darkening and the sea

becoming streaked with purple, and set off on a path that led up the mountainside. A fierce sadness welled up inside me because I was riding off with strangers whom I'd never met before. I couldn't help but think of the palace where my parents and all the servants lived, of the dinner that my nurse would prepare for me and set on the table. But then my curiosity at meeting these people and seeing places I'd never seen before won out.

'Don't you have anything to say to your grandfather?' asked Autolykos. He was sitting in front of me, but didn't turn around.

'I've waited a long time for this day,' I answered.

'Why?'

'A man who makes an invitation fifteen years ahead of time isn't an ordinary person. And if that man is my grandfather, it means a part of him is in me and I'd like to know which.'

'Have you been told who I am? The most wicked of men: thief, liar, bloodthirsty plunderer and oath-breaker.'

'I've heard those things . . . but my parents have always spoken of you with respect. And they told me that it was you who gave me my name.'

'That's right. Because I was full of hatred for everyone.'

I couldn't say anything else. I wasn't ready to know the reason for such bitterness.

My uncles didn't say a word for the whole journey. Their eyes never stopped darting around and their hands stayed on the hilts of their swords. In the end, we reached a house of stone which was set back in a clearing in a thick oak wood and we spent the night there after eating some bread and cheese with a cup of red wine.

'Tomorrow you'll eat better,' said my grandfather and I nodded my head as if to say that anything was fine with me. I was surprised that we'd stopped in such a solitary, unprotected place, but then I thought that grandfather Autolykos had such a terrible reputation that no one would dare come close unless they had sufficient forces to attack or challenge him.

I slept in a bed that smelled of pinewood and I woke up several times in the middle of the night, roused by the sounds coming from outside: grunts, whistles, the cries of nocturnal animals. My hand fell on my dagger more than once. The second time I awoke I saw a sight I would never forget: the peak of Mount Parnassus lit by the full moon. A thin cloud was passing across the snow-topped peak and the reflected moonlight created a play of translucence that enthralled me. I would have climbed to the peak, then and there, but I was certain my grandfather had already done that, and that he knew everything that a mortal man could possibly know. The time after that I was awakened by a rustling of wings: an owl had settled on the windowsill. I got out of bed but she didn't move. I took a few steps towards her but the bird just seemed to regard me with curiosity. Why didn't she fly away? We looked at one another for a long time, or maybe a short time, a time suspended, unreal. Maybe I was dreaming. But today I am sure it was my first encounter with my green-eyed goddess, Athena . . .

Where are you?

The sky was light long before the sun rose from behind the mountains and I went outside. The birds were beginning to twitter and when I turned towards the sea I saw the blue expanse stretching out before me, rippling in the morning breeze, and the tips of the islands being lit up by the sun, one after another.

'The one down there that's still dark, that's Ithaca, your island,' said a voice behind me. 'Do you know why it's still dark? Because the peak of the mountain behind us is still covering it with its shadow.'

'*Pappo*,' I said, turning around and amazing myself at my use of such an intimate, familiar word with a man who despite being my mother's father was a stranger to me.

He smiled saying: '*Pai* . . .' and gave me a piece of pork. 'This is food for men, have some.'

I was finally eating meat and bread for breakfast. I could consider myself a man. '*Pappo*,' I started up again, 'have you ever been up there, on the peak?' pointing to the summit of Mount Parnassus.

'I certainly have. And I didn't see anyone playing a lyre surrounded by nine beautiful maidens.'

I dropped my head. 'Even if they were there you couldn't have seen them. We mortals don't have the power to command the waves of the sea or the wind, to stop the stars from wandering in the sky, to change the cycle of the seasons or to defeat death. There's someone, I think, who rules our world. Someone who's there but doesn't show himself, except in disguise.'

'Listen to my words well, *pai*: I've challenged them time and time again and they've never taken me up on it. I've done every evil thing a man can do: I've murdered, terrorized entire regions and cities, sworn oaths that I immediately broke, and no one has ever punished me. I'm strong and powerful and afraid of no one. If they've never answered, you know what? They don't exist.'

I thought about his words for a few moments and replied: 'They've never even noticed you.' *Challenging the gods is something else.*

He said nothing.

We resumed our journey up to the highest part of the mountains and finally reached the home of Autolykos: a palace made of big squared-off boulders like my father's, surrounded by a wall with a single entrance. When we went inside I saw that someone had got there before us: the servants had killed a bull and were quartering it. 'Our lunch,' I thought, 'and maybe our dinner too.' A big fire was blazing in the middle of the room and the meat was already roasting on spits. We ate and drank until late that night but I held back; I didn't want to get drunk or overload my stomach. I'd always preferred to feel vigilant and at the ready. Ready for what exactly, I couldn't say, but my instincts have always made me careful. I considered who my table companions were: only my uncles and my grandfather were present at the banquet, because – I thought – they could trust no one else. I participated in the conversation when I could. Especially when they talked about the next day's boar hunt.

'It's a dangerous pursuit,' said my grandfather. 'Have you ever taken part?'

'King Laertes my father . . .'

'Whoever taught you to talk that way?'

'Mentor, my educator. I was saying that my father engaged a Thessalian instructor to train me. In the use of the bow, dagger and javelin.'

'So how many boars have you killed?'

'None.'

My grandfather broke out laughing, imitated by his sons. One of them gave me a slap on the back that nearly sent me sprawling. I turned sharply and gave him the sternest look I could, letting him know he should never try that again.

'Tomorrow you will kill one. The first of your life, but not with those needles you carried here with you. You'll need this to stop a three-hundred-pound beast.' He got up, went to the wall and took down a heavy, solid spear. He threw it at me and I caught it in flight. 'But tomorrow you could die instead,' he continued. 'Shall I have someone take you back to the port? You're still in time.'

'Have them wake me before dawn,' I replied and began walking off, spear in hand, towards my room. Before entering, I turned. 'I have a question for you too. Why weren't you invited to hunt the boar of Calydon? All of the greatest heroes of Achaia were there.'

'Tomorrow night, if you're still alive, you'll have understood on your own.'

What did he mean by that? I went to bed but kept hearing the laughing and shouting of the revellers until sleep won me over.

There was no need to wake me the next day. The dogs barking, the servants calling to one another, the weapons clanging; all roused me when it was still dark. I got dressed, put on my leather corselet and wristband, pulled my belt across my hips, added my dagger, grabbed the spear in my hand and slung my bow, two javelins and a quiver over my shoulder.

'I see you've decided to come,' said my grandfather when he saw me appear. 'We'll see how you handle yourself. Follow me.'

We walked alongside one another in silence through the forest. I kept thinking of the things he'd said to me the night before and he was surely aware of that. Before the sky started to turn white we had reached a clearing and we stopped there.

'By this time,' said grandfather, 'my sons will have taken position and the beaters will be on the other side of the forest. There are three trails that the boars always favour: the biggest pack come from the south, and will be driven towards my sons, the small pack tend to come up along the little stream we just crossed and they're for me. Any that separate from the rest will end up here and you'll be waiting for them. Don't move from this position; this is the only spot from which you'll be able to take aim.' He picked up some boar droppings and rubbed them on my legs and arms: 'This way they won't smell you. The wind is against us. Remember: you'll find them in front of you.'

He walked back towards the stream and disappeared among the oaks. I looked around and tried to apply Damastes' advice. I needed to seek cover behind a tree trunk to stay safe but the nearest trees were all far in front of me. The ones behind me were at least a hundred paces away and that was too far. I felt like calling my grandfather back to ask him how I could find a safe position but I was ashamed. I had no choice but to remain where I was. I looked around to work out how I could protect myself if one of those animals charged me, but all I could see was a small depression in the ground. In the distance I could hear horns blaring and sticks knocking and thrashing. The beaters! From the sound of it, there must be more than one boar. I gripped my spear tightly. My heart started pounding but I tried to control it. The sounds were getting closer. Without even realizing what I was doing, I had instinctively begun taking steps backwards. I would need more room to take aim.

All at once, a rush of broken branches and uprooted under-brush. I drew my bow and assumed my stance, planting myself firmly with my legs wide apart. Nothing. More branches snapping. I backed up. Nothing. Drops of sweat dripped into my eyes, burning them. Then a group of boar suddenly broke into the clearing at a gallop. Not in front of me, not behind me, but at my left side. I turned that way but the rising sun blinded me. I let fly regardless and a female collapsed abruptly. Instantly a dark shadow, enormous, loomed; I hurled my spear. A tremendous snort of pain. I threw myself on the ground and found him on top of me. A gigantic male. I felt an acute, agonizing spasm and was overwhelmed by a foul stench. With my right hand I pulled the dagger from my belt and plunged it hilt-deep into the animal's belly. I was drenched in blood. I neither saw nor heard anything else.

It was my pain that awoke me, piercing, at the bottom of my thigh, near my knee. I opened my eyes and saw.

A mighty albino ram, with great curving horns, enormous horns. Perhaps I was dreaming. But the pain was real and getting stronger. I was lying on the ground in the middle of the grass. I was all covered with blood. A voice:

'You've killed your first boar.'

The voice of Autolykos, my grandfather.

'Is it real?'

'What?'

'That.' I pointed to the ram standing absolutely still in front of me.

'The ram. Of course. He's the leader of my herd. He's magnificent. No other ram this big exists. I stole him from the Aetolians who live in the interior. They offered to pay a ransom to have him back but I refused.'

'It hurts, so much . . .'

'The boar ripped your thigh open,' he said, and turned away.

A downpour of water hit me. Then another and another. They were taking buckets of water from the stream nearby and throwing them over me. I was being washed.

Autolykos reappeared and in his hand was a red-hot knife. 'I have to cauterize your wound and sew you up or you'll die. Don't scream, it irritates me.'

The blade burned my flesh, the pain rent my heart, my eyes clouded over.

Only the albino ram remained, a white vision standing out against the darkness.

5

THE FEVER RAGED WITHIN ME for five days and five nights, then left me. It was then that I met my grandmother Amphithea because it was she who stitched my wound, not grandfather, and who nursed me. She spread an ointment on the flesh scorched by Autolykos' blade that greatly eased the pain and calmed the itching of the scab that was forming. When she felt I had begun to heal she allowed me to get out of bed so I could try to take a few steps. I was careful not to betray my fear: the gash had been very deep, all the way to the bone. I knew that many, under similar circumstances, had remained crippled their whole lives. I tried to take heart by telling myself that even though I hadn't been wounded in battle I could say I'd had a close encounter with a wild animal, so at least it had been an honourable fight.

I touched the ground first with one foot and then with the other and . . . I was standing. A servant handed me a cane but I refused to take it. I took one step and then another: my muscles and tendons didn't seem to be severely damaged. My gait was halting and quite stiff, painful but normal. My spirit filled with joy. This wouldn't prevent me from doing battle, from running, from competing, on land or sea. In my heart of hearts I thanked Athena, who had appeared to me that first night in the form she most often takes when she wants to hide from mortal gaze. And I thanked my grandmother, who had cured me.

My grandfather came to see me as well and since I'd had plenty of time to ponder what had happened I told him what I thought: 'The attack didn't happen by chance. I was expecting the boars to come from the north and that animal charged at me from the east. You were the one who told me to take position at that spot, without any cover. You had them drive that animal at me knowing that I would be blinded by the sun. Was it the beaters who did it, or did you drive him at me yourself? Is that why you invited me to hunt with you when I was still an infant? So you could watch me die? At least now I know why no one wanted you around when they were hunting the boar of Calydon.'

'I told you that first night that you would soon understand why I hadn't been invited on that hunt despite the fact that I was the best hunter, and that should have put you on your guard. It was meant as a warning. It was I who saved your life, actually, no one else. You are a wise and courageous boy: two virtues that are rarely found in the same person. Many courageous men are stupid; many a shrewd, clever man is a coward. What happened was my will. You've learned that you can trust no one in this world and you'll never forget that as long as you live. That's why I called you here. In Ithaca you would never have learned what you now know. Now your flesh bears the indelible mark of your credulity. That scar will be a reminder forever.'

'I could have died.'

'But that didn't happen. I've been observing you since the first moment we met: how you take in your surroundings, how you listen to the men, the animals and the world around you. I haven't missed a single one of your words.'

'What if it had happened? If I had lost my life?'

'We are all mortal beings, but no one can say whether living a longer life is a boon or a curse. For me it has been a curse and I have met many men who are sorry they were ever born. I have a terrible reputation because I don't hide who I am. Others, many who are much worse than I am, manage to hide their true natures. I'm exactly who you see I am. And I came to your father's palace when you were born because I had waited so long for you.'

'You came to give me this dreadful name.'

'No, a sincere name. I wanted you to remember what the world is like, what human beings are like. Hatred is by far the most common emotion felt by mankind.'

'And why were you so eager for me to be born?'

'Because I don't like any of my own sons and I was hoping that the new heir would be different.'

'Well then?'

'What I desired has come to be. You don't know what happened that day during the boar hunt: I saw everything. I had my bow aimed at that big male, ready to take him down but I didn't need to do that. Your instinct was faster than the beast's, your spear struck a vital spot with precision. And your bow did not fail either. The arrow that felled the female penetrated her right shoulder, very close to her heart. All that was missing was a bit of strength, but that will come as you finish growing. Your body fitted perfectly into a hollow of the soil so you wouldn't be crushed by the weight of the boar. You are perfect, Odysseus, the son I would have desired.'

I couldn't answer or say another word. My grandfather lived in his own reality of hate-fuelled folly. He was violent, arrogant, maybe even cruel, but not evil. I learned in the days that I spent with him that a truly wicked person is a coward who doesn't have the courage to look his victims in the face, who prefers to charge others with the loathsome task of inflicting suffering. In his own way Autolykos wanted to make me understand that he loved me and that he wanted to protect me from a world he despised, to provide me with the weapons to defend myself even when he was no longer alive. The old wolf certainly had a secret he was bent on carrying to his tomb, but I was in no hurry to find out what it was.

The day before I left he pulled me aside and asked me: 'Your mother. Didn't she leave you a message for me?'

'Yes. I was going to give it to you tomorrow morning before my departure.'

'You have to give it to me now. I won't come to the port. I won't like seeing you go.'

I took the minuscule terracotta amphora from my bag and gave it to him. He crushed it in his hands. Inside was a thin bronze leaf with a carved inscription. As he was looking at it, I told him: 'The way you should start is with the star.'

The symbols must have represented some secret language because I understood nothing of what I could see, and what I'd just said was the phrase that my mother had asked me to learn and repeat to him.

He looked at the little bronze leaf for a long time and then tucked it into his belt and looked straight into my eyes. 'You'll tell your mother the names of three animals, the ones that come to your mind . . . No, say nothing to me,' he added when he saw me opening my mouth. 'I don't want to know. Be careful, those three names could mark your destiny.'

When it was evening the three of us ate a meal together: Amphithea, Autolykos and me. The uncles were off on some venture. I thanked my grandparents for their hospitality, for their care and for everything they had taught me. My grandmother kissed me on the head and eyes and took my face in her hands for a long time, then retired to her rooms. Grandfather stayed with me a little longer. He said: 'I don't know whether we will ever see each other again. A man like me lives in constant danger and when my strength starts to wane someone will be eager to take advantage. But to ward off this eventuality, let's say I invite you to return for another round of hunting when you've entered your twenty-first year. That way I'll have to stay alive to welcome you back. Don't let me down.'

'I'll come, because this time I'll know what's waiting for me.'

'You knew then too. I'm certain of it. And . . . I wanted to give you a female tonight but I can see you're not too expert about such things yet and you might have left me a bastard to bring up, something I have no time for.'

We said goodbye.

'Farewell, *pappo*.'

'Farewell, *pai*.'

The next morning I saw only my grandmother, Queen Amphithea, and together we ate the breakfast prepared by one of her handmaids. Then, when the sun came up, a man arrived to take me to the port. Grandmother hugged me tight with tears in her eyes: 'Will you come back to see us, my child?'

'I will, grandmother, if the gods allow it. I've been invited.'

'Say hello to your mother and father for me. Tell them they are always in my heart.'

We separated and I followed my guide to the harbour, where the ship that would take me back to Ithaca was waiting for us. Only one month had passed.

I had my own standard hoisted at the prow and when I arrived at the port of Ithaca, the scene was identical to when I had left: my parents had come to receive me with an escort, along with the island dignitaries, Damastes my trainer, Mentor my educator and Euriclea my nurse, who cried and dried her eyes with a handkerchief, repeating, 'My child, my child', just like grandmother had.

Another bull was butchered at the palace to celebrate my return. My father's friends were invited, and some of my childhood friends as well: Antiphus, Eurylochus, Euribates and Sinon. They were good lads, swift runners and skilled with weapons. This time it was I who had a story to tell and I proudly showed off the scar above my knee. 'He was truly enormous, with a black hide and tusks as long as swords. He came at me from the east: I had the sun in my eyes and all I saw was this massive black shape descending on me like a boulder rolling down a mountainside. I had just enough time to hurl my spear, because I'd already felled the female with my bow, but he was too close . . .'

Everyone listened raptly, even my father, who had won immortal glory for himself as one of the Argonauts. You could see he was proud of me. At that moment I thought that if grandfather hadn't done what he had, I would never have had such an amazing, exciting tale to tell. Who knows, maybe our poet Phemius would even sing of my doings one day to entertain the guests during a banquet. I understood that grandfather had done the right thing; he'd made a man of me and he had taught me things I'd never forget. He himself, a wolf . . .

We ate and drank until late that night. By the end of the evening, my friends seemed more dead than alive and they had to be taken home by their servants. I also asked my father permission to retire and I went to my bedroom, where I found my mother waiting at the threshold.

'Did you give the message to my father?'

'Yes, of course.'

'And what did he reply?'

'He said that when I saw you I would have to tell you the names of three animals and to be careful which ones I chose because those three words could mark my destiny.'

'Well then?'

'The animals are the bull, the boar and the ram.'

'Are you certain?'

'Absolutely certain. The bull was the first animal sacrificed to celebrate my arrival, the boar wounded me and I will forever bear the signs of that encounter. The ram was the first thing I saw when I opened my eyes again, after the attack. He was an albino that grandfather said he'd stolen, a gigantic animal with huge curving horns and red eyes. I don't know why but he looked like a demon to me. He wasn't moving at all and he looked more like an idol than a living animal. He just stared at me with those empty eyes.'

'My son,' replied my mother, 'it is written that these words will have a special meaning for you one day. They may even be the key to your life, and to your death.'

I've never forgotten the way she was waiting there and what she said to me, because no mother, I believe, could speak like that to her son without giving him a chill, making him feel the weight of the unknown. She seemed to realize that and feel sorry for me; she smiled a little, gave me a kiss and told me to sleep well.

I collapsed exhausted onto the mattress and slept a long time. Then something woke me up and my hand crept to my dagger: I could feel a presence in my room. I made sure I wasn't dreaming and then I smelled . . . my father. I didn't move but I wondered how long he'd been there, sitting in the dark, watching me sleep.

He must have sensed that I was awake because he got up to go to the door, silent as a ghost.

'*Atta.*'

He turned.

'*Atta*, do you know what happened in grandfather's house?'

'Something so important that you've waited until now to tell me about it, in the middle of the night, in the dark?'

'I saw the goddess Athena.'

'Sleep, my son,' he answered.

6

IN THE DAYS THAT FOLLOWED Euriclea took care of my wound, applying an ointment that she had made herself, and as time passed the scab grew softer and fell off; even the redness faded until it was completely gone. It left a scar, but my knee showed no sign of damage. I could walk and run for days on end as I always had down the woody paths and trails that criss-crossed my island. Damastes, my weapons instructor, never left my side: he ran alongside me, forced me to scale the steepest slopes and descend from the rockiest cliffs. He would have me dive from the top of a bluff and swim for hours along the coast. Between one activity and another, he taught me to handle a spear and to use a bow until my aim became sharp, clean. Perfect.

'A bow is a powerful weapon: it allows you to take shelter and kill from a distance. Many think that a true warrior should use a sword and confront his adversaries in hand-to-hand combat. They believe the bow is the arm of a coward.'

'Isn't that so?'

'Not at all. In battle, the most important thing is to win. All weapons are equal if they serve their purpose: taking your enemy's life. If you win, you survive; if you lose you die or end up as a slave for your whole life. The bow is a noble weapon. An arrow flies whistling through the air, faster than the wind, swifter even than a bird, even without their wings. *It strikes your target at a great distance and allows you to procure food for yourself* in situations where any other weapon is inefficient or useless.'

We stopped only once a day. Damastes would take some bread

and goat's cheese from his bag, we'd drink water from a spring and then continue until dusk. When we got back to the palace, we would report to my father about the progress I'd made.

Last of all, Damastes taught me to use a sword.

'This is the most terrible of weapons,' he said. 'To strike you have to be close enough to the enemy to look into his eyes, to feel his breath on your face. When you deal the blow you will run him through from one side to the other; his blood squirts out at you, his bowels burst out of the wound, the smell is nauseating. The screams of battle become overwhelming, the clanging of bronze deafening. And that's what men call "glory". That's what the poets sing of when they celebrate the deeds of heroes, accompanying their words with a lyre.'

I wasn't sure what he meant by that. It seemed however that the toll of my passage into manhood was learning about all the ugliest aspects of life and of other human beings.

Sometimes we slept out in the fields or in the forest, wrapped up in our cloaks, on a bed of dry leaves. Before I fell asleep I would watch the stars glittering between the leaves on the trees and ask myself what they really were. Had they been put up there by the gods *to guide sailors on their route home*? Mentor had taught me to recognize the constellations: the Bear and Orion and the Pleiades and even more, and I knew that one day I would have to use that knowledge out at sea, to navigate a crossing or make a long voyage.

One night I saw the owl again: for a moment it was only her eyes with their golden reflections staring at me, and then the goddess emerged from behind a trunk. She wore a dress the colour of the moon, her bare feet skimmed the grass of the field. Pale flashes danced across the tip of her spear. A fragrance accompanied her, a scent of forged metal, of olive and cedar and wild flowers. I hung on to those notes that I could barely perceive and became inebriated. I wanted to call out to her, but nothing came out of my mouth: mortals are not allowed to address a god unless they will it. And yet she turned as if she had heard me; she smiled and disappeared. The owl left her perch on the branch and flew off through the sweet-smelling night.

'You were talking in your sleep last night,' Damastes said to me in the morning. 'What were you dreaming?'

'I wasn't dreaming anything,' I replied. 'I was too tired to dream. I was sleeping, that's all.'

ALL THAT YEAR, for as long as the season held out, my father went to sea for voyages of fifteen, twenty days; sometimes with a few trusted friends, at other times with his warriors. I suppose he was going to the nearby islands that constituted our kingdom: to Same, Dulichium, Leucas, maybe even to Zacynthus, to meet with the noblemen who provided spears for our army and ships for our fleet. Black, shiny ships, superbly crafted. Once, I believe, he went out for plunder and took his warriors with him. They returned with the signs of combat on their bodies and faces, and brought back coppery-skinned slaves, jugs full of wine, timber, richly coloured fabric and hundreds of beautiful glass beads. The booty was split up after the king had taken his share.

Some of the slaves wept, surely thinking that they would never see the day of their return. It upset me to see their despair. My father put his hand on my shoulder: 'This is the law of life. The same thing could have happened to me or my comrades – to become the slaves of worthless men, of merchants or fools, or to be exchanged for a handful of coloured glass beads. And no one would have taken pity on us. Save your feelings for people you love, if one day they should suffer ills or lose their lives or their freedom.' Having said that, he walked off without waiting for me and headed to the palace, where the women were waiting for him with a bath and clean robes taken from the cypress chest.

I followed him and watched while he was bathed. 'Father,' I asked him, 'what happens to a king if he is captured; does he become a slave?'

'A king has a good chance of being freed because he can pay a considerable ransom: gold, silver and bronze, weapons, livestock, precious fabrics. No one would want to hold on to such a slave when they could buy themselves dozens of slaves, just by sending him back.'

'But what if it did happen?'

Laertes paused thoughtfully for a few moments and when he spoke again his face had an enigmatic expression, as if someone else were talking through his mouth: 'He would become a slave like the other slaves; he would obey his master so as not to be beaten and he would try to please that master in order to have better clothes and food.'

'Anyone else,' I insisted, 'not you.'

'Who can say? When a man loses his freedom he loses everything. There's only one thing worse than losing your freedom: losing your life.'

I went out into the corridor, climbed to the upper terrace and waited for night to fall.

ONCE THE AUTUMN had arrived and the season for voyaging at sea was over, King Laertes had the heavy steering oar removed from his ship and hung over the hearth so it could absorb the smoke and harden in the heat.

We often had visitors and guests. Some of them, not many to tell the truth, had come from afar, on ships which sought shelter in the port. My father felt these were the most interesting, because they had sailed through bad weather and that made them brave or desperate or both things together.

One of them brought us news of Hercules.

The king of Mycenae, Eurystheus, not daring to take on Hercules directly, had ordered him to cleanse his guilt by carrying out a number of impossible tasks. Hercules made no objection and departed forthwith. No one had seen him since. I asked my father what these tasks were, but he didn't know or he didn't want to tell me. He wasn't even sure that Hercules had ever owned up to killing his whole family. I could tell that my father still refused inwardly to believe his friend had been responsible for such a heinous act. He did tell me that Eurystheus was capable of any iniquity and that anything could be expected from a villain like him.

I would have liked to know what my father was referring to but I didn't insist any further. I imagined Hercules with his club in hand wandering through desolate and deserted lands to seek out an adversary who was worthy of him, be it man or god or monster, for a fight to the death. Perhaps the only way for him to find peace.

'I imagine that next summer we'll learn more,' said my father. 'We'll be making a voyage.'

'A voyage?' I said. 'And you'll take me with you?'

'Yes. It will be something you won't forget.'

'Can't you tell me more?'

'In time,' replied my father, and that meant no more questions.

WITH THE RETURN of the good weather, we took the oar down from its place over the hearth and fitted it back in position. The ship needed work to make it seaworthy again. The servants had to clean away all the encrustation and pull at the ropes that held the planks together to tighten them. I watched them using pumice to scrape and smooth the stern, the bow and the hull, and then oil to buff and polish all the wood.

We departed one day at the beginning of the summer. I said goodbye to my mother and my nurse, who kissed my eyes again and again and wept as she always did on these occasions, calling me 'my child', until my father made his voice heard, meaning that it was time to go. I grasped my spear and walked out alongside the king. We crossed the mountainside on foot as the sun was rising and brightening thousands of yellow and blue flowers in its clear, dazzling light. Turning towards the coast we were confronted with a sweep of asphodels crossed by the same slanting light that made them translucent and incredibly luminous. I asked myself why such lovely white flowers were planted on tombs and considered the flowers of the dead.

We descended to the main port and set sail. The wind was in our favour and we put out to sea at a good speed. The ship creaked under the force of the wind and the sail was full and taut. Mentor was with us this time and I was happy about that. He knew so many things and he enjoyed my father's trust. He and I sat down on the rolled ropes to talk, conjecturing about where we were bound. Not even Mentor knew, but one thing was certain: we were distancing ourselves from the mainland and heading out to the open sea.

I asked Mentor what lay in that direction.

'There's another land covered with forests, inhabited by savages who do not respect guests or fear the gods: it is the land of dusk and darkness, and few dare to journey there.'

I didn't ask any more questions but I could see that behind us the coast was getting lower and lower until it vanished as it if had been swallowed by the sea and I felt flooded by a sort of dismay I had never felt before. The horizon was empty in front of us, and yet my father was intent on keeping to the course. Mentor had got to his feet and was holding on to the rail behind the bow; it looked to me as though he was trembling. Time passed until the sun was smack in the middle of the sky and our shadows had shortened until they were practically under our feet. It was then that my father ordered the sailors to strike the sails and cast the anchor; it was so heavy it took four men to drop it overboard into the sea. The sea was calm, almost motionless, and patches of light undulated in the water, blinding us.

Nothing in any direction. The horizon was an empty circle.

There were no longer any birds hovering above us and the wind had dropped as well. No one said a word. I was left alone with my thoughts for what seemed like a very long time. Would we stay there until darkness fell? And then how would we find our way back if all the paths of the sea were darkened?

'Mentor . . .' I whispered, 'Mentor . . .'

'Your father wanted this. He wants you to know what nothingness feels like. Infinity . . . bewilders us. Leaves us hanging between the sky and the abyss. Do you know how many sailors' bones are lying on the bottom of the sea? *Do you know how many of them have drowned?* Their spirits find no peace because they haven't been buried . . .'

'Stop,' I told him, 'I don't want to hear that. I don't want . . .'

I didn't dare say another word and I let myself sink into silence. I thought of how I would feel if the ship were destroyed, if I found myself submerged in the water, amidst the raging waves of a storm, alone, no land in sight, no bearings, no strength. And yet, instead of feeling anguished, I found myself becoming enthralled by that boundless, shapeless expanse. I imagined the sea creatures crossing it, traversing impossible spaces, risking encounters with the monsters of the depths or the blue gods with their hair of seaweed, liquid themselves. Transparent. One day I would defy the shoreless sea, the boundless space, I felt it. I, the son of an Argonaut.

My father finally gave the order to lower the oars into the sea and to alter course. The bow was pointed eastward. We spent the night at sea and I heard the breathing of the blue god as he shifted on the bottom of the sea. *He must not be wakened.*

We beached in a little bay in an unfamiliar land.

'Where are we?' I asked.

'This is the land of the Eleans,' replied the king. 'At a day's sail from here we will find ourselves in Messenia, the kingdom of Nestor. You will meet him. His greying temples reflect his wisdom, and he is respected by all the Achaian kings. I have brought gifts for him and his wife which you yourself will set before them. The time has come for you to be recognized as the man who will one day become the king of Ithaca. Nestor has a palace that overlooks the city of Pylos and a vast bay protected by a long island, providing a safe, ample port for all the vessels that seek shelter there. The king has many sons, some begotten by concubines and others born of Queen Eurydice. Some are almost my age, others, the youngest, are as old as you are. Befriend them – one day one of them will sit on the throne. It's good for the kings and princes to be friends and allies as long as we all respect the confines and dominions of the others, because if a common enemy were ever to challenge us, we could face him together.'

Sandy Pylos stood at the foot of a hill and Nestor's palace was similar to our own, although it was much bigger, because it had no walls or fortifications. From such a vantage point, they'd seen our ship and its standards at a great distance. We donned our best clothes. When we berthed we were met by a squad of warriors commanded by Prince Antilochus, who was a little younger than me; they had been waiting to welcome us and escort us to the palace. We followed them and climbed the steep path, the bay opening beneath us, bordered by a long wooded island.

It was my first visit to a king.

7

We were received in the great hall by the king and queen of Pylos. They were standing, and came towards us as one does with friends, expressing great joy at our arrival.

The king embraced my father and the queen nodded graciously when I put our gift at her feet: a coral necklace belonging to my grandmother Chalcomedusa, whom I had never seen, although according to my mother she had held me in her arms when I was very small. We'd also brought a woollen stole expertly embroidered by the women of Same, who were very skilful weavers. It depicted the divinities of the four seasons crowned with flowers, with golden ears of wheat, with fruit and grapes and finally with reeds tipped with white frost.

Queen Eurydice was much younger than Nestor and she asked one of her handmaids to bring her a mirror so she could try on the necklace at once. She seemed very pleased and she thanked us.

That evening an enormous banquet was laid, even more abundant than the one that my grandfather Autolykos had prepared when I went boar-hunting with him. All of the princes of the royal house participated as well, including Antilochus, who had greeted us at the bay, and Pisistratus, who was just taking his first steps. My father was seated on Nestor's right side and I could see them leaning close together as if they had many confidences to share. The servants came by continuously with spits of roasted ox and kept pouring wine, but my father ate and drank in moderation as I had always seen him do. He'd visited and explored many a wild, faraway place and had always taught me how important it was to stay alert.

I wondered what the two kings were speaking about. About their past adventures? Or about the family affairs of the other kings and their consorts? Nestor had been an Argonaut and had taken part in countless great exploits with my father despite the difference in their ages. The weapons won and plundered hung everywhere on the walls of the room: shields, spears, axes and swords; belts adorned with silver ornaments and shining bronze buckles. Outside the palace gate I could already hear the clamouring of the beggars who had gathered, waiting for the leftovers of our banquet. They knew they would have to fight the dogs for their rightful share.

I spent the evening speaking with Antilochus, who sat next to me, and asked him whether he had ever journeyed away from the palace, by land or by sea.

'By land,' he told me, 'I've been to Sparta and Argus. They are beautiful cities with great palaces but I like it better here because we have this bay full of fish where so many ships can moor. They come here from everywhere, you know: from Asia and the lands of the second sea, and from Crete, which is ruled by King Idomeneus, a friend of my father's. One day I'll go to Crete and even further than that. What about you?'

'I went to the mainland to hunt boar with my grandfather, and I was wounded here, on my thigh, see?'

'Your grandfather? Isn't he that old plunderer and livestock thief?'

'If you weren't such a child,' I replied, 'I'd make you swallow that insult.'

Antilochus apologized: 'I didn't want to offend you. You are my guest and I must honour you. But if Autolykos has such a terrible reputation, it's no fault of mine.'

'My grandfather is not a plunderer, he's a predator, and if he lives as he does he must have his reasons. I was very happy with him and I'm going back as soon as I can.' Having done my duty in defending the family honour I tried to turn the conversation to less controversial subjects: 'This is my second journey away from home and I'm proud to be visiting the house of *wanax* Nestor. Our fathers are bound by a great friendship and we must follow their example.' My thinking was that Antilochus might well be king one day and that we should become allies. I had yet to learn that the future is ruled by fate.

WE SPENT three days in Pylos, then left for Sparta. The king gave us chariots and horses and we left our ships in his care, with part of the crew. I was amazed by the horses, animals of great mettle, accustomed to the battlefield, with twitchy tails and shiny coats. It was Antilochus who brought them to us, and I understood that this was an honour reserved for the most illustrious guests.

I mounted the chariot next to my father and held on to the rail. Mentor followed behind us with the commander of our ship. Three more chariots followed with six of our men, armed with spears, who would act as our escort. The final chariot had a lone driver, to allow room for the gifts we were taking to all the other kings. To reach Sparta we had to travel a very steep road that crossed a mountain range and then descended into the valley on the other side. At times the passage was very narrow and cut into the mountainside, so that the chariots were forced to proceed carefully, one at a time. When we got to the summit a marvellous sight met our eyes: a vast plain with thousands of olive trees, fruit orchards, meadows and pastures with flocks of sheep and herds of horses. I'd never seen anything so wondrous in my life; so many horses all at once!

'This is the kingdom of Tyndareus,' explained my father, 'the lord of Sparta. His queen, Leda, is renowned for her beauty. They have four children, two boys and two girls. Even though Leda has given birth to twins twice, her body is as perfect as a goddess's. And her daughters, young as they are, promise to outdo their mother! When we are in their presence, pay your respects to the queen first, and then to Tyndareus. I will do the same.'

It took us nearly a day to descend from the mountain, cross the plain and travel up another small hill opposite the first, where the city of Tyndareus and Leda stood. We reached the gates of Sparta at dusk and I realized that the day ended much sooner there than it did in Ithaca because of the huge mountain looming to its west, whereas in Ithaca I could watch the sun shine until it sank into the sea.

We were welcomed by the royal guard lined up on both sides of the road that led to the main gate. As we made our way, my father began speaking again: 'Tyndareus reconquered his throne only seven years ago, after his half-brother had tried to banish him from his own city. He never would have succeeded in winning it back without the help of Hercules. His support in the battle was decisive but even his mere presence would have done the trick. Anyone who finds himself up against Hercules knows that he is doomed to defeat – fighting him would be like combat against the gods.'

'Is that really true, father?'

'It is indeed. No mortal can stand up to him. He's like a boulder that rolls down the mountain and tears up pines and hoary olive trees on its way as if they were twigs. His battle cry is like the roar of a lion. I've never seen him wear armour: he fights half-naked and yet no one has ever succeeded in piercing his skin . . .'

I didn't ask my father anything else. But I thought that a man who has massacred his own family has crossed an extreme limit and entered into a territory impossible to return from; he can go nowhere except towards his own destruction. I understood my father's admiration but I couldn't understand how Hercules could still be considered a hero after having carried out such an atrocious crime. Or could the horrendous cruelty required for such a deed actually be a part of his nature? I surmised that men like my father, like Hercules, belonged not only to another generation but to another era: to a race of heroes that had the last drops of the blood of the gods in their veins. We would be different. We would only be men.

When we arrived at the palace, the footmen took care of our horses and we were taken to the baths, where we would be washed and scented and then change into fresh clothing before being admitted to the presence of the king and queen.

Leda had big, luminous eyes and long, wavy hair that fell to her shoulders and hung down her back. I felt my heart miss a beat in my chest. Her look was green and daunting, producing in me a dumbfounded amazement. Was that the gaze of Medusa, who turned anyone who looked upon her to stone? It was a song I heard when I looked at her, a complex song, with many voices combining to form a single melody. The evening breeze entered the palace, carrying upon it the scent of far-off lands, a hint of hay and violets and the distant hooting of the scops owl.

I was shaken from my rapture when my father elbowed me sharply in the side and we stood to pay homage to Tyndareus. The two princes, the youngest of the Argonauts, were shown in; they were about twenty-five years of age and named Castor and Pollux. They were twins and so identical that nothing but the colour of their eyes set them apart: Castor's were more like his mother's, Pollux's more like his father's. They had earned the fame of being unbeatable athletes, and you could see it in their build. Ignoring protocol, they ran to my father and embraced him, and he hugged them back tightly, overcome by emotion. It made me realize how striving together in a common endeavour created a bond that could never be broken.

The king had us sit at his table for the banquet and I looked around to admire the room. Here, like in Pylos, shining weapons hung from the walls – huge oxhide shields, bronze-tipped spears. Parts of the walls were painted with scenes of hunting and combat. One of them represented Hercules in the act of attacking the usurper who had seized Sparta from Tyndareus. It was amazing how every act Hercules performed became legend, even before the echoes of its telling had died away. My father observed the paintings as well with a look of wonder.

'*Atta*,' I whispered, 'does he look like that?'

'No. No artist can depict a hero for what he is, he wouldn't be capable of it. He paints the things that are recognizable about him.'

'Like the club . . . his bulging muscles. Will I ever get to meet him?'

'I don't think so. His road has taken him far, far away from our world, to a place from which *no one has ever returned.*'

I remember how deeply his words struck me. Words like many others, but coming from a mariner they spoke of sheer pain.

The banquet was a display of how immensely powerful the king of Sparta was, with its abundance of roast meats, of fragrant bread, of wine poured into embossed golden cups. There were many guests wearing fine linen gowns interwoven with purple threads, precious belts, buckles of gold, ivory and amber. The queen herself donned a stunning necklace and a wealth of bracelets. How poor our little island kingdom seemed to me then! My Ithaca, rocky and covered by forests, grazed by goats and pigs.

At the end of the banquet, one of the queen's handmaids brought out her two daughters, Helen and Clytaemnestra, to introduce them to the guests. They were thirteen or fourteen years old and were very different from one another. Helen seemed like a supernatural creature, with her perfect face, the violet reflections in her eyes and hair that shone like orichalch, rippling and reflecting the light. When she moved her head, her hair swung in a wave over her body, which flexed languidly like a flower in the breeze. Her lips looked like the buds of mountain poppies when they are about to open, and when they parted revealed white teeth joined in a smile without love, but all the more thrilling for that very reason. I yearned to have the inspiration of a great singer like Phemius in order to express what I felt and saw; how beauty, absolute beauty, held me in its sway. She was slim and much taller than other girls her age. A bud not yet open: what would the rose be like?

My father the king read my thoughts: 'Don't even think about it, my boy, she's not for you. She's made of gold, but you are . . .'

'Made of wood, *atta*. The wood of our oaks on Mount Neritus that only one of Zeus' thunderbolts can shatter. Wood always stays afloat while gold sinks to the bottom.'

My father smiled.

Clytaemnestra was very different from Helen, although they were twins, with a haughty, icy beauty that was disconcerting in someone so young.

I met Helen the next day, towards evening. I was sitting on a stone near the horses' pen, admiring those magnificent animals that we could not breed on Ithaca. I was fascinated by their imposing frames, the powerful curve of their necks, the harmony of their movements, their proud gait and big damp eyes, the way their manes swayed in the wind. I realized all at once that she was approaching and I tried not to look at her. I had begun to think that anyone who looked at her would remain her prisoner, or perhaps unhappy all his life.

'You are Prince Odysseus of Ithaca, aren't you?'

'Yes,' I said without turning. 'And you are Helen of Sparta.'

'Did you know that King Theseus of Athens has asked me to marry him? He's that warrior down there on the black steed.'

'I see him.'

'But he's too old for me.'

'He who challenged and defeated the man-bull in the labyrinth will never be old. What have you done in your life? Nothing. You're just a pretty girl and that's certainly not your doing.'

She smiled without showing anger. 'My doing? What does that matter? Isn't being pretty enough?'

'Well, yes, of course, but . . .'

'Would you ask me to marry you if you could?'

'No.'

She planted herself directly in front of me then and stared at me intently: 'Why do you hate me? Do you have to, because of your name?'

I jumped to my feet and flushed deep red: 'I don't have to do anything because of my name, and I don't hate you . . . I wouldn't ask you to marry me because . . .'

'Why?' she insisted.

'Because, when the gods have finished moulding you, you will

59

be too beautiful to love anyone but yourself. And that's why I think you will be the ruin of many men.'

Helen's eyes seemed to turn the colour of amaranth as the rays of the sun descended behind the peak of Mount Taygetus. A hint of melancholy veiled her expression.

'These things depend only upon the will of the gods,' she replied. 'We are mortals and we have no power. I'm not a bad person, Odysseus. If you could stay here with me I'd talk to you every day.'

'About what?'

'The sun and the night, hate and love, life and death. There's a light in your eyes that I've never seen before, not even in my brothers, handsome as they are. I envy the bride you will take to your chamber, whom you will bend to your bed with the force of your love, prince of Ithaca. Farewell.'

She dissolved in the light of the sunset.

8

WE LEFT TWO DAYS LATER bearing many precious gifts on our chariots. Thoughts of Helen came back to confuse me now and then but I'd look over at my father and think of how happy I was to be on this journey with him; to be learning so many things, hosted by powerful kings and splendid queens. Seeing places that I had never seen: rugged mountains and plains, rivers and forests, flocks at pasture, herds of horses at a gallop, flaming sunsets and silent dawns.

We crossed another mountain chain.

'Where are we going, *atta*?' I asked him. 'Are we beginning our return?'

'You're already eager to get home? Our journey has just begun! No, we're going to Mycenae.'

I couldn't help but shudder when I heard that name: 'That's a cursed place, *atta*. Why there?'

My father continued to look straight ahead as we proceeded along the dusty white path that led to the mountain pass from which we would descend towards the plain of Argus. He replied some time later: 'Because I have heard from both Nestor of Pylos and Tyndareus of Sparta that the king of Mycenae, the biggest and most powerful city of Achaia, is a despicable man, a monster. And so I've asked him to receive me.'

'Why, *atta*?'

'Do you remember that night the messenger came to the palace with that terrible news?'

'I remember it well. I didn't sleep all night.'

'It happened at Mycenae. I'm thinking that only by entering the palace where the massacre took place can we understand what went on that night.'

'You don't think he did it, do you?'

'Hercules? No, as a matter of fact, I don't.'

'Would it change something if you discovered the truth?'

'Greatly, even if the dead cannot be brought back to life.'

I asked no more questions and for many hours we made our way down the road, crossing an immense plain where herds of horses were grazing. At times we came so close I could almost touch them. When we stopped in the evenings I was the one who took care of our steeds. I would free them from their yokes, give them the hay I gathered in the fields and cover them with woollen blankets to protect them from the damp night air.

When we reached Mycenae night was falling. The city was not visible from the road we were travelling on, which led to the port instead. Mycenae was hidden at the end of a narrow valley that had to be crossed, heading north, until we came within sight of two hills: the first one was tall and quite massive, while the second was lower but much rockier; it was on this second hill that the city stood. The palace itself was built on a sheer cliff wall, overhanging a chasm. It towered above all the other buildings, the valley and the distant plain.

We made our way uphill along a road flanked by majestic stone tombs until we reached the gate, a lofty construction made of two jambs topped by a gigantic lintel that not even one hundred men could have moved. Only a god, had he so wished. On the architrave were carved the figures of two lions rearing up to face each other; their bodies were painted a tawny colour and their heads were glittery gold.

'This is Mycenae,' said my father. 'Do you agree that no man should die without having seen it at least once?'

He knocked three times at the gate with the shaft of his spear. It opened for us.

Twenty warriors, ten on the right and ten on the left, saluted us and escorted us to the palace. My father pointed out, to our right, the funerary enclosure that held the tombs of the Perseids, the first sovereigns of the city, and then the palace, up on high, illuminated by torches. Every step that took us closer to the grand royal dwelling made me feel more anxious and uneasy. I walked close alongside my father but I dared not say a word, so as not to be heard by the men escorting us. I also didn't want him to think I was afraid. No one crossed our path save a few rare passers-by; all we could hear, now and then, were doors opening and closing on creaky hinges, and I asked myself why the inhabitants of such a dismal place didn't just leave. Who wouldn't rather live on a hillside planted with olive trees or a meadow crossed by flocks and herds? Or was it just the gloom of the night that made me feel that way?

I was sure that any small village of farmers or shepherds would have seemed more inviting, but perhaps my father had brought me here so I could understand something that words could not explain. At the heart of the most powerful kingdom of Achaia everything was inverted: evil standing for good, defiance and insult taking the place of justice, perhaps even darkness replacing the light. I started thinking that while night descended on the walls of Mycenae, the sun was still shining on Ithaca and sandy Pylos, and I feared that day would never break over the mute roads of this city.

I would have done anything to avoid meeting Eurystheus because I knew deep down that he was evil and sensed we would also be in danger if we ate his bread and spent the night under his roof. But we'd already reached the entrance to the palace.

He received us, alone, in the armoury. I had never seen so many spears and swords, so many shields, so many helmets with their crests. They completely covered the walls. Scores of full suits of armour, lit up by oil lamps, seemed the ghosts of fallen warriors. He sat down with a sigh on a bench and gestured for us to take seats as well. He offered us no wine, no bread, no salt.

'What brings you here, king of Ithaca?' he asked my father.

'My son and I are directed to Argus and, if time permits, to Salamis, to meet with the kings of those cities and to exchange tokens of friendship with them. To pass by your splendid citadel without stopping to pay our respects would have been a failing that, were you to hear about it, you might very well have held against us.'

My father was lying, concealing his true motives. At the same time, I was learning how to feign telling the truth and how to deceive those more powerful than me while avoiding damage and offence.

'I'm grateful to you,' replied Eurystheus without looking at me. It was as if I didn't exist.

There was not a sound to be heard in any of the surrounding rooms or those above us; and yet it was dinner time, the hour of the day at the palace in Ithaca when the lamps were lit, the women set the tables, the servants set the spits into the fire so the meats could be roasted and the handmaids took golden loaves of bread from the ovens. Was this power? Standing watch alone over deserted rooms? That's the way it seemed. I was certain that Eurystheus would be wakeful and alone until dawn, too wary to fall asleep, afraid of being killed or of being visited by nightmares or by the divinities of the Night and the Underworld. He would not close his eyes until first light, but even then he would not sleep, nor carry out the tasks that daylight imposed.

My father spoke again: 'Perhaps we've come at an inopportune time, Eurystheus, a time when you would have preferred to be alone. No king can afford to shirk the duties of governing his kingdom to entertain visitors.'

'Let it not be said,' replied the king of Mycenae, 'that such an illustrious guest did not receive a fitting welcome. I have not had a banquet laid for you and your son, but the reason is another. I am tormented by an affliction that gives me no respite: a shooting pain in my head, as if a fiery arrow were burning my temples. But I will have you served every sort of food and strong red wine, the kind that warms the heart, in a large, richly decorated room, and tomorrow you shall leave with the customary gifts.'

Two warriors escorted us to our quarters. We walked down a long corridor lined by bare walls made of big blocks of stone. Our footsteps rang out in the silence and the palace seemed deserted, and yet several times I had the feeling we were being followed. We were finally shown into a large hall adorned with paintings. Wooden chairs were placed against the walls. A window opened like a flaming red square in the middle of the grey surface of the longest wall, still reflecting the sun which had already set. In front of two of the chairs were tables with bread, roasted meats and pigeons' eggs. On the side, grapes and figs.

'Father,' I said as soon as the steps of the two warriors had faded away down the long corridor, 'didn't you hear someone behind us? Following us, or maybe spying on us?'

'No,' he replied, 'but I had other things on my mind. Why did Eurystheus have us taken to this room? Why is there no member of the royal family here to keep us company?'

'Perhaps he trusts no one. If he can't – or doesn't want to be – present, he won't let anyone else be with us either. Perhaps he senses that we've come here looking for something.'

A servant entered with a jug of wine and he poured some into our cups. Both were finely crafted in gold embossed with images of birds in flight. My father put the cup to his lips.

'It's strong and undiluted,' he said. 'Don't drink more than a cup.' As the servant turned his back to him in order to fill my cup, father let his bronze ring fall to the ground.

The servant did not turn.

'Mistrust abounds in this house,' observed my father. 'He's deaf, and probably dumb.'

I nodded.

The servant lit an oil lamp that he was carrying. Along with the others hanging from the walls, it cast a warm light, making the place less gloomy. But dining alone with my father in the house, perhaps in the very room, where Hercules had slaughtered his family made me feel terribly uneasy and even made my flesh creep. I had felt a thousand times more comfortable in my grandfather's house in Acarnania, despite his dreadful reputation. Even after he had loosed a boar against me.

'The walls can speak, though,' said my father in a low voice. 'And hear, as well.'

I understood what he meant: I wasn't to say another word about the reason behind our visit. There was no need. We spoke of other things: about Argus, where I had never been, and about Salamis, the island kingdom of Telamon, another Argonaut and a friend and comrade of my father.

'He has a son who is just a little older than you: he's gigantic, as strong as a bull. His name is Ajax. And another younger boy called Teucer, who is good with a bow and arrow, like you are,' he told me. 'I'm sure you'll be friends. You know, one day it will be you lot ruling over our kingdoms, when we've died or become too old. That's why we are making this journey: so you can meet and perhaps even befriend the other princes. This will prevent wars.'

Even as we spoke, I could feel that his mind was on other things. He stood abruptly, walked towards the door and opened it briefly, then continued: 'I don't like this place. I don't like the welcome we got from Eurystheus and I don't like this isolation. At the end of the corridor one of his warriors is standing guard. And there are two at the other end. We won't be allowed to speak with anyone, nor will anyone be able to speak with us under these circumstances. Staying here makes no sense. Tomorrow we'll leave, at dawn.'

'Father, how did Eurystheus come to rule over this city?'

My father was silent at first, then walked over to the window and looked out at the dark night. I could almost read his thoughts: he had come certain to find some sign, some clue that would allow him to absolve Hercules of such a monstrous crime, at least in his own heart. Leaving without achieving this would mean defeat. A mute city, a sullen king, a segregated room, a still, stifled atmosphere, were all that we had seen and heard.

'Eurystheus and Hercules are cousins . . . Many, many years ago, an oracle had decreed that the last descendant of the Perseids would reign over Mycenae and Tiryns. Now, that should have been Hercules, but a priestess of Hera stepped up and swore that Eurystheus had been born first. She claimed that the goddess Hera herself, who is present at all births, had revealed this fact to her. Eurystheus became the lord of the two cities; Hercules was forced to leave and to begin a life of wandering.'

'Then why should this terrible crime have happened at all? What possessed him to return here?'

'That's what I'd like to find out, but Eurystheus has done his best to make that impossible. We're not free to go anywhere or speak with anyone. But you are certainly right, my son: that is the heart of the matter. Why did the massacre happen here? Perhaps in Argus we'll learn something more. There are some things that can only be whispered by one king into the ear of another. Not here.'

We finished eating and I didn't see the bottom of my cup. We retired into the adjacent room where two beds had been prepared with linen sheets woven through with purple threads. My father laid his sword and sheath on the floor next to him and I kept my dagger under my pillow. I fell asleep, although scenes of the blood-bath kept throbbing under my eyelids.

Then in the middle of the night I heard a noise in the next room. It was coming from the foot of the door, and it sounded like a dog trying to scratch his way in. I put my ear to the floor and listened. Someone was scraping something hard and rough over the stone, to make a noise that could only be heard at a short distance. Someone who wanted us to hear, but no one else?

I got up and made my way to the other room, following the dying light of the last oil lamp left burning. I lifted the bolt very slowly, without making the slightest noise, and then swiftly pulled open the door. What I found outside was a boy, his eyes flashing with fear.

9

I TOOK HIM BY THE HAND and pulled him in.

'Was it you making that noise? With what?'

He showed me a nail stuck in a piece of wood.

'Who's there?' asked my father from the other room.

'It's just a little boy . . . What's your name?'

'Eumelus.'

My father approached and our little visitor backed up to the door, clearly frightened.

'We don't want to hurt you,' he said. 'We're friends. Where do you come from, Eumelus? And what are you doing in this place?'

'I'm from Pherai, in Thessaly . . .'

My father turned towards me: 'This isn't just any child; look at his clothing. He's a young guest of this palace, a prince, most likely. A guest, perhaps, but more likely a hostage . . .'

Then, turning back to the boy, he said: 'Why have you come here? Is there something you have to tell us?'

The boy was struck dumb, and I motioned to my father to step away: his presence was too intimidating. He understood without me saying a word and he went back to the other room. I looked in my knapsack for something the child might like; I found a little wooden horse I'd carved with my knife and showed it to him: 'Look, I made this myself. It's pretty, isn't it? Would you like to have it?'

Eumelus nodded. I stretched out the open palm of my hand with the little horse. He hesitated for a moment, then snatched it up and put it in his belt.

'This is my gift for you: remember Odysseus of Ithaca whenever you take it out of your belt to play with. Do you know what that means? It means we're friends. Friends exchange gifts.'

'I don't have anything to give you in exchange,' the boy replied.

'Your friendship is the best gift. And then, who knows, maybe some day you'll receive me in your palace and you'll give me a gift to remember you by. But now, tell me why you were scraping the floor under the doorway. You wanted me to hear you and open the door, didn't you?'

Eumelus nodded again. I came close, took his hands between mine and looked into his eyes: 'What did you want to tell me?'

Eumelus started to speak, very quietly, without ever changing the tone of his voice or the expression on his face, and to describe what he'd seen one night some time in the past in the very hall we found ourselves in. He'd been awakened that night by strange noises and then by moaning and gasping. He'd got up and followed the direction that the noises were coming from, opened the door a crack and had then seen something so horrible that he turned and ran back down the corridor as fast as his legs could carry him, desperate to get back to his room and jump into his bed before anyone saw him.

When he'd finished talking he just stared at me with those eyes: so big, so black, so open, as if he wanted to let me look all the way into his heart.

'Are you sure you weren't dreaming?' I asked him.

He shook his head: no, he hadn't been dreaming. Then he showed me what the nail stuck in the piece of wood was for. He scraped between one stone and the next on the floor and gathered the dirt that had collected in the cracks. He poured some into the palm of my hand and then he showed me that the little sack hanging on his belt was full of it.

'You have to leave with us, tomorrow. We'll take you back to your parents. They can't have imagined what a situation you would be in.'

I beckoned for my father to come close, certain now that the child trusted us, and showed him the dirt. 'He uses the nail to scrape at the cracks in the floor: look, this isn't dirt, it's dried blood. The floor was cleaned but not everything was washed away.'

My father sniffed at the specks in my hand and nodded solemnly. 'It's blood, no doubt about it.'

'We have to take him with us,' I said. 'We can't leave him alone in this place with this secret in his heart. It's too much for him.'

'They won't let me go,' said Eumelus, 'and there's not enough room on your chariots for you to hide me. If they found me, they'd kill all of us.'

'You are Admetus' son, aren't you?' said my father. 'I'll tell him what we've seen here and the state you're in.'

'He can't do anything either, not even if he wanted to,' protested the boy. 'There's only one man who can free me from this prison.'

None of us said a word because we were all thinking of the same person: Hercules.

The next day, at dawn, we went down to the palace courtyard. Eurystheus was already waiting, surrounded by his warriors. Two men bore his gifts for the king of Ithaca: a bearskin and an antique ceremonial sword whose burin-engraved blade was inlaid with gold. It had a gilded hilt as well, its pommel ending in two lion heads. I'd never seen such a wondrous thing. We reciprocated with a bronze and amber staff that my father had taken as booty in Asia.

As we were leaving I happened to look up and then caught my father's eye. I said, softly: 'Up high, third window.' There was a child leaning out slightly and seemingly waving his hand.

Eurystheus' gaze shot to the window and his mouth twisted into a smirk. Perhaps he wanted to make sure that his young guest was staying put.

My father dropped his head, I think to hide his impotent outrage. Leaving a child in such a place, in the grip of such a ruthless, ferocious man, was against his nature. The heart inside his chest was certainly howling like a dog. We passed under the gate of lions, still shrouded by darkness, then continued down the ramp until we reached the fork in the road. We turned left, towards Argus.

'Go slowly, now,' I said to my father. 'Set the horses to a walk.'

The time had come for me to tell him everything the child had said.

'There was a great banquet in honour of Hercules. Eurystheus had sent him word that he wanted to make peace and restore good relations. He wanted his cousin to bring his whole family to the palace, and Hercules accepted the invitation. As the evening wore on, his wife Megara and his children retired to their chambers, while Eurystheus insisted that Hercules and the other table companions remain to enjoy the feasting and revelry. Hercules drank and drank, until he lost consciousness. Perhaps his wine contained a drug that caused him to lose his senses. They carried him into his room and left him there.

'The palace sank into silence.

'But late that night, Eumelus, who was sleeping in a room at the end of the corridor, heard screaming and moaning, ominous thuds, objects being overturned. He strained to hear, imagining that cries of alarm would soon be filling the corridors, expecting to hear the pounding tread of the guards on duty rushing by. Instead, nothing. No one moved, no one called out. What was happening could not be interrupted. The child got up from his bed then and made his way, barefoot, down the whole corridor until he found himself in front of the room where all the noise had been coming from. Now he could hear them distinctly: the horrendous sounds of slaughter.

'He pushed the door open a crack and saw what was happening. Hercules lay unconscious on the floor and three armed men were finishing off the members of his family who were still breathing. His wife and his children. Then one of them put a sword in Hercules' hand. Eumelus fled back to his room, terrified that the three killers would leave the room and discover him. He didn't close an eye for the rest of the night. At dawn, the shrieks of a woman woke everyone. The palace resounded with cries of horror, groaning and weeping.'

My father was turned to stone by that story. He asked me: 'Why do you want me to go so slowly?' The thread of his thoughts always ran in the direction that he wanted, not in the direction that anyone else would expect.

'Father, do you remember seeing the boy at the window?'

'Yes, I saw him. It was Eumelus.'

'He was sending me signals.'

'What? What kind of signals?'

'Like the ones shepherds use to communicate at a distance. We use them on the island too.'

'Of course we do. And what did he say?'

'Two cypresses.'

My father pulled on the reins and stopped the chariot. Mentor, behind us, and the others of our escort did the same.

'What does that mean?'

'A place, I think, along the road we're taking. He knows where we are headed. A place marked by two cypress trees.'

'A tomb, perhaps. And something might happen there?'

'I think we'll understand when we get there.'

We started up again, at a slow pace. We reached another fork: left to Tiryns and the sea, right to Argus. We looked around: no one was following us, no one was ahead of us.

The fields were full of farmers already at work, reaping the barley and gathering the hay. The herdsmen and shepherds were taking their animals to pasture. Behind us rose Tiryns, at the top of a rock towering over the tilled fields. I turned to see it better, white and blue in the middle of the green countryside, so beautiful. And I saw the two cypress trees.

'There they are, father! Look!'

'Open land, and we're not very far from Mycenae . . . what shall we do?'

'I'll go alone. If all of our chariots turn in that direction, we'll be visible from a distance. I don't think anything escapes Eurystheus' men. If the boy is there, he and I will return together. If he's not there, I'll wait until the sun is two spans above the horizon and then

I'll come back alone. You wait for me here, behind those trees, so you won't be seen; it will look like we've stopped for a rest. In the meantime, tell Mentor what I've told you.'

I set off on foot, keeping up a good pace, towards the two cypress trees. A path led through the fields, planted with crops that I didn't recognize. The cypresses were two big trees, visible at quite a distance, rising alongside an ancient burial mound which perhaps marked the tomb of some ancient hero. I approached warily, looking all around, but the place was deserted. I let some time pass, checking every now and then how far the sun had risen from the horizon. My father and his men were well hidden in the forest and even I couldn't see them at this distance.

I found him suddenly at my side, as if he'd appeared from nowhere.

'Where were you?' I asked.

The boy pointed to the entrance to the tomb.

'There? Weren't you afraid the dead would pull you underground?'

He shook his head. He wasn't afraid. He knew that he had much more to fear from the living than from the dead.

'How did you get here?'

He pointed at a path that snaked through the fields in the middle of high rows of elms and poplars. From a distance no one would have been able to pick him out. He must have got out of some window at the back of the palace, dropped down and taken a shortcut to get out to the fields.

'Let's go,' I told him. 'Once they discover you're missing they'll be looking for you everywhere.'

He nodded and let me take his hand and lead him to where my father was waiting.

The time he'd spent in the palace must have taught him to keep his thoughts to himself, for he avoided talking whenever possible.

'Listen,' I told him, 'when we're with the king my father you'll have to tell him everything you know: he's risking a lot to help you and so am I. You know that, don't you?'

'I know,' replied Eumelus. Enough said, in his mind.

My father emerged from the forest as soon as he saw us crossing the road. 'We'll leave immediately,' he said, 'but we'll split up. You and I will go to Argus with the child on a byroad. Mentor and the others will continue along the main road, but they'll split up again as soon as possible. We've already discussed it. We'll meet up on the isthmus in six days' time, at dusk. This way we won't attract undue attention. Now let's get moving.'

We said goodbye and separated. Each chariot left a long wake of dust behind it, racing off down the main road. We took a lesser road that wasn't heavily trafficked. In no time, our route became a mere footpath that climbed up towards the hills. Eumelus seemed to be having a lot of fun, and he wanted to hold the reins and drive the chariot himself.

'This boy is full of spunk,' said my father, letting him have a go. 'He'll have a chariot of his own one day!'

In the meantime I was thinking: Eurystheus would be more or less certain by now that the boy had somehow managed to join our party. We'd taken this byway, counting on the fact that Eurystheus and his men would see the wake of dust from the other chariots heading north and would decide to follow them in an attempt to catch us. It was also reasonable to assume, however, that Eurystheus would credit us with a bit of cunning, given our family tradition. It would make perfect sense, then, for them to search for us on the less busy and less practicable thoroughfares, which was the way we'd logically choose to go if we were trying to hide the child. Actually, they would most likely decide to go both ways, and then we would truly have no way out. We needed another stratagem.

The first time we stopped, I asked Eumelus to repeat everything he'd told me about the night of the massacre to my father, leaving nothing out. He agreed. He told the story with a wealth of details, and even told us that the bodies of Hercules' wife and children had been dumped in a common grave outside the city walls. That's why he had decided to scrape up the blood that had dried between the cracks in the flooring, so that he could bury the little leather sack in the shade of a pine tree overlooking the sun-drenched valley.

'A better place for them.'

'What were you doing at Mycenae in the first place?' asked my father.

'The king had asked my parents. Why would they refuse? It's customary for a prince to spend time as a page in another king's court.'

As they were speaking I had wandered off to check the path that climbed up from the valley and I'd spotted Eurystheus' men. I returned to my father. 'They're on their way,' I said. 'We could have expected as much, right?'

'Yes. But now what would you do, you who are so clever?'

'We have two choices: try to make them believe that we never came this way at all . . .'

'. . . By wiping away every trace of our passage. Gather the horses' dung, take apart the chariot, hide the pieces and hide the horses. Find a hiding place ourselves. Until they've gone on.'

'Complicated, time-consuming and difficult. Perhaps we don't have the time. If they're coming this way it means they've seen us and if they find us in hiding, things can only get worse. Easier to hide him,' I said, turning to Eumelus. 'Do you see that pine down there, halfway down the hill?'

The boy nodded.

'Are you good at climbing?'

He nodded. 'That's all I did when I was little, living on Mount Pelion.'

'Good. Run as fast as you can. By the time they get here, you must already be at the top, and you'll stay there until I come looking for you.'

Eumelus disappeared into the woods.

'He's Thessalian,' said my father. 'Their land is covered with forests: they learn to climb trees even before they learn to talk.'

I opened the bag with our provisions and gave some food to my father. 'Let them find us here sitting calmly and enjoying a meal, but we'll be ready for anything. The first thing they'll be asking themselves is why we separated from the others. So, what shall we say?' This time it was me soliciting the inventiveness of Laertes' mind.

'Because we're going to Arcadia,' he replied instantly. 'Haven't you ever heard of the Sanctuary of the Wolf King? Your grandfather's name strikes fear into everyone's heart. Let me do the talking.'

THERE WERE a dozen of them, well armed, on five chariots. We'd seen them at the palace and we greeted them.

'Has something happened?' asked my father.

'We're searching for a child. A young prince, entrusted to the care of the palace.'

'And you're looking for him here?'

'That's right. He disappeared when you left. Why have you separated from the rest of your party?'

We exchanged a glance, King Laertes and I, and our heart laughed because we'd foreseen everything.

'Why, we're going to Arcadia. To the Sanctuary of the Wolf King . . .'

The smiles were wiped off the faces of our pursuers.

'It's a family matter, I'm sure you understand. My son's grandfather, my father-in-law, of whom you will have heard speak, has the blood of the wolf mixed with his own, and I want to avoid a similar curse for Odysseus. No one wants to see his own son turning into a wolf once a month, only to surprise and slaughter lonely wayfarers in a deserted place late at night.

'We would happily join forces with you searching for your precious guest but, you see, we're in a hurry. We have to make it to the sanctuary before the full moon. If we don't arrive in time the consequences could be very unfortunate indeed; not only for us, but for yourselves as well. Trust me.'

That was all that was needed. They took a hasty look around and went back to where they'd come from. I waited until I could see them back at the start of the path on the plain before going to Eumelus, but only to tell him to follow us without leaving the forest.

Until night had fallen.

10

WE WENT ON UNTIL THE SUN set and we were completely certain that no one had been following us except for our young prince walking in the woods. Our path had led us high up the mountainside and the night air was chilly. We came across a fire that some shepherd must have abandoned. My father pulled on the reins and stopped the horses. The embers of the fire were still glowing under the ashes, so it was easy to rekindle the flames with some dry leaves and twigs. I called out to Eumelus to tell him that it was safe to leave the forest. No answer.

'Where are you?' I called then turned to my father: 'Where could he have gone? I told him to follow us, without leaving the forest. He can't have got lost.'

My father dropped his head and sighed. 'He's a strange child,' he said. 'Maybe he changed his mind. I thought he trusted us. Maybe he was frightened by what happened.'

'So am I, *atta*, I'm more than just afraid of that story you came up with! Tell me the truth: what does the Sanctuary of the Wolf King in Arcadia have to do with how grandfather got his name?'

'Nothing, those are just stories that people have made up because your grandfather has such a nasty disposition and he has a name . . . well, he has a name unlike any other. But perhaps I shouldn't have told Eurystheus' warriors that story.'

'Of course you should have: it made them turn back.'

'Quiet!' said my father, laying his hand on his sword. I heard the sound of twigs breaking and Eumelus appeared. His left hand held a rabbit he had captured and killed somehow.

'Do you have a knife?' he asked.

I handed him mine. He skinned the rabbit and removed the entrails, separating the heart, liver, spleen and kidneys from the bowels, then skewered it with the knife and set it over the embers to roast. We watched in amazement.

'Where did you learn that?' I asked him.

'Where I live, they leave you in the forest when you're little and you have to learn to survive. Some don't make it back. Most learn.'

When we had satiated our hunger and wrapped ourselves in our woollen cloaks, the urge to talk came upon us. The sky was full of big, luminous stars, and light puffs of wind rustled the oak leaves. I heard the screeching song of an owl. Athena! She was close, watching over me. I felt her presence in the forest, her green and gold eyes seeking me out.

'Young prince,' began my father, 'are you certain that you saw what you told us? Might you not have dreamt it? Sometimes dreams seem truer than reality.'

'What about the blood? Have you forgotten that I brought you their blood?' said the boy.

'That's true. The blood,' admitted my father.

'But why did they do it? Why didn't they kill him as well?' I asked.

'Eurystheus is too shrewd to have made such a mistake,' my father replied. 'The townspeople would surely have accused him of the misdeed. They would have rebelled against him and brought him down. Hercules has always been close to the people's hearts; everyone adored him and would certainly have wanted him to take his cousin's place as king of Mycenae and Tiryns. Eurystheus did this to demolish Hercules' reputation as a hero whose generosity knew no limits. He had to turn the hero into a bloodthirsty monster who would slaughter his own family. And spread the news everywhere, not only among the people but among the kings.'

My father turned back to the boy. 'And afterwards? The morning after? What happened then?'

A spirit passed in the night, the oak trees shivered. Eumelus took a deep breath and began speaking and both my father and I were astonished. He seemed like someone else: the little boy who had said so few words up to then suddenly began to describe what he had experienced in great detail, like a raging river breaking its banks, like a singer inspired by the gods. I think it was Athena who freed the words that now tumbled from the circle of his teeth. Even the timbre of his voice sounded different.

'Hercules awoke with his sword in hand, surrounded by the slain bodies of his wife and children. He let out a roar of anguish and horror that I will never forget. The entire palace trembled, the horses broke out of their pens, the crows fled the towers, cawing. I crept down the corridor just in time to see the king's guards taking the sword from Hercules before he could turn it on himself. Eurystheus then appeared out of nowhere and cried loudly: "How could you? How could you have committed such a heinous crime?"

'Hercules looked as if he'd lost his mind: he let himself be bound in chains and dragged underground to a prison chamber. As they were hauling him off, the king shouted after him: "What you have done is too terrible to be judged by any man. Only a god can judge you and inflict the punishment you deserve."

'There was great despair in the palace. People wept because they could not believe what they had heard. Or because they did believe it, and Hercules was the one man on all the earth they had thought was good and just. I badly wanted to find a way to get into the prison and tell him the truth. I was certain that he would snap his chains and break down the door, and then after chasing Eurystheus through every room of the palace he would crush him like a cockroach. But no one could get close to him.

'Days and nights passed in this way. From the window of my room I saw them carrying the corpses of those innocents out in darkness and tossing them into a nameless hole they'd dug in an unmarked spot in the valley. I saw the monster himself standing on the tower rising over the chasm and watching against a red sky.

'I learned to hide, to escape his sight, to live as if I didn't exist. If anyone found out that I had seen everything, my life would be worthless. I stopped speaking, sometimes I was even afraid to think, afraid that Eurystheus could read my mind.

'In the end, the verdict that everyone has become familiar with was pronounced. Eurystheus solemnly declared that the Oracle had been consulted and had condemned Hercules to atone for his crime by liberating the world of all the monsters infesting it: wild beasts, evil giants, savage predators that feed on human flesh. "If you do so, and you survive, you will perhaps have expiated your guilt. If you die, as you deserve to, no one will weep for you: you will have paid your debt," said the king his cousin.

'This was certainly what Eurystheus had hoped for; that his rival would be killed off in one of those impossible labours, his memory and his honour stained for all time. He had Hercules released from his chains.

'Since that day, Hercules has wandered through the spheres of nightmare, taking on these seemingly impossible tasks. He has given up all his weapons, all his clothing and ornaments, and lives like a wild man. He dons nothing but the pelt of a lion that he killed with his bare hands near Nemea, he brandishes an uprooted tree trunk as his club and he feeds on whatever he finds.'

My father laid a hand on Eumelus' shoulder. 'You acted bravely and wisely, and the most important thing is that you lived to pass on the truth. Eurystheus had us followed because he is tormented by doubts about how much you know, and he'd have no scruples about killing you for that. Now that you're free, he'll have no peace until he does away with you; we'll have to be extremely careful. Remember: on the day that you meet Hercules, it will be your duty to tell him everything you saw.'

'But how will I ever be able to meet him? No one knows where he is.'

'You will surely see him again, when the time comes. Your testimony will lift an unbearable weight from his heart. Try to rest now. Tomorrow a long journey awaits us.'

They lay down near the fire. I, instead, ventured into the forest, hoping I would meet my goddess. The owl's song had inspired me, as if Athena herself were calling to me, just like the first night I'd slept in my grandfather's house in Acarnania. I walked for a short while but it felt as though I had travelled a long distance when, in the moonlight, I saw a nest of leaves at the foot of an enormous ash tree. I felt that she was close, so close that I was a little afraid. Then I was overcome by a sense of deep fatigue and I lay down on the bed of leaves.

Behind closed eyes, I saw seven armies laying siege to the walls of a city with seven gates. Each army was led by a great warrior. Seven more warriors were on the inside, trying to drive them back. At the fourth gate I saw the goddess, armed, protecting the city. None of the attackers could hope to defeat her. She was dreadful to behold: a crested helmet on her head, a gorgon on her shield and the aegis on her breast.

My vision was fragmented into a thousand shards, into a frenzy of blood, of neighing and shrieking, of horses dashing at a gallop against the ramparts and walls of the stronghold. Duels of man against man, king against king. I saw one of the skirmishers climbing the wall and hurling himself at his opponent. They plunged their blades into each other's bodies. The attacker took a blow to his side but sank his own sword into the neck of his adversary, who crashed to the ground lifeless. The victor raised a cry of triumph but suddenly fell to his knees as he saw his own blood flowing copiously from his side onto the ground. I realized that this man was beloved by the goddess and she, springing from one tower to the next like a sparrowhawk, had come to save him from death. Tydeus was his name. Melanippus his enemy.

Tydeus dragged himself with a final spurt of energy to where Melanippus lay and then he beheaded him with a single stroke of his sword. He smashed the skull on a stone until it split open and then he gulped out his enemy's brains. Athena was so outraged and disgusted that she took flight, vanishing into the air, leaving Tydeus to the jaws of the Chaera of death.

I jumped as if hit by a thunderbolt at the sight of so much horror and I found myself awake and covered with sweat on my bed of leaves. Silence all around me; the air was undisturbed by any breeze, and yet I felt her close to me. Had she flown here from the city of the seven gates?

'O goddess of the cerulean eyes that witnessed this atrocious act,' I prayed, 'do not reveal yourself to me in your true form, a mortal cannot bear the sight of a god. But guide me, please, assist me and I promise to think only of you. I will have no one but you in my thoughts and in my heart.'

I looked up and saw the owl perched on the highest branch of the enormous ash tree. She was looking at me. I was certain that the goddess had heard me.

I wandered back to the fire without even knowing where I was going, as if I were walking in my sleep. My father was sleeping with his hand on the hilt of his sword, as always. Eumelus was curled up next to him and he finally seemed serene, deep in an untroubled sleep as if he were home next to his parents. I was still completely shaken by the vision I had had in my dream, no less horrifying than what Eumelus had seen in Eurystheus' house. I was certain that this hadn't happened by chance: the goddess had carried these visions with her in her flight from the city of the seven gates, brought them to me. Why?

I finally understood the true purpose of my journey: I had to experience the wide world, so different from the peaceful island where I had grown up. I had to learn what lengths a human being will go to in order to achieve power or to maintain it and how hate can drag a man straight to the bottom of the abyss.

I tossed another piece of wood onto the fire, gathered some dry grass and lay down upon it, covering myself with my cloak. In the end I let the peace of that place seep into my head. I realized that the images of horror would not be back, not that night anyway, and that I could abandon myself to sleep near the fire, under the stars, next to my father.

THE LIGHT of day awoke us and I watched the moon grow pale until it faded into the glow of dawn. Our horses, free of their yoke, were grazing on the woodland underbrush. Sparrows hopped between blades of grass and mountain flowers while flocks of starlings rose from the treetops. They sought a direction at first, then followed their instincts and veered down towards the plain. I didn't have the courage to tell my father what I had dreamt because, now that the sun had risen, I was confused, and couldn't have said whether what I remembered was real or not.

We set off, driving along the ridge of the mountain for as long as we could. When the path seemed to come to a dead end in the middle of a wood, we began our descent, searching for a road wide enough for our chariot. Once we had found our way again, we continued at a much faster rate and before evening we saw the walls of Argus appear with the palace on Larissa Hill. Argus . . . how often had I heard that city spoken of! The sight of it was no less than I expected. A mighty citadel, with high walls and towers covered with slabs of white stone. These had earned Argus the name of 'bright city', famous in all of Achaia. But as we drew closer an ominous sight appeared before our eyes: banners of black wool were hanging from the bastions and towers in a sign of deep mourning.

We didn't have to wait long to understand why: the body of a warrior in full armour, wrapped in a red cloak, was being carried on the shoulders of six of his comrades up an earth ramp to the top of a tall pyre made of pine trunks. The bier passed quite close to us, and from my elevated position on the chariot, I could see him quite clearly.

'That's Tydeus,' said my father, 'an Argonaut, the son-in-law of King Adrastus. He returns from an unsuccessful expedition, as you can see.'

'That's the man I dreamt of last night,' I whispered. The man that the goddess, horrified, had abandoned to his death. Why had she come to me with those visions? Why?

'Look,' said my father again, 'see that boy with the blond hair and the black cloak following the bier? Tydeus' son. He's just a bit younger than you are, and he could become the king of Argus one day.'

'What's his name, father?' I asked.

'His name is Diomedes. As young as he is, he's a formidable fighter, I've heard.'

'I can tell,' I answered. I watched as he followed his father's bier up to the pyre. Diomedes walked with a firm step, his back straight, his hand resting on the hilt of his sword, crafted from bright bronze. His colours were black and gold. It was he who went to the base of the enormous heap of wood and set it ablaze. Immediately it was wrapped in a vortex of flame. And it was he who ritually bent Tydeus' sword and handed it to the priests so they could put it in his tomb when they buried the ashes.

I caught his eye when he passed in front of me and bowed my head as a sign of respect. He barely gave me a glance, but I knew he'd seen me.

We slept under the portico of the market square, on the straw they used for the animals because we had arrived at a very bitter moment for the city and the family of the king. What was more, had we appeared at the palace, everyone would have noticed that the king and prince of Ithaca were travelling with the boy sought by the king of Mycenae. The next morning, as soon as the market filled with people, my father learned what had happened to Tydeus and the six other great Argive warriors who had laid siege to the city of Thebes with seven armies.

And I learned that I had dreamed the truth *or maybe I only know that now in this play of mirrors that is my mind every real thing is reflected a thousand times like an echo on the sides of a rocky valley.*

We also learned that young Diomedes, along with six friends and comrades, had sworn to dedicate every day of their lives to training for combat, so as to be ready for the moment when they would return to the gates of Thebes to avenge their fallen fathers. I thought that I would never see him again; I didn't know that the gods had a different destiny in store for us.

We started out again on our journey after buying food and blankets for the night. We journeyed northward for four days, until we saw the great rock of Corinth and then, finally, the sea.

That same evening we met up with our travelling companions, who we found waiting for us in a wood sacred to Poseidon, lord of the Isthmus.

Mentor came first to welcome us. His beard was bristly, his hair dry and tousled by the sea breeze and the sun. 'We were in such distress,' he said, 'we'd heard such terrible things! I thank the gods that brought you here safe and sound, *wanax*.' He kissed my father's hand. 'Seeing you arrive was like seeing the sun rise.'

'We're very happy to see you as well. Appointments of this sort almost never end well. But you acted judiciously and all went for the best. Tell me, then, what news have you heard?'

'Hercules has been seen in Crete, where he is pursuing an enormous, invincible wild bull that has been devastating the countryside, destroying the crops and then eluding capture. It has evaded the best hunters and killed many of them. One man alone succeeded in wounding him, but that very same night the bull charged into his house, trampling everything he found in his way. All those inside were crushed under his hooves, gored by his horns . . . No one but Hercules can find him and take him on, but he will surely meet his own death in doing so.'

'It is death he seems to be seeking,' replied my father. 'But even though he doesn't know it yet, he has a reason for living. What else?'

'Seven kings laid siege to Thebes of the seven gates, where Oedipus' sons Polynices and Eteocles had supposedly agreed to take turns reigning over the kingdom in alternate years. The attackers were defeated . . .'

'I know. We saw Tydeus' body being placed on the pyre, his sword being plucked from the blaze and bent in two.'

'The two brothers killed each other, each plunging his sword into the other's chest. An unspeakable atrocity. The new ruler decreed that their bodies be left unburied, prey to dogs and worms. Their sister Antigone violated the edict by scattering a handful of sand over them, but she was discovered and sentenced to be buried alive! First Mycenae, ruled by a monster who has slain innocent creatures, and now Thebes . . . O *wanax*, my king, why has Achaia been cursed with such horror? What is happening to our land?'

'I don't know. Neither mortals nor gods can stop fate from taking its course. But it is in our power, at this moment, to save an innocent child. You'll board a ship with the boy and sail as far as Iolcus. There, get yourselves a couple of mules and disguise yourselves as merchants until you reach Pherai. You, Mentor, will be responsible for everything. Your escort will carry arms, but keep them hidden; no one is to know they are warriors. Once you are in Pherai, make it known to the king that you have important news for him. If he agrees to receive you, you'll take the boy to him.'

'What if he won't receive me?'

'You'll take Eumelus to the palace door. He will know how to make himself recognized and how to bring you into the presence of the sovereigns. Then you will tell them, and them alone, about what happened, and the boy will be your witness. Let them know that you were sent by Laertes, who reigns over Ithaca and other islands. Go now. May the gods lead you down safe paths.'

We watched him leave. We hadn't spent a single night together eating and drinking wine by the fire and recounting everything that had happened to us in the time since we'd left each other. My father and I left before dawn as well, after stocking up on food and water, following the seashore westward at first and then heading inland, where steep rocky gullies awaited us.

'*Atta*,' I said, 'wouldn't it have been better to return to Sparta, where we can rely on the friendship of King Tyndareus?'

'No,' he said, 'because we're going to Arcadia.'

'Arcadia? But I thought that . . .'

'That it wasn't true? That I'd invented it all just to scare off Eurystheus' guards?'

'Yes, that is what I thought.'

'I was telling the truth,' he answered. 'We're going to the Sanctuary of the Wolf King.'

11

THE MOUNTAINS. They certainly weren't any higher than those I'd seen in the kingdom of grandfather Autolykos, but they were rockier, steeper, more inaccessible. Many of the peaks were whitened by snow.

'Will I be able to see it up close, father?' I asked. 'The snow?'

'No, we won't have time to go that high, nor can we leave the chariot and horses unguarded. You'll see snow when you go back to Acarnania to visit your grandfather. Ask him to take you up to Mount Parnassus; you'll be able to touch it there. It's like sea foam, but it's very, very cold: if you sink your hands into it they become red and then purple and after a while you can't feel them any more. Your grandfather doesn't fear the gods. He'll be delighted to take you up to the peak and he'll say to you: "See? There's no Apollo, no Muses, none of those other false creatures."'

The snow . . . so much of it . . . infinite, cruel. Even then it was in my dreams, nightmares.

They were wondrous, actually, those glittering silver spires that rose to the left and right of the deep gorges. Beneath us the river gurgled and sparkled over multicoloured gravel, boulders, stones, pebbles, sand which was red or grey or as green as a meadow. We travelled on the banks, sometimes fording a passage from one side to the other. For a long time, we saw no men. But we did see eagles. A group of deer. A wolf. I would use a sharpened stick to capture crayfish, or impale fish on my arrows. We were accustomed to eating fish on the island and my father knew which of the aromatic herbs growing alongside the river were best for roasting with them.

'Was it like this, the world after the great flood?'

'I think so. When the mud had been washed away by the rains, the rocks shone, the rivers ran clean and clear, the trees were radiant with green and silver. The bodies remained where they had found rest, on the bottom of the sea.'

Long silences between us. I would remember them one day in the heat of battle, my mind fogged with the terror of lying unburied. Golden silences, translucent, sparkling, scented with mint and rosemary. Words came too, when the mysteries of those rocks and woods touched me with fear.

'Father, you were serious, then, when you said we'd be going to the Sanctuary of the Wolf King in Arcadia.'

'We are going to Arcadia, my boy. You have nothing to fear. We will perform the rituals as tradition wants and nothing terrible will happen.'

'But why must we carry out any rituals at all? I'm absolutely certain that grandfather doesn't believe in such things. So why should they be true?'

'No one can say with certainty what is true and what isn't true. That which really exists and that which doesn't. And so we shall go.'

'Just because grandfather has that name?'

'Yes, because he has that name. And because your mother believes, even if your grandfather doesn't.'

Arcadia was even more beautiful. Hills and mountains, ravines and forests, wild flowers and sunsets, the disc of the moon streaked with thin clouds. The sanctuary, my father said, wasn't too far off, but it was best to rest in a peaceful place before approaching it. We prepared to spend the night at the mouth of a big cave where a spring delivered up its waters into a mountain torrent.

'What do you think? Will Mentor and the boy have arrived at their destination, with our men?' I wondered.

'Mentor is sensible and cautious. He'll find the right roads and he'll manage to return the boy to his parents. I would have liked you to meet them, Admetus and his wife Alcestis. She is the daughter of Pelias, king of Iolcus. She was very beautiful and very proud as a girl; everyone desired her but only Admetus, another glorious Argonaut, was able to win her as his bride.'

'How did he manage it?' I asked. I couldn't help but think of Helen, of the words she'd said to me in Sparta.

'By proving he was the best, I believe, although I've heard singers tell extraordinary and incredible tales of what happened, as is their custom. Perhaps only the king of Pherai himself could tell you the truth. If he wanted to. But there is one story I've heard told time and time again; there was awe in the voices of my comrades when they would whisper it, as we were stretched out on the benches of the ship on the nights we were awake at anchor, along the route for Colchis.'

'What was it?'

'One day, a handsome young man, a stranger whom no one had ever seen around before, showed up at Admetus' palace asking for work. The king hired him as a herdsman for three years. He grew quite fond of the youth; he treated him with generosity and esteem because the boy did his work conscientiously, and since he had begun taking care of the herd, it had grown greatly, had almost doubled in size.

'The youth had also become quite fond of his master and did everything he could to please him. Until one fine day, before the contracted time was over, in the same sudden way as he had originally appeared, the boy decided to go . . .'

My father interrupted his tale, straining to hear something.

'What is it?'

'Don't you hear it?' he replied. 'Can't you hear that long call? It's a wolf.'

I could hear it. A baying, getting louder and closer. The horses were frantically trying to free themselves from their hobbles. '*Atta*, do you suppose he'll try to attack? That howling is enough to chill a man to the bone.'

The voice of the wolf still wounds my heart . . . in another place covered with snow . . . in another time I cannot measure . . .

'This is a region of flocks and herds. Where there are sheep, there will be wolves. But you mustn't fear. We are not sheep, we're warriors and we have our weapons.'

The wolf fell silent, taking warning from the words of King Laertes.

'You didn't finish your story . . .'

'Well, before leaving, the youth wanted to say farewell to *wanax* Admetus. It is said that in order to repay the king for his affection, he left a gift, a great and terrible one . . .'

'What was the gift?'

'What you're about to hear is a tale that poets sing to instil men's hearts with wonder, when they wander from palace to palace to entertain the kings and heroes at the banquet table. No one can say whether any of it is true . . .'

'What was the gift, father?' I insisted.

'A gift that only a god could give. Apollo, some say. His gift was this: he told the king that he had convinced the Moirai, the three Fates who spin the thread of life for every mortal man, to allow Admetus to escape death, but only once; and only if, when his time came, he found someone willing to die in his place: then he would be spared.'

'And did this ever happen?'

'Not yet, at least from what I know. One thing is certain: the gods are always putting us to the test and imparting lessons. We can rarely recognize them by the way they look, because they are always disguising their true appearances, but they leave signs . . .'

He sighed and then began speaking again: 'Who but a god could promise you the most precious gift that exists: life . . . living for even a single instant more than the time you've been allotted . . . but, at the same time, pretend that you pay with the life of another? And not just any other; that of a person who loves you so much he is willing to give up his own life in order to prolong yours.'

'So what is the lesson?'

'You're asking me? The lesson is that even the briefest moment of happiness has its cost. If you're given a gift, even if it comes from a god, one day other mysterious forces, or even that god himself, may demand that you pay a price that could make you sorely regret ever having accepted the gift. But you must sleep now, son. Tomorrow will be a day you'll never forget.'

We fell asleep in the shadows of the cave, but not before making a votive offering to the nymphs who inhabited it. When we were awakened by the morning sun, I left the horses inside the cave so they couldn't be seen, and my father and I set off, without having eaten, towards the sanctuary.

'Can't you tell me why, father?' I asked. 'I must know why we're doing this. You'd already decided before we left Ithaca, hadn't you?'

'You're right, I had. To satisfy your mother. She is . . .'

'Different from other women. I know. She's her father's daughter.'

'Yes. She has premonitions . . . visions, sometimes. She believes that your grandfather, as a young man, was initiated into the rite of the wolf. Do you know what that means?'

I did not know and at the moment I was not eager to find out.

'Do you see that mountain?' my father continued. 'It is the tallest in all Arcadia. It was up there, a long time ago, that the wolf-king lived. The people called him that because he fed on human flesh. Everyone in the neighbouring lands lived in fear of his evil habits. When a man, or a maiden or a child disappeared without leaving a trace, every community, every village, every out-of-the-way house, was prey to absolute terror. Their eyes would rise to the mountaintop, their thoughts would fly to the bloodthirsty king who had made his home there. They couldn't stop thinking of their loved ones becoming the victuals of his gruesome banquets.

'Then one day, the wolf-king vanished. Perhaps he died, perhaps he was killed, but his memory did not disappear with him. People thought he must somehow be living on in some other form. The fact is that, to this day, in that sanctuary, a terrible rite is performed on certain men who are marked by a sign that only the priest can recognize. From that moment on, the man becomes a wolf one night every month, for seven years. When those seven years are up, he returns here to the sanctuary. He is offered different kinds of meat, including . . . human flesh. If he refuses it, he is set free. If he devours it, he remains a wolf for seven more years.'

'No, it's not possible,' I whispered, 'I can't believe that . . . Are you saying that my mother's father is, or has been, a wolf?'

As we drew closer, the sanctuary became visible: an enclosure made of tree trunks which surrounded an entrance that seemed to lead deep inside the mountain.

'Not that way. But your mother has told me that on certain nights she saw him take on the appearance of a wolf. She said that once she saw him writhing on the floor, groaning, his mouth yawning open to show sharp fangs . . .'

'My mother sees ghosts! I admit that my grandfather is harsh, unbending, even ruthless, but he's a man. I'm sure of it.'

'Nonetheless, I made her a promise. And as your father and your king, I order you to submit to this test. You mustn't worry; I will never leave your side.'

I had no choice. We entered and found ourselves in a vast cavern. At its centre, a large slab of polished stone was set on four squared-off boulders. It was dark but at the far end I could make out a flickering light. Was it a fire? Perhaps a torch or an oil lamp. The deep silence was abruptly broken by the howl of a wolf. I tried to tell myself that it was only a man imitating a wolf, but I couldn't believe it: it was too loud, too intense and raucous. A figure emerged from the shadows at the far end of the cavern: a man – the priest? – whose face was covered by a wolf mask. I shuddered as he walked towards me. He held a cup from which steam, and a sharp odour, were rising. He handed it to me and my father gestured for me to drink it.

I obeyed. My mind vanished.

I find myself in an infinite, white, freezing expanse and I move forward with great difficulty, the wind pushing me back and slashing my face. The horizon is deserted in every direction, the sky empty. The light is still.

Perhaps it is morning, or daytime or perhaps evening, there's no difference. Then, suddenly, a black dot far in the distance. It's coming towards me fast; it's getting bigger and bigger. I can't make out who, what, it is. I have no idea how much time has passed when finally it is close to me. It is him, the wolf-king himself on a chariot, pulled by wolves that seem to fly!

When I regained consciousness I was lying on the grass, in a meadow at the edge of the forest and I could see the hooves of our horses.

'Now you can be sure,' my father's voice was saying, 'that even if your grandfather was a wolf, nothing of his nature has remained in you. Your mother will be satisfied and she'll sleep easier.'

He was in front of me, laughing.

'Does that mean I didn't eat human flesh?'

'It means what you want it to mean. There was an exchange of messages between your mother and her father and you were the intermediary. A rite was performed in an ancient sanctuary and you took part in it; as did, perhaps, your grandfather before you. The man who gave you your name. You conserve all of this in your heart, my son. Today you feel that you can't remember but the moment will come in which the memories will return to you and everything will have a meaning.'

'Why can't I remember it now?'

'Because you were somewhere else and now you are back in your world. But the gateway to the other world will open again. When that will be, I can't say. Our world is unstable, Odysseus. But eat now, and drink. We have a long journey ahead of us.'

The sun was high now and lit up the mountain peaks. The images of darkness were forgotten and our destination was sandy Pylos, the palace overlooking the wide bay, with silvery fish darting in that vast liquid mirror. Wise Nestor would set a rich banquet for us.

We crossed Arcadia and then Messenia. In five days we reached our destination. The king and his sons came to welcome us. Nestor embraced my father and Antilochus greeted me: 'Odysseus, the colour of your gaze is strange: I'm certain you have many things to tell me.'

'And much else to ask you,' I replied.

'Where is your escort?' asked Nestor. 'What happened to them?'

'They took another route,' replied my father, 'but they'll be here.'

And so we stopped for many a day and night, until one evening towards sunset we saw a cloud of dust rising on the hillside.

'It's them!' I cried, and ran towards the three chariots that the horses were pulling at a gallop.

Mentor got out first and hugged me. I leapt onto one of the chariots, holding the rail fast, and we descended swiftly towards the bay. The two kings awaited us on the golden sand and their hearts were cheered to see that everyone had made a safe return.

'We've returned Eumelus to his parents,' said Mentor. 'They now know the truth. *Wanax* Admetus and Queen Alcestis send this message: "There is no limit, King Laertes, to our gratitude. A god surely sent you to save our son. As long as we live, our house will be your house, our heart your heart. Let us make a vow to the gods so that the destiny of our children will be united in the future as ours is today."'

He showed us the gifts the king and queen had sent, including an Egyptian cup for my father made of gold and quartz and exquisitely crafted. It had belonged to a king whose home was on the banks of the Nile and had been brought to the palace by Phoenician merchants. For me, a pin for my cloak, a thing of wonder, made of gold and amber.

Nestor welcomed the newcomers with great joy, already imagining how the tales of Mentor and the other guests would gladden the family and friends gathering at the banquet table in the palace. Indeed, we stayed awake until quite late, enjoying the wine and food that Nestor had served to us in great abundance. That evening, Mentor had the attention of two of the most famous kings of Achaia, like the greatest of poets.

When weariness had overcome us and we stood to go to bed, my father spoke to Mentor: 'From your words I can tell that you've become very fond of Eumelus and think of him often.'

'That's true,' he replied. 'And I'm sure he misses me as well. Our journey after we left you in Corinth was a long one, and we were always together. He wept inconsolably when it was time for me to go!'

My father smiled. 'Well, I think we can make do without you for some time in Ithaca, but not forever! You can return to Pherai, if you like, but don't forget us. The day will come when Eumelus feels comfortable with his own family again; he won't need you any more and you'll feel nostalgia for Ithaca. Come back to us then, and take up your place at the palace again. You can keep two of my warriors as an escort and I will ask King Nestor to leave you the chariot for as long as you need it. He won't refuse me, I'm sure of it.'

Parting from sandy Pylos was very sad, but leave we did, three days later. We left the chariots and returned to our ship, having loaded it with all the many gifts and mementoes of a journey that I would never forget. We set sail north.

Towards Ithaca.

12

THE WIND WAS IN OUR FAVOUR: we sailed all day and all night and we reached our destination the evening of the following day, passing between the mainland and the island. Our Ithaca welcomed us at the port closest to the palace. My trainer Damastes was unfailingly waiting at the port with a four-wheeled cart drawn by a pair of oxen that would take us to the palace. My nurse Euriclea embraced me, weeping for joy. She kissed me on the head and on my eyes, but not before she had kissed my father's hand. Damastes and the palace dignitaries rendered homage to the king and paid their respects to me as well, realizing that I was no longer the boy I had been before we departed. I was a man now, like they were, capable of reigning over the kingdom if it became necessary.

The warriors escorting us loaded the gifts we had received onto the cart. Damastes sat in front and drove the oxen. Two huge white oxen with big horns. At first I felt like I was crossing a new, unfamiliar land, and it wasn't until I had become accustomed to the landscape that I truly felt I had returned. I couldn't understand why it all seemed so alien to me, until I realized that I had seen so many extraordinary things, lived through so many wondrous experiences, that I was somehow rejecting the small, restrictive island where nothing ever happened. Although I'd delighted in seeing my mother, my nurse, my home, my closest friends again, now I could find nothing interesting in what I had returned to.

It got worse. For days on end I nursed a feeling of true repulsion for my land, along with no small measure of discomfort, because I realized it wasn't fair and because I couldn't even justify feeling this way. I forced myself to comprehend what was happening. For nearly two months (how the time had flown!) I had journeyed through a large part of Achaia at my father's side. I had met three sovereigns, two queens, any number of princes and two royal princesses, one of whom was extraordinarily beautiful. I had seen fascinating landscapes, mountains and rivers, snowy peaks, impenetrable forests and vast, fertile plains. I had received gifts of unimaginable cost and craftsmanship; single objects that were worth as much as an entire flock of our sheep or herd of our pigs.

I had been pursued, I'd had dreams and visions, I'd had to face real fear, horror, admiration, tenderness, doubt and, finally, mystery. I had explored the world in all its variety, and also the diverse and often disquieting aspects of the human soul. I knew now that even the most violent emotions, the most terrible and frightening, were preferable to the rigidity, the inertia, the tedium of a life that was always the same. Even though I was still very young, my father had spared me nothing, just like my grandfather before him.

My father must have noticed that I was often restless and distracted, and sensing my malady he spoke to me: 'Don't think I don't know what you're feeling, son. It's a kind of sickness that gnaws at you, that won't leave you alone, but there's a deep contradiction in it; when I was off on the *Argo* in faraway Colchis, all I could think of was my island and its scents, of my wife, of my house and of you, my only son. I missed all of that terribly, I felt a really acute yearning to be back. Stretched out on my rowing bench, I would look at the distant stars and I could not fall asleep. I'd wait, aching, for the dawn. But when in the middle of the night the alarm trumpet sounded and my comrades put on their armour, I did the same. I clad myself in bronze, threw the sword belt over my shoulder, unsheathed my sword and steadied my heart, impatient for the battle. In the fury of combat I forgot all else, my mind was drunk on the frenzy and the delirium of the fray and I could think of nothing but the fierce, bloody fight, the victory, the spoils. That's how it is, son: our hearts long for our loved ones, reach out for memories, envisage the family and the hospitable, lovingly built house we left, but what lies at the bottom of a man's heart is an abyss of darkness populated by monsters that not even Hercules himself could defeat. Your heart has only just grazed the darkness. You saw the madness in Eurystheus' eyes and the terror behind the gaze of little Eumelus. You've had nightmares, but you have never had the experience of combat, of a situation where each man seeks to inflict the most damage and the most suffering possible on another man he has square in front of him. You haven't faced the unknown, son, and that's the one thing that strikes more fear into a man than anything else.

'Be calm and wait. Go fishing with your friends. You'll soon become accustomed to Ithaca again. Remember: what you have here is good. When we come home, live in our houses, eat our food, sleep in our beds with our wives, hunt in our forests, the best part of us gains the upper hand. The monsters sink back down into the darkness and it's as if they were dead. It's good to sit at the table in the evening with friends drinking strong red wine and listening to stories, especially on those winter nights when sailing is impossible and the wind of Boreas blows cold and impetuous!'

'Father,' I asked him, 'has the frenzy you speak of ever descended upon Ithaca? Have pirates ever tried to bring death, plunder and rape to the island? Has an ambitious pretender never tried to take your throne, or your father's before you? Has Ithaca ever been stained with blood?'

'No, my son, not within living memory. This, too, is good, a privilege afforded us by the gods. The sea protects us, perhaps because I never forget, on stormy days, to sacrifice to the blue god Poseidon. But also because the inhabitants of our island are valiant and fearsome warriors and because we live simply and do not flaunt what riches we have.'

'It's a great fortune,' I replied, 'to grow up next to a father like you, who has an answer for all questions. Even the ones that don't get said.'

'I've only showed you a part of what awaits you when the time comes, but I've done so loving you, as a father loves a son, and this will remain in your heart.'

He looked into my eyes as he said these words, his gaze as deep as the sea.

I still miss him now, I need his voice, his advice.

Then he called Damastes to tell him to prepare the hounds for a boar hunt.

MENTOR DIDN'T come home for two years. His return at the beginning of spring was a great event. King Nestor had given him a ship to cross the sea with. The sailors at port had recognized the ship by its standard, and they accompanied Mentor to the palace. It was dusk and the servants were preparing the tables for dinner. When my father learned that Mentor was arriving, he wanted to be the first to greet him at the gate. Mentor bowed to kiss his hand. Then I greeted him as well, embracing him like a friend I had greatly missed.

'Don't tell me anything yet,' my father told him. 'You'll speak after we've eaten. Once the tables have been cleared, we will linger and bring out the best wine.' He was certain that Mentor had long, jaw-dropping stories to tell. He couldn't have remained at Admetus' palace for two years unless important events had held him there.

When we had finished eating Mentor waited until the king had drunk of the best wine and ordered the servants to refill his cup before beginning to drink himself.

And then he began:

'When I returned to the palace in Pherai, the king and queen were very surprised to see me, but Eumelus ran towards me and hugged me tightly as if he were afraid I would want to leave again. His parents understood, and entrusted him to my care. I soon realized why he wanted so badly to be with me. I think he hadn't been able to forgive his parents for sending him off to Eurystheus' dark palace in Mycenae. I still don't know why they did it, but I imagine that the king had invited him to come as a page, and his parents had no reason to refuse. What mother would ever want to separate from her son, what father?

'I realized, in fact, that after my departure from Pherai, Eumelus hadn't spoken any further with his mother and father about what he had seen and heard when he was in Mycenae. And even though they longed to unburden Hercules from his insufferable remorse, what could they do? Where to find Hercules, hero of boundless strength? How far had his heavy heart taken him? No one knew. The echoes of his exploits reached our ears, certainly distorted, in the songs of the poets. Was he in Thrace? Crete? In the Peloponnese or Boeotia or Iberia, or at the extreme edges of the world? Would he ever return? Could he survive so many superhuman labours?

'And so we waited. I'm not sure for what. For Hercules to return, I suppose, and pay them a visit? Perhaps. It is said that the Argonauts meet up every now and then – but only you can confirm this, my king – all of them except, of course, for Jason of Iolcus, their leader. In the end he married his savage princess, Medea, the daughter of Aeetes, king of Colchis, and from what I hear it's like living with a Caucasian tiger. He'd like to be rid of her but doesn't know how he can do that because they have had two children together and blood is a strong bond. I'm afraid that sooner or later something terrible will happen.'

'Move on,' my father urged him. 'There's no need for you to tell me what I already know. I want to know what has happened in Pherai these two years.'

The king had spoken sharply as if to reprimand Mentor for overstepping his rank; it was not his place to speak of Laertes' fellow king using such a familiar tone.

Mentor humbly began again:

'One day *wanax* Admetus fell sick, with an ill-defined ailment that seemed to pass from one part of his body to another without pause. So it wouldn't be recognized, I imagine. And, in fact, the healers could find nothing. They said that only Asclepius would be capable of suggesting a remedy, but no one could say where he could be found just then. Some claimed that he had died. What an absurdity! Healers do not succumb to death or illness, of course.

'Days passed, and long nights, and more days, and the king continued to waste away. He was cared for by his sweet bride, Alcestis, the daughter of Pelias, king of Iolcus. Tears fell unbidden from her eyes. Many a time I saw her weeping as I passed in front of their bedchamber with Eumelus. Once I stopped, so the boy could observe them and understand that what he was seeing was a great love: the greatest love, the same love that had brought him to life. Eumelus paused thoughtfully, and then, light-footed, he approached the bed. He hesitated a moment, but then took his father's hand between his own, in silence.

'I understood that he was becoming reconciled with his parents and thought that I would soon be able to return to Ithaca, but I instantly realized that my reasoning was, in fact, nonsense. Wouldn't it be even more dreadful for the boy to lose his father after he had made his peace with him?

'What happened after that is not entirely clear to me. What I'm about to tell you comes mostly from what I have heard, and only partly from what I directly experienced. I can't be sure of the truth of it, and I myself hesitate to believe it.

'With each passing day, Admetus felt closer to death. He said he could see the Moira approaching his bed and feel the chill of her creeping into his limbs. The news spread through the city and the whole kingdom. Laments could be heard issuing from the forests and the mountain peaks. I swear to you, the shadow of death seemed to be descending on the whole city, the entire kingdom. The light of the sun was veiled by a dark mist.

'Finally, the visit of the king's parents was announced. Alcestis, exhausted, had gone off to rest and was not present when they entered Admetus' room. The poor woman was depleted of energy, depleted of tears. But there was a servant in the bedroom with them and it was he who told the story I am about to tell you.

'Perhaps the king was delirious, or perhaps he was lucid and in his right mind; there's no way we can know. His voice was hoarse but the words he pronounced were perfectly clear. Admetus told his parents that a god had once worked for him as a servant, attending to his herd. Since the king had treated him well, this god, upon leaving, had given Admetus a gift, a rather terrible one: if, when his last moment was upon him, the king found someone willing to die in his place, he could escape the Moira who had spun out the thread of his death.

'The king implored his father first, and then his mother: "You have already lived almost your whole lives! I have a wife who adores me, a young daughter, a son who has finally been returned to me after so long. I don't want to leave them. I beg of you. You, my father, or you, my mother: take my place at the gates of Hades! It will not matter to the Moira whether she is offered the life of an old person or of a vigorous man still in the fullness of his life."

'But Admetus' father was unshakeable: "We gave you life once, we cannot give it to you a second time. How dare you even ask for such a thing! Act like a man, instead, and face your destiny with courage."

'At that very moment Queen Alcestis appeared at the door to the bedchamber and heard the father's cruel response. "I'll go," she said. "I shall go to the gates of Hades and save my dear love."

'The maidservants following her burst into tears. They knew that their lady never spoke in vain and never made a promise she couldn't keep. Admetus was struck by those words, at the thought of the immense gift his wife was ready to give him. The news flew around the palace in a flash and from there spread throughout the town. Alcestis was going to her death to save the life of the husband she adored. A chorus of laments echoed along the roads and in the squares of Pherai.'

My father – only he could do so – interrupted Mentor's narration. 'How is that possible? I know Admetus. He's an Argonaut. I've seen him risk his life in battle, time and time again, in bitter, harsh combat. He's no coward.'

Mentor listened respectfully, then answered: 'Oh, king, if you allow me to say what I think, we are speaking of two very different things. Dying in battle is like being struck by a thunderbolt. There's no time to think in the thick of the fray, let alone meditate. Imagine, instead, that you learn that you must die. You don't know when, but soon enough, you don't know how, but probably in a bed soaked in your own humours. You can only watch as your body wastes away, hour by hour; your limbs shrivel up, your muscles disappear, until you can see your skeleton under your wrinkled skin. Even if we know that we are born mortal, this is unbearable. Even more unbearable if you know that there's a way you can avoid all this, or at least put if off to an unknown, unknowable time. If this is hard for a man still in the bloom of youth, it is even worse for an old man, because the closer he gets to death, the harder he holds on to life.'

Wise Mentor! He had come up with the only possible answer: not even a god can give you a gift like that without making you pay an exorbitant price for it. My father fell silent and Mentor continued his story:

'Her maidservants began to prepare the queen to enter the kingdom of shadows, although she was still alive and as beautiful as she had ever been: her perfect lips stood out scarlet against the waxy pallor of her face, her blue eyes, shining with tears, looked like the sky after it rains. She embraced her children and wept; she had wanted just a moment to say one last goodbye but there she lingered, unable to break away. Eumelus, who had finally understood, was crying as well. Not a youth yet, no longer a boy, yet he was forced to witness this terrible event: the woman who had given him his life was going to her death, alive.

'King Admetus, in the meantime, felt vigour flowing through his veins again as life slowly seized possession of his body. He felt appalled and yet overwhelmed by a shameful joy, by a sense of endless gratitude for his wife's heroic, sublime gesture. He blurted out ridiculous things, pure folly. "I promise you," he said, "that I will never touch another woman for my whole life. I will have a perfect likeness sculpted of you by a great artist and I will put it next to me in our bed. No woman will ever take that place." His daughter looked at him without understanding, his son with disgust.

'Finally, Alcestis broke away. Accompanied by her usher to the Underworld – dressed all in black, black streaks on his face and black rings around his eyes – and by a host of weeping mourners, she took her place on a chariot drawn by four horses, all black as the wings of a crow. She was taken away.'

'Away?' asked my father, once again interrupting the story. 'Where away?'

Mentor sighed. 'Many are the mouths of Hades. Many caves echo with the howling of Cerberus and let off fetid sulphurous vapours from deep underground. But I could also say that although there are many ways of ending up in the Underworld, it is also true that one is alive until the instant of dying. And if one is young, he or she is even more alive.'

His voice was tremulous. The words he had offered came from the inspiration of a poet, but also a true witness to the events; he was leaving it up to us to seek their real meaning. Silence reigned over the hall. I saw my mother leaning against the wall in the corner. She was weeping.

'Continue,' said the king my father.

'The procession disappeared at the end of the road that led westward. None of us moved, no one let out as much as a sigh. A profound silence fell over the city. All our tears were mute. Even those of Eumelus and his sister, who tenderly held each other's hands.

'I don't even remember how long we stayed that way. Hours? Days? Because, in truth, time had stopped: life was death and death life. I only know that all at once we saw the mourners returning, with the death usher. Where was Alcestis? Where had she been taken? Had she descended underground, while still alive? Had her throat been slashed by a sacrificial blade and her ashes cast to the wind? No one asked. No one said a word.

'Something passed through the air. Not time, there was no passing of time. It was regret, a sharp nostalgia for simple things, for joys forever lost. Then a voice, I don't know whose, I don't know where it was coming from. The voice was saying: "Hercules is here."

'I thought I was dreaming. A wish that turned into a dream and thus seemed real. A hand gripping my arm, a face with bewildered eyes searching for my own, a voice repeating itself: "Hercules is here. He's in the palace and he's asking for food."

'Only then did I jump and realize what was being said to me. "Where? Here, in the house? Where's the king?"

' "The king is there," replied a servant. "Out there, at the door. He hasn't been told."

' "What about the guest who just arrived? What does he know?"

' "Nothing. No one has had the courage to tell him what just happened. But the news of his arrival is spreading through the palace and outside as well. He says he is just passing through, heading somewhere else, off to accomplish one of his tasks."

' "Take me to him," I said, "and send someone to take care of the king and keep him away for the time being."

'The servant obeyed and took me into the kitchens. Hercules was already there. Sitting at a table, devouring a roast kid. I'd never seen the likes of him before: gigantic, he was clad only in the pelt of a lion, his feet bare, dirty and dusty. He had a cloudy, lost look in his eyes, as if they were searching for distant images, or escaping from them. In a corner, leaning against the wall, was his club. It was covered with branch stubs that had been filed to sharp points and bore visible traces of bloody combat. I couldn't manage to open my mouth.

' "Who are you?" he asked me. "I've never seen you in this house."

'I lied, making up a false name, but I told him the truth when I added that I had been in the king's service for two years, assisting him in governing the house and educating his son. I approached him and poured some wine into a wooden cup for him. He drank it, then wiped his moustache and beard with the back of his hand.

' "What are all these dark faces? Why is no one laughing, no one having fun, in this place? What is this deathly silence? Where are my friends, King Admetus and Queen Alcestis? Why haven't they come to greet me?"

'All of us in the kitchen looked one another in the eye, including me. No one had the courage to open his mouth.

' "Where are they?" he shouted. His voice was like thunder. And since still no one dared to speak, he took his club and smashed it on the table made of solid, seasoned oak; the wood went flying in a thousand splinters. I had to answer, or he would have demolished the whole palace in his anger.

' "The king is outside, in front of the gate. The queen has . . . gone away."

'He got up and came so close to me I could smell the feral odour of the lion pelt mixed with his own sweat. I didn't have much time to search for an answer. I started talking without waiting for him to ask again.

' "Queen Alcestis has gone to die. To deliver herself, alive, to Thanatos."

'The roar that rang out in the kitchen seemed to come from the mouth of the lion. Then he grabbed my throat with his left hand and I realized that he could break my neck like a child snaps a stalk of barley. I promised to tell him everything, without omitting a single detail. It was only then that he loosened his grip and let me free. He had a strange, incomprehensible grimace on his face.

' "He promised he would never again touch another woman? He swore that?" he asked me after I told him of Admetus' oath. I hadn't noticed the colour of his eyes before then: they were amber, with green reflections, and they burned with dark desperation.

' "That's right. He swore to it."

'As I answered him, trembling, I realized that I hadn't yet had an instant to let him know that he wasn't to blame for any crime, that the massacre of his family had been an abomination plotted and executed by his cousin Eurystheus. Hercules was already gone, grabbing, as he ran out, weapons from the walls, from the racks, from the chests. I tried to catch him up, to speak to him, but at that point he had already run down the steps leading out of the palace, jumped onto a quadriga and was driving the four-horse team down the road at a reckless speed.

'"What did he need those weapons for?" I asked myself, paralysed with shock, overwhelmed by the fury of events. "How can he think to defeat the god of death using human weapons?"'

Mentor paused so that all those present in the great hall could ask themselves the same question. Everyone surely yearned to hear that Hercules had made it back from wherever he had rushed off to . . . an unknown place at the ends of the earth, perhaps? Or perhaps somewhere underground, populated by idle shadows.

'His return was announced seven days later, after seven days of anguish and trepidation. King Admetus never slept and the nights rang with his cries and shrieks. Eumelus came to my room time after time, holding his little sister by the hand. Sobbing and scared, she couldn't help repeating: "Where is my mother?"

'He entered the city through the south gate. The crowd that parted to let him through was mute and staring, with none of the cries of joy and exultation that I would have expected. I soon understood why. The hero moved forward on his chariot, drawn by the four horses at a walk. His body was full of scratches, bruises and wounds, his skin looked burnt, his eyes were fixed straight ahead. At his side, immobile, was a veiled figure. So still that it seemed lifeless, like a statue. Perhaps it was the likeness of Alcestis crafted by a great sculptor that Admetus had wanted to put in his bed? That's what I thought of when I saw them.

'The king had been alerted by his guards. He had already exited the main door and had walked down the stairs to receive his friend and embrace him, finally, after so long a time. Hercules had already got out of the chariot to greet the king. I was close and I saw them meet. The hero's expression had changed; he seemed different now, relieved, and when he greeted his friend, his voice was warm.

'"I know that you have lost your wife and my dear friend Alcestis, but you cannot spend your life weeping and despairing.

Your people need you, as do your children. And so, be it reluctantly, you must start living again, as you always have." Admetus
glanced over at the mysterious veiled figure, still and straight on
the chariot. "I've had my share of trouble, of pain," continued
Hercules, "but I've learned to live again. There's no alternative.
You're still young, and a man like you can't live without the
pleasure of love. And so I've brought a gift for you: this woman.
I bought her at the slave market in the last city I crossed. She's
beautiful. Never cleft by delivering a child, high-hipped and firm-
breasted. Her eyes are like the morning stars. She'll cure you of
your melancholy. Take her."

'But Admetus turned to Hercules with eyes full of tears. "I don't
want her, friend. It was contemptible of me to allow Thanatos to
take Alcestis in my place. How could I not have understood that?
My life without her is no life at all. There is no joy in me; not even
my own children bring me relief or consolation. Please do not be
offended, but no woman bought at the market, beautiful as she is,
can take the place of my bride. What I had was priceless: the scent
of her hair, the light and warmth of her gaze, her love so passionate that she gave her own life to save mine. What folly have I
committed, what shame have I brought upon myself! If I didn't
have these children, I swear to you, I would join her where she
is now. I can't promise that I won't do it, because life to me now is
nothing but a burden."

'Hercules smiled, despite his friend's harsh words: "I see that
you are sincere in what you're saying and thus you deserve to be
pardoned. There's no need for you to go to join her because . . ."

'We all waited without taking a breath while the invincible hero
removed the veil that covered the woman.

'It was Alcestis!'

13

ALL THOSE PRESENT IN THE great hall rejoiced over the happy conclusion of the events narrated by Mentor. He finally smiled himself, at seeing the effect that the epilogue of the story had had upon his audience. Phemius, the king's bard, was also present, but although I observed him carefully I could see no emotion in his expression. I turned then to my father and I saw him signing a personal message for Mentor: two fingers of his right hand making a brief horizontal line in the air: stop. Then a half-circle, in Mentor's direction: you'll tell me later.

Neither of these gestures escaped Mentor, who stopped talking, returned to his seat and drank a cup of wine.

'So?' clamoured many voices. 'What happened to Hercules then?'

'What about Admetus? And Alcestis? Are they living together now as husband and wife?' asked others.

Mentor excused himself by asking his listeners for a chance to rest and sate his thirst. He would, he promised, continue his story and answer their questions as soon as the opportunity arose. Since the king seemed to be in agreement and, what's more, had ordered more wine to be mixed, no one dared to make any more requests.

When all our table companions had announced their intention to retire and the voices of the retreating guests had melted away into that summer night, there were just three of us left sitting close to a lamp that hung from the ceiling: my father, Mentor and me.

I was the first to speak: 'Where is Hercules? Did he learn how he had been tricked by Eurystheus? That he was innocent of killing his wife and children?'

'Yes. I told him myself,' said Mentor. 'He left for Mycenae that very day, on the same chariot he'd used to bring Alcestis back. And I swear that the Furies, their heads wrapped in snakes, were running at his sides. The four black stallions seemed to breathe fire from their nostrils and sparks flashed under the rims of the wheels as the quadriga crossed the stone pavement on the square.

'Admetus ordered his guards to follow him, thinking perhaps that the man could use help, and I took the opportunity to jump on one of the fifteen war chariots that, one after another, flew off in pursuit of Hercules. Everyone knew me, and I had been at the palace for such a long time this seemed natural to me. We raced on, practically without stopping. Some of the chariots were lost along the way because they broke down or because the horses couldn't keep up. And yet none of us ever caught up with Hercules' quadriga, which seemed to have taken flight. Perhaps those four black stallions truly came from the Underworld, sent by Persephone herself.

'Only three of the fifteen chariots arrived at the destination, shortly after the invincible hero had halted his quadriga and freed the steeds of their harness. But it was soon evident that he would not need anyone's help. He scaled the city walls easily and dived inside like a sparrowhawk. For a time that seemed endless to us we heard nothing. Then we were startled, all at once, by a loud creaking noise: the hinges of the great gate of the lions. The gigantic doors burst open and there was Hercules, dragging Eurystheus by one of his feet. The king of Mycenae was still alive, but barely recognizable; we knew it was him only because of his royal robes. His face was a shapeless mask of blood. Hercules smashed his body up against the city wall, holding him up by the neck with his left hand so he would not slip to the ground. With the fingers of his right hand he put out both of Eurystheus' eyes, then squeezed the king's neck harder and harder with his left until it snapped. Hercules summoned one of the men and handed over the eyes of his enemy, who had died without even having the strength to open his mouth. "Take these to Thebes, to my mother. Tell her who they belonged to, and that justice has been done."

'Eurystheus' body lay disjointed on the ground like the carcass of a slaughtered animal, while Hercules jumped onto his chariot and disappeared in a cloud of dust. Heading north. He hasn't been heard from since.'

'Eurystheus got what he deserved,' said my father after a long, heavy silence.

'Where did Hercules go? What will he do now?' I asked.

'I don't know,' replied Mentor. 'I'm afraid that the truth that I revealed to him about the death of his family did nothing to heal his wounds, but merely refuelled his wrath. His wife and children were murdered and no one can bring them back. Not even the gods. They would have already done so if they had wanted to or, better yet, they could have prevented it from happening in the first place.'

Another long silence followed. The sleeping household was so utterly quiet that we could hear the cries of a flock of wild ducks passing in the night.

'What will become of Admetus and Alcestis?' I asked. I was wondering how a man and a woman who had survived such events could recreate a serene life together.

'No one will ever be able to answer such a question,' replied Mentor. 'Least of all them. Sunlight and night, joy and agony, shame and pride . . . and love exceeding every limit, beyond time and beyond life. These were the banks wherein flowed their lives. Sometimes we ordinary mortals are fated to experience passions that push the heart to its extreme limits, passions that not even the gods can experience . . . because the gods do not know what it means to love another to the point of distraction, to desire life so strongly it becomes your undoing. To tremble with fear in the dark, to suffer solitude and abandonment. Admetus and his wife lived through all of this. Perhaps they will find the strength to forget, to forgive each other, to walk together again towards a death that will not be an abyss of shadows but a quiet sunset.'

The night was already half gone when we finally surrendered to our weariness. Before I fell asleep, I thought that Mentor had spoken like a man laden with the wisdom of years, not like the youth he still was. I knew that, whatever befell me in the future, he would always be my support and my succour, whether he was near or far.

That night I believe my dreams revealed the true answer to my questions but when I awoke the next day I had neither the strength nor the will to remember.

I went hunting with my father.

HERCULES, as far as we were able to learn, had simply disappeared, much like he had appeared from out of nowhere that day at the court of Admetus in Pherai. All traces of him were lost. I imagined that he had decided, in any case, to complete the labours that Eurystheus had assigned to him, because in doing so he was liberating the world of ferocious, deadly creatures that threatened men and devastated the countryside. One day, when Mentor and I were alone on board a ship, I asked him one of those questions that demands that you either tell the truth or refuse to answer entirely.

'Tell me, what do you think happened to Alcestis from the time she was taken away to the moment when she reappeared on Hercules' chariot? You were there. You must have asked yourself what actually happened.'

'It's as I said the night of my return to Ithaca: there is no answer to this question. Only Hercules and Alcestis know the truth. But he has disappeared and she has never spoken of it. Where was she taken? The closest gateway to Hades is in Ephyra, which is not very far from here. That's where the Stygian swamp is, and the Acheron river.'

I said nothing more but my question hung in the air between us; it had piqued Mentor's interest. He spoke up again: 'Have you ever seen someone lose his senses? Appear entirely dead to the world and then reopen his eyes? The border between life and death is very ill-defined. Dreaming, for instance, takes you to a territory that has no borders and is free of the limits that this world places upon us. In fact, dreams are inhabited by people living and dead. There's one thing I'm sure of, however: Hercules knew full well where Alcestis was; he knew where to look for her and how to bring her back. When they returned on his chariot she was covered by a grey veil from her head to her feet. She looked like . . . a ghost.

'And when Hercules removed the veil to show her to her husband, her skin was pale, her eye sockets dark, her face was expressionless. Death was still inside her; it hadn't left her completely.'

Mentor managed now and then to send messages to the palace at Pherai to be recited by voice and he would sometimes receive replies. But these contacts became rarer and rarer until they stopped completely.

More than three years had passed since his return, when one evening Mentor told me that he had to talk to me about something my father the king had already been informed of.

'MANY IMPORTANT events have been taking place on the mainland. In Mycenae, the throne left vacant after Eurystheus' death was occupied by Atreus, son of Pelops, who had taken shelter at Eurystheus' court along with his brother Thyestes. He is now the mightiest sovereign in all Achaia. He has two sons: Agamemnon and Menelaus. You may even have seen them while you were in Mycenae: Menelaus has tawny red hair and a powerful build. His skin is the colour of bronze. He wears his hair gathered at the nape of his neck with a leather tie. Agamemnon is his older brother, and is even more strongly built than Menelaus, but his eyes are black and sullen and he wears his long hair straight on his shoulders. He's very good with the spear and trains every day in the palace courtyard. Atreus also has a daughter, Anaxibia, a proud, beautiful young woman. She has been promised to the king of Phocis.

'In Argus, there is no heir apparent to the throne of King Adrastus; during your visit to the city you saw for yourself how his son-in-law Tydeus, who had fallen in battle in front of the walls of

Thebes, was burned on the pyre. Tydeus' son, Prince Diomedes, has become a formidable warrior. Ever since his father's death he has done nothing but train for combat, together with the sons of six other warriors who died in the siege of the city of the seven gates. It is said that they live only to avenge their fathers. Those who have seen them describe them as a pack of young lions thirsty for blood.

'I know that you met Nestor's sons when you visited Pylos, and the twin sons of Tyndareus and Leda, Castor and Pollux, as well, in Sparta. You may have seen Atreus' sons in Mycenae without knowing who they were, and Tydeus' son, Diomedes, at his father's funeral. But even if you don't remember them, it won't be long before you see them again, because all the young princes of Achaia are setting off for Sparta, you included.'

'Me? Why should I go to Sparta? I've already been.'

'Because, as it turns out, many of the most valiant princes of Achaia have asked for the hand of Helen, Tyndareus and Leda's daughter, in marriage. She has just turned seventeen, and her beauty is such that any of them would be willing to risk his life to be able to carry her in his arms to his wedding chamber.'

'Not me, Mentor.'

'Wait until you see her, prince of Ithaca. You may lose your wits as well.'

'I doubt that, precious adviser. My wits are what I care about most; I wouldn't want to lose them for any reason.'

'I'm happy to hear you say that, because the other princes of Achaia seem ready to cut each other's throats for that female. They have me quite worried, actually.'

I fell silent and pondered the situation. This could lead to war, and that had to be avoided at any cost. I had gone to the mainland with my father, Laertes, to consolidate an alliance based on friendship with the other kings and princes. If blood was shed now in any way, for any reason, people would certainly take sides, and I wouldn't be able to stay out of it. I would have to join up with one group or another, even against my will.

As far as I saw it, the greatest result of the adventure of the Argonauts was not winning the treasure of Colchis, the golden fleece, as everyone had come to call it. It was uniting fifty kings and princes of Achaia in a single endeavour in which they fought side by side and had to defend each other's lives. My father was everyone's friend, everyone was my father's friend, and that was the way it had to stay. He had taught me that war usually brings only grief and misfortune, but that there were conceivable justifications for a war, as long as it was fought outside Achaia. Never within. In that case it would be a calamity.

'When are we to meet in Sparta?' I asked.

'On the day of next month's new moon.'

'Then I'll leave now. Find me a ship and summon my friends: Eurylochus, Perimedes, Polites, Euribates and the others. You'll come as well, you will be of great use to me.'

'No, I can't go with you. I'm sorry,' he replied. 'I must remain at the king's service. This is a matter you'll have to resolve on your own.'

While Mentor made arrangements for the ship and crew, I went to look for my father, to tell him what I meant to do. The sons of the Argonauts were starting out badly. We needed the wisdom of our fathers. Each of us, including myself, would have to do whatever was necessary to prevent war from breaking out in Achaia and destroying everything that our fathers had built.

I told father what Mentor had told me and he didn't seem surprised. 'Have you ever seen rams in springtime butting each other until they've broken their skulls to win a female? And deer, and boars? Well, we're not so different, not when we're young, anyway. Find a solution, if you can: your mind can find its way down many roads, and I don't think it will be difficult for you. Remember this: when you convince someone stronger than you to do something you feel is necessary, make him believe that he was the one who found the solution. Be sure to come and say goodbye before you leave, *pai*.'

'I will.'

'You'll have to take gifts for Helen, even though I'm fairly sure she won't become your wife. She is . . .'

'Made of gold, *atta*. And I'm made of wood. Oak.'

The following days were spent at the port, readying the ship along with my friends. We even slept on board, all together, feeling like we had already begun our journey. The first one all on our own. I was the leader and the sovereign and everyone treated me as such. We would eat, swim, fish and even hunt together if there was time, but they showed me signs of respect, like saving the best parts of the prey we'd caught for me, or asking my opinion before taking the initiative, and this filled me with pride.

The first thing I did when we arrived at Pylos, our first stop, was to render homage to King Nestor, who welcomed me like a son. I set off again, leaving the ship to my friends and turning over the command to my cousin Eurylochus. The four-day voyage had passed quickly. I had enjoyed myself thoroughly and tried not to think of what was waiting for me in Sparta: it had felt like being with a group of friends out on a tuna-fishing expedition. But every now and then, the evening by the horse pen came to mind, that evening when Helen had surprised me and spoken to me.

King Nestor wanted me to accept an escort of bronze-clad warriors with crested helmets, more for the sake of prestige than necessity. Among them was his son Antilochus, whom I'd met years before. During the journey we became fast friends. The king also gave me a chariot and a big tent which would serve as my abode during my stay in Sparta, along with provisions and splendid robes that I would wear when I was invited to the palace. All things I was not accustomed to.

The long procession of men and chariots slowed our march considerably, but there was no hurry, for the moment. Once we reached Sparta, the commander of my guard went to the palace to announce my arrival and returned with an invitation to dinner the following night.

That afternoon I bathed in the Eurotas and donned the robes that Nestor had given me but I felt embarrassed. I'd never worn such luxurious clothing and it didn't feel right for me. In the end, I decided to wear the robe that Euriclea, my nurse, had put in my travelling chest. It seemed beautiful to me but it was very simple. Just two stripes of purple edged in gold, attesting to my dignity as the son of a king.

Antilochus wanted me to go to the palace escorted by two gigantic warriors from his father's guard, but I convinced him that a couple of servants, bearing the gifts I'd brought for Helen, would suffice.

King Tyndareus and Queen Leda welcomed me with signs of great respect and esteem, as my servants opened an ivory box to show them the prince of Ithaca's gift for Helen of Sparta. It was a diadem of gold with dozens of pendants mounted with magnificent stones: cornelian, jasper, lapis lazuli, red amber, light blue quartz and pearls.

'Helen will be enchanted,' said the queen. As she closed the box and handed it back to me, she warned the maidservants present not to ruin the surprise by telling the princess about it, should I be the one destined to offer her my wedding gift. Then the king took me into the armoury, where a table had been set with two golden cups full of red wine.

'Your gift is truly splendid, Prince Odysseus,' the king said.

'It's certainly not suitable homage to the beauty and grace of the most splendid maiden on earth. But it's what I have to offer her,' I said, 'and it comes from my heart.'

Tyndareus' mood changed as if an ominous thought had crossed his mind. He sighed and said: 'Her beauty represents a danger.'

'I know. But not for me. I do not intend to put my hand to the sword to conquer her, even though she is surely worthy of it.'

'Why not?' asked Tyndareus. 'You are the son of a king, like her other suitors.'

'Because a betrothal should be a celebration, not a bloodbath. As for me, I know well that I couldn't even hope for the slightest glance from Helen. Ours is a kingdom of small rocky islands, *wanax*; we have no plains rich enough to nourish horses and grow luxuriant crops. We're happy with very little and when our men leave port with plunder in mind they may be away for a very long time. Helen can have so much more: there are many princes of the Achaian people who have mighty kingdoms, endless riches, grand palaces. But there is something that worries me, *wanax*.'

'What might that be?'

'I fear that the princes of Achaia who are vying for Helen's hand will first lavish countless gifts upon her and then fight each other to the death, since only one can carry her off to his wedding chamber. Those who lose will be humiliated and end up hating the victor and strife will surely ensue. Bloody battles and endless grief.'

'My same fear. But listening to your words and your reasoning, so complex despite your young age, gives me hope. In my heart, if I could choose as her father, I would want you to have my daughter, for your mind and your heart are worth far more than mere brawn and quick swordplay, *pai*.'

I was moved that *wanax* Tyndareus, the sovereign of mighty Sparta, had called me by the name that only my mother and father and my dear nurse used. Just then, a herald asked to be received and, once he had gained entrance, he announced: 'Ajax Oileus has arrived, *wanax*, and raised his tents on the right bank of the Eurotas. The sentries have also sighted the banners of Prince Diomedes of Argus; they shine in the sun like ripe ears of wheat.'

'Reserve a suitable place for him, with abundant water and a large space for his tents.'

'Prince Diomedes?' I asked.

'Yes,' replied Tyndareus as the herald left to carry out the orders he had been given. 'Diomedes is second in the line of succession, because his mother is the king's daughter and she is a widow. After Tydeus' death, King Adrastus called young Diomedes to the palace, but the boy refused. He apparently prefers to live in an austere fortress at the edge of the forest together with six comrades who will one day fight at his side to avenge the deaths of their fathers at the siege of Thebes of the seven gates. They do naught else but train for combat, from dawn to dusk. He is certainly a force to be reckoned with. And he comes asking for my daughter's hand.'

I had seen him in my dream: mighty Tydeus, as he devoured the brains of Melanippus like a starving lion at the seventh gate. The goddess fled, horrified, from the sight . . .

'As do many others,' Tyndareus continued, 'from Pherai, Arne, Mycenae, Salamis, Phthia . . . from the islands and from the mountains . . .'

'The sons of the Argonauts,' I replied. 'Our fathers contracted an alliance that united all the kings of Achaia, and here we are destroying their achievement. If only Hercules were here! He would sort out all these brawling pups! In any case, I've thought of a solution, *wanax*, that might fend off the discord we are envisaging.'

'A solution? Oh, Prince Odysseus, son of great Laertes, you have a solution that might avert this quarrel? If that were so, I would cover you with gifts and vow a perpetual alliance with your father. He would never again be wanting for wheat or wine, the most precious fabrics or high-hipped slaves instructed in the arts of love. And for you I would reserve a beautiful city, on the coast if you like, with fields rich with pastures and crops. Speak, please, I beg of you.'

The king was sincere. He understood that disaster was in store because the gods had caused all the beauty of the world to shine in a single woman, so that anyone who saw her would be willing to kill to have her.

I said: 'The greatest gift would be lasting peace in Achaia and that the house of Tyndareus be blessed with heirs.'

Then continued: 'This is my plan. You will speak to the princes after each of them has introduced himself to Helen. Or I can speak in your name, if you so wish. I will say that your daughter's beauty must not be conquered with any test that involves violence, reminding them that blood begets blood and that a chain of implacable vengeance would end up staining Achaia for centuries to come. It will be she, luminous Helen herself, who chooses. But before she expresses her decision, all of the contenders must swear that regardless of who she picks, they will respect her choice. You, her father, will sacrifice a bull to Zeus, the custodian of oaths. You will have the animal skinned and then you will gather all the princes. They will stand on the freshly flayed hide and make an oath, one by one, that should anyone try to carry Helen off, away from the husband she herself has chosen, the others will all be prepared to fight at his side to bring her back to her rightful home.'

'You are incredible, *pai*,' exclaimed the king. 'How is it possible that you, so young, already know men's hearts so well? You have understood that they will all accept because each of the princes is certain in his own heart that he is the only one worthy of bringing Helen home to his wedding chamber; thus each of them will happily give his word, convinced that the oath will bind all the other contenders to him, to his own advantage. But only one will be chosen. And the others will have to respect their vow.'

'I am devoted to Athena, the green-eyed goddess,' I replied. 'She sometimes lets me feel her presence. Perhaps a reflection of her infinite wisdom sometimes illuminates my heart, so that the words I speak are judicious. At least that's what I like to think.'

The king embraced me: 'This house is your house, this land is your land. You are the son that every father wants, the son-in-law he would desire for his daughter. Promise you'll stay with me, Odysseus, until everything is resolved.'

'I will stay, *wanax*, not only because you bid me to do so, but because the goddess sent me a vision last night: a water bird with green and amber feathers made its nest in an olive tree in Laertes' palace, my home.'

The king smiled: 'Water birds do not make their nests in olive trees.'

'No, they don't, and that's why I must stay until I recognize the meaning of the dream. I'll know then that I have acted as Athena the all-knowing warrior and virgin has ordained.'

My green-eyed goddess.

14

I TOOK LEAVE OF THE PALACE wondering in my heart how the princes would take such a solution. When had it ever happened that the woman chose and not the man? How could they give up the idea of winning the most beautiful woman in the world by dint of their swordplay? I needed to convince them with my words alone, by offering friendship. There was no other way. I would have to prepare my words with great care and, above all, avoid meeting Helen. I couldn't be certain that I would not succumb.

And so, weighing words and ideas, I left the palace and was walking towards the valley which opened, golden with grain blowing in the wind, along the banks of the Eurotas.

A song stopped me:

> Fly, fly away,
> Eye the river from above
> Eye the sea from on high
> As the sun sets
> and the air tastes of salt
> End the sting of nostalgia,
> Bring him home to me!

A girl's voice carried on the air, clear as water, soft as a caress. Where was she? I looked around but saw no one. I spotted walls covered with flowering jasmine which surrounded a garden of apple and olive trees; I could see their foliage. That's where the voice was coming from. I approached and walked along the walls to find a point from which I could peek in. I stopped where several well-squared stones had been removed; perhaps someone had taken them for the foundations of his house. There I saw a girl dressed in a light, short-sleeved gown, cinched at the waist with a wide band. The neckline bared her perfect shoulders and the checked pattern of the dress was embroidered with a brightly coloured duck in every square.

She was picking field flowers, but she sensed my presence, straightened up and approached me without fear.

'Who are you?' she asked. 'Your robe looks like a prince's. Have you come to claim Helen? Others have already arrived and are camped along the river; they're there practising for the bloody duels.'

'And I say you're a princess. Your gown looks fashioned by expert weavers and embroiderers, and your song touched my heart. Were you thinking of someone as you sang those words? My name is Odysseus.'

'The prince of Ithaca. What a strange name you have.'

'So they say. Perhaps I wouldn't have chosen it, but now I wouldn't exchange it with anyone.' *With no one?*

'Will you battle for her, Odysseus? How will that happen? Will the adversaries be drawn by lots? I hope you get one who's not too terrible.'

'Were you singing those words for someone?'

'For no one,' she replied.

For No One. 'Why are you worried about my adversary? Are you afraid I won't be able to handle him?'

'Because you have beautiful eyes. They change colour when you smile.'

'You have beautiful eyes, too. Luminous. A man could get lost in them. Who are you?'

'The daughter of Icarius, King Tyndareus' brother. So I'm Helen's cousin.' She gave a naughty smile. 'I've seen her naked, many times. Do you want to know what she's like?'

'I want to know your name. Why won't you tell me?'

'Penelope.'

123

'Now that's a strange name! Is that why you have those little ducks embroidered on your gown?'

'Don't you like them?'

'I do, very much. They look like a rainbow. Will I see you again?'

'If you don't get killed. Do you know how big Ajax, the son of Telamon, is? Gigantic. A walking mountain. And his cousin Achilles? A thunderbolt. He'll cut you in half before you even lay a hand on your sword.'

'I'm faster than they are,' I replied. 'I've already beaten them all.'

She stood looking at me without saying a word. The flowers fell out of her hand. I resumed my walk.

'Odysseus!' her voice rang out behind me. I turned.

She smiled. Dusky and luminous.

I ARRIVED at the camp of the suitors as the sun was just beginning its decline, after having stopped several times along the tree-shaded bank of the river. I needed to think, to repeat the words out loud, again and again. Only the cicadas answered me, and the voice of the river. I finally decided to enter the camp. The first tents I saw were those of Achilles, prince of Phthia of the Myrmidons, then those of Ajax, son of Telamon, prince of Salamis. The tents of Diomedes, prince of Argus, came next, and then those of Ajax Oileus, prince of Locris, Idomeneus of Crete and Menelaus, prince of Mycenae. He was accompanied by his older brother, Agamemnon, who was not a contender. He had already asked for and obtained the hand of Helen's twin sister, Clytaemnestra. This would certainly have its importance, but for the moment I couldn't predict how. I instantly felt sick. I knew that my mission would be much more difficult than I had thought: all I heard was the clash of weapons. All I saw was young men facing off, in training for much harsher duels. Lethal ones.

I reached a point where a space opened up between the two lines of tents, coinciding with several rocky outcroppings on the riverbank. I thought that would be the best place to make my speech. Tyndareus' warriors were there as well, patrolling the entire extension of the camps, perhaps to guarantee that the noble guests would not attack each other in brawls or skirmishes. I wasn't ready to talk yet, so I walked through the camp to see who these youths who wanted to win Helen were; did they truly only want to possess the most beautiful of women or something more instead? I studied their attitudes, their posturing. If I could understand, perhaps I'd be ready to speak.

When I saw that the sun was drawing close to the horizon, I called over one of the heralds, standing under a banner with the king's colours in a clearing that was free of tents. I told him that I was Odysseus of Ithaca and that King Tyndareus had sent me. I ordered him, on behalf of the king, to call the princes to assembly. He looked into my eyes and recognized me; perhaps he had seen me at the palace. He nodded and climbed onto one of the rocks, the highest one. His thundering voice rang out from the tents of Achilles all the way to the distant tents of Protesilaus. Then a bugle call sounded where his voice alone would not carry.

One by one, the contenders arrived at the clearing by the river and I climbed up on the rock to address them.

'Princes of Achaia!'

Their voices quietened to a buzz.

'Noble princes, heed my words! I am Odysseus, son of Laertes, king of Ithaca. I know why you are all here: to vie for Helen, the most beautiful woman on the face of the earth. There are many of you. Only one of her!'

'We had already worked that out!' shouted one of them. 'No need to muster us here to tell us that.' The others laughed.

'Good, I'm happy to hear that. Then you'll also have worked out what happens afterwards, right?'

'Why are you talking about us, prince of Ithaca? Don't you share the same intention? Aren't you interested in Helen?'

I recognized the youth who had spoken: it was Diomedes of Argus. And he recognized me: 'I've seen you before!'

'You have,' I replied, 'in Argus, on the day your father was set on the pyre! Are you ready to die now as well?'

Diomedes dropped his head and then looked up, staring straight at me with a defiant expression: 'And who says I have to die?'

'Right, who says that?' I said, looking out among them. 'Achilles of Phthia? Ajax of Salamis, perhaps? Or you, Philoctetes . . .'

'Or me!' said a voice I thought I recognized.

'Who are you?' demanded Diomedes.

'Eumelus of Pherai, son of Admetus,' said the same voice.

It hit me who was speaking and I stopped short for a moment, my heart pounding: 'Eumelus? What are you doing here?'

'The same thing as the others,' he replied curtly.

'You don't know what you're saying. You can't last. Diomedes has done nothing for years but train for combat.' I didn't allow him to answer, or let anyone else speak, for the moment. 'The challenge of this young man whose beard has just sprouted shows you how far this has gone. Now, listen to me, all of you, and then you'll decide what you want to do. I'm not here of my own initiative; I've been sent by the king in person, *wanax* Tyndareus, lord of Sparta, Helen's father.'

The clamour of voices that had begun to rise died down at once, giving me the chance to take a good look at the men I found standing before me. Achilles looked more like a god than a man; completely clad in bronze as if he were about to stride onto the battlefield, his bare arms shone as if they themselves were made of metal. His muscles contracted spasmodically as though animated by uncontrollable energy and his hair rippled like a lion's mane at every passing puff of wind. Ajax of Salamis was simply huge. Only Hercules, perhaps, could match him in size, although I'd never seen Hercules. Menelaus had red hair but his skin was dark and his eyes amber: he was the second of his dynasty, after Agamemnon, and would never become king. There was Philoctetes, infallible archer: everyone said that he had inherited Hercules' bow. Antilochus, my friend, Nestor's son: he had no hope against these giants, but how to convince him to return to his Pylos, mirrored in the sea? Ajax

Oileus, bold and arrogant, agile and lightning swift. Idomeneus, lord of Crete, heir of Minos, as mighty as Zeus himself. And there was Eumelus, Alcestis' son more than Admetus', little more than a boy: did he perhaps imagine he could make up for his father's lack of spine by facing off against one of these colossuses in an impossible duel?

I had to force them to reason.

'It won't be a bloody duel that decides this contest. Each and every one of you who falls, or remains disfigured or wounded, will bring nothing but disgrace and grief upon the land of the Achaians and all its people. It will be Helen who decides!'

The princes looked at each other incredulously. That was the last thing they'd expected to hear, and the worst.

'Fine, there is no need to shed blood!' shouted Diomedes. 'Why don't we wrestle instead, or race chariots or compete by seeing who can hurl his spear the furthest? Anything is better than letting a woman choose!'

'What you're proposing wouldn't change much. None of you would accept defeat; vengeance and war would be the next step. We're not talking simply about any woman, but about Helen of Sparta. It will be she who decides which of you she will follow as her husband. All the rest of you will swear to respect this marriage as if Helen had married you Talone. You will make your oaths one after another, as you are called by the herald, standing bare-footed on the freshly skinned hide of a gigantic bull, sacrificed to the gods of the Underworld. And be glad of it: from this moment, until Helen pronounces one of your names, each of you can dream of being the chosen one.'

'Will you be with us, prince of Ithaca?' asked Ajax of Salamis.

'I cannot ignore the privilege offered to me by the king and queen of Sparta, and so I will also lay wedding gifts at Helen's feet and swear with the rest of you but I am certain that I will not be chosen; the islands of my Ithaca are poor and rocky, and I lack your prowess. The king and the queen, with their resplendent daughter, will await you all tomorrow in the palace courtyard, after the sun has set.'

For an instant I saw, standing between Antilochus and Achilles, my counsellor Mentor, who stared at me with an enigmatic smile on his lips. I was about to call out to him, but he vanished, like the mist.

Athena!

I trembled at that vision but my heart was joyous. I was sure I had won; I had averted the disaster.

I returned to the palace, thinking of Penelope. I walked through the halls and corridors hoping to catch a glimpse of her but I knew that was impossible. Surely such a flower would be under watch in the women's quarters, now that the sun had already sunk behind the ridges of Mount Taygetus. I went back on my steps and out into the great courtyard where the servants were preparing food for dinner. I felt something tumble around my feet and bent to pick it up: a little pebble of red sandstone. I looked up and saw her leaning on a windowsill. Her smile looked sad, or was I imagining that? I motioned for her to come down. She pointed to the southern wall of the palace and disappeared.

I looked around to make sure no one had noticed anything, then turned the corner and tried to find the place she was suggesting for such a unexpected, secret meeting. A group of holm oaks and box trees created a small, secluded space: it must be there she had been thinking of.

I stepped in and soon saw her furtively exiting a little door and calling my name softly. She reached me in three agile steps and there she was in front of me.

'What a funny gift you've given me!' I greeted her. 'I wouldn't think of repaying you in the same way. But if I'd had a flower I certainly would have brought you that.'

'Why are you saying that? You're famous for having a way with words and making people believe what's not true.' Her eyes were glittering, in the shadows.

'I don't know what you mean. My words are sincere, they come from my heart.'

'Oh really? Well, then listen to this: just a little while ago I heard Helen speaking with her nurse. She was saying: "*Mai*, I had a dream last night, a dream I think might come true."

'"What did you dream, my child?" asked her nurse.

'"I dreamed that I was with the prince of Ithaca, Odysseus, in a bath chamber whose walls were all covered with a rare stone, glowing with a green reflection; there were alabaster vases filled with oriental perfumes in the room. We were acting like . . . husband and wife."

'"What do you mean?" asked her nurse but then Helen whispered something into her ear that I couldn't hear. And then Helen added: "Do you think it's a dream that will come true?"

'"That depends on you, my child," replied the nurse. "Only you can make it come true."

'"But don't you think that the gods have sent me a sign to help me make my choice?"

'"No one can say, but if it is this that you desire, then it is your heart sending you these dreams."'

Here Penelope broke off and burst into tears. I tried to pull her close but she pushed me away as if I had betrayed her.

'If Helen said that, it's because she has already made her choice and you've consented. I know her too well. She always takes what she wants.'

She didn't give me a chance to say a word before she ran off, crying.

THE NEXT EVENING, after sunset, everything was ready in the palace. The priests dragged the big bull to the middle of the courtyard, while the young heroes entered one after another garbed in their most stunning attire, with their armour shining brightly. I joined them, wearing my finest as well and carrying the weapons my father had given me for the day of the contest. We all held our helmets under our arms so our faces would be recognizable.

The king and the queen came through the main gate, followed by dignitaries and warriors. They accompanied their daughter, who wore a veil that descended all the way to her feet. The king's brother Icarius followed with his wife. Last came Princess Clytaemnestra with her husband Agamemnon, the elder son of Atreus, king of Mycenae.

Struck by the axe, the bull collapsed all at once, flooding the pavement with its blood. It was flayed immediately and its hooves, innards and head were set upon the altar and burned in sacrifice to the gods. The flesh was cut into pieces and carried away for the great banquet that would follow. The hide was stretched out on the ground, with the flayed, bleeding side upward. Then the nurse unveiled Helen. The light blue drape that had covered her fell to the ground and all of those present gasped. She was more a goddess than a mortal woman, a beauty pure and perfect as a golden rose, fiery as a lightning bolt, diaphanous as the moon.

One by one, treading the bull's hide barefooted, we swore the same oath. Achilles was first:

'I, Achilles, son of Peleus, lord of Phthia of the Myrmidons
Have come bearing wedding gifts for Helen of Sparta
And I hereby swear that, even if she should choose another
    of the princes gathered here,
I will defend her honour and her person as if she were my
    own bride.'

Once each prince had vowed to defend Helen, he signalled for his shield-bearer to lay his wedding gifts at her feet, and then joined the others who had already made their oaths, lined up in the middle of the courtyard. To my right was Menelaus, to my left Diomedes. A heap of treasure had accumulated at Helen's feet, but only the gifts of the man she married would be kept. The others would be returned. When each of us had finished making that solemn oath, Helen was called upon to make her choice and in the chest of every prince, including my own, hearts beat furiously, as if it were time to enter a terrible battle – that fierce fray that can give victory or death.

Helen moved and she seemed more fearsome than a panther as she descended the steps, one by one. She walked towards the first of the young heroes at the beginning of the line, Achilles, who blazed with his own light. There, everyone thought, she would stop, but she only paused for an instant with the merest hint of a smile. Achilles bit his lower lip. She passed by Philoctetes, the infallible archer, Eumelus, son of a mother who had returned alive from the threshold of Hades, Protesilaus, lord of the untameable Thracians, Antilochus, the most valiant of the sons of Nestor, Menestheus of Athens, Ajax Oileus with his impassible gaze, even Diomedes, the proudest and brightest after Achilles.

She had reached me, the prince of a small rocky island, pasture of goats; my gift had been modest compared to the other treasures. She would pass me by now as well . . .

She stopped.

She drew closer, seeking out my gaze, looking for an answer. I saw her as a girl, talking to me in the pen of those spirited steeds. I knew. I looked straight at her and shook my head so slightly that only she could see me. Ardent tears sprang to her eyes as soon as she understood. She abruptly took an almost imperceptible step to her right and chose the first man she saw: Menelaus, skin of bronze, hair red as copper.

A shout arose from the crowd: of jubilation, of incredulity, of delirium. The tremendous contest had taken place and nothing terrible had come of it.

Helen had a husband, a prince without a kingdom.

In no time the palace was buzzing with preparations for the great wedding feast. That very night Menelaus Atreides would possess the most beautiful woman in the world in his bedchamber. No one was paying any attention to me and I darted off, skirting the courtyard and racing down the corridor to the little garden at the back. I didn't have to wait long: Penelope ran towards me with her beautiful face full of joy and of tears. She embraced me tightly as if *her white arms could never let go of me.*

'Take me away with you,' she said, 'now, Odysseus. You are the man I want and I will want for my whole life.'

'Run,' I shouted, 'run as fast as you can, follow me!' By the time we got to the stables we were panting. I yoked the horses to my chariot, helped her on, and whipped Nestor's magnificent chargers with the reins. They flew off down the road.

But we instantly heard a shout louder than the sound of their galloping: 'Stop! Stop, daughter!' as Icarius, her father, threw himself into our path. Perhaps he'd understood, perhaps a god hostile to me had warned him. Now he barred my way. I had to pull on the reins and halt the chariot to stop from running over the king's brother.

'Get out,' he said to Penelope. 'This is not the husband your mother and I have chosen for you. We want a mighty king, lord of a vast and fertile land, with numerous ranks of warriors at his orders. The son of Laertes will only rule over small islands in the western sea, rocky and sterile, living off plunder, like his father and his father's father before him. To survive he will have to give rise to much hatred, as his very name suggests. Come back with me, daughter of mine, while you are still in time. I beg of you!'

I was humiliated by his insults and I would have challenged him with my sword in hand but he was the father of the woman I loved and I repressed the ire in my heart. I also felt sorry for him. He was weeping because he was losing the daughter he adored. But Penelope was adamant. She pulled the veil she wore at her shoulders over her head and face, like a woman already betrothed through a solemn promise of marriage, whose wedding day was approaching. I took my whip to the horses, trying to drive them off the road and leave Icarius behind me, but with an unexpected burst of energy he grabbed a handle and tried to leap onto the chariot. He was dragged over the grassy field for a while but could not sustain his grip and soon had to let go. We heard his desperate cries continuing on and on, as he called and called for his daughter.

15

I STOPPED THE HORSES IN the shelter of a crumbling wall, because I understood that going any further would have been dangerous. Clouds had covered the moon and I had Penelope with me. Besides that, I felt sick at leaving Sparta the way I had, like a thief. I had perhaps stopped Helen's suitors from facing off in a series of bloody duels, but now I was running off with a princess of royal blood, against the will of her father, and leaving the men of my escort in an impossible situation. Nestor himself, he who had helped me so generously, could suffer damage because of my behaviour. My mission, which had begun with the best of auspices, had ended up quite badly. And yet at that moment all that mattered to me was that I was alone with the girl I loved, the girl I had lost my heart to the moment I heard her voice.

Both she and I were eager to savour our love without waiting another moment, carried away by the ardour of our youth and by our emotions. I breathed in her scent, the fragrance of her dusky skin made more precious by Arabian perfumes. I sought her eyes in the darkness and she mine. The kisses we'd dreamed of could not sate our passion and our desire; on the contrary, they set us on fire, like when the wind blows on the flames devouring the forest, but I held in check the heart that coveted her so fervently, and holding her close, I said: 'Penelope, there is no creature in this world that I could desire more than you, because it is not only your beauty that I love; I love everything that makes you the way you are: gentle and sweet, proud and luminous. The gods have surely made you for me because I will never ever desire another, now that I have met you. I would never take another woman as my bride.'

'I know,' she replied, caressing my face. 'You turned down Helen. No one noticed but me. No one else in the world would have been capable of doing that. That is why I veiled my head and my face for you, so you would understand that I wanted you and no one else, not now and not ever.'

'That's why we can't flee. We have to turn back. I'll speak to King Tyndareus and ask him to speak to his brother so that he will not curse me and will consent to you becoming my bride. He'll listen to me. That's why I won't take the pleasure of love from you in this dark, squalid place. I want to take you to a place you will cherish, sweetly fragranced like the nest of a dove in the springtime. A place worthy of you and of me, my joy and my love. Come now, let us go back.'

I held out my hand and helped her back into the chariot. I turned in the direction of Sparta and urged the horses onward at a steady pace. The white road appeared before us as we proceeded slowly and the clouds let through a dim but diffuse glow. We made our way up the slope of a hill but when we got to the top we saw a scene that made us catch our breath: thirty war chariots were coming towards us in a fan formation. Tens of lit torches were fixed to the points of the warriors' spears to light the ground as they advanced. I stopped and they stopped as well. For a few moments there was a silence as heavy as the sky hanging over us. All we could hear was the crackling of the torches and the snorting of the horses. Then one of the chariots, the one at the centre with the royal insignia on its standard, came forward until it was in front of us.

The king of Sparta spoke: 'Where are you going at this late hour, prince of Ithaca, after deserting my daughter's wedding? And who is this girl so shameless as to flee with you in secret, at night?'

I took Penelope by the hand. We got out of the chariot and approached the king's carriage.

'We are not fleeing, wanax, and the honour of your niece,

Princess Penelope, has suffered no offence, even though love is a god that no mortal can resist. He overwhelmed us and impelled us to take flight, but then we realized that we could not leave your house this way and we were coming back to ask for your forgiveness. And also to ask you—'

'What?' asked the king.

'To intercede with your brother Icarius, who tried to stop us fleeing, so that he might agree to his daughter becoming my bride. King Laertes my father will send a great quantity of wedding gifts, worthy of his noble house, and will welcome Penelope with every honour. He will love her as a daughter. I beg of you, *wanax*.'

Tyndareus seemed to listen indulgently to my words. 'I found you as you were heading back, Odysseus, and so I believe what you've told me. I cannot forget that your help has been precious to me. Helen now has a husband and all of the princes of Achaia are bound by an oath. Although you have offended my house by carrying off my niece—'

'He didn't abduct me!' exclaimed Penelope. 'I went with him willingly and even if you tried to keep me from him I would escape to be with him, for he is the man of my life.'

Tyndareus didn't answer. He turned to me instead: 'I do not think that my brother Icarius would be willing to listen to you now and allow his daughter to become your wife. But I will arrange for the two of you to meet his wife Polycaste in secret. She'll know how to speak to her husband. I will tell Icarius that King Laertes will pay him a personal visit to ask for a bride for his son.'

I kissed his hand and thanked him and Penelope did the same. Then we resumed our journey, escorted by the war chariots that returned, following the king, to Sparta.

We were very tired when we finally arrived late that night and I was accompanied to my room in a secluded part of the palace. Penelope, veiled, was whisked away to the queen's quarters under the cover of darkness.

Although I was bone weary I could not sleep. Penelope and I had been together for a very brief time, but being separated from her made me anxious and profoundly uneasy. I felt that if I lost her, my life would never be the same, and that I would mourn her for the rest of my days. I got up and went out to walk in the olive grove outside the palace near my quarters. I'm not sure how much time had passed when I noticed that the clouds had cleared and the moon shining in the sky was nearly full, casting many shadows onto the ground. One drew up next to mine and a voice rang out behind me: 'Why wouldn't you have me?'

In the moonlight Helen was so beautiful it hurt. Like a sword entering my flesh. Only a goddess could be the way she looked to me at that moment. The sublime curves of her body showed through the light gown she had donned for the night. Her wedding night. Her hair hung loose on her breasts and shoulders, caressing her perfect face as its golden reflections sparkled even in her eyes.

'No man could ever resist your extraordinary beauty and your radiant gaze. I trembled before such splendour—'

'You wounded me, prince of Ithaca, and now you won't answer me. Why didn't you want me?'

'It was Penelope, your cousin, that I was thinking of, and now I'm sure that I love her. She is made for me and I for her. You would have been unhappy on my little rocky island and you would never have forgiven me. You are made of gold in my eyes and as distant as the moon, too distant for me to even think about having you. I am not great, nor powerful; none of the magnificent heroes who vied for your hand would ever have tolerated you choosing me. They would have cursed you, and me for deceiving them . . .'

'Say nothing else,' she replied, 'but know that you have made me unhappy. And a woman like me, when she is unhappy, can do more damage than an entire army.'

I suddenly felt my courage failing me and my vision fogging over, and I knew that I had to leave. 'You have married a strong, handsome young man who will make you happy. Happiness is what I wish for you. Farewell, Helen.'

I walked towards my room but her voice stopped me and she approached me again, coming so close that the scent of her made my heart tremble. 'And yet you and I will see each other again, alone, in a beautiful place. You and I alone, like husband and wife. I dreamed it. I don't know how or when but it will happen.' She vanished in the moonlight, among the shadows of the olive trees.

THE NEXT MORNING I met Polycaste, Penelope's mother, in secret, to ask her to try to sway her husband's feelings. Penelope's destiny was joined to mine and nothing could change that. I still nurtured hope that one day Icarius would accept our union and consider me his son. Tyndareus promised me that he too would speak to his brother and that he would send me a message when his sentiments had changed. I thanked the king again for believing me and speaking up on our behalf and defending us. Penelope and I were ready to leave with my escort for Pylos, our first stop on the way to Ithaca.

I had already asked my cousin Eurylochus to set off before me and to travel as swiftly as he could, so he could tell my parents that I would be arriving with my betrothed. Happy as I was that my father and mother would soon be meeting Penelope, I couldn't put the memory of Helen's night-time apparition and her bitter words out of my mind for many days and nights.

At Pylos I greeted Nestor and thanked him with all my heart, for he had always treated me as a son, and we set sail for Ithaca on one of his ships. But he, the knight of Gerene, as everyone called him, insisted on sending another ten ships as my escort, with a hundred warriors clad in gleaming bronze on board, so we would not run into any danger. Eurylochus had taken my own ship, so he could reach the island more quickly.

The sea was calm, the wind in our favour. I felt content, because I'd had to make many decisions and they were all good ones. But there must have been something about me that made Penelope realize that my mind was wandering because she often asked: 'What are you thinking about?' As if she could read my heart.

'I'm thinking of us, of the life we'll live together, of the children we'll have, of the day in which we will be the king and queen of

Ithaca and the western islands. My father will be my counsellor and his wife Anticlea will be like a second mother to you.'

'Are you truly not sorry you rejected Helen? I'll never forget that moment. The entire world came to a stop. Even the gods were looking down from on high to see who the chosen one would be.'

'I didn't reject her. I gave her a look that made her realize we'd never be happy together. I'm very relieved about the way things went. What could have been a string of duels ending in the deaths of many of the most valiant young princes of Achaia was instead resolved without violence. Now the sons of the Argonauts are at peace amongst themselves, like their fathers were before them.'

'Is it peace that you see, Odysseus? May the gods heed your words. Do you know who Agamemnon and Menelaus really are? Do you know who their father Atreus is? Do you know what he did to his wife, who betrayed him with his brother Thyestes, and what he did to his brother when he found out? He invited him to a banquet, feigning a desire to make peace, and when Thyestes was seated, he served him—'

'I don't want to hear these things!' I shouted. 'Even if it's true, it's of no interest to me. Atreus was not an Argonaut.'

WE ARRIVED on the evening of the third day of navigation at the main port and I could see instantly that Eurylochus had succeeded in arriving well before us. Thirty ships, fifteen on the right and fifteen on the left, emerged from behind the promontory and joined the others escorting us. The oars beat the foam-rimmed waves in perfect rhythm. The banners of the most powerful families of the kingdom fluttered from the yards, and shields polished to a mirror-finish hung at the sides, reflecting the last red glimmers of the sun which was sinking into the sea. Then, as soon as the ways of the water and land were darkened, hundreds of torches took flame on the prows and sides of each ship, so that it looked like vessels of fire were ploughing the waves of the gulf. The fires set even the sea ablaze! As we sailed closer and closer to land, a sweet sound was carried on the air, and a chorus of girls dressed in white and crowned with flowers appeared on the shore. They were singing the wedding song: they sang of the beauty and grace of the bride and the vigour of the husband who would lift her in his arms to carry her into his home. At their centre was the king, my father, surrounded by his guard. He was wearing the armour he'd worn in battle in Colchis: the breastplate was embossed and the shin guards gleamed. His invincible sword hung at his left side from a baldric adorned with silver and tawny copper. Covering his shoulders was the same light blue cloak he'd worn the first time I saw him descending from his ship. At his left, the queen my mother was wearing a gown I'd never seen before: yellow with wide purple stripes. A veil was fastened to her hair by a finely crafted clasp of amber and gold.

Tears came to my eyes.

'See?' I said to Penelope. 'I told you my parents would be honoured to have you.'

The sailors lowered the gangplank onto the wharf made of oak boards and poles and we walked onto dry land, Penelope and I. I bowed in front of my father, kissed his hand and greeted him, then bent my knees in front of my mother and kissed her hand as well. I said: 'Father and mother, I beg you to welcome my betrothed, Penelope, daughter of the noble Icarius of Sparta, with benevolence and affection, and to bless her so she may gladden our house with children.'

'My daughter,' my father said to her.

'My child,' said my mother, embracing her and kissing her on the eyes and cheeks, 'you are most welcome here. We will love you.'

'We will love you,' repeated my father.

Behind them I caught a glimpse of my nurse Euriclea, who was weeping tears of joy, continually dabbing at her eyes with a handkerchief without managing to keep them dry.

On the ships, the sailors were waiting for a signal from the herald. When it came, they all lifted their oars from the sea at once, raised the blades and pounded the rowing benches with the handles, making the hollow of the hull resound with a deep rumble, sounding like the thunder roaring down from the mountain peaks and descending on the sea.

We got onto a cart pulled by white bulls, and hundreds of warriors holding lit torches escorted us to the palace, the walls and windows of which were already brightly illuminated.

A beautiful celebration awaited us. All of the noble families of the kingdom were invited and the great hall had been adorned with flowers and garlands of pine, myrtle and juniper twigs. Meats of all the best cuts were roasting on spits and baskets were filled with freshly baked breads. There were even flute players and dancers who had been called from the mainland.

Everyone's eyes were on Penelope. But she was looking at me and I at her.

THE NEXT DAY my father took me to the side of the palace that faced east and said to me: 'This is where you will build your wedding chamber. I would have taken care of it myself but I could not imagine that you would return already engaged! To such a flower, if I may say so. Look, here she is, coming this way. An early riser! She hasn't seen us yet.'

'Thank you, father. Don't worry. If you can spare a few servants to help me, I'll get the work done in no time. Woodcutters, first of all, so we can get rid of that olive tree that's taking up so much room.'

'In no time . . .' replied the king, smiling. 'You must be very eager to bring her into your wedding chamber.'

No sooner had he said this than the servants arrived, with two hardy woodcutters. They were already lifting their axes when Penelope spotted us and shouted: 'Stop them, I beg of you!'

I had a flash: the dream I'd had of a water bird alighting on an olive tree in my house.

I raised my hand to stop the axes as Penelope reached my side. 'It's so beautiful, that olive tree. Please, don't destroy it. Let it live. Do it for me,' she said.

'I will do it for you, gladly. This fulfils the destiny that was revealed to me in a dream.'

I turned to my father then: 'You know, *atta*, when I saw her for the first time she was in a garden of apple and olive trees and she was gathering flowers.'

IN THE DAYS that followed, I used white flour to mark the borders of the walls, ordered stones to be squared and sent for expert stone-cutters. Others were already at work carving out the foundations with pickaxes. All around the olive tree that Penelope loved they built walls, straight and well connected with big cornerstones. Enough room was left inside to install the ceiling beams that other craftsmen were smoothing and squaring. And I left big openings for the windows. In spring and summer, the sunlight would pour in and light up every corner; I would close the shutters only in winter, to keep out Boreas' breath. Then I was ready. I sent all the workers away so that I could finish the work myself. No one was to see what I was doing.

I raised the ceiling beams into place and secured wooden boards over them, using bronze nails. I fitted them carefully to leave an opening big enough for the olive trunk to pass through, and I left room for the stair as well. The moment had come to carry out my plan. I removed the tree's biggest branches with a saw and trimmed them with clippers, leaving only the lighter boughs all around. When I'd finished I used a chisel to make openings in the cut branches where I'd be able to fit the legs of our wedding bed. The legs were secured, so they would never budge, with long wooden pegs that I hammered into horizontal openings I had drilled from one side of the branch to the other. I nailed four big wooden planks onto the legs and on this framework stretched strips of cowhide, interweaving and pulling them with great force so that they would provide support and not sag when weight was set upon them. On top of this web I placed the mattress that the maids in the house had already prepared, made of pressed, quilted wool covered with linen fabric. Then I laid out sheeting made of finely woven wool whitened with ash. Lastly I put a precious purple bedcover over the mattress and pillows. It had been part of my mother's dowry when she entered Laertes' house as a young bride.

Our wedding was celebrated as soon as our abode was ready, before the priestess of Hera who protects hearth and home. I lifted my bride in my arms and carried her over the threshold of my house. Then, when evening came, the maidservants arrived with lit torches to prepare her and accompany her to the door of the bedchamber upstairs. After she had entered, they retired.

When I heard her cries of wonder and joy, my heart filled with a happiness I had never felt before. From the darkness downstairs where I'd been waiting alone, I looked up now, to the opening at the top of the stair, from which the rosy glow of an oil lamp filtered. The pounding of my heart was almost suffocating me, and I had to wait to catch my breath before I went up to the perfumed wedding chamber where the woman I loved was waiting for me.

She was smiling, lying on the purple cover, her glossy raven-black hair spread over the pillow, her divine body barely veiled by a light weave that felt the night breeze. She was crowned all around by tiny olive branches; their shiny green leaves stood out against the bright purple. Penelope's eyes gleamed fire in the darkness.

'You made me a nest in the branches of a tree! No other man in the world would have even thought of such a thing. If it were only for this, I would love you forever,' she whispered.

'A water bird settled on an olive tree in the house of Laertes. You were given to me by the gods, my love.'

She opened her arms to me and I lifted the delicate veil to contemplate my bride, to caress her as she closed her eyes and the desire for love overwhelmed her.

Never in my life have I been so happy, never has my heart beat so hard, never again has a mortal woman or a goddess given me as much pleasure as my bride that night, gentle, smooth, ardent. The aurora found us still intertwined. I darkened the bedchamber and sleep fell on our eyelids. The scent of her filled my dreams.

I heard her voice whispering: 'The gods will envy us for this. The immortals will never be able to understand the intensity and fire of our ecstasy, splendid Odysseus, prince of Ithaca, my husband.'

16

I GOT UP ALL THE SAME the next morning before the sun was too high on the horizon, so I wouldn't give the servants and handmaids, my dear nurse and even my own parents, too much reason to speculate about what had gone on that night.

I found my father hoeing in the garden, as he sometimes took pleasure in doing. He stood up straight, wiped away his sweat and walked towards me.

'Son, I must tell you that you've brought an exemplary bride to this house, respectful and modest; you would never know she was the niece of Tyndareus and Leda, the sovereigns of Sparta. And I'm proud of you, Odysseus. The news of what you accomplished has already reached my ears . . . yes, it was Nestor's men; they told me. You've made the impossible happen: you've restored peace and unity among the sons of the Argonauts before a quarrel with disastrous consequences could even get started.'

'Father, I—'

'Do you know what this means for me? It means that soon I'll be able to retire to my farm in the countryside to plant grapevines and prune olive trees, because you will be able to govern in my place with far more wisdom than I'm capable of.'

'No, *atta*,' I replied, 'you'll sail the seas and sit on the throne of Ithaca for as long as you live. There are still a great number of things I need to learn before I even think about taking your place.'

'Don't worry, I'll always be with you if you need my advice. And so will your mother. Look, here comes Euriclea with your breakfast, nice and abundant from what I can see,' he said with a wink.

Our hearts laughed, with a joy that knew no shadows. The sun shone brilliant on our island, the air was sweetly scented. I had my parents and my wife who loved me, and I loved them. The people all over the island were absorbed in their daily occupations . . .

'You're missing something; you know that, don't you?' my father said abruptly. I was sure he could read my thoughts.

'What is it, *atta*? What could be lacking in my life?'

'I don't know, but your grandfather certainly does. In fact, he's sent a message that he's expecting you to come and pick up your wedding present.'

'Grandfather . . . Of course! I'll leave with the new moon, in five days' time.'

'Tomorrow, *pai*. That cantankerous old man doesn't like to be kept waiting.'

'Tomorrow?'

He nodded.

When Penelope learned about it, she was surprised, or more likely peeved, but she said nothing and came to say goodbye at the port when I weighed anchor with the same comrades who had come with me to Nestor's Pylos. 'I'll be thinking of you every moment,' she whispered in my ear. And then she added, smiling: 'Once good and once bad.' I smiled as well and kissed her.

During our crossing, we spoke at length of what had happened in Sparta, and my friends all wanted to know the same thing: 'How beautiful is Helen?' Once that was out of the way, they queried me as to how enormous Ajax of Salamis was, and if Peleus' son, Achilles of Phthia, was truly invincible.

'No man is invincible,' I replied, 'but for now it doesn't look like there's anyone capable of beating him.'

They didn't mention the bride I had brought from Sparta, nor did they ask any questions. For the sake of respect. They already treated me as though I were a king and, if on one hand I quite enjoyed it, on the other hand I was sorry.

We arrived at port that very same night, thanks to a stiff, steady westerly wind. My uncles were waiting for me, with a couple of servants who offered abundant food to my comrades on board the ship. We barely said hello. They'd become no less taciturn with the passage of time. I got on the chariot and we headed up to Autolykos' stronghold. The sun was setting into the sea at our backs, staining the mountains in front of us red. For a moment everything around me took on a red tint, and I became quite uneasy. There was something in the air and in the sky, in the ground and the rocks looming nearby that I could not understand. Until I was brought into the presence of the lord of the fortress of Acarnania: Autolykos walked up to me smiling. From within came the fragrance of roasting meats and fresh bread. He embraced me and all my fears vanished.

'*Pappo!*' I said. 'Here we are again!'

'Yes, it seems just yesterday that we were out hunting together and you were just a boy, and here you are married now with a princess of the most powerful dynasty of Achaia. You're a grown man! I know what you did in Sparta and I'm proud of you. But . . . don't you want to see your present, *pai?*'

'Certainly,' I replied. 'Isn't that why I came?'

Autolykos laughed, took me by the arm and led me to the stables where he kept the horses.

'Here he is: his name is Argus, he's three months old, and he's yours.'

A puppy! Tawny-coated, with a lighter spot between his eyes.

'He'll be a great hunter, like his father and his mother,' continued grandfather. 'They're from a very sturdy, long-lived breed that comes from Thrace. Go on, pick him up, you have to become friends.'

I did pick him up and it was love instantly. He licked me and wagged his tail as if we'd known each other forever.

'Thank you, *pappo*, it's a wonderful gift. I like him so much and he likes me too, doesn't he?'

'How long are you staying?' he asked me.

'Not long. I've only been married two days.'

'I understand, but I'm happy you made it.'

'So am I, *pappo*,' I answered.

We were silent for a while and then we walked back to the house. 'Let's go to dinner now and speak of happy things. You know . . . I think this will be our last.'

'Why, *pappo*? You're strong as a bull and not afraid of anybody.'

'Not because of me, *pai*. Because of you.'

This caught me unawares and I didn't know what to say. I felt a sudden surge of fear, what they call green fear; you can't even defend yourself from it. My happiness from the days before vanished in an instant. The old wolf had spoken to me with a firm, tranquil tone of voice. I had to answer him the same way: 'I know that a man can die young, before his parents and even before his grandparents. I'm ready.'

'No, that's not what I mean. I simply don't think you'll be back to see me again before I die. I can feel it. And that's why you'll find a chest on your ship with my true wedding gift. Don't tell anyone it was me who gave it to you, don't open it until you're back in your own home and don't let your men open it either. *Sailors are curious. You can't trust them.* And now, listen well. Whatever happens, make sure it never leaves your home. Never.'

'*Pappo*, before we go in and get drunk I have to ask you something.'

'If I've ever been to the Sanctuary of the Wolf King?' he said, baring his teeth in a grimace. He still thought it was funny to scare me. 'Yes, and I don't know what kind of meat it was I ate, but don't worry, I never grew a tail. Let's just say that this story helped earn me a certain respect.'

We entered and he had me sit on his right. He broke bread and carved a slice of the best meat for me. I watched him and wanted to think that he'd told me the truth, because that was the most natural thing to believe. On the other hand, I knew that lying was the art he loved best. Argus yelped now and then at my feet and I'd throw him a bit of boar skin or a bone with a little meat to gnaw on. I think that our bond of reciprocal loyalty was born that night.

When grandfather was so drunk he rolled, burping, under the

table, the uncles took him to bed, and I never had the chance to say goodbye. We had said everything there was to say and he'd given me my gifts, and so there would be no reason to see him the next day. He hated farewells anyway and I thought I knew why. He preferred for us to picture him alone in his den, snarling at the whole world.

As soon as they saw me, my comrades were quick to point out that something had been delivered for me, pointing to a sealed wooden chest sitting at the stern, near the helmsman's post. They were greatly disappointed when I left it there without even touching it; they didn't dare even ask me if I knew what was inside.

The voyage back turned out to be more difficult, because there was a northerly wind which abruptly whipped out from in between the islands, striking the right side of the ship. We even had to haul down the sails at times and use the oars. When we arrived it was quite late and nearly dark. No one was there waiting because they surely thought we'd be arriving the next day. Two of my comrades bound up the chest with a rope and knotted it at the sides to create a couple of handles and carried it home for me. It wasn't so heavy, but long and very bulky. I held Argus in my arms so that he wouldn't get lost.

At the palace everyone was sleeping except for Penelope, who was up waiting and apparently not in a good humour. Things did not improve when she saw the puppy.

'You're not thinking of keeping him here with us in the bedroom, are you?' she said.

'We can leave him outside but you'll hear him yelping all night and no one will get any sleep.'

She gave up, but it wasn't easy to wrap her up in my arms. She was afraid that the dog was watching.

After we'd made love, my bride fell asleep and I left the room barefooted without making a sound: the floor planks had been fitted and nailed so precisely that they didn't creak or groan under my weight. Argus lifted his head and padded down the stairs after me, to where the chest had been placed. I went into the corridor and lit an oil lamp, put the chest on the floor and broke the seals securing it.

A bow!

A huge, magnificent horn bow. The bowstring was loose: it was made of bull's tendons cut into strips and wound up into a fine, thin braid. I took the bow out of the chest and grasped the top end with my left hand. Leaning my knee against the grip, I held the end of the string fast with my right hand, straining to pull the two together, until the top ring of the string hooked on to the end of the bow. How long had it been since that weapon was strung? I tested the string: a first light touch at its middle produced a dull rumble that became more strident when I pulled it tauter and let go. This had to be a tremendously powerful weapon. Argus yelped softly as if he had an idea of what the object was used for.

I closed it back up in the chest and went back to lie down next to Penelope but I couldn't close my eyes in the dark. Autolykos' gift and his words of warning filled my mind: 'It must never leave your home: never.' Both he and my mother had a gift: they couldn't exactly foresee what would happen, but they would feel things a long way off, like when animals feel an earthquake before Poseidon shakes the ground with his trident. I don't have the gift and so I couldn't understand the reason for his words. *When the time came, I would understand.*

I got up early and darkened the windows so Penelope could sleep as long as she liked, then went out with Argus and got him some fresh milk from the stables. My father came out soon afterwards and instantly saw the dog.

'Is this your grandfather's gift?'

'Yes,' I replied.

'You're good at lying, just as he is. I heard a bowstring vibrating last night. I know the voice of a weapon like that one. How often they sowed death among my comrades when we descended from the ship to plunder some unknown land!'

'This is my grandfather's gift,' I repeated, pointing at Argus.

'Show it to me. I heard its voice last night. Every bow has his own and this one strikes terror into a man's heart.'

I couldn't continue denying the truth: I took him to the room where I kept the chest and opened it in front of his eyes. Laertes the hero was stupefied at the sight and held out his hand to stroke the horn, black and shiny.

'This weapon comes from very far away,' he said. 'Perhaps the gift of a chieftain or a king, perhaps a spoil won in the sacking of a foreign city.' His hand closed over the grip.

'Grandfather told me this weapon must never leave this house. What did he mean by that?'

'It means that it must never be taken to sea; it must remain on the island. Perhaps it's a talisman, a magic object that can keep misfortune at bay. Your grandfather has been generous. This is a gift worthy of a king, my son.'

MY LIFE resumed quietly again on the island. Mentor often journeyed to the mainland and brought us news about what was happening there. In Mycenae, Atreus had been killed by his brother Thyestes and the story Mentor had to tell recounted such an atrocious chain of vengeance that certain parts of it were actually hard to believe. Agamemnon had managed to banish his uncle Thyestes from the city with the help of his brother Menelaus and it was said that he wanted to claim the throne for himself. Menelaus and his wife Helen were still living in Sparta. King Tyndareus was hoping that upon his death his two twin sons, Argonauts Castor and Pollux, would reign together in Sparta.

Argus was growing fast, well fed thanks to the abundant leftovers from the banquets we frequently held for visitors and guests. I had started to take him hunting. I always carried the great bow that grandfather Autolykos had given me. I'd learned to handle it well; it felt like it had always been mine. Even Damastes was amazed at how light and manageable it became in my hands: it was as if the bow gave me strength and not the opposite. Argus had learned to drive deer to where I lay in wait. I never missed a single one.

One day Damastes came to see me as I was skinning a buck and cutting the meat into pieces so that the cooks could purge it of its gamey odour and prepare it for roasting.

'I've come to say goodbye,' he said. 'I have nothing more to teach you, my prince. If I stay I'll only end up becoming bored or feeling useless.'

'I'm sorry,' I answered. 'I owe you so much. The days we've spent together have been full of adventure, and of hard work as well! You forged the boy who was put in your charge into a man. If you wish, I'd like you to stay here with us as a member of the family and as my counsellor. Think about it, please. You'd be happy with us.'

'I thank you. But as I've just said, my prince, I would only become bored waiting to grow old. It's best that I return north, to my home on the mainland, to live among the bold horsemen and adventurous sailors who dwell there. I come from the land of the centaurs, you know. A man like me cannot wait for the sun to set forever; I have to chase after it, remain in a beam of its light until my strength serves me, and then die on my feet, if I can.'

My rough and ready instructor knew how to speak like the most learned sage and his words would remain in my heart for the rest of my life. My father rewarded him with ingots of copper from the mines of Cyprus, along with a sword taken from his personal armoury, made of sharpened bronze with an ivory hilt, and gave him a ship that would take him home. Argus barked loudly as he watched the ship leaving the port as if to say goodbye, and Damastes replied with a wave of his hand. I never saw him again, but I liked to imagine him walking through the dense woods and the rugged mountainside, waiting in silence in the evenings for the centaurs to descend from the heights and drink at the springs. My youth went with him. That evening Penelope told me she was carrying my child.

I loved her even more then, if such a thing were possible. A child would crown our perfect life. It would be such a gift to see how much of me and how much of his mother would come alive in him! I wanted a son, but a little girl who resembled the only woman I'd ever loved in my life would fill me equally with joy. Euriclea was more attentive than ever to Penelope, fretting that she'd lost weight or that she looked pale, and nagging her to take better care of herself. At the end of the year, when the day of the birth was drawing near, I built another bed on the ground floor with the pretext that it would be easier for Penelope not to have to go up and down the steps all the time. In reality, both of us were jealous of our wedding chamber, and we wanted no one to discover our secret. Only Euriclea was allowed in.

A boy was born, and I gave him his name, before someone else could show up and give him a name I didn't like. I called him Telemachus, because one day he would become an archer and I would leave him the bow that grandfather Autolykos had given me, the most powerful and extraordinary weapon in all the palace. All of the men in the house said he looked like me, all the women that he looked like my mother, and everyone agreed that he would be a handsome boy. One day I went to the peak of Mount Neritus to offer a sacrifice to Athena: a lamb that I'd had my shepherds choose as the fattest in the flock. I immolated the lamb on a rock in the centre of a clearing full of blue flowers and red poppies and made a burnt offering of its flesh. My mother made a sacrifice to Hera, who assists women in childbirth, to thank her that all had gone well.

Argus immediately adapted to the new arrival and often, when he wasn't out hunting with me, he would curl up at the foot of the cradle and whenever the baby let out a wail he would put his paws on the side of the bed and lick Telemachus' little hand, as if to say, you aren't alone, there's someone here watching out for you.

Penelope chose a nurse from among the maidservants to make sure the baby got the best care possible, but she liked to keep him with her as much as she could. Sometimes they even kept me company on my boat when I went out fishing.

One day, as we were sitting on the palace steps and watching the sun set over the sea, she said to me: 'You've paved the way for a long period of peace in Achaia, so that your son will live as long as possible in a world without bloodshed. The bad omen in your name has never come true. Look at the sun sinking into the sea, listen to the voices of the children playing in the village! I'm so happy that I veiled myself for you, Odysseus. We'll be able to go back to Sparta soon, and my father will understand that it's not power and armies that make people happy, it's wanting the same things, living in peace, watching your children grow so they can have a better life than you had.'

I took her hand between mine and held it there until the sun had disappeared into the sea and Euriclea had called us for dinner. But Mentor told us that my father had important matters to discuss with me and Penelope preferred to have her dinner served in the women's quarters. My father and I ate together in the great hall.

Some of my friends were there too, the ones who had come with me when I visited grandfather on the mainland: Eurylochus, Perimedes, Elpenor and Euribates. My father's advisers were also present, as were his gamekeeper and Mentor. I was sorry that Damastes' place was empty. Lamb on a spit was served, with toasted bread, olives and partridge eggs, and good red wine from Messenia. Nestor always remembered to send it to us, every year, and we thanked him with sheep and goat hides and pork sausages.

When the tables were cleared after dinner, Mentor turned to the king and said: 'Prince Odysseus, our guests and I are all anxious to hear what you have to tell us.'

My father had wine poured for everyone and then began to speak: 'At the end of the summer you, Mentor, will summon all the people of Ithaca to gather in the main square of the city. Each of you present here will convince all those you know to be present. The herald will visit every household to announce the date of the assembly. I wish you all a serene night.'

I glanced at him to try to gauge from his look just what he was thinking, but I didn't ask questions. A buzz ran through the room.

Everyone was wondering what could have happened to cause the king to call for an assembly of the people and what would happen next. But since my father had dismissed us, there was no excuse to linger and everyone said goodbye then left to go to their own homes. Once all our friends had left, only Mentor and I remained with my father, who poured more wine with his own hand and continued.

'Son,' he said, 'you're a man now and have shown that you can handle great responsibility . . .'

I shot an inquisitive glance at Mentor, but it didn't seem that he had any idea of where my father was going either.

'. . . on your mission to Sparta you showed great sagacity and skill. All of Achaia should be grateful to you. You refrained from courting the most beautiful woman in the world, but chose the bride who was most beautiful in your own eyes, most judicious and deserving of you. You built your wedding chamber with your own hands, you possess a formidable weapon which attests to the consideration and esteem of the most irascible and arrogant man I've ever met, your grandfather. And finally you have generated a son, you are the head of a family. You can be the head of your people . . .'

'No, *atta!*' my heart cried out, but no voice came from between my teeth. My father stared, with those iridescent blue eyes of his, into the depths of my soul.

'. . . You can be the king of Ithaca!'

17

I TRIED IN EVERY WAY I KNEW to dissuade him. I begged him not to make the decision. I never wanted the moment to come, because I had never imagined succeeding my father. He was still a very strong man, held in great esteem by all the kings of Achaia; he could count on powerful allies and enjoyed enormous prestige. He could reign for many a year to come. I had carried out no exploit worthy of praise, except for killing a boar and getting myself wounded in the process.

'You've accomplished much more than that!' he answered me. 'You headed off a violent struggle among the princes of Achaia and bound them together with an oath. This was a far greater feat than winning a duel or even a battle. You mustn't think that I've come to this decision without reflecting on all of this.'

I spoke all night long with Penelope, who tried to convince me to accept my father's decision.

'Your father is also your king, Odysseus. You cannot shirk the responsibility he's offering you. To do so would be ungrateful and disrespectful as well. I'm a happy woman; I have no desire to become queen. But I am certain that you will be a great sovereign because I know you. When you laugh your eyes change colour like the sun in the morning. I told you that in the apple and olive garden . . .'

'I remember,' I replied, 'as if it were now. You were laughing, while I was trying to assume an expression befitting a great warrior.'

'You are a great warrior. So great you have no need of

demonstrating it. So, accept the will of your father and honour him for the rest of his life. As far as Queen Mother Anticlea is concerned, I already know how happy this will make her.'

I dropped my head and my heart flooded with sadness: others would have yearned for the sceptre and the throne. Not I.

The event was announced by the herald throughout the kingdom on the day of the last new moon of the summer. My succession to the throne of Ithaca would take place on the spring equinox; sufficient time to make all the necessary preparations. All of the noblemen of the kingdom were invited and my father long pondered whether he should invite the other kings, or at least some of his fellow Argonauts, but he felt it would be impossible to offer hospitality worthy of such powerful sovereigns. The kings would bring with them wives, children, a retinue of dignitaries, bodyguards, maidservants and slaves; his house was simply not big enough.

'Ithaca is too small, my son. But it will be a great day nonetheless. The kings will be notified afterwards by a message that Mentor will personally take to the mainland.'

I looked into his eyes, so transparent, so deep. There were so many things I wished I could tell him. I wanted to plead with him not to place such a heavy burden on my shoulders, to make him understand that I still wanted to be free to go hunting on my own or with grandfather, without an escort of Ithacan warriors. All that came out was a choked, 'I'm sorry, *atta*, that's too bad . . .'

He sighed, Laertes the hero, my father. He gave me a slap on the shoulder and didn't reply.

I spent the time that separated me from my succession talking to him every day, trying to glean all I could from his experience and his wisdom, his memories and his mistakes, his secrets, his adventures, his heart's most hidden feelings.

I spent the time hunting with Argus. He was a magnificent animal: powerful, swift, untiring. He would flush out the game and drive them towards me and as soon as I saw them coming I'd let fly with the horn bow that Autolykos had given me. A single shot could pierce the tough hide of a boar and cleave its heart.

I spent the time alongside my bride, who every day seemed more desirable and beautiful than ever. And I went to the pastures and the stables so I could take stock of my wealth in sheep, cattle and slaves.

One day Eumeus, the swineherd, who wasn't much older than I was but who had been taking care of the pigs for as long as I could remember, said to me: 'Will you still come by to chat once you've become king?'

'I certainly will if you invite me to dinner and roast a nice pig's haunch!' I replied.

He kissed my hand. I would often pass by, when I could, especially after I'd been hunting. I felt like I could breathe around him, and he did have a way with roasted pork. He didn't remember who his parents were or where he had come from; my father had bought him when he was just a child from Phoenician merchants. We were his family. He would have sacrificed his life for my father without batting an eye.

I spent much time with Mentor as well, and it was he, on the day of my succession, who took the sceptre from my father's hands and gave it to me. The sceptre was made of ivory and decorated with finely carved amber set in gold and silver. King Laertes my father – *yes, I'll keep calling him that for as long as I live, because a king is a king forever* – placed the blue cloak he'd been wearing when he returned from the expedition of the Argonauts upon my shoulders.

My mother cried, Euriclea cried, certainly because they were happy for me. So little time had passed since they had held me as a baby in their arms. I held out my left hand and Penelope took her place at my side. A cloak was placed upon her shoulders as well; it was white, embroidered with a rich purple thread at the hem and belt. My mother gave her a necklace made of diaspore with three rose-coloured pearls harvested from distant seas and a ring of yellow quartz set in orichalch that had belonged to grandmother Chalcomedusa. She was incredibly beautiful, my queen, her hair gathered at the top of her head with a bone comb, and yet I could not feel happy. I felt my father's eyes upon me, I heard the voice of the people, but in my heart I could not help but feel certain that all those cheering for me would be far safer with my father on the throne than with me.

A solemn procession took us to a sanctuary on the seashore, a sacred grotto inhabited by nymphs, and I offered them a propitiatory sacrifice. But then I continued on alone to a site on the steep, bare, rocky mountainside, where I immolated another victim to Zeus, who protects kings.

But it was to Athena, not Zeus, that I directed my most heartfelt prayer. I asked nothing from the goddess except that she stay close by me. 'Do not ever abandon me, goddess of the green-blue gaze, remain by my side always and show me the way. Give me, I implore you, a sign that you have heard me and that you will answer my prayer.'

As I was returning to the city and to the palace, I saw a shepherd boy taking a single lamb to pasture. There was something strange about him; first of all, he was too young for such work. A blast of cold wind suddenly struck my left side, as if a storm were coming up, and I turned in that direction and said: 'Where are you?' When I turned back again, the shepherd boy was gone and the lamb had been transformed into the enormous albino ram that belonged to grandfather Autolykos.

From my mouth came a sound, and I didn't recognize my own voice when it said: 'The storm shall come, and the lamb must become a great ram . . .' Was this the message from my goddess?

That evening a rich banquet had been set at the palace for the noblemen of our kingdom and the nearby islands. They were introduced one by one, and each paid homage to me and Penelope. My queen's close ties to the king and queen of Sparta made her a person of great prestige and importance. Each swore loyalty and allegiance to me, and having my father by my side certainly had a strong influence. There were some of them, however, men of my father's age, who could not manage to conceal a certain attitude of superiority towards me.

Many of the guests were given hospitality in the palace, others stayed at the homes of the Ithacan nobility: an excellent occasion to strengthen friendships, contract marriages, strike up alliances between families. When they had left the banquet hall, I joined my father in the courtyard, where he had gone to take in the cool night air under the portico before retiring for the night. He smiled at me and said: 'How does it feel to be king?'

'*Atta*, first of all I need to understand. Why did you decide to turn over your sceptre? You are at the peak of your energy and experience, and I didn't want to become king. How could I desire such a thing while you are so strong and can govern the kingdom with such a steady hand? Sitting on the throne while you no longer enjoy the prestige due a sovereign makes me feel unworthy.'

'I know. I understand you. But it was necessary. Many things have happened. King Adrastus of Argus, having no male heirs of his own, has given over the throne to his grandson, Diomedes, whom you've met. It's not easy to understand why, but I believe that Diomedes is convinced that where the Seven failed, he and his comrades can succeed in re-establishing the prestige of Argus. Diomedes is bent on waging war on Thebes to avenge his father, but only a king can declare war.

'In Mycenae, Agamemnon has banished his uncle and for all practical purposes is already acting as king. To think that just three years ago no one had even heard of him and now he is one of the most important sovereigns, if not the most important, in all Achaia. Do you see what I mean? And that's not all. Tyndareus, in Sparta, is anguish-stricken: Castor and Pollux seem to have disappeared. He has had no news of his twin sons, who once fought by my side, for months now. They departed on a trip to the north without giving any reasons for going, and they have not returned. As you know, they were the heirs to their father's throne, and everyone is gravely worried that this will make the kingdom of Sparta unstable. For the time being, the palace has managed to keep the secret and the people have been reassured about their absence. But if the situation doesn't change, Menelaus, Helen's husband, will succeed Tyndareus. At least that's what people are saying and that's what I know to be true.

'Do you realize what that means? It means that Menelaus and Agamemnon together will have a power greater than anyone else in Achaia. The entire southern peninsula will be in the hands of a new generation of young sovereigns, and we have to be equal to the other royal families. That's why I left you the sceptre and the throne. But don't worry, son. I have no intention of disappearing. I'll always be here to support you with my counsel and my arms, if need be. But I'm sure that won't be necessary. We enjoy a secluded, tranquil position here and we are everyone's friends. We are the sentry of Achaia on this side. And there is nothing on the horizon that need worry us.' He patted my shoulder. 'Rest easy, *pai*, all will go well. And remember, even if you are King Odysseus for the people of our island, for me you're still my boy and that's how I intend to treat you!'

He embraced me, the hero Laertes, my father, and for a moment I felt like a little boy again.

THERE WERE a great number of obligations involved in my coming to power, even if our kingdom was a small one. First of all, Penelope and I had to visit all of our islands. I had already met the noblemen who had come the day of my succession and had kissed my hand. Many of them were my father's age, but others were younger. My father knew everything there was to know about each one of them, and when they had been introduced to me at the palace, he greeted them fondly first and then whispered into my ear what he really thought of them. Now that I was meeting them again in their own homes and palaces, it became clear to me that even as they rendered me homage, their gestures of deference were always accompanied by a certain show of power. It was obvious that my kingdom would last for as long as I could prove that I was stronger than they were. No one would even consider challenging me or rebelling against me if that remained clear. And so I travelled without guards.

None of my friends lived on the surrounding islands; they were all Ithacans. I soon realized that as we journeyed from one island to another it was a shortcoming. It was better to have friends, people you could count on, all over your territory. At the end of our travels, when we left Same to cross the channel that separated it from Ithaca, I felt satisfied. The islands were peaceful, people lived a good life, and the noblemen had been given the chance to see for themselves that my father had made a wise choice. Most of them were certainly loyal to him. Many of them had followed him on his exploits and had witnessed for themselves that Laertes had always been the first to put himself in harm's way.

After I had reigned for six months, Telemachus had started to say his first words, but for a while only Argus could understand him. Penelope played with him every moment she was free from palace duties. I would have liked to join her, but I supposed that a king must show a certain detachment from human feelings. One evening I formally invited my father to dinner. I told him that I'd decided to visit my grandfather in Acarnania and that he would have to sit on the throne to administer justice and receive guests – that is, to replace me during my absence from the palace.

Mentor was not with us but on the mainland announcing my succession. No one knew when he would return; we were well aware of what delight he took in such duties and in the elaborate protocol of the courts. And most of all, in dealing directly with queens and kings, princes and princesses. I had given him gifts to deliver personally to Achilles, Diomedes, Ajax of Salamis and Ajax Oileus, Eumelus, Nestor's son Antilochus, Menelaus and his brother Agamemnon, the king of Mycenae.

'Why do you want to visit your grandfather?' asked my father.

'I haven't seen him for a long time.'

'No one visits the Wolf of Acarnania without a very precise reason.'

I was silent for the amount of time it took me to cut a piece of calf's liver and put it on his plate.

'Well?' he insisted.

'I'll tell you if you promise not to tell mother.'

'You sound like a child. In any case, I won't tell.'

'On my last visit, he told me that it would be the last time we saw each other, not through any fault of his own, but mine.'

'So you want to show him he was wrong. That you can reverse his prophecy, change the course of fate? You're mad, *pai*.'

'No, I just want to show him that one person is determined to see another . . . Fate has nothing to do with it.'

'He's capable of refusing to receive you, if only to prove that he was right.'

'Fine. As long as he's happy, so am I.'

'I'll stand in for you, *but don't stay away long*. There are chores that need doing: I have to sow the broad beans, shear the sheep, chop the wood for this winter . . . or simply idle about. It's a fine life, I've found. I quite enjoy it.'

'I won't be gone long, *atta*.'

We sat up until late, talking and drinking wine. The next day I gave orders to prepare my ship so I could set sail before the new moon, but just two days before my departure, a messenger announced that a ship had arrived from the mainland, flying the Spartan flag. My father was present and he frowned upon hearing the announcement, then gave me a worried look.

'Why that look? Sparta's our friend; we have nothing to fear.'

'Sparta is Helen's city, and you know what that means. Mark my words, your grandfather is never wrong.'

'What shall we do, go to the port to receive them?'

My father hesitated a moment before answering: 'No. We'll wait for them here at home. Don your judicial robes. You are the king.'

I had my servants dress me and sent them to call for the queen. Penelope soon arrived in all of her beauty, wearing a light blue linen gown sashed at the waist with a black wool band fringed with threads of gold. A veil of the same colour as her gown was pinned to her hair with an orichalch clasp. She sat to my left. Twelve warriors in shining bronze armour joined us, lining up six on each side of the throne. My father sat on a stool of olive wood laminated in gold, placed at the bottom of the steps, a position of honour for he who had been the king and still enjoyed all the privileges of his rank.

A wave of agitation flew through the entire court at the news that Mentor had been on the ship and that he was making his way to the palace using a shortcut. He soon arrived, panting and sweaty, and blurted out: 'King Odysseus, King Menelaus of Sparta is ascending to the palace and asks to be received.'

'King of Sparta?' My father's prophecy had come true even sooner that we had thought it could. I tried to meet his eyes and saw behind his troubled gaze the thousands of thoughts flitting through his mind, none of them good. Penelope looked at me with foreboding as well. I motioned for Mentor to come closer and asked in a low voice: 'What's behind this sudden visit?'

'Something terrible has happened,' replied Mentor quietly. 'Helen has been abducted.' Penelope and I gave a start, shocked at such an unexpected revelation, and exchanged a look of utter dismay.

Abducted. Suddenly my kingdom, the peace of Achaia, my family and my home, all happy up until that very moment, were in grave danger. I wanted to ask him more but the arrival of the king of Sparta was already being announced, and the courtyard rang out with the pounding of heavy steps. A herald entered first and declaimed: 'Menelaus, son of Atreus and king of Sparta, asks to be received by Odysseus, son of Laertes and king of Ithaca!'

I stood and walked towards him to embrace him. Menelaus was strikingly handsome, tall and wide-shouldered, his long red hair gathered at the nape of his neck by a leather string. He was clad in shining bronze armour but the expression on his face was grim, almost scowling. As I clasped him to me, I thought of what Mentor had just said. Abducted? How could that be? Who would be so mad as to abduct the queen of Sparta? Might she have got it into her head to flee on her own? That seemed quite possible to me: she was as unpredictable as she was beautiful.

We stood facing each other: two young kings who occupied thrones that perhaps neither of us had desired. Penelope stepped up then, and hugged Menelaus. Pretending to know nothing she greeted him warmly: 'Cousin! What a pleasure to have you here in our home. Have you brought news of my father?'

'I'm sorry,' Menelaus told her, 'but the news I bring is not good. It's not about your father; it's your uncle, Tyndareus, who has died. A sudden illness took his life . . .'

'King Menelaus will certainly stay with us for some days,' I said to Penelope. 'I'm sure you'll have plenty of time to talk about your father. But I fear he brings other news no less distressing than that of Tyndareus' death. Could you please have rooms prepared for the king of Sparta and his retinue and arrange for dinner to be served for us in the Hall of the Argonauts?' That was what we called a room set away from the others where my father had had the *Argo* portrayed on one of the walls as she weighed anchor and set sail from Iolcus. The ship's figurehead was the goddess Hera and Prince Jason was standing at the prow. It was the room the king favoured for confidential meetings with his guests. It was he I was thinking of when I said to Menelaus in a low, unceremonious tone: 'From your forthright manner and the look in your eye I take it that this is anything but a visit of courtesy. Would you mind if I invited King Laertes my father to have dinner with us? He is a wise man and has a wealth of experience. He may be of help to us.'

'I would be honoured to have dinner with King Laertes,' Menelaus replied.

'Please follow us,' I said to Menelaus. I led the way to the hall. I felt there was no time for ceremony or protocol. As far as I could see, he hadn't even brought the customary gifts exchanged at such moments of hospitality. A sure sign that he'd left in a hurry, and with great urgency, I thought, rather than a sign of the proverbial arrogance of the Atreides brothers.

Penelope had us served roast kid, sheep's cheese and red wine. The servants placed the food before us, bowed and disappeared.

'What has happened, Menelaus? What brings you to Ithaca?' I asked as I cut him a piece of meat.

'Helen has been abducted.'

'When?' I asked.

My father's blue eyes had darkened like the sea under a stormy sky.

'Fifteen days ago. I was in Phocis visiting my sister Anaxibia. I am told that while I was away a ship from Troy put ashore one day at Gythium, our port. Aboard the ship was Prince Paris, son of King Priam. A courtesy call, I suppose, but not just that, certainly. Priam must have wanted to gather information about the situation in Achaia, where so much has changed recently. In my absence, it was the elders who received Paris and listened to what he had to say.'

'And what did he have to say?'

'That has no importance,' he replied curtly. 'That bastard violated my house and my hospitality. He has dishonoured me in the eyes of the whole world. You, Odysseus, can vouch that we princes solemnly swore a pact, in the presence of King Tyndareus and in the name of the gods of the Underworld. That's why I'm here. You are the guarantor of that oath and it's your responsibility to make sure it is respected. You must summon all those who swore to defend not only my own honour, but the honour of all Achaia. If any foreigner can get away with carrying off our wives and not be punished for it, that means that the fate of this land is sealed. I want to strangle that bastard with my bare hands, raze his city to the ground, exterminate his people and drag the women of Troy, every last one of them, back here to Achaia, to sell them off as slaves and concubines . . .'

'Wait, my boy,' said my father with a tone and a timbre of voice that commanded respect and attention. Menelaus turned towards him. His expression was sullen but there was a ferocious, deranged glint in his eye. He looked ready to tear into anyone who didn't happen to be Laertes, the hero of the Argonauts, friend of Hercules, Telamon and Peleus, and master of the house he found himself in. He halted his tirade, nodded, and let my father continue with what he was saying.

'War is always a catastrophe. Everyone loses in war, some more and some less. A kingdom is deprived of its king and princes for months, or even years; its best men are forced to leave. Many fall and never return. Each of the contenders is certain of victory when he first sets out, unaware that the outcome is, sadly, never certain. For one thing, powerful allies may intervene, completely over-turning the course of a war even at the very last minute. And even then it is not finished. He who is defeated swears revenge, calling upon friends and allies, invoking the gods themselves.

'War can only be the final solution, when everything else has already been attempted in order to obtain the desired result. It's never right to sacrifice thousands of young men in the prime of life to placate the anger of a prince, no matter how justified that may be. Heed my words, my boy: a king is the father of his people and he cannot plot to bring about the death of his sons, unless it is absolutely impossible to avoid conflict.'

I could see that Menelaus was about to say something that would offend my father and put me in an impossible situation. I stepped in just in time: 'What do you suggest he do, then, father? We cannot imagine that the king of Sparta would suffer a similar insult without reacting.'

Menelaus was momentarily placated by my words and he considered my father with an expression that could have been diffi-dence but might have been curiosity.

King Laertes spoke: 'Go to Troy, the two of you, immediately. You, Menelaus, and you, my son. Make a show of benevolence; tell Priam that you know that behind his son's ill-considered act are a people who have done no harm: men, women, old people and children who seek to live in peace and whose lives would be cut short or forever ruined by a war. Menelaus will demand, simply, that Helen be returned to him. If the king should refuse, you will speak to him, Odysseus. I'm sure you will find a way to convince him to avoid the grief and destruction of a war. Remind him of the blood ties that join him to the Achaians: the King of Troy's sister is married to Telamon of Salamis. If Priam still refuses, ask to speak to him in private; that will make things easier for you.'

I turned to my guest: 'What do you think, Menelaus?'

'You would do this for me?' he asked me in turn.

'I would do it for you, for myself, for my family. I would do it because it's the right thing to do and because I trust in the wisdom and experience of my father.'

'When will you be ready to leave?'

'In ten days' time I'll leave for Gythium.'

'In ten days' time. From this moment on, consider me a true friend, Odysseus.'

We embraced and each of us retired to our rooms for the night. None of us had so much as touched our food.

18

TEN DAYS PASSED IN A MOMENT, and it was time for me to leave Ithaca, Penelope and Telemachus. My heart ached but my eyes were dry; I was learning to act like a king. I embraced both of them together and it was agony to break away. I couldn't say a word. It was my wife who broke the silence: 'Are you taking many warriors with you? You may run into danger down there.'

'No. He who brings warriors brings war, and that's just what I'm trying to prevent. For a mission like this, you either leave with an invincible army or you go alone. When it's time to meet the king, we'll go alone, with our heralds. Priam is a wise old king. He rules over a wealthy city: all the ships that pass through the straits have to pay taxes to him. Many of our own ships have helped to line his coffers. It won't be a problem for him to offer reparation for his son's reckless act. He'll return Helen and this will all be over. I'll be back in a month's time. But every day I'm away I'll be thinking of you.'

'Take the dog with you,' Penelope urged. 'Animals can sense danger; he'll be able to warn you.'

'No . . . Argus is so attached to our little boy, and Telemachus would be miserable without him. They're always playing together.'

'Come back to me as soon as you can, Odysseus. Come back to sleep at my side in the bed you've built in the branches of the olive tree. Come back to breathe in my arms. Every day that goes by without you will be a grey day.'

'If I can manage to avoid a war, the day of my return will be a bright one for all of us. We'll celebrate here on Ithaca and on all the islands. Athena will help me. I can feel her close to me.'

I kissed Penelope, so I could take the taste of her lips to sea with me. I let my eyes sink into hers, black as the bottomless deep, and I kissed the son she carried in her arms.

I watched her for as long as I could as the ship drew away. Her slender figure seemed the shadow of a goddess and I could almost hear the song that acquainted me with her voice before I had even seen her face, in a garden of Sparta: '*Fly, fly away . . .*'

They didn't set Argus free until the ship had pulled away from the shore, and I watched him running back and forth along the wharf. He tried to jump into the water but he was too afraid. I could hear his long, desperate howling for ages.

When evening fell I felt a sharp pang of desire for my wife; I already missed her so terribly. The swelling sea, the still sky mirrored within it, made my solitude even more bitter. Why hadn't my father offered to come with me, at least as far as Gythium? He could have sailed back on this same ship. Where were Castor and Pollux, the invincible twins? Where was Hercules, how far away could his despair have driven him? Why were the Argonauts slipping one after another into the shadows? How had Tyndareus, king of Sparta, died? Why was I venturing far from home to petition one of the great kings of Asia, to try to win a war without fighting it?

My friends governing the helm and manning the sails were taciturn, as the approaching night flooded us with darkness and fear. Ithaca was at our backs and had sunk into the water; only the coast of the mainland could be seen, a dark bastion at our left. A light twinkled faintly, tremulously, in the distance between the folds of the mountains.

'Athena!' my heart called out. 'Daughter of Zeus, powerful virgin, ne'er defeated! Come to me!'

And Athena did come. She heard my voice and inspired different thoughts in my head, the same ones that had given me courage on my very first voyage at sea. More than courage, even . . . desire, for what I had never seen, never known; desire to pursue fleeing horizons . . . *To the point of no return?* To where the water covered everything and no land dared to raise its head above the waves. To beyond the sea, to the shores of another continent. To magical, mysterious, fantastic lands where anything can happen. Damastes came to mind, my master of arms: he had decided to return to his mountains . . . to meet life's end in the dawns and twilights there, to roam among those ancient oaks, to catch a glimpse of centaurs as they descended to the valley, to spy on the chimeras at dusk as they crossed an impossible sky and delved into the confines of the night. To listen for their shrieks echoing in the remote valleys.

Weariness at last prevailed over my thoughts. Perhaps it was the goddess who closed my eyes, to give me rest and inspire me for what I would have to do the next day.

Rocked by the waves and the lapping of the water against the side of the ship, I slept deeply as my comrades kept watch at the sails and helm. The day was slow at breaking: the shadow of the mountains lengthened over the sea like a dark curtain, protecting me from the light and prolonging my rest. When I opened my eyes and looked up I saw Nestor's palace, white and ochre on the hillside, looming over the sandy beach and the wide bay. The shadows of the mountains on the sea shortened little by little as the sun rose, and when it crested over the sharp peaks they disappeared completely. The sea turned silver and the ship seemed to slip more swiftly over the waves. The wind pushed us towards the shore and was most welcome. The first face I saw as I got to my feet was Eurylochus'.

'I thought you'd never wake up, *wanax*,' he said to me, 'and while you were still sleeping I ordered the sails to be taken in. We're approaching the coast of Pylos.'

'Good,' I replied, 'but don't call me that. You're my cousin and my friend. You are all my friends. Call me by my name. What makes a man a king is being capable of selecting the right decisions and of surrounding himself with men who can do the same thing while he's sleeping.'

The others heard as well and gathered around me. 'We're proud that you consider us your friends and that you ask us to call you by name even though you are our king,' said Perimedes. 'We consider it a great privilege. We want you to know that your destiny will be our own. We will face the same dangers as you do, but you will always be in command and will enjoy all your rightful privileges at the table and in claiming the spoils after an attack or a victory on the field. If, upon returning from this mission, you choose to depart once again to plunder crops or wine or women or slaves in distant lands, you already know that – in the big chest at the bow and the other at the prow – we will always have our weapons ready.'

'Don't worry about all that for now, friends. This ship has set sail on a crucial mission. If it goes well, we'll all live tranquil lives. If it goes badly, then we will need our weapons, and I'll have to rely on your loyalty and your valour for a very long time.'

That tied their tongues; they had no idea what I was talking about, since I hadn't revealed the goal of my mission. But Eurylochus promptly set to work, giving orders to the men and taking the helm himself. With the wind in its sails, slicing the smooth skin of the sea in two, the ship entered the mouth of the harbour between the hill of Pylos and the long island that closed off the bay. We docked at the wharf as Nestor's sons were just arriving from the palace: Antilochus and his brothers, even young Pisistratus. They'd been alerted by the sentinels, who had spotted our ship and standard.

'King Odysseus,' Antilochus welcomed me, 'it seems but yesterday that you were a boy like me, travelling with your father Laertes, and now you reign over Ithaca, Same and the other islands of the west. How long will you be able to stay with us? King Nestor has ordered a fat bull to be slaughtered for you and your men.'

'I thank you, my friends, but I fear I cannot stay. I will go to the palace to pay my respects to your father and ask him for water to drink and fish just caught, bread and fruit.'

'Go,' replied Antilochus. 'Everything is ready for you. When you return to your ship, you'll find it full of whatever will make your voyage easier.'

Nestor, knight of Gerene, greeted me like a son. He already knew many things. 'Menelaus' ship stopped here on its way to Ithaca and then again on its return,' he told me. 'What an unhappy man; you could see his torment in his eyes. To know that the woman who you had never dreamed would be yours, the most beautiful in all the world, is far away, in the hands of another, a young man, capable of seducing her over time . . . And so you will go to Troy with him. That's what I've heard. May I ask you to confide in an old friend of your father's, young king?'

'How could I refuse?' I replied. 'My father thinks you are the wisest of all men and he is certainly not mistaken. I know that you will keep my words in your heart.We will go to Troy together, Menelaus and I, and ask to be received by Priam. Menelaus has bid me to speak to the old king and ask him to return Helen freely without demanding a ransom. On the contrary, I will ask him to make amends for his son's offence, for his violation of the sacred law of hospitality. It is I who will speak because it was I who vouched for the oath that the Achaian princes swore in Sparta, at the court of Tyndareus and Leda.'

'The fame of your multifaceted mind, my son, has reached the opposite shore of the sea and will precede you in Asia,' said Nestor. 'Speak honestly with Priam, if I may give you my advice. You have the force of law on your side. Menelaus was offended, wounded, after offering hospitality and a hearty welcome. King Priam is a just man; he will listen to you.'

'That's what many think, but reality is often different from our expectations. Thank you for your advice, I shall surely follow it. Thank you for your welcome here and for your friendship, great king. I will stop again at this port and visit this home upon my return, and I pray to the gods that they will allow me the joy of bringing you good news.'

King Nestor embraced me as if I were his son, and said: 'If you do not succeed in your mission, an age of mourning and carnage awaits us. Young warriors are always spoiling for a fight, they can't wait to show how strong and powerful and courageous they are, but they don't know what war is. You are the only one who seems aware of this because you know the value of life. Find a way to come to an agreement with Priam, even secretly if necessary. Bring Helen back to Achaia and forestall this war.'

I wanted to depart that same day but it was impossible to refuse the king's hospitality. Not one of my comrades slept on the ship. They were all guests at the palace or in a home close by. We set off again the next morning before dawn, but Nestor was already on his feet and insisted on accompanying us to the port. His straight figure was visible standing on the wharf for a very long time after we sailed off in a southerly direction.

Two days later we rounded Cape Malea and then turned north again, pushed by the southerly wind. Our destination was Gythium, at the end of the Laconian Gulf. Shielded to the east and west by high promontories and by the mountain chains that emerged from the water like the backs of dragons, the ship advanced swiftly. We reached the port of Gythium five days after departing from Ithaca, brandishing our standard. We had obviously been sighted while far from shore, for King Menelaus was waiting for us at the wharf, surrounded by his friends and the warriors of his escort. They had come to render honours to the king of Ithaca.

Two warships were docked at the wharf and were being loaded with water and provisions. They would get us to Troy whether the winds were favourable or unfavourable, fair or foul. I embraced my comrades one by one and watched as they began the manoeuvres to exit the port and point the prow south. *They would share my destiny for many years, in good times and bad, through luck or misfortune.*

'Tell my father I will be back soon, and that he should not think ill thoughts. Tell the queen mother, Anticlea, that I will bring magnificent gifts back to her, and to my wife as well.'

They assured me that they would do so and that they would anxiously await my return from Asia. Before the ship had put out to sea, I had already reached Menelaus' side. Scowling as always, decked out in full armour, he nonetheless gave me a little smile and greeted me with kind words. A month had passed since Helen had forsaken Sparta.

We left two days later. Both of us were on the same ship, so we could speak during the long hours at sea. Menelaus was mainly worried about proving that Helen had been abducted forcefully and had not chosen to flee with another man by her own free will. He told me she had only recently given birth to a girl, Hermione, and she wouldn't have left the baby for any reason on earth, let alone to run off with a stranger.

'She was the one who chose me, after all,' he said, 'not the contrary.'

'Is that love I hear speaking,' I asked, 'or your wounded pride?'

I couldn't help but recall that moment when Helen, the most beautiful of all beauties, had seemed to linger in front of me, only to veer away at the last moment when she saw me shake my head, so slightly that no one else noticed.

Menelaus replied: 'I can't separate one thing from the other! Helen is mine! Helen has made love with me and given me a daughter. Do you think that any man who has lain with such a woman can turn around and forget her? Can ever be free of her? A woman like her gets into your blood, Odysseus, like a disease. No other woman could ever replace her or even awaken your desire; her absence is an unspeakable torture for me. Every night when I close my eyes, I see her naked in the arms of another man, doing with him what she did with me, and it feels like a wolf is devouring my heart.'

I had asked an inopportune question. I stopped talking about her so as not to aggravate him any further. We did speak of many other things during our long crossing, as we rounded Cape Sounion and sailed along the coast of Euboea. We passed close to the bay of Iolcus and could see the gleaming white city and Pelias' palace rising on the hillside. I wondered what had happened to the ship, the *Argo*, that had set sail from Iolcus to retrieve the golden fleece from distant Colchis. Perhaps it lay toppled over on its side like a beached whale, its keel encrusted with mussels, its masts and railings chopped up to burn for heat in the winter. Too big, made for men who were too big. Useless now.

'I think that ships have a soul, you know?' I said to Menelaus. 'They sing in the wind, sigh in a storm, whisper in the night breeze. And when they give up the ghost and are abandoned as sad wrecks, they weep, and their voice mixes with the voice of the waves. Tears fall from the eyes they have painted on their prows and are lost in the sea.'

When we had sailed beyond Thessaly, Menelaus held his arm straight out and pointed to a peak surrounded by storm clouds. 'Olympus,' he said. 'From there the gods can see the whole world.' A brisk western wind pushed us along the peninsula of the three promontories and then towards Thrace, and in just seven days' time we had arrived within view of the Asian coast. In my heart I thanked the goddess who was helping me and I begged her to come to my aid when the most difficult moment arrived.

An unfamiliar mountain came into view, rising up massively to dominate that part of the world. I felt the need then to ask Menelaus a question I could have asked him much sooner but I had always put off: 'If Priam returns Helen, will you be satisfied? You won't demand more reparations and thereby provoke him into refusing? Will we be able to return home and live in peace?'

'Are you afraid of fighting?' asked Menelaus. When a man answers your question with one of his own, I thought, it's because he doesn't want to give you an answer you won't like. I felt a shiver in my heart.

'I'm not afraid. I've been brought up and trained to be a warrior, like you were. I'm saddened by the thought of leaving Penelope and Telemachus, of not seeing them for a long time, or perhaps never again. I fear that in my absence someone may try to prevail over my house, my wife, my father, who is no longer in the bloom of youth. Invaders, pirates, who knows? My kingdom would be vulnerable, stripped of its best men; the strongest and bravest would be far away, engaged in a war with no certain outcome. Is that so hard for you to understand? Do you remember what my father King Laertes told us when you came to visit our house? I feel exactly the same way he does. Menelaus, you came to Ithaca to ask for my help, knowing full well what my position was, and still is. You said you would be my true friend your whole life.'

'I did,' said the king of Sparta.

'Then answer me using clear words: will you support me in my attempt to get Helen back, and will you return with her to Sparta? If this is really what you want, will you help me convince the Trojans and King Priam? The truth, Menelaus.'

'I will help you,' replied Menelaus, and he said nothing else for a very long time.

We came within sight of the island of Tenedos and then of the Rhoetean promontory on the sixth day after leaving Gythium. The gulf that opened before us was wedged between the two bodies of land for about four leagues. The waters at the far end of the gulf lapped at the base of a hill upon which a mighty citadel rose, and a great palace.

Troy.

19

THE CITADEL ROSE ON TOP of a hill that overlooked the bay and was surrounded by ramparts reinforced by mighty buttresses. Somewhat lower down the hill was a second wall, older and less massive, less striking, than the first and connected to it by a ramp. A construction with a wide battlemented terrace and two towers must have been Priam's palace. Looming before us was one of the two gates, the western one. It appeared to be open.

There was a lively traffic of carts, livestock and pack animals: a lot of donkeys, but also other animals I'd never seen before. I later learned they were called camels. Many were making their way up from the port, others came from the fields. There were warriors posted up on the towers and the walls and alongside the gates, heavily armed with helmets, breastplates, shields, swords and spears. The city and her king made a proud display of power to anyone coming from the sea, whether they were merchants, travellers, pirates . . . or us.

From the very top of the hill, a steady plume of smoke rose, most likely from sacrifices being offered to the gods from the sanctuaries and sacred enclosures. A river that I later learned was called the Simoeis flowed into the bay from the east, and the other, which flowed from the west, I would one day call the Scamander. Their banks were flanked by tall, slender poplars, lush thanks to an abundance of water.

At the foot of the citadel I could see an extended built-up area filled with one- or two-storey houses, encircled by a massive wall of sun-dried bricks, tilted at an angle and reinforced here and there by stones, especially around the doors. The main road to the city led up to the citadel's impressive main gate. It was set at an oblique angle and the jambs were on different levels. I had never seen such an extraordinary construction. Its name would one day become a symbol of massacre and slaughter, a bulwark soaked with the blood of so many young heroes: the Skaian Gate. The name itself sounded harsh, perilous; a gate askew, inviting any enemy to stumble.

There were warriors present at the port as well, along the piers, at the fish market and among the stands selling other wares. They seemed unconcerned; leaning on their spears, they chatted amongst themselves and scanned their surroundings every now and then. Everything else faded from my sight at that moment; I saw only them, unreal creatures. I took it as a sign from my goddess. A warning.

All at once, one of them pointed at our ship, shouted something and the docks suddenly sprang to life, teeming with men and voices. Loud cries, a horn blowing . . . in greeting or in alarm? Ours was a warship entering the port. Aboard we had twenty warriors lined up on both sides of the ship with shields, spears and high-crested helmets. Flying at the prow was the standard with the colours of Sparta, red and ochre with two lions facing each other: the symbol of the Atreidae, the same as I had seen hanging from the lintel of the gate of Mycenae.

I gave the order to pull in the oars and prepare to moor the ship. The helmsman threw out a line and two servants secured it to a mooring. A good number of Trojan warriors had, in the meantime, gathered along the wharf. The sky was thickening as well: grey, sullen clouds, damp, suffocating heat. My brow was dripping sweat, my arms were shiny.

'Did they know we were coming?' I asked.

'We didn't warn them,' replied Menelaus, 'but they were certainly expecting it. What Paris did was no less than an act of war.'

I summoned the heralds. The first was one of my men from Ithaca; his name was Euribates and he was the son of a nobleman from Same. The other, who accompanied Menelaus, spoke the language of the Trojans. He turned to the warrior whose stance and insignia identified him as their probable commander, and announced: 'This vessel is a royal ship and carries two sovereigns from the land of Achaia.' The commander stared at me and Menelaus, while the herald continued. '*Wanax* Odysseus, son of Laertes and king of Ithaca, and *wanax* Menelaus, Atreides, king of Sparta. The man they seek is King Priam, lord of this powerful city. We wish to speak to your sovereign and request, on their behalf, an audience with him. The two kings will wait on board this ship for his response.'

The commander spoke to two of his men in a low voice. They accommodated our heralds on a chariot and raced off towards the city and the citadel. Menelaus and I waited in silence; we had no desire to talk. The solemn words which the herald had used to introduce us only roused my fear, for the moment. I looked towards the citadel and I realized I was already exploring its weak spots; I was looking at the fields and beaches and thinking of where I would land a fleet, from which direction an attack could be launched. In my heart I was already acting like a man who no longer thinks peace is possible. Menelaus was certainly doing the same. I suspected that our mission had been compromised from the start, and yet I had no intention of surrendering. I just wanted to leave no stone unturned.

I watched the gates, the people, the mists, the dust. The life of a peaceful city flowed before my eyes: trading, traffic, ships entering and leaving the harbour. A storyteller roaming the docks and looking for listeners. No one stopped. Time never passed. I felt neither hunger nor thirst, only a hard knot in my throat. The sun had begun to sink at our backs. As the light changed, colours became more saturated and tinged the world around us with beauty. The heat broke, clearing the air for the swallows, and the sea turned wine dark. Fish darted under the surface of the water while low-flying seagulls shrieked, disagreeable and ravenous.

'They're coming,' I announced.

I had just spotted our heralds: they were heading to the port from the crooked Skaian Gate. The two of them were on a chariot being driven by a charioteer. Two more chariots followed, without passengers. For us.

'They're coming to get us,' I answered.

We got ready. 'Make no show of arms, Menelaus,' I warned him, 'except for self-defence. Breastplate, greaves, helmet under your arm. Nothing else.'

He nodded and we descended from the ship, escorted by our guard, as the chariots arrived and the heralds descended. My eyes were desperately searching for my goddess, for any sign of her presence. *Where are you?*

'Here,' said a voice inside me and my eyes raced upwards, swiftly. Racing like young impetuous warriors, beyond the Skaian Gate, beyond the bastions, beyond the ramp, beyond the second circle of walls and up to the sanctuary. A figure arose over the citadel, aflutter in the wind, a shield reflecting the small, scarlet, setting sun.

'Help me, I beg of you,' implored my heart, beating fast, my breathing slow. The tang of the sea and the shrieking of birds. The time had come.

The heralds approached: '*Wanax* Menelaus, *wanax* Odysseus, King Priam has consented to receive you and hear your words. For as long as you remain in our city, you will be the guests of Antenor, one of the most eminent noblemen of the city, adviser to the king, father of many sons.'

We departed. The drivers turned the chariots towards the city and urged on the horses. We left the warriors of our guard to watch over the ship. Our chariots went through the gates, the wheels easing over the misaligned surface on movable wooden tracks, and then started up the ramp, which was so steep that the horses had to arch their necks as the bronze rims thundered over the stones. Menelaus' chariot was first, mine second. Once we had arrived at the palace, we descended and the Trojan warriors escorted us inside, twelve on each side. The corridors echoed with their pounding steps, with the loud clanking of their weapons. They accompanied us all the way to the great hall and up to the king's big ivory throne. Priam was sitting there, awaiting us. His hair was white but his neatly trimmed beard was grey, streaked with black. A golden circle crowned his head and he held a silver sceptre in his right hand.

Everything around him spoke of his power. He was surrounded by immense riches, beautiful women, wives and concubines, certainly capable of generating strong, handsome princes. I knew what Menelaus was thinking: Helen was nearby, maybe watching him unseen, perhaps begging Prince Paris to prevent him taking her back to Achaia.

Surrounding the king were the elders and advisers who would also listen to our words. Menelaus spoke first: 'Priam, king of this great, glorious city, hearken to my words. I have come beseeching justice. I hosted your son in my home; he ate my bread. And he, while I was far from my home visiting my sister Anaxibia, abducted my wife Helen, my legitimate bride who had herself chosen me as her husband. He has offended my hospitality and mortally wounded my honour. I ask that my wife be returned to me so that I may bring her home, back to the daughter born of our union that she has not seen since the moment of her abduction.'

The king replied immediately: 'Noble sovereigns, I recognize your claim, but here in this city it is customary for the assembly to decide such matters. You will speak to the people yourselves and attempt to convince them. The people will decide. We pray that the gods will inspire in you and in my people the fairest words and thoughts. For as long as you remain here, in the sacred city of Troy, you will be considered sacred as well, your persons inviolable. Noble Antenor, a man very close to me and very dear to me for his great wisdom, will host you in his home. There you will receive an announcement when it is time for you to address the assembly.'

Thus our first meeting with one of the most powerful kings of Asia had already ended. I couldn't understand why he had not offered to convince his people himself. His great prestige, his imposing presence, his authority as father over his son Paris would certainly be sufficient to loosen the knot that threatened to tighten like a noose around his magnificent city. I couldn't help but feel that there were invincible powers all around us that would not be bent to our will; an obscure fate was gathering, milling around us like a storm at sea.

I tried to fill my mind with thoughts of Penelope, of her gown embroidered with a hundred little ducks, of Telemachus speaking a language that only Argus could understand, the language of the innocents. They had never felt so far away.

We were taken to Antenor's house, a palace with many windows that stood at a short distance from the top of the ramp. We'd been told that he had many sons; there must have been a window for each of their bedrooms.

Our host was an impressive-looking man, very tall, with a thick dark beard despite his years. He dressed in the luxurious style typical of the East, earrings dangling at the sides of his face and rings on his fingers. Bronze, gold and silver filled his house; who knew where all those riches had come from? I couldn't separate that vision of luxury from other visions of plunder and pillage. It was thus that my father's ship would return from his armed forays: loaded with objects taken as booty in distant lands, where conquering unknown peoples and taking their treasures were somehow always justified.

Antenor welcomed us surrounded by his numerous sons, and treated us as befitted our standing. It was clear that he'd been alerted to the king's decision to house us there, because the servants were scurrying here and there preparing dinner, and the scent of roasting meat from the fireplace soon spread through the whole house. A separate bath was readied for each of us, with maids sent to serve us. We even found fresh clothing to wear, suited to our different sizes. Menelaus was taller and more muscular than I was. I'd always asked myself what had made Helen flee from such a man. We felt her presence wherever we went; it was hovering everywhere in the city. A sensation that weighed heavily on my heart. It was me who had made everyone swear to the pact of the princes: how far would the repercussions of that act ripple out? It was difficult to understand how beauty can unleash violence and lead to such terrible consequences. I couldn't stop thinking about the moments I had spent with Helen, how close I'd been to her, how she'd surprised me the night of her wedding, after I'd tried to run away with Penelope. How would I feel if I saw her again?

The dinner took place with all due ceremony. The guests must have been the cream of the Trojan nobility, to judge from the way they were dressed, their arms and their ornaments. I watched them walk in one by one to take their places at the table. Last of all came an old man, carried in by four servants and accompanied by a young warrior.

The Trojans spoke a language that was very similar to ours, although the accent was quite different. Antenor made himself understood perfectly and when something was not intelligible he used the aid of an interpreter. In this way, it was possible for us to carry on a conversation. About hunting, dogs, horses, weapons, game and archery. Is this what we'd come to Troy for? We realized instantly that this was not the case when the guests had retired for the evening and only four of us remained. King Menelaus and I, our host, and the young Trojan prince who assisted the old man with such filial devotion. A young man with a dark complexion, wavy brown hair and shiny black eyes. His name was as rich and fluid-sounding as a cry of war or the song of a woman, depending on how it was pronounced: Aeneas.

Antenor spoke first: 'Prince Paris is Priam's son. Out of respect for the king, I will not say openly what I truly think of him. Let it suffice to say that were he my son I would have punished him harshly and returned King Menelaus' bride to him immediately, with a recompense proportionate to the offence.'

Menelaus and I exchanged a look, taken by surprise at such an affirmation. I began once again to hope that I might be able to return to my island and take my wife into my arms among the branches of the olive tree, raise my son, nurture respect for my parents, take my dog out hunting.

'Noble Antenor,' I said then, 'your words encourage me, for we have come in peace, merely asking for what is King Menelaus' right. May I ask you now if you intend to repeat in front of the assembly of the people what you have said to us now between these four walls?'

Aeneas gave a brief nod, as if to say that he approved and expected our host to act accordingly.

'It is exactly what I plan to say,' said Antenor. 'Furthermore, I'm happy to have this opportunity to offer you my hospitality. The last thing I want is for our sons to fight you in battle and end up losing their lives or taking yours. But let us put aside such sad thoughts now. We should retire; you must be tired after such a long journey. Consider this house your own.'

We spent three days in Antenor's house and I continued to hope that the dispute might be settled peaceably. I dedicated much of my time to Menelaus, to instruct him in how to address the assembly before it was my turn to speak.

'This is a proud city,' I warned him. 'Do not challenge that pride. Even if the people and the warriors of the city realize that you have been wronged, they may give in to the temptation of demonstrating that when there is force there's reason. We'd do the same, in their place. Remember this: deciding to go to war is easy, for each side is sure of emerging the victor. Waging war is another thing.'

On the day of the assembly, I convinced Menelaus not to wear his armour. He donned a simple robe, without ornaments or jewels. He had to look like a man offended to the quick, pleading in the name of justice for what was rightfully his. A large crowd had gathered in the square and King Priam had already arrived and was seated on his throne next to Queen Hecuba. One of the elders, accompanied by a herald, led Menelaus to the centre of the throng and called for attention. The buzzing ceased and silence fell over the assembly.

Everyone I had met during our stay inside the walls of Troy was present, including all of the king's sons except Paris. The most powerful and valiant was Hector, the heir to Priam's throne; he stood alongside his cousin and ally, Aeneas the Dardanian prince, both in full armour. Aeneas' old father, Anchises, was also there, along with Antenor and many of the other noblemen I had met in his home. It was Antenor who invited Menelaus, with a sweeping gesture of his arm, to take the floor.

The king of Sparta advanced to the centre of the square. He wore a long green robe hemmed in gold and his deerskin sandals had silver laces. The sun made his flaming red hair shine. His gaze was like that of a lion warily regarding its surroundings before pouncing; his gait was like that of a bull preparing to charge. Just looking at him aroused one's admiration. I thought that only the gods could have muddled Helen's mind and convinced her to leave such a husband for a feckless, spoiled young boy. It couldn't have been the same Helen that I met when she was little more than a girl at the horses' pen one evening at dusk. Or maybe it was precisely that Helen, whose devastating beauty even at that young age had struck me as a cause for the ruin of many men.

Menelaus began to speak: 'King Priam, Queen Hecuba, men and women of the great city of Troy, heed my words!

'I am here to ask you to redress a wrong. Prince Paris, who had come to pay a hospitable visit to Sparta, was welcomed as a guest in my house, but taking advantage of my absence he carried off my wife, Helen, took her aboard his ship and fled to Troy. Perhaps he is here among you and he doesn't have the courage to show himself, to face me man to man!' A loud buzz accompanied his last words and I feared that Menelaus' impetuous nature would betray him. I shouted in my heart, 'Careful!', hoping that his heart would hear me.

He continued: 'Return my bride to me and make reparation for the injury I have suffered and I will forget what happened. If you do not do so . . .' he thundered, ignoring my frantic signal to stop, 'it will mean war!'

There was a long, grievous silence during which the dozens of heralds and interpreters gathered near the king and scattered among the people explained Menelaus' words. Then a roar erupted from the crowd, with yelling and shouting and scornful taunts, which Menelaus perhaps could not understand but whose tone wounded him nonetheless. Their words were clear to me; I had already managed to understand how their language was different from ours and how it was similar, or perhaps Athena was whispering what they meant into my ear. I watched as Antenor paled, then stood and walked to the centre of the assembled crowd. Silence fell again as he approached the podium. He bowed to the people and to his king and asked for attention: 'O king, and beloved sons of Troy, lend your ears now to *wanax* Odysseus, king of Ithaca. He asks for your attention. Let him speak.'

My heart trembled. Now the burden of avoiding a war already unleashed by Menelaus lay squarely on my shoulders alone. I called upon my goddess to assist me, to hasten to my side and inspire my speech. I opened my mouth and I spoke in their language, certain that this would be a sign of respect for them, certain that Athena would make this miracle happen. I said: 'King Priam, Queen Hecuba and all you noble inhabitants of Troy, great and glorious!' The assembly hushed all at once.

'*Wanax* Menelaus, who reigns over Sparta, has spoken in bitterness and anger. Wouldn't each of you have done the same if you had suffered such humiliation? If your hospitality and friendship were repaid with insult and betrayal? Wasn't your prince received as befits the son of a friend and king? Are not our countries joined by bonds of hospitality and even of blood? Is not your king's sister the wife of one of the kings of Achaia?

'If all this were not enough, try to imagine for a moment that no other solution remains except going to war: how many ills would we have to face then, both you and us? How many of our sons and your sons would fall in battle? The soil would drink their blood! Their mothers and fathers – you who are listening to me now! – would have to bear the unspeakable horror of watching their sons burning on a funeral pyre! How many other mothers and fathers would spend their days scanning the distant horizon, sighing and longing for the return of sons who are lost forever?'

I saw Helen. I saw her, in the distance, on the highest tower of the palace. Haughty and beautiful, watching me. I think she heard me. I wanted to shout: Bitch! Other words spilled out instead.

'If you refuse to give us what we ask for, honour and duty will force us to take up arms. Wouldn't any man – every last one of you seated here in this assembly – do the same, perhaps, if deprived of his dignity? But consider, I bid you, how long would such a war last? How many families would be plunged into grief and despair? And all of this . . . for a woman?

'Let us find an agreement, Trojans, there are a thousand ways to avoid war if there is a will to do so. King Priam has many sons and he surely wants to see them grow and thrive, sit in the assembly, find joy in their wedding chambers and perpetuate his race. I hope that your king's wisdom will provide you with counsel. We will remain in the house of noble Antenor until you have come to a decision.'

We walked out. As we were leaving the assembly, I could hear Antenor exhorting his fellow citizens to return Helen.

'Will he succeed?' Menelaus asked me.

'I hope he will,' I replied.

We followed the guide, who led us back to Antenor's house in silence. Antenor himself did not return that night. We dined alone, served by a Phrygian attendant.

As he was clearing the table, I turned to him: 'Can you understand me?' I asked him.

'Yes, my lord,' he said.

'Do you know why we are here?'

'For Princess Helen, my lord.'

'And what do you think about this story?'

'I would prefer not to reply, if I may.'

'You may not,' I said.

'She won't be returned to you.'

'Why not?'

'Because Prince Paris always obtains what he wants from his father the king. And he wants Helen.'

Menelaus exploded in anger. He would have strangled the man if I hadn't stopped him.

The servant made a fast retreat. Escape, I should say.

'He's only a slave,' I said to Menelaus, letting go of his arm.

'Even a slave can tell the truth, and he has.'

'I don't believe it,' I replied. 'The king will not risk a war just to make his son happy.'

THE NEXT morning we were taken back to the assembly. There was absolute silence, and the sun was veiled by high, thin clouds. The heat in the square was suffocating. A dog barked in the distance. The king rose to his feet and all those present stood as well. Thousands of people. Hector was next to his father, clad in his splendid armour. Aeneas stood behind him.

Priam spoke: 'Noble sovereigns, the people have pronounced their verdict after having listened to Prince Paris' plea. We cannot return Helen to you because she doesn't want to go. She followed my son freely by her own will. Now she is his bride and my daughter-in-law. She is, indeed, like a daughter to me.'

I swiftly approached Priam before the guards could try to stop me and when I stood before him I said in a low voice so no one else could hear: 'Great king, this means war. Bloodshed and infinite mourning. Why? We can stop this while we are still in time. I have a mandate to negotiate with you privately. We can find an agreement.'

'We cannot negotiate the freedom of a person who decides her own destiny, King Odysseus, but I thank you for trying to avert war in every way possible. I would have done the same. And before our weapons have begun to spill blood, please take my regards to King Laertes your father. I met him when he passed here on the *Argo* heading for Colchis and I was struck by his courage and his wisdom.'

'I shall.'

I turned back and stared into Menelaus' eyes, shaking my head. The king of Sparta grimaced and his face twisted into a mask of fury as he shouted with all the force of his thunderous voice: 'This means war! We will return with an army the likes of which you've never seen and, mark my words, I will take back my legitimate wife. We will raze your city to the ground and drag you all back to Achaia as slaves!'

I don't know how well the Trojans could understand him, but they reacted as if they had caught every word. They charged headlong at us, some of them brandishing clubs and stones. The death I could see rushing my way was not the one I desired for myself. Menelaus looked over at me and I saw an instant of bewilderment in his eyes, but I was sure that he would fight tooth and nail before letting himself be slaughtered, and I the same. All of a sudden, one hundred warriors stepped out and positioned themselves between us and the ferocious crowd.

'No one will touch a hair on your head,' said Hector with an arrogant smile, 'as long as you are on our territory and under the protection of King Priam. You may return to your ships.'

We left the city accompanied by Trojan warriors. As soon as we got to the port, they were replaced by our own escort.

I spent my last night in Troy on the ship, waiting, wide-eyed, for dawn to break. As soon as the sun appeared at the horizon, I gave orders to cast off the moorings.

'Oars in the water!' I shouted. 'We're going home.'

The wind was in our favour and we sailed along the coast of Asia until we reached Cape Mimas and then turned west, passing between the islands until we had crossed the whole sea. We entered the Laconian Gulf on the seventh day of navigation and dropped anchor without hoisting the standards and colours. There was no cause for rejoicing.

There I separated from Menelaus to embark on the route that would take me home. We embraced, because that luckless journey had nonetheless consolidated our friendship. Before getting onto my own ship, I realized that there still was one possible way out. 'You have the power to release the princes of Achaia from the oath we swore,' I reminded the king of Sparta. 'Will you do it? For me, for them, for all the mothers and wives who will weep for their fallen sons and husbands.'

'No,' he replied.

20

My ship seemed to fly over the waves, pushed by the east wind and even more so by my desire to get home. I had expected Menelaus to refuse to release the princes from their oath, and yet there was still something in his stubbornness that eluded me. Granted, I had never lain in Helen's arms, never taken pleasure in the golden flower between her thighs. How could I understand what it meant to be crazed with desire and rage, out of my mind with jealousy? Oh, Menelaus of the mighty voice and coppery hair, what a privilege and what a curse!

I was reminded of my own words to the Trojans: 'All of this . . . for a woman?' Yes, exactly. In the end, didn't all of our longings lead us to that dark, torrid, blissful place? Wasn't Helen all the women of the world? All their beauty, all their grace, all their fragrance in a single body? All of their looks in a single look, certain to drive any mortal or any god mad?

Anyone except me.

I could think, reflect, ponder all I liked, but even I had to admit that a war for the most beautiful woman in the world was the only war that could ever make sense.

My mind drifted back to the last night spent on our ship in the port of Troy, on the eve of our return. A sad return, robbed of hope. I had been very agitated all night, and I got up again and again to go to the prow and watch the enormous red moon slowly sinking towards the sea. It was very late when I left the ship to walk through the port, breathe in the salty air, take in the silence.

'You can't sleep, *wanax*?' sounded a voice from a dark corner.

The street poet, the singer of tales that no one wanted to hear.

'What a foolish question, old man. If I could sleep I wouldn't be walking along the wharf at this time of night.'

'Won't you listen to my song, then? It will calm the anguish that burdens your heart. I'll sing it just for you. I don't want anything.'

'No, leave me alone. This isn't a good time.'

'You'll be at peace afterwards. I can't make you happy but I can give you visions that will fill your spirit with a soft, gentle light, like a sunset on the sea.'

I walked on, but I could hear his song, his solitary voice, accompanying me in the dark.

There were no words: a single unending melody, aching and infinite. He was crying, that's what it was, the poet was singing and crying, tears and drops of light in the darkness. I understood that what I had in my heart, what oppressed me so – boulder, millstone, unendurable anguish – was melting away into that invisible, immaterial song of the night.

When I turned back he was no longer there, but his song was alive with its own life. Would it echo forever? I wondered . . .

I lifted my eyes to where the song seemed to be drifting now, carried by the wind along the dusty roads of sacred Troy, over the walls built by the gods . . . and I saw her again, a figure hovering between being and nothing among clouds transparent and thin as blades . . . 'It's you, Helen, isn't it? Sublime creature, shall I curse or implore you? It's you who summon armies of bronze to crash into the Skaian bastions. It is you, isn't it? Helen, divine and despicable? For you thousands of young men will give their lives, driving their spears into each other's chests, descending too soon into lightless Hades.'

KING LAERTES my father had trained his gaze on the sea every day, from the top of a cliff, scanning the horizon to catch a glimpse of the sail of my ship, like Aegeus, king of Athens, had done before him, waiting for Theseus, who had gone to kill the man-bull in his labyrinth.

He embraced me tightly now and whispered in my ear: 'Bad news. Am I right, my son?'

'Bad news, *atta*. Menelaus wants war. And so does Priam, and his people both.'

'Well then, if that's the way it has to be, so be it. You will fight, king of Ithaca, you will clad yourself in bronze, gird your sword and raise your shield. Your weapons adorn the walls of our palace; flawless arms which belonged to the ancestors who came before you and before me. In the days that remain before your departure, stay close to your mother and to your bride and give them all the love they won't have for years to come.'

We made our way up to the palace at the top of the mountain where the queen mother was waiting for me.

She wept when I told her the outcome of my mission. 'I did all I could, mother,' I told her. 'I tried to convince them, and one of their own, noble Antenor, also tried to persuade the Trojans to return Helen and avoid the infinite grief of war. In vain.'

My mother cursed Helen and her beauty and cursed the folly that seizes men and pushes them into war. She cursed the lure of weapons, the craving for power that carried men far away, forgetting their children and abandoning their wives, who wasted away with longing for them. Penelope was nowhere to be seen. I knew where she was: waiting for me among the olive branches, waiting for when the lights went out in the tall house on the mountain and it was swallowed up by silence and darkness.

She knew, she had heard. She wept.

'Don't go, my love, don't make me curse the day that I met you, your eyes that change colour when you smile; don't leave us alone, me and Telemachus, on this dark island; suddenly it's so very dark here.'

I came close and she curled up on the edge of the bed. 'You're the daughter of a warrior, and you know the rules. I made an oath on the gods of the Underworld, the most powerful oath there is. The reason I did it was to stop war from being unleashed, to end discord, to prevent blood from being shed. And now that has all turned against me. Do you think, perhaps, that any of this has happened by chance?'

'Your grandfather,' she went on, 'has always broken any oath he made; he's never taken part in any exploit.'

'And he lives alone, like a dog, hated by everyone. I couldn't do that.'

'When it comes time to decide, a man has to choose what is important and what isn't important, or what is less important. What could be more important than your home, your wife, your son and your parents? A war over a woman who betrayed the husband she herself chose?'

'Listen to me. A king lives in a palace, he receives hospitality from other kings and he exchanges that hospitality, he enjoys many privileges. But he has to demonstrate that he is the best and the bravest, willing to give his own life if necessary. How could I bear the scorn of my comrades, my friends, my people and the other kings? My father himself told me clearly what he expects of me. It isn't so simple.'

'It is simple. As simple as water, as day and night, as love and hate. Simple, Odysseus, my lord, my king, my only love . . .'

She hid her face in the folds of the bedclothes. I tried to hold her in my arms and pass my heat and my passion on to her. Sometimes I thought I could hear the strains of that melancholy and heart-breaking melody sung by the poet who had followed me through the night in Troy. As solitary as the song of the nightingale in the dark.

Neither of us slept. We wept in each other's arms, in silence, in our bed nestled in the branches of an olive tree, because there was no way out. Any expedient would lead only to misery and shame.

The first pale light of dawn found us tangled, naked, in the embrace of love, so intense and deep that it hurt. When I loosened myself from her arms so white, from her *eyes so black, black, black,* when I had pulled out of her fiery womb, so hot that my fear and anguish melted away like a furnace melts bronze, we collapsed next to each other and Athena, I think, filled with pity, poured sleep onto our eyelids. And I thought I heard, through my light, thin sleep, that Penelope was singing, whispering, her song.

How often would she sing that song in the times to come? How long would I be away from her? When would I come back to her? I thought of how I felt as a little boy, waiting for my father to come home, I thought of the time his warriors had to carry him off the ship, his chest wrapped with bloodied bandages, his face pale as death, the wailing and weeping that met his return. My body jerked on the bed as if I'd been pierced by an arrow, and then I sank back into a sleep that felt like death.

My mother was inconsolable. Why? She'd been through this before: watching and waiting, alone, for someone she felt might never return . . .

'I'll be back, *mama*, and I'll bring you precious gifts, jewels and coins crafted by great artists,' I promised.

She wept, her chin drawn close to her breast, she didn't want to listen, didn't want to talk. But now and then, for a brief instant, she'd lift her eyes full of tears and gaze at me with an expression of despair that broke my heart.

'It's only a war, just like so many others. Some will die, but others will come back. I'll be one of those, you can be sure of it. I promise you. Wait for me, help Penelope, stay close to my son, he'll need you, you and *atta*. Please, mother, don't cry. Don't cry as if I were already dead!'

She stopped crying then and stiffened. Like a statue.

Where was Mentor? *Why can't I remember where he was?* Far away on one of his journeys? Wandering, perhaps, through wild and desolate lands? Was he searching for traces of lost, forgotten heroes? I tried to imagine Hercules: had he started greying at the temples? What about Admetus, lord of Pherai, how was he living his second life after having once escaped death? And his wife, Alcestis: what part of her heart had been frozen by the breath of Hades when she had leaned into the abyss? Where were Castor and Pollux, invincible wrestlers? And Jason, the hero of the *Argo*? Did he still bask in the love of his wild princess?

It felt as though those stories were as far away as the light of the stars. I spent entire days walking, meditating, through the forests that covered my island. Argus followed me. He would listen to me and look at me with moist eyes . . . as if he understood. Sometimes we'd sit, as it was getting dark, on a rocky outcrop to watch the sun set the sea on fire. I talked to him and he answered me in soft growls.

I thought of taking him with me. No! I had to leave him with Telemachus, so he could protect him and follow him, step after step. It wouldn't take long, after all: we would win the war in no time. Weren't we the strongest and the bravest? And then we'd be back.

One day a light, speedy ship showed up in the small port, announcing a visit from a person of great prestige: king of Messenia, lord of Pylos, knight of Gerene. Nestor!

The king arrived the next day at sunset and found waiting for him a cart pulled by a pair of pure-white big-horned oxen that young Philoeteus, the son of our cowherd, held by the halter. Ready to escort him were twenty warriors in shining bronze armour and, representing me, my father, *wanax* Laertes, wearing his best robes, his sword girded at his side and his spear in hand.

I welcomed Nestor from my place on the throne with Penelope by my side. She was no longer just my wife; she had become a queen, and her expression bore the weight of responsibility and authority. Her eyes were rimmed with bistre, her forehead encircled by a jewelled diadem that my father had given her as a wedding present, and the ring on her finger was the one my mother had received from her own mother, a red cornelian set in gold. She wore a flame-red gown and a white belt interwoven with gold and purple threads. My robe was long and white, with two stripes of gold. I wore my father's diadem and grasped the sceptre. I had arranged to have a finely crafted chair, as tall as my own, positioned opposite my throne for *wanax* Nestor, who had chosen to honour our kingdom by this visit. My father would sit alongside him, in a chair only slightly less impressive.

As soon as he crossed the threshold of the great hall, while my warriors and his own were fanning into position, the king of Messenia strode up to me with arms wide open.

'My boy! What a pleasure to see you. Let me take a look at you in all your majesty, in your royal finery! And you, you divine creature,' he said then, turning to Penelope, 'if your cousin had a mere crumb of your wisdom, I would be here to enjoy a banquet in your delightful company instead of acting as the harbinger of war, on a mission entrusted to me by the Atreidae.'

He clasped both of us to him in a strong embrace without considering protocol in the slightest, just like a father. Penelope was moved, and kissed him on the cheek, murmuring: 'Wanax, kind father and friend . . .'

'My king,' I said to him, 'the joy that I feel in seeing you comes from my heart and my affection for you is no less than what I feel for my father, Laertes the hero.'

Having completed the ceremonial greeting and honours reserved for such a high-ranking guest, we retired to the Hall of the Argonauts – our guest, my father and I – to speak freely, without being seen or heard.

'My reason for coming here,' began Nestor, 'is a mission of the utmost importance. I need your help.'

'Of course. Whatever you need,' I replied.

'You must come with me to Thessaly, to Phthia, the kingdom of Peleus, a dear friend of mine and your father's. He has a son, Achilles . . .'

'I know him well. He strikes like lightning, runs like the wind. No one can measure up to him. He swore the oath of the princes with me.'

'Yes, but there's someone who's bent on doing everything possible to keep him from leaving for the war.'

'Who?'

Nestor hesitated a moment. 'I'm not sure. His mother, perhaps. Nothing is known of her. No one has ever seen her; anyone who says he has is lying. People attribute supernatural powers to her. The only thing that anyone knows is her name: Thetis. Only Peleus knows where to find her, for she bore him his only son. No one can fail to notice what an amazing creature Achilles is. And they say that she . . .' here he broke off. 'Will you come with me?'

'I will, *wanax*. I've done everything to prevent this war but now that it has been decided I will do everything to win it. Without Achilles we have no hope. I've seen Priam's army.'

'Will you come as well, Laertes?' Nestor turned to my father. 'Your presence would be precious. Your prestige is great and all the young men respect you.'

'Ask him,' he replied, pointing to me. 'He's the king of Ithaca.'

'My father knows that he can decide anything for himself,' I said, 'but he also knows that in my absence, the fact that he is seated on the throne to administer justice, to lead the army if necessary and to protect my family is a great comfort to me.'

'As you've heard for yourself, I've been ordered to take care of the kingdom in the king's absence,' said my father with an ironic smile. 'Luckily I'm familiar with the job. You'll have to make do with my son, but I'm sure that will be good enough.'

That's what he said, but then he went on at length offering me advice of every kind. He ended up by reminding me to give his best to King Peleus, his friend and companion-in-arms, and to invite him, once the war was over, to come and hunt with us on the island of Same with his boy Achilles.

We left the next day. As I said goodbye to Penelope I thought that this temporary separation might help her to prepare for the much more difficult one that would soon follow. She kissed me on the mouth but shed no tears. 'Come back as soon as you can,' she said. 'I want to take pleasure in every moment of every day and every night that we have together before your departure.'

'I'll be back, my queen and my love. I'll come back this time and next time too, I swear to you.'

She smiled and her eyes sparkled like black pearls. 'I'm beginning to think that you can tame fate and that your goddess must really love you. But not even she, who is immortal, can love you more than I do.'

She stood on the pier waving goodbye, her hand as slender and white as a silver leaf, and I didn't take my eyes off her until she disappeared behind the crest of a wave.

'I know what you're feeling,' sounded the voice of the wisest of kings behind me.

'Do you think so, *wanax*?'

'I know so. This is love, a terrible disease that you will never be free of. I've always gone from one woman to another: wives, concubines . . . when one's beauty faded, I simply found another, younger one. I've never known any other way. But I envy you, you know. I felt love once, a long, long time ago. A feeling that transforms a mortal woman into a goddess and makes her beauty and charm eternal. Unfortunately, the spell didn't last long for me. I lived in the mountains then, I had been sent to garrison the passes that led to Arcadia. She didn't survive the bitter winter there, accustomed as she was to the warm sun of Crete. Her skin was dark, shiny and smooth as bronze, and her smile was radiant. Sinuous, she was, like a panther. She painted her lips and the tips of her breasts red, like the ancient queens of her homeland.'

I turned and saw that the lord of Pylos' eyes were shiny with tears.

'You are a fortunate man,' he said again. 'Your Penelope is gentle, wise, very beautiful and as sweet as honey.'

We were sailing along the coast of Locris, ruled by Oileus, who had a son named Ajax, the same name given by Telamon of Salamis to his gigantic son. We continued to Corinth, which I thus saw for the second time. Here we learned that Jason, the hero of the *Argo*, was in the city!

'I want to see him, *wanax*,' I said to Nestor. 'I'll never have another chance to meet the hero who stole the golden fleece from Colchis and who sailed on the biggest ship in the world with a crew of fifty kings and heroes.'

The old king's brow wrinkled. 'Do you really want to see him?' he asked. 'Do you not know what has happened?' He had his men drop anchor and we descended onto the wharf. 'We're now going to cross the isthmus at its lowest point. On foot. On the other side another ship will be waiting to take us to our destination. This will save us a long trip sailing around the southern peninsula of Achaia with its promontories and cliffs.'

'This is why,' I thought, 'King Nestor is so highly considered by all the Achaians. He knows so much, has so much experience, and is so wise.' The fact that he wanted me by his side for the most important mission of that moment, to convince Achilles to participate in the war, filled me with pride. We marched for hours across the isthmus, taking with us mules laden with our supplies and everything else we needed for the journey. We went on until we reached a place from which we could see the eastern sea, the gulf and the second port.

We stood there for a few moments, at the point separating the two slopes. The view that opened up before me was astonishing. Nestor pointed to the cliffs on the northern shore of the gulf.

'Look down there,' he said. 'See that enormous wreck run aground on the rocks?' Cold terror nipped at my heart. I didn't have the strength to let a single word come out from between my teeth.

'That is the *Argo!*'

We started treading down the hill with heavy hearts, continuing until we reached the shore of the eastern sea and the pier where the ship that would take us to Phthia was waiting for us.

'We can go aboard now,' he said. 'We'll sail past the *Argo*, but remember what I'm telling you: you won't like what you see. And you'll like even less what you hear.'

'I can't believe that, *wanax*. What are you saying?'

Nestor ordered the helmsman to direct our ship towards the huge beached hull.

'Have you ever seen a ship of this size in your whole life? Listen. After Jason had returned to Iolcus, he soon realized that his savage princess, Medea, could not live a life like any other woman's. In fact, his people feared and detested her; they whispered that she could work dark magic. She was hated by all but still madly in love with Jason. He was the only person she would obey and she bore him two children. But then one day, she spotted old King Pelias, who she knew had seized the throne during Jason's absence. Using trickery, she lured him to a secret place, where she murdered him and cut him into pieces. They found her cooking up his sorry remains so she could devour them.

'Jason fled from the city in horror. He set sail with his wife and children and a crew of mercenaries and escaped here, to Corinth, whose king was his friend. He fell in love with the king's daughter, a beautiful young woman named Glauke, and she with him. Medea went crazy with jealousy and transformed herself into a tiger, like the ones who roamed her homeland. She pretended to accept Jason's new bride and even gave her a gown as a wedding present. The day of the wedding, Medea dressed her children as pages, crowned their heads with flowers and had them accompany her. Holding a sacred torch, she approached Glauke and touched it to her gown. Imbued with some kind of noxious substance, the gown burst into flames, turning beautiful Glauke into a human torch. Her screams of agony echoed through the whole city. She melted into a shapeless mass, a charred black firebrand. Not content, the savage princess murdered the two children she'd had with Jason under their father's eyes. She cut their throats. Then she jumped on a chariot, whipped the horses into a run and vanished. His men gave chase, searched everywhere for her, but she was never found. Jason went mad. He boarded his ship, all alone, waited until the west wind started to blow and then heaved out the sail. He took the helm and crashed the ship onto the rocks.'

He hadn't finished speaking when, from the gloomy, rotted wreck of the *Argo*, all covered with algae, an inhuman scream was heard, a cry of anguish and folly that froze my blood. For a moment I thought I could see in the false light of dusk a spectral figure lurching behind the shredded sail, among the mouldy shrouds.

'There,' said Nestor, 'that is the voice of Jason, the hero of the golden fleece. And this is his last landing place.'

I wept.

21

THAT ANGUISHED VOICE AND THE SIGHT of the smashed hull of the *Argo* tormented me for days as we made our way up the eastern coast of Achaia towards Phthia of the Myrmidons. We rounded Cape Sounion and sailed down the channel that separated the mainland from the island of Euboea. Nestor had plenty of time to tell me what he knew about those lands and the people who reigned over them, although much of what he told me I'd already heard when I met the other princes vying for Helen's hand in Sparta.

'Peleus of Phthia is the older brother of Telamon, the king of Salamis, so that means that Achilles and Ajax are first cousins. Both are exceptional young men; there is absolutely no one else in all of Achaia that can measure up to them. The fact that they are so closely related has led to much conjecture about their ancestry. Achilles was born when his father was already very advanced in age, and no one has ever seen his mother. You can imagine how many stories about her have sprung from the lips of poets and singers!'

'A goddess?'

'A sea goddess. Thetis.'

Nestor continued: 'Peleus' city, Phthia, dominates the southern plains. And on the other side of that plain is Pherai, the city of Admetus and Alcestis. But we won't be going that far. Their son Eumelus has already said that he will come to the port of Aulis in Boeotia, where all of our forces will gather to set off for Troy . . .'

'Eumelus,' I thought to myself, 'the brave young witness of Hercules' innocence . . . ready to take his place among us.'

Nestor heard me thinking, I suppose, because he said: 'He swore the oath of the princes, but he also knows of the pact between his parents. He was there when Hercules dragged his mother back from the gates of Hades. Perhaps in his mind throwing himself into the burning jaws of the war is better than living alongside a father who trembled with fear in the face of death, a mother who can never be more than half alive and half dead . . .'

I nodded. 'You're right, *wanax*, tremendous things have happened in our land. And I can only wonder what still awaits us.'

'You will convince Achilles to join us. You're the only one who can carry this off. If Achilles comes, his cousin Patroclus will come as well; the two of them are inseparable. Patroclus lives in Phthia, in exile. He was forced to flee his city after he killed a man during a quarrel over a game of dice; the man's relatives are still seeking revenge. His fate would be sealed if they had their way, but they won't dare come forward as long as Patroclus is with Achilles.

'But what I don't understand,' Nestor continued, 'is why Achilles wasn't the first to take up the challenge. War is his element. Like water for a fish, the air for a bird. He was born to slaughter.'

'Have you ever seen him in combat, *wanax*?'

'I have. Just watching him is enough to strike fear into a man. The armour he wears is blinding, his shield reflects the light of the sun like a mirror, and all you can see behind his helmet are those ice-coloured eyes. He is as swift as lightning, and no one can guess his next move. He usually gets his kill on the first try; if he doesn't, it's only because he wants to prolong the fight, and the agony of his adversary.'

'Then how do you explain his reluctance?' I asked.

'That's what you'll have to discover,' he replied.

We sailed by the bay of Iolcus on our left and the port from which the *Argo* had once set off to go to the ends of the earth. We berthed in a small protected cove beneath the striking bulk of Mount Othrys, disembarked and began to climb up the mountain path that led to Phthia. They were certainly expecting us; it was clear that no one could hope to get close without being seen by the invincible Myrmidon warriors. When we got to the pass, they fell into step alongside us, silently escorting us to the city. I was impressed: these could be the automatons built by the god Hephaestus! They marched with precisely the same step, their armour was burnished to the same sheen, their crests fluttered as one in the light breeze. They looked like giant ants, as their name suggested. Perhaps they had been ants once, long ago, who could say? Finally, Phthia appeared, towering above us on the peak of the mountain. It nearly took my breath away.

Peleus welcomed Nestor like a brother, but it didn't take long to realize that no preparations had been made for a great banquet or feast. The shadow of the war made any revelling impossible.

'May I introduce the king of Ithaca?' said Nestor, motioning for me to come forward.

'You are the son of Laertes . . . Achilles has told me about you,' said Peleus thoughtfully. 'How is your father?'

'He sends his best wishes and he hopes that you will one day accept an invitation to Ithaca when . . .' I hesitated, 'when the war is over.'

Peleus sighed. 'From the moment you all leave Achaia, your father and I, and all the fathers like us, will think of nothing but the day of your return. And even if you weren't to leave, where could you hide?'

'I don't want to hide,' I said. 'I did everything possible to prevent a war being fought, but now that it is inevitable, it must be won.'

'So you've come to get Achilles?'

'We cannot win without him.'

'This is his curse.'

'Where is he now?'

Peleus pointed at a spot on the slope of the mountain looming before us. A cloud of dust was moving swiftly across the hillside. A war chariot. A figure clad in dazzling metal, a red crest, two horses, long fringed manes, bronze frontlets spiked like the horns of unicorns.

'There,' he said.

From the way he looked at me he'd already understood that it wouldn't be Nestor doing the talking.

I was fascinated by what I was seeing: Achilles' chariot plunged downward at a frightening speed and then burst onto the plain, slicing through the fields full of crops, scattering the herds of cows and flocks of sheep.

The roar of wheels and the roll of hooves got louder and closer, until the chariot entered the courtyard and Achilles jumped to the ground. He took off his helmet and his armour and went to wash at the fountain. He wet the muzzles of his magnificent chargers.

'Balius and Xanthus,' he said, pointing at them as he came towards me.

'They're amazing, Achilles,' I replied as the servants loosened them from the yoke and dried them off.

I walked towards him and soon we were face to face.

'Welcome, king of Ithaca.'

'Achilles! It is a joy for my heart to see you again.'

'Are you alone?'

'Nestor is with me. He's talking to your father.'

'And you?'

'I've come to talk to you.'

Achilles dropped his head for a moment in silence, then said: 'Follow me.'

We left the palace and walked down a path that led towards an oak forest. The horses followed us, step after step, alongside each other. We stopped near a spring that gushed from an enormous moss-covered boulder. Achilles sat on a toppled tree trunk. He touched its gnarly bark. 'Hit by lightning,' he mused. 'This used to be a beautiful, vigorous tree.' I knew what he was getting at.

'I've come to ask if you'll fulfil the promise you made at Sparta.'

His long silence unsettled me.

'What are you thinking?' I asked him.

'A pact can be interpreted in many ways.'

'I'm here because I think the oath we made was clear. The

Trojan has carried off Menelaus' wife. He and I went to Troy together, to ask that Helen be returned. We were met with a refusal. The townspeople mocked and insulted Menelaus.'

'Helen left freely. Our oath would be binding if she had been abducted.'

'She was abducted. Helen belongs to Menelaus and she was taken from him. I would have expected different words from you.'

'So why do you want to go?'

'Because the oath was my idea. I can't back out now. I tried to prevent this war, but that's no longer possible, and all I'm thinking now is that we have to win. But without you that's simply not possible. Tell me why you're hesitating, Achilles!'

The horses came close and nuzzled Achilles with their noses. They seemed to hear the voice of his heart.

Achilles stroked them. 'For me, they're like people. They talk to me, you know? In their own way, they talk to me.'

'I can see that . . . Answer me, Achilles: why are you hesitating? You are like the god of war. There's no one who can stand up to you. Why weren't you the first to step forward?'

Sad smile.

'You know, each one of us, when war is in the offing, can choose to go down one of two roads: you either go to war, die young in combat and are remembered forever by those who hear of your exploits, or you don't go, and you choose obscurity: a tranquil, meaningless, never-changing life.'

'There's a third possibility, Achilles: you can win glory and come back alive to your home and family. That's what we'll do.'

'That may be so for you, Odysseus, ingenious and astute as you are, but not for me. It's either one or the other for me.'

I couldn't understand. 'What you're saying doesn't make sense. Who told you such a thing? An oracle? A soothsayer? Was it your own mother, perhaps, the mysterious being that no one has ever seen? I have to know, Achilles, because what you decide is key to the life or death of thousands of young combatants, and to the future of our world.'

'What difference does it make? These are my possible destinies and I've already made my choice. When we die all that remains of us is our name. The rest is consumed by fire. I want my name to be remembered forever. Glory is the only light of the dead, Odysseus. Farewell. We'll see each other at Aulis, in the spring.'

We were both too choked to continue, or perhaps there was simply nothing left to say. Nestor and I were leaving the next day and so I didn't have the chance to talk to Patroclus, although I did see him in passing. He looked much older than Achilles, and I realized that he had been among Helen's suitors in Sparta.

When the time came, Nestor and Peleus embraced; when they separated both had tears in their eyes. I overheard Nestor whispering: 'I just can't watch this happen from behind the bastions of my palace, waiting for my boy to return, torturing myself in the meantime. I'm going with them. Maybe they'll be able to use some wise advice from an old man.' He and I walked off in silence, flanked as we had been at our arrival by a host of Myrmidon warriors.

It wasn't until we were back on the ship that Nestor spoke to me: 'Will he come?'

'Yes. He'll be at Aulis, in Boeotia, in the spring.'

Nestor nodded without saying another word. He accompanied me all the way back to Ithaca.

TIME PASSED, much too quickly, and the day arrived. Agamemnon and Menelaus' heralds landed at the main port and I summoned all of the best youth of my island, the sons of the most important families. My friends. They came from the nearby islands as well, all young men in their prime, shining in their armour, ready to answer my call to arms. They seemed not to realize that in that distant land, on those fields of battle, death would be lying in wait. They were anticipating, instead, a great adventure of which poets would sing, and minstrels would tell fantastic tales. They were sure they would come back laden with booty and fame. Joking among themselves, they bragged and talked about treasures waiting to be plundered, and beautiful Asian women to be brought back as slaves and concubines.

We armed twelve ships. We filled them with food, weapons, tents and clothing, and everything that would be necessary for a long war.

Since my return from Phthia, my heart had been preparing to say farewell to Penelope. Telemachus was too little to understand; too young to remember me. Or perhaps he would recognize me one day, the way I recognized Laertes my father when he returned from Colchis.

But Penelope . . . how could I say goodbye to her? I would have preferred to fight a dragon than face the anguish in her gaze, that expression of a wounded deer in her eyes. Because I was the one who had shot the arrow. And yet, incredibly, she helped me. She came down to the port, just like any other woman on the island, with the same acute pain in her heart. She waited until my parents had embraced me, until my mother had cried all her tears, her face buried in my neck, until my father had said: 'You will win this war, king of Ithaca. Make us proud of you and . . . come back, *pai*, come back to us. We'll be waiting for you.'

Euriclea, my nurse, overcame the impulse to embrace me like a mother. She lowered her head in front of Penelope, her mistress, and accepted the baby from her arms. My queen threw her arms, so white and perfect, around my neck, and she gave me a long, intense kiss, shamelessly, like a lover, and then she put her mouth to my ear and said: 'Remember these lips, my king, remember how I took you into my arms last night, remember with what passion I gave you my body. No woman in the world can love you as I do.'

She stepped back and, aquiver with tears, looked at me and then said: 'Now smile, so I can see your eyes change colour one last time.'

I forced myself to smile. She took out her final gift to me, a magnificent red cloak, threw it over my shoulders and then fastened it using a golden pin shaped like a deer in the clutches of a hound. I whispered into her ear: 'I will think of you every moment.

Remember me every night when the moon rises from the sea. Take care of our son, our bed, my dog and my bow.'

Euriclea knelt at my feet and kissed my hand. 'My child, my child,' I could hear her say through her weeping.

I gave Telemachus a kiss and began walking down the pier until I reached the steps to the royal ship, but as I put my foot on the first one, I heard barking and I turned: Argus!

'I can't take you with me,' I said. 'You have to stay here with Telemachus. You have to protect him while I'm away. When I come back we'll go hunting together.'

He seemed to understand my words. He licked my hand and whined as I got on board. A sailor cast off the moorings and my ship pulled away from the shore, pulled away from Ithaca and everything in the world that was dear to me. I felt my heart splitting in my chest, but I remembered that my men at the oars and at the helm were waiting for the triple shout from the king of Ithaca that announces the start of a war, and I walked up to the prow. The other ships were fanning out so that each one of them was equally distant from my own. The sailors pulled in the oars and raised them up as if they were warriors' spears. I donned my bright armour then, and shouted at the top of my lungs:

'He – ha – heee!

'He – ha – heee!

'He – ha – heee!'

And they replied to my cry with a roar, beating time with the oar handles against the wooden benches.

We departed.

22

I can remember, I can see, as if it were now, how the expedition unfolded.
The first thing that I realized was how fundamental my role in the
war was. My small kingdom was the northernmost of all, and I
sailed at the head of the western branch of the army. *I remember*
how from the stern I watched the other eleven Ithacan ships
follow the royal vessel I commanded, built by Laertes. In my
mind's eye, *I can still see* the other fleets uniting with ours one by
one from the other ports, from the gulfs and from the coves, like
streams flowing into a great river as we sailed south: the ships of
Meges from Dulichium, of Thoas from Chalcis, of Ajax of Locris,
son of Oileus, and finally of Kings Polyxenus and Amphimakhos,
who shared the throne of Elis, a coastal kingdom with a great gulf
at the north and the open sea to the west. We continued our
descent, and by the time we arrived at the entrance to the bay
that lay before the palace of Pylos, we were an impressive fleet
indeed. Nestor's ships were waiting there to join us. We divided
into two formations and entered the inlets on either side of the
harbour that lay between the island and the mainland. We then
reunited in two lines, and faced the Messenian fleet drawn up in full
force. There were ninety ships, brimming with warriors: they
matched, even surpassed, the entire squadron we had assembled up
to that point.

I personally went aboard the royal ship to turn over command
of our formation to Nestor. It was his right as the eldest among the
kings and because his fleet and his army were the most powerful
and numerous.

'We meet again, *wanax*,' I greeted him, 'and I bow to the power manifest in this display. I've never seen such a thing.'

'Look who's here with me, *pai*,' he replied affectionately and he called over Antilochus, the son most perfect for this war. Perfect to fight it, win it, perfect to die.

'Antilochus . . . we were just boys, it seems like yesterday, and look at us now . . .' I said.

'You're a king now,' he replied.

'And you, my friend, are the pride and the boast of Messenia, of glorious Pylos and of *wanax* Nestor, the knight of Gerene.'

He smiled: 'It will be an honour to fight at your side, king of Ithaca.'

We clasped each other, each of us pounding his fist on the other's bronze-clad back. There was a tremendous vibration in the air, the odour of pitch and of pine, the clatter of bronze and the crash of the sea. In that moment, among those tens of thousands of youths, there was no one who didn't want to be part of this, no one who would have preferred to be back at home, perched safely on a boulder watching the ships parade down the coast and listening to the lapping of the waves.

Not even me.

We rode at anchor for three days, so as to finish loading up all the extra provisions that Nestor had prepared; he seemed to have an abundant supply of anything we could desire. The third night I remained awake until very late, well aware that we'd be leaving the next morning. There was a thought that had been nagging at me ever since I'd left Ithaca: why hadn't I seen Mentor at the port as I was leaving Ithaca? My faithful counsellor had not come to say goodbye. Why not? Where could he be? Why hadn't he come to hear my plea to watch over Telemachus and my whole family? Why hadn't I sent someone to look for him? I could sense an odd state of consciousness coming on; that same feeling I'd had on certain nights in Acarnania and Arcadia. I was hovering between two worlds: one visible and the other invisible, but just as strong and as present.

In the middle of the night, when the stars had already started to set and the waters of the bay were a slab of marble, I saw a light flashing out at sea. A boat was approaching my ship, as silently as if the oars were not touching the water. Who could it be at that time of night? And why hadn't the sentries noticed? We were safe and in friendly territory, but there still had to be someone standing guard, especially at night.

'Who goes there?' I called out when the boat pulled up alongside the right flank of my ship. A man grabbed the anchor rope to hoist himself aboard and a voice replied: 'Don't you recognize me?'

'Mentor? What are you doing here so late at night? Where are you coming from?'

'If you help me get on I'll tell you.'

I held out my hand and I helped him climb over the railing. He was as light as air.

'Are you hungry? Thirsty?' I asked.

'Neither hungry nor thirsty,' he replied.

'How did you find my ship in the midst of so many others, in the dark?'

'Usually *wanax* Odysseus doesn't ask questions, he gives answers,' he said in a teasing tone. 'I saw your standard.'

'In the dark?'

'In the moonlight.'

'Yes,' I replied. 'You're right, the moon is out now.'

'It was out earlier as well, believe me. Perhaps you couldn't see it because your thoughts were elsewhere.'

'Why didn't you come to the port to say goodbye in Ithaca?'

'Why didn't you send someone to look for me?'

'I've been wondering that myself. The thought has been troubling me since I left the island, and yet I'm unable to come up with an answer.'

'Because you felt in your heart that we'd be meeting again anyway?'

'Perhaps. Where are you coming from?'

'From a long journey. And I bring news.'

'Sad news? I can see it in your eyes.'

'Terrible. But I won't tell you if you don't want to hear it. I won't let the words out from between my teeth; I will keep them in my heart.'

'I want to know.'

'Hercules. He's gone.'

'No! It can't be true!'

'You know I'm not lying. You know that if he were alive he'd already be waiting for you at Aulis in Boeotia, his homeland. Do you think you'll see him there?'

'No. You're right. Achilles will be there, but he won't.'

'He is no longer part of our time.'

'How can that be, if there is no man or animal strong enough to triumph over him? Did an insidious illness drain his life force before killing him?' My heart was weeping because Hercules had lived, fleetingly, in my time, but not in my place or my space. I had never been able to meet the greatest man who had ever set foot on mortal ground; I had only imagined him.

'I saw him die,' said Mentor. 'It was not so long ago. There is a cliff which overhangs the foaming sea of Pallene on which Mount Olympus casts its shadow. He stood there, as still as a stone column, looking like a god, in front of a gigantic pyre. A young shepherd stood next to him, holding a lit torch. Hercules nodded, and the boy set the pyre ablaze.

'An earth ramp led to the top of the pyre. Hercules must have built it himself, I thought. I watched as he threw his club on the ground. It bounced twice and then lay there. He stripped off the lion's pelt that covered him and walked naked up the ramp and into the midst of the swirling flames. They rose roaring towards the sky, erupting in a storm of smoke and sparks against the twilight clouds.

'With every step he took, I could hear savage cries, see inside the flames images of the monsters, ferocious beasts and wild creatures that he had fought and slain . . . I could see the spirits of Hades that he had challenged and won. Now they all wanted revenge. They were ripping him apart.'

'Why didn't you try to stop him?' I cried. 'You yourself brought Eumelus to Pherai so he could declare Hercules' innocence. You were there when he brought Alcestis back from the Underworld single-handedly, and restored her to her husband's side.'

A breeze blew softly close to the surface of the sea, making the shrouds quiver like the fingers of a practised singer barely skimming the strings of his instrument. My heart was swollen with grief at the story that Mentor told: the end of the greatest of all heroes.

'There was nothing I could do. Hercules was walking into his own funeral pyre, alive, because even though he was innocent, he never got over the sight of his murdered family, nor had he been able to bear the solitude he had been condemned to. He knew he had to join those whom he had loved and never forgotten. When he got to the top of the ramp, he threw himself into the flames . . .'

'I don't want to listen any more!' I shouted. 'I can't take this!'

Mentor did not pause: 'His howl of agony shattered the solid mountain rock and a landslide crashed to the valley, uprooting the pine trees that tumbled down one on top of another with a roar like thunder. His scream rent the clouds that the night had turned black.'

A long, mournful silence fell over the sea and the ship. Now my mind was transparent as alabaster, as Egyptian glass. My thoughts were like stones on the bottom of the bright sea.

'Who are you?' I asked.

Mentor did not open his mouth but I could nonetheless hear his voice say: 'Don't ask questions you already know the answer to.'

'Athena . . . Where is Mentor? Tell me, please tell me.'

I had the impression that her lips were moving: 'He's sleeping. In a secret place that only I know. This way I can take on his likeness.'

'How long have you been Mentor, for how long has Mentor been gone? When did I meet you thinking it was him? When did I meet him?'

'Do not grieve for him. I must do things that he couldn't do or wouldn't know how to do. Don't fear, I will always be at your side.'

Having said this, she plunged into the sea and emerged instantly in the guise of a pure white seagull. I watched as she flew far away, almost transparent in the light of the moon.

A profound bitterness overcame me. I thought with infinite melancholy of how Hercules had given in to his desperation . . . of how Jason, prince of Iolcus, had run his ship onto the rocks, smashing it along with his mind and his heart. Of how Mentor, my faithful friend, had disappeared so that my goddess could hide herself in his skin. Was he dead, perhaps?

I waited anxiously for dawn, I waited until the sun rose and the wind had made its voice heard among the shrouds. I saw Nestor's royal ship crossing the bay, pushed forward by many oarsmen, who sang an old song to keep time as they rowed. All of the ships followed and I entered their wake, with my eleven ships behind me and behind them other kings and other ships.

I tried to forget the images and sounds of the night, telling myself that it had been a dream, but a voice inside me told me it was all real, that I had never fallen prey to sleep, and that there was no escaping truth.

We passed the furthermost tip of Messenia, where there was said to be one of the entrances to Hades. After two days of navigation we reached Cape Tainaron. Between Cape Tainaron and Cape Malea, we were joined by the contingent of Menelaus, king of Sparta, with sixty ships. I steered my ship alongside his, and we met on my vessel.

'Hail, *wanax* Odysseus, my friend,' he said, and embraced me.

'Hail, *wanax* Menelaus, my friend,' I answered.

King Nestor, Ajax Oileus and the other kings joined us and I had wine poured for everyone. I stored it in a large clay jar that I had my servants continuously wet with seawater, so it would stay cool. We all had dinner together on the ship at anchor, on a quiet sea. Everything seemed to favour our voyage. The gods knew who was right and who was wrong.

'I've never drunk a finer wine,' announced Menelaus. He poured some of it into the sea to propitiate the god of the abyss, to help our journey.

It was late at night when each of my guests returned to his own ship. We set sail again at the break of dawn. In the gulf of Argolis we were joined by the hundred ships of *wanax* Agamemnon, the Achaian king of kings, the lord of Mycenae, who I hadn't seen for some time, as well as the fleet of Menestheus of Athens. Diomedes of Argus arrived with his ships as well: he was the commander of the Epigoni, who had sworn to avenge the deaths of their fathers, the Seven who had dared to challenge Thebes. Last of all we were met by Ajax of Salamis, who like me was from a small, poor island. Like me, he had only twelve ships, but his glory and fame were immense: he was the first cousin of Achilles and he was huge and powerfully built. From the prow of his ship hung his shield, made of seven layered bull hides; it had been created just for him, to cover his colossal frame. As one after another of these fleets were added, the army grew tremendously in size and I suggested to Nestor that the lines of ships should be distanced, so that if a storm broke out the ships would not be dashed against one another.

After four days of navigation, we reached Aulis in Boeotia, where Achilles and Patroclus were waiting for us, along with Automedon, the charioteer who governed Balius and Xanthus, the horses who were as fast as the wind. The prince of Phthia of the Myrmidons had kept faith with his promise and honoured the pact of the princes. There in Aulis was also anchored the great hundred-ship fleet of Idomeneus, the lord of Knossos and all of Crete.

I climbed up the mountain that overlooked the bay and I beheld a spectacle that I could never have even imagined. One thousand ships at anchor, perhaps fifty thousand men. I nearly couldn't believe my eyes. The best of Achaian youth, gathered there so we could cross the sea and wage war on Priam's city. But the sight of such an enormous force brought other thoughts to my head. When had so many ships and so many warriors ever been assembled for a war? For how long would the memory of such an incredible endeavour be handed down from generation to generation? And was it truly possible that the reason for the incredible show of power that I was witnessing before my very eyes was merely to avenge the offended pride of one of the princes of Achaia? Not only were all the princes who had made the oath present, but so were many more who hadn't been present at Sparta, even though they were ready now to claim they had. Perhaps Agamemnon had convinced them.

I couldn't stand the idea that there might be a reason behind the waging of this war that was different from the one I knew about, a reason that remained hidden from me.

When the sun set behind the mountains behind me and the routes of land and sea were darkened, I counted the number of nights that I'd already spent at sea, apart from Penelope, and I was struck by how much I already missed her love, her scent, her eyes and her hair, her white arms and shapely breasts. I realized how much I missed Telemachus, the touch of his little hands, the sound of his tiny voice that would one day be booming, shouting out the triple war cry of the kings of Ithaca. How many more nights and how many more days would I spend away from them? When would I receive news of them and they of me?

After our initial enthusiasm, the banquets, the invitations from the other kings and the celebrations of the warriors, the days that followed began to weigh on us all like stones. The sun would rise without a dawn to announce itself, already blazing. An unbearable heat suffocated the land, and the water of the bay was still and stagnant in the swelter of noon. It seemed that the chariot of the sun had stopped in the centre of the sky and that nothing could move it from that position. Sweat flowed copiously on men's brows and thousands of Achaians sought relief in the water. The ships were as motionless as the cliffs and rocks, the standards drooped from their yards. Sails were furled and shrouds loosened. Not a breath of wind, not a ripple on the sea. It seemed like a curse, and this was the rumour that started to snake its way among the men. Someone had surely provoked the wrath of the gods, but no one knew why or how. Who had offended them and how could the wrong be righted?

We met: Achilles, Diomedes, Ajax Oileus and Ajax of Salamis, Nestor, Menelaus, Agamemnon, myself. King Idomeneus of Crete was also very uneasy: there was the real risk that the men would become convinced that our endeavour offended the gods. Too grand, too haughty, too arrogant? My own worry grew so great that it sometimes made me forget my family, my parents, my island, in my efforts to find a solution.

But there could be no solution, unless it came from the supreme head of the glorious expedition himself: Agamemnon, the king of kings.

Those were my words as I left the council of kings and returned to my tent on the mainland. I climbed up to the promontory and looked out over the bay teeming with ships and the moon rising over the sea. I remembered what I had said to Penelope before I left her. I thought of her so intensely that I could feel her skin under my fingers, her lips on mine. I could hear the sound of her voice. I turned and saw Mentor, making his way slowly down the path towards me.

He looked older. I noticed a few white hairs at his temples and even in the beard that framed his face.

'I bring you news of your family,' he told me.

'Thank you, my friend. Tell me then: how are they?'

'Penelope . . . you broke her heart but she is playing the part of a true queen. Your father is performing your duties as he promised you but he shows your wife great respect and always asks for her advice. Telemachus is walking faster and faster now; I made him a little wooden spear and a sword and we practise fighting together . . .'

I smiled, trying hard to keep back my tears. 'I know what a good instructor you are, although I would have put more faith in Damastes for the swordplay. Who knows where that cranky old bear is now.'

'At home. He goes hunting, lights a fire for himself and cooks what he has killed, in the forest, where he has built himself a little wooden cottage, his home.'

I looked deep into his eyes as they flickered green and then I spoke without holding back: 'Why this dead calm? What must we do? We are at war, and if we remain in this stagnant pond we'll be defeated before we ever set out. Help me!'

I heard a voice inside my mind, clear and sharp: 'Stay out of this. Yours is not the supreme power. A prophet will make a suggestion. Then the wind will begin to blow again. From the land towards the sea.' Then my friend was gone before I could bid him farewell.

Soon enough, a seer was consulted and the truth was told. An offended divinity was keeping the wind prisoner in the distant caverns of Haemos and would not release it unless the commander-in-chief of the army agreed to perform the supreme sacrifice: immolating his own daughter at the altar. The daughter he loved most: Iphigenia, who had already been promised to Achilles when she became of age.

None of us saw, but Pheme of one thousand mouths spoke to us all.

It was said that at the moment in which the blade descended on Iphigenia's tender neck, the offended goddess was placated. She whisked the maiden away to a sanctuary in snowy Taurus and replaced her with a deer. No one would ever see Iphigenia again. Her own mother, Clytaemnestra, never saw her again. The hatred which bloomed in her heart was implacable, and it grew, like a monster, with time.

Then, one silent morning, the wind blew. The shrouds vibrated, the wood creaked, the water rippled with a myriad of shiny shivers. Then the long, long blare of a horn, a standard flapped in the wind, followed by many others, fluttering with stupendous colours and fantastic figures. The sails swelled. One ship moved and then put out to sea, another followed suit, then ten, then one hundred, oars flashing, picking up speed, sails as white as butterfly wings which instead were intent on bringing death beyond the foam-tipped waves. I set sail behind Menelaus' squadron. I could hear his loud shouting, see the red cloud of his hair as he raged at the helm. My other ships flocked around me, like when a flight of wild ducks soars up to migrate far away, a single force behind one leader.

A thousand, in the end. One thousand ships.

23

THE SIGHT OF THAT IMMENSE FLEET, of the hundreds of ships and thousands of oars beating the surface of the sea seething with foam, filled me with wonder. This was truly an enterprise that dimmed any other human adventure. The world of Hercules, of Jason, of the seven kings against Thebes, of Theseus of Athens who had defeated the man-bull in his labyrinth, faded away in the mist that the wind lifted from the cresting waves. A world had been lost forever and was dissolving in the haze of an early summer morning as the sun which rose over Asia lit up a vast sweep of vessels, a forest of standards, a myriad of flashing shields. The rumble of drums beating time for the oarsmen, the trumpets raising bronze blasts towards a clear sky in which white clouds galloped. This was the voice of the greatest army that the world had ever seen. Thousands and thousands of men were setting out to traverse the sea and their crossing that day would be forever impressed in the hearts of each one of them, and would be passed down to their sons and the sons of their sons for centuries and centuries to come, for thousands of years.

They were leaving their brides and young children, babies even, behind them, abandoning their parents weakened by age and by an anxiety which would never again leave their sides for as long as they lived. But now they felt part of the multitude, of the shouts and the blasts, of the incessant pounding of the drums, of the crashing of waves against the prows, of the spumy sea, of the shrieking birds. They denied it now, but the time would come. The cruel toil of battle, the bitter, bloody brawl. Nights without sleep, eyes staring in the dark. The time would come for wounds and death and, far worse than death, fear!

Many of them, too many of them, would never make it back, but descend inexorably into Hades instead. The vision that now filled my eyes and my heart would be the last vision of greatness and glory, I could feel it. Nothing else would be this luminous. Destiny had been set free to take its course. The route was carved out, the wind blew strong and steady. Its enormous force pushed one thousand ships in a single go, pushed tens of thousands of bronze-clad men. Where was my goddess? Was she sitting on her throne of ivory on high Olympus contemplating the spectacle as well? Were the other immortals seated beside her: Zeus and Hera, Apollo, Ares who could already pick up the smell of blood, and Aphrodite, naturally, Aphrodite who protected the woman, sublime Helen, for whom this war was being fought? O, Athena! Is your blue-green gaze searching for me even now, perhaps, in the sea froth, among the swaying sails? Here I am, standing straight at the prow, gripping the spear that *wanax* Autolykos, lord of Acarnania gifted me. I'm searching for you. Can you see the flashing tip of my spear?

The wind continued to fill the sails with no change in direction for two days and two nights. *Oh, how many days, how many nights, would be needed to cover the same ground on the way back!* The men at the oars added speed and the helmsmen held the prows unwaveringly, heading west. It was as if a god had suddenly opened the gates of the great cave on Mount Haemos where the wind had been kept locked up so long, and the prisoner, released, had rushed out in an unbridled gallop like an eager steed, aching for infinite spaces.

Each of the royal ships was at the head of its own squadron. Some were faster, others lagged behind. I could see them all, the sovereigns of Achaia, resplendent at their prows. Sometimes our ships would nearly touch and we'd greet each other, shouting over the hiss of the wind. At my left I saw coppery-haired Menelaus and it felt like that day when Helen had chosen him, unlocking her eyes from mine at the last moment.

Achilles' ship drew up alongside mine and we spoke. He had a favour to ask of me: he wanted to go ashore at Scyros to see the young son he'd had with a princess, daughter of King Lycomedes, when Achilles had lived as a page at his palace. The child was called Neoptolemus but Achilles preferred to call him Pyrrhus because his hair was the colour of fire. He had advised Agamemnon, and suggested that the fleet wait at anchor in the shelter of a promontory, and take the opportunity to stock up on water and provisions.

Achilles and I alone, followed by two Lapiths from his guard, made our way up to the palace. He didn't want to meet the little boy; perhaps he was afraid to upset him. He merely looked on, from behind a parted curtain, as young Pyrrhus slept peacefully, nestled in his mother's arms. Achilles watched his son for a long time in silence.

Instead, I met the little boy myself and gave him a small suit of armour I'd had one of my shipwrights craft using the copper from an urn. I told him: 'This is a gift from your father, who is leaving to go to war. Start getting ready, one day you will join him and fight at his side.' The boy gave a shrill laugh, grabbed the sword and started making slashing movements like a tiny warrior. His eyes looked like a wolf cub's, cold and expressionless.

'He'll grow up to be like you!' I said to Achilles later. 'But he'll need someone to instruct and train him. We'll have to leave your Lapiths here.' Achilles nodded but didn't say a word.

I went to pay my respects to King Lycomedes. '*Wanax*, thank you for your warm reception. We can't stay any longer because we have the sea still to cross, but we'll be back. We're leaving these two warriors who can begin at once to train young Neoptolemus in the art of weaponry. They are ready to repay you for your hospitality.'

I don't really know how I came up with such a plan or what made me say those words: it was as if I were obeying the voice of a stranger whispering in my ear. Even today, I can't resign myself to what I did.

'He's my grandson,' responded the king harshly. 'I'll decide how he should grow up.'

'It's the will of his father Achilles,' I replied.

The name alone was enough to intimidate even a king into obeying, without protest. I said nothing else to him, but spoke in secret to the two Lapiths: 'Listen well to what I'm telling you. The outcome of this war is completely uncertain. The boy will become our weapon of last resort, when all else has failed. You must bring him up to be an implacable warrior, a slayer of men. Use no pity, no affection. See that he is separated from his mother tomorrow.'

The next day Achilles and I rejoined the rest of the fleet. The crews heaved out the sails and they were soon bellying in the wind as the rowers urged each other on, bending their backs in a race to see who could make the sea boil under their oars, who would reach the shore first. Troy was already visible in the distance on top of the hill.

It felt like a contest, like the day we traditionally celebrated Poseidon, the blue god and lord of the abyss, by stripping our ships of their masts and sails and launching forth by dint of our oars alone. Their hulls furrowed the waves and the prows fought over the space that separated them from the finish line.

As we neared land, Agamemnon had his heralds proclaim the order in which the ships would put to shore, arranged by kingdom and point of origin. I was to draw up at the centre, equidistant from Ajax at one end and Achilles at the other. We began to prepare our tents, along with everything else we would need to set up camp. Meanwhile the walls of Troy were filling up with warriors but also with townspeople: old men, women, youths, even children. After the unhappy outcome of our first visit no one could have imagined we would accept the abduction of the queen of Sparta without a fight. Priam surely had his ways of getting information and knowing exactly how many men and ships were on their way.

I could see, even before we set ashore, that reinforcements had been built up on either side of the Skaian Gate. But I was mostly struck by the fact that the Trojan fleet had not advanced against us on the open sea. Why hadn't they thought of attacking us as we were landing, when they would have had stood a good chance of succeeding? Could a city so powerful that it controlled the straits not have a huge fleet? How was that possible?

The first to touch ground was the ship of Protesilaus, who commanded the Thessalians; he ran onto the beach, followed by his men. Achilles was next, then Menelaus with his Lacedaemonians. Next it was my turn to touch shore, with my comrades. Then came Agamemnon with his Mycenaens, Diomedes with the Argives, Ajax Oileus with his Locrians and Ajax the Great with the warriors of Salamis alongside the Athenians commanded by Menestheus, and then all the others. I ran straight to Agamemnon, to warn him to call back Protesilaus, who was too exposed, but it was too late. An arrow had already pierced the king of the Thessalians in the middle of his chest. A formation of Trojan warriors, who had been laying in wait behind the defensive palisade at the second city gate, surged out right and left to surround Protesilaus' army. His men had gathered around the body of their fallen king to protect him, but they were open to attack from every side, and the Trojans were charging forward on chariots!

'Achilles!' I shouted. 'Achilles!' But the prince of the Myrmidons had already seen. His warriors had rolled their chariots off the ship and were yoking Balius and Xanthus, Achilles' splendid steeds, one dappled brown and white, the other blond as wheat, on to the hero's own chariot. Other comrades were preparing to charge forth in the same way. The Myrmidons, all of them armed with burnished greaves and shields, had mustered rapidly and were running among the chariots in squads of fifty men. I shouted for Diomedes and Menelaus to go to their aid, and their men followed as well, in a second wave of chariots and warriors on foot. I drew up my archers to be ready to cover their return to camp.

The counter-attack slammed into the Trojan ranks, fragmenting them. They were not unified or numerous enough to withstand Achilles' furious charge nor the vigour of Diomedes and Menelaus following close on his heels. The king of Sparta certainly hoped that Helen was watching from up high on the walls, and that she would recognize him by the splendour of his weapons and the colours on his chariot.

Diomedes burst upon the Trojan ranks right after Achilles. He hurled an anchor that he'd grabbed from the ship and hooked the wheel of an enemy chariot, while Sthenelus, his charioteer, pushed the horses forward on an oblique path and ruinously threw their already crippled adversary off balance, toppling him into a shrieking tangle of men, horses, splintered wood and broken limbs, as black blood stained the ground. I was moving forward with my archers when I saw the Skaian Gate open on our left, vomiting forth thousands of fresh warriors onto a field already soaked with blood. How many of them there were! I gave the triple war cry of the king of Ithaca and wheeled to the left. The archers immediately formed up in three rows either side of me. They planted their quivers in the ground, raised their bows, cocked their arrows and waited.

'He – ha – heee!

'He – ha – heee!

'He – ha – heee!'

My throat burned like fire.

They were pouring with sweat, their foreheads gleaming. The sun blazed down on us from the right. None of the others, engaged in combat, had noticed the new threat. I was reminded of the boar of Acarnania and the wound on my leg started burning.

'Let fly!' I shouted, and a cloud of arrows rained down hard as hail on the steps in front of the gate, beating down on the Trojan ranks.

They buckled.

'Let fly!'

They shouted.

'Let fly!'

They turned towards us. We drew our swords, raised our shields. The din was hellish, I couldn't tell the shouts from the sounds of the clashing metal; the weapons spoke different languages but they all pronounced the same word: death, death, death! I was gasping for air in the fray, my breath was short, broken, painful. But then racing rumbling chariots were cutting the ground between us, their rims carving deep furrows in the earth. Our own! Achilles' chariot! Diomedes' chariot! Menelaus' chariot!

'Skaian Gate!' roared a Trojan warrior. Powerfully built, helmet glowing in the sun, high crest. Hector!

The gate opened again with a deafening screech. The city swallowed up her sons so they would not die.

They closed themselves in.

Great Ajax advanced. A shower of arrows greeted him; he raised his huge shield, thick with the hides of seven bulls. The other hand brandished a two-headed axe. The earth trembled beneath his feet. He went all the way up to the gate.

'Let fly!' I shouted again to my men. 'At the bastions! Protect Ajax! Cover him!'

He was already under the parapet. He swung the enormous axe and banged it on the gate, one, two, three times. He made the doors shudder, made the bronze hinges groan.

My heart laughed inside my chest: Ajax was knocking at the door!

Many of their men were strewn on the ground, fewer of ours. Too many, in any case. The Thessalians carried back their king on their shoulders, singing a funeral dirge. Before evening the Achaians had raised a pyre and laid his body upon it. The days of bitterness had already begun. Protesilaus had only just been married, had spent only one night of love with his young bride, and had lost his life the moment he set foot on Asian soil. This is how he would be remembered: as the one of us, the Achaian, who had first touched ground and been first to die.

The Trojan warriors could oversee our whole camp from the highest towers of the city. A few of them cautiously pushed open the gates and ventured out to gather hastily their fallen from the field of battle so they could be given proper funeral rites.

As soon as night fell, high plumes of smoke and flames shot up from a hill dark with black cypresses near the eastern bastion of the citadel of Troy. If I had taken a group of bold warriors up there and attacked all those who were attending to the funeral honours for their fallen, we would have caught them completely unawares and killed a great many, but I told myself there had to be a limit to the wickedness of war.

Not enough time had passed yet. Things would change, later.

Columns of smoke rose from our camp as well. Young men reduced to ashes who would never return home, whose mothers and fathers would never see them again. Their ashes were gathered in bronze jars and buried. This was what we had decided: we would not send back ships carrying the ashes of the dead. Their families would have to build empty tombs on the seashore to wet with their tears.

Late that night, Agamemnon sent heralds to summon the kings to a war council. He wanted to know how many had fallen on our side and theirs, and to get information on how the Trojans fought: were they good in the fray? In hand-to-hand combat? How many chariots had they sent out onto the field of battle? He praised Achilles, Menelaus, Ajax and Diomedes and finally me as well, for protecting our warriors and keeping the Trojans at bay. We all congratulated each other, then sat down to eat and drink; we had to regain our strength. Nestor asked me then what I made of the fact that the Trojan fleet hadn't sailed out against us.

'Yes,' Agamemnon said as well, 'how do you explain that?'

'I think they've hidden their ships,' I offered. 'They knew they couldn't get the better of us, and instead of witnessing the fleet's destruction they must have scattered their ships among the coastal cities allied with Priam.'

Agamemnon pondered my words for a while and so did Nestor; it was he who spoke again: 'Maybe we should attack and seize those cities one by one. We would eliminate Priam's friends and destroy the fleet wherever we find it. We could lay siege to each of the cities in turn until it falls.'

The kings began to discuss this idea and others, and their opinions differed greatly. Achilles wanted to assault the walls of Troy without delay. Menelaus was behind him, and everyone could understand why: he wanted to take the city by storm, exterminate its inhabitants, chop Paris into little pieces and feed him to the hounds, get Helen back, take her home and forget about everything, if he could manage it.

But it wasn't so simple. The city was defended by a mighty wall with ramparts and by palisaded gates. The Trojan army was powerful and Priam certainly had many friends, perhaps even the great king of the Cheteians, who sat on a stone throne in his city of stone in the heart of Asia. In the end, the prevailing opinion was that it was best to start by raiding the cities allied with Priam or at least those closest to our position. But the bulk of our forces would remain to hold the siege of Troy.

The decision proved to be a wise one. Over the first year of war, Achilles and Patroclus, at the head of their own fleet and that of Protesilaus, attacked a number of cities on the coast and plundered them, destroying all of their ships. The only thing that stopped the onslaught was the winter, when the cold breath of Boreas began to sweep the sea with violent gusts. They brought a great deal of booty back to camp with them, a part of which was left to Agamemnon, his right as supreme commander of the army.

The following spring, Achilles, Patroclus, Menestheus and others seized the greatest and most prosperous city of the coast near Troy. It was called Thebes and it rose at the foot of a mountain called Plakos inhabited by Cilicians from the southern sea. Achilles himself killed the king and sold the inhabitants as slaves. It was a great victory, but I took no joy in it. The murdered king was called Eetion and he was the father-in-law of Hector, Priam's firstborn and heir to the throne of Troy. I had seen Hector's wife Andromache when I first went to Troy to try to stop this war and to ask for Helen's return. I remembered her as being very beautiful, with a deep, melancholic gaze.

The violent death of her father, Eetion, king of Hypoplacian Thebes, kindled even more hatred for us in Troy and made the fight even more vicious. The Trojans made continuous sorties to try to force us back into the sea or set our ships on fire. We responded by trying to wipe out their army and attacking the defences they had built outside the city, aiming to breach the walls of the lower city. The struggle was becoming more bitter by the day.

I suffered my first losses as well. It had never happened to me before, and my grief was made worse because the dead were from Ithaca. I knew their parents, their wives, I had seen their children born. I would avenge them by killing the same number of enemy combatants, for this was the law of war: to perpetuate the slaughter, although we knew it would not serve to bring those who had been killed back to life. What hurt me most was looking at their faces; they'd always been so ruddy, their colour deepened by the sea air and the sun. They were so pale, the dead. A colour hard to define but one that only the dead have. *Pale heads!*

Achilles relentlessly continued to attack cities and pillage them. He came back from one of these rampages with a beautiful maiden for Patroclus, to give him pleasure on long nights – her name was Iphi; long-legged, she was, with high, firm breasts – and another for himself, splendid high-waisted Diomedea.

What I remember most from the beginning of the war, more than the battles and the blood, more than the victories and defeats, more than my own exploits and those of my comrades, are the words. Everyone talked to me.

Even Ajax of Salamis, who was not a talker, but a man of unbeatable strength, a walking mountain. I believe that none of the kings and princes of the Achaians ever achieved feats as prodigious as his, or bore up under such great toil alone, without asking for help from either man or god. And yet he was as simple-hearted and innocent as a child. While Ajax occupied his place on earth like a boulder, Achilles was light, swift as the wind, deadly and ruthless, yet as fragile as a clay cup. He killed so as not to be killed; he fought to escape the Chaera of death, who was always present at his side. He saw her, sometimes, racing beside him on a chariot pulled by four stallions as black as a crow's wing, wielding her scythe. Only she could keep up with him, as he urged on Xanthus the blond and Balius the dappled, making them fly over the field of blood, his steeds answering him with words that only he could understand. It wasn't that he wanted to cheat the Chaera of her due, but he was holding out for glory. The last moment of his life would be, had to be, like a dazzling strike of lightning. He would not be forgotten, would not vanish into oblivion.

Menelaus, consumed with bitterness and humiliation . . . he often confided in me: his nightmares, his doubts, his dreams. He didn't talk that way to anyone else. One day he said to me: 'You were next to me that day. Why did Helen choose me? Why did she choose me, only to betray me and abandon my home?' I looked into his eyes and he seemed sincere. Was it really possible, I asked myself, that a thousand ships and fifty thousand warriors had crossed the sea to Asia for the sole purpose of reclaiming a man's wife? I searched my heart for other reasons, truer reasons, reasons which were not apparent. The real motives of men and gods. But I couldn't find them. Not then, not yet.

'Don't torment yourself,' I answered. 'Look around you: one thousand ships have crossed the sea with myriads and myriads of warriors. Do you really believe that all of this – the finest youth of Achaia pouring their blood onto this sun-scorched field – has happened for the reason we pretend to believe? Is there any way to explain this? No, Menelaus, there is not. You may think you know why we're here, but you don't. We're here without knowing why we came, or what we're doing here. We're like twigs at the mercy of a raging river. We endure hardships, fear and hunger, we toil and strive, suffer wounds . . . only to finish in the mouth of implacable Hades. Someone else wanted this . . . something else, something that is irresistible and overwhelming. Something faceless and voice-less. Our only defence is to stay together, like we are now, to stay with our comrades and friends and ward off darkness and fear.'

'But we'd made a pact . . .'

'There's no mere pact that could keep fifty thousand warriors here for all this time, is there? Can you explain why we didn't sail back before the winter began? What has kept us here? I don't know. Do you, perhaps? Does Agamemnon, king of Achaian kings?

Menelaus, if you know, tell me, now. I want to know why I'm here to lose my life. Helen's not enough.'

Menelaus was silent, and I'll never know whether it was because he didn't want to say or because he didn't know.

I spoke again: 'Haven't you noticed something strange going on? Something that makes you uneasy, fills your heart with anxiety?'

Menelaus looked at me as if he were seeing me for the first time, as if he were realizing that I could feel things that escaped other people. He said: 'They say that the goddess Athena speaks to you. Is that true?'

'It's not important what people say about me, what's important is what's happening here. Can't you see that time is escaping us? Can you remember what happened just seven days ago? Or four, or two? How long have we been here?'

Nothing but a blank stare met my words.

ONE NIGHT I ventured as far as the walls of Troy to see if I could hear the voice of the city. Nothing, not a sound; nothing but silence hovered over the sleeping city. It seemed to be uninhabited, empty. That silence made me shiver. Could we be besieging a ghost city? But then I remembered that I'd seen the city myself, gone through the gate, lodged in Antenor's house, spoken to him for long nights. I walked and walked until I found myself under the citadel and called out Helen's name. I wanted her to hear our voices as she lay in Paris' arms, I wanted her to remember a day long ago: a boy and a girl in a horse pen as the sun was setting . . .

When I got back to camp it was the middle of the night and I called out to my sentries so they wouldn't kill me. That night, *which night?*, I felt my father's absence acutely. How many nights had he lain awake, like I did now, his eyes staring wide into the dark?

DIOMEDES WAS CERTAINLY not a man of many words, but I'll always remember them nonetheless. After the initial attack, when Agamemnon was reviewing his vast army for the first time, the high commander turned to Diomedes and said, to rankle him, I presume: 'Why do you hesitate? Why are you afraid of jumping into the fray?'

'I fear nothing,' Diomedes snorted. 'Don't forget that I'm the only one who fought and won a battle before coming here. I avenged my father at Thebes of the seven gates.'

Agamemnon fell silent and continued to advance on his chariot in front of the drawn-up ranks of the Achaians. Diomedes turned towards me and it was as if he were seeing me for the first time.

'You were there,' he said, and I understood what he meant.

'Yes,' I replied. 'I was.'

'What were you doing at Argus?'

'I was with my father. We were taking Eumelus of Pherai back to his parents, Admetus and Alcestis. You remember, don't you?'

'Yes, I do,' he replied. 'Everyone was looking for that boy . . .'

'But no one ever found him.'

'You have something that I don't have,' said Diomedes. 'What is it?'

'I know that the mind is a weapon more powerful than any sword or spear or claw or fang.'

'Together we could be invincible.'

'I could be invincible on my own,' I answered, 'but if you like I'll very happily be your comrade. Our fathers were together on the *Argo*.'

'All of our fathers were together on that ship,' he replied with a smile, and he got on his chariot alongside Sthenelus, his driver, ready for combat.

24

ACHILLES CONQUERED CITY AFTER CITY on the coast, but the war wasn't going any better for us. Even more warriors flocked to Troy from other countries to assist Priam in driving off the foreign invaders. Even the gods, at that stage, had decided whose side they were on, and you could feel it in the air and in the turns of events. The weather. Unexpected manifestations of the earth and sky, thunder and lightning, even an earthquake that made our horses restive and made the sea boil around us. Messages from the gods that the soothsayers were only too eager to interpret. Agamemnon had brought his own seer to Troy, Calchas, a man he despised but whom he kept at his side, afraid to do otherwise; it was Calchas who had pronounced that horrific prophecy when the dead calm of the sea had left the fleet wind-bound in Aulis at such length.

Once, fed up with the priest's manner and his empty words, I challenged him myself: 'Tell me something useful, o prophet, how many figs are on this tree?'

He regarded me icily, and drew close: 'My art does not serve to count figs, but that's something you know well. Do you think I haven't heard you when you speak to a certain someone that the others don't see?'

I was stunned. We had been under a great, lush fig tree and I don't know how or when we had come to find ourselves walking along the seashore as the moon was rising. I knew in that very moment Penelope was searching for my thoughts, *the sting of nostalgia* . . .

'Isn't that true?' he continued as if we still found ourselves under that fig tree.

I did not answer. I didn't want others to get between me and my goddess.

'She loves you and protects you. You feel when she is close, but I can feel her when she's present as well, you know. I envy you seeing her. Tell me, what is she like?'

'Be careful of what you ask,' I replied. 'If she wanted to be seen by you, you wouldn't have to ask me anything.'

He dropped his head and we continued walking. 'I have a proposal to make,' he said, breaking the silence. 'You tell me what will be the day of my death and I'll tell you yours.'

'No one wants to know when the day of his death will be,' I replied.

'Then we'll tell each other without moving our lips, without pronouncing a word. That way each of us will know the truth, but will be free to ignore it.'

'What good would it do us?' I asked. 'Here it's easy to die. Every day.'

'It will allow us to understand if we really are different from all the others. It's a very rare gift that the gods have given us. There are borders that only a very few are allowed to cross. You are one of them.'

'I'll accept your challenge if you will answer this question of mine: why does the passage of time escape me? Why don't I know how long I've been in this place, and why don't any of my comrades ever talk about it either?'

'Because there are two borders in our world: time and place. You have crossed the border of time and what feels like a month for you can be a year for the others. Or the opposite. And one day you will cross the other border as well. You'll cross an invisible line to reach places that no one else can see. Athena . . . perhaps it is she who wills this. I know no more than that.'

I turned towards him and as soon as I looked into his eyes a dark, bottomless well opened up. I gave him an answer, and he to me. But his answer was not a day or a year. It was an image, one I thought I'd already seen. I wouldn't think about it again for a very long time afterwards.

THE WAR went on, ever harsher, ever more violent and cruel, ever more difficult. We hated it. In order to sustain such a huge army we had to sack everywhere around us. We took crops, herds, flocks, while the bronze and copper, the silver and gold and the beautiful women were all for the kings. I wanted the war to end, so I fought on the field with all my might, and my men with me. I had to be an example for them: I had to share the strain, the danger, the long nights awake on guard. I shared their food as well. Only when I was invited to the table of Agamemnon with the other sovereigns did I eat roasted meats and drink pure, inebriating wine, in endless banquets which perhaps helped us to forget what was happening.

One night I realized that there was a guest whom I thought I would never meet again: the minstrel without listeners from the port of Troy, the one who had offered to sing for me alone. I remembered his song as a long lament, as a mysterious, harmonious weeping, a melody he had drawn out of my own heart. How could he have entered our camp? Was it a divinity in disguise, plotting calamity for us? Or a friendly god coming to our aid? Would Calchas notice him?

He didn't sing until the banquet was over, and I leaned close to hear every sound that came from between his teeth. No one else listened, not Diomedes, not Achilles, not Great Ajax, not the handsome king of Crete, Idomeneus. Not Nestor, knight of Gerene. Beautiful slave girls had joined us and even Nestor, who was so old, was eager to indulge in the pleasures they offered. I noticed that the poet was looking straight at me and that his lips were moving without making any sound. I saw, and I understood a single word: *Antenor*. When he walked off I ran after him. 'When?' I asked.

He did not turn. 'Now, at the wild fig tree,' he said and disappeared into the darkness before I could say another word.

I went to my tent, put on a dark, hooded cloak and girded my sword. I left the line of ships dragged up on the dry beach and started off into the countryside. I could feel the presence of many troubled shadows as I walked, ghosts of heroes fallen in the cruel fray, and I could feel their pain inside me as they mourned their lost lives.

The wild fig was an enormous tree, so big that one hundred men could have found shelter in the shade of its leafy boughs. Ever since we had come ashore so long ago, it had been a landmark for us in the middle of the plain, and it bore the signs of our many battles: arrowheads still stuck in the trunk and spear tips as well, deep wounds and gashes in the bark and wood. And yet it was thriving, and laden with fruit that the birds ate. I saw a shadow and remained at a distance, saying: 'A poet asked me to come to this meeting, noble Antenor. I came because I was certain you would not betray the bond of hospitality.'

'*Wanax* Odysseus . . . I recognize your voice even though you keep your face hidden. No one but you could come to this place at this late hour. I knew you would accept.' We stood opposite each other now, dark statues sculpted by the moon. 'We were the only ones who fought in the assembly to avoid this useless massacre.'

'In vain, *wanax* Antenor. What has urged you to summon me to this place?'

'Both Trojans and Greeks are suffering terrible losses. It's clear from the pyres incessantly burning at the edges of your camp and on our cypressed hills. Young men in the bloom of their youth are falling on the field every day, their mothers clasp the urns with their ashes to their breasts and weep inconsolably. Our two peoples are bleeding to death without one prevailing over the other. There must be a solution, a way to stop all this.'

'Do you know what that is, noble Antenor?'

'A duel . . .'

'. . . between the main contenders,' I finished his thought. 'Paris and Menelaus. But how can Paris be convinced? He is a coward. He has allowed thousands of young men to go to their deaths to pay for a passing fancy.'

Antenor hesitated, meditating silently in the shadow of the fig tree streaked by the moonlight. 'It's no passing fancy; it's love. But that doesn't change anything. Hector will convince him. Paris always stays close to his brother in combat; he's afraid to fight alone. Listen to my words, Odysseus, and swear to me that you will not use what I'm telling you now to unfair advantage . . .'

'I swear it. I'm just as eager as you are to end this meaningless war.'

'Tomorrow Hector will be drawn up on the right, his cousin Aeneas will be at the centre and his brother Deiphobus on the left. Convince Menelaus to challenge Paris to single combat. He will be easy to recognize: he wears a leopard skin on his breastplate. Tell Menelaus to step forward and to shout in a thunderous voice to overcome the din of the battle. It would be best for him to make his challenge before the two fronts engage. Paris will want to flee at the mere sight of Menelaus, but Hector will stop him and force him to fight; he is too proud, too noble and uncompromising to allow his brother to refuse, and he has no esteem for Paris. He'll force him, if necessary, to show that he's ready to face danger personally, and not to let only those who are not sons of a king to die for Helen's thighs. Paris will have no choice and Menelaus will be satisfied.

'I don't care who wins. A pact will be sworn and I will convince King Priam himself to vouch personally that the outcome will be respected. The king is grief-stricken by the great number of deaths, with many of his own sons among them, and I do not believe he will oppose a duel no matter how much he loves that wretched son of his. You convince Menelaus and Agamemnon, it won't be difficult for you. At that point, no matter how the duel turns out, the war will end.'

My heart exulted at those words. Our return was imminent. In perhaps just a couple of days we'd be checking the hulls to make sure our ships were still seaworthy, and hauling them to the water. Just eight more sunsets before I'd be sleeping in Penelope's arms, in the wedding bed suspended between the olive branches. I'd see my son, my parents. I couldn't believe it, and I prayed in silence for my goddess to help me. Everything depended on me now.

We shook hands, and before we separated, I said: 'If Agamemnon accepts, you'll see a yellow banner flying at the prow of my ship.' Antenor nodded. Each of us retraced our footsteps in the darkness.

I went to Agamemnon's tent. The banquet had finished but he was not sleeping yet, so I had Menelaus summoned as well. As soon as the king of Sparta crossed the threshold into his brother's tent, I told them about the meeting and about Antenor's proposal. Menelaus' face lit up.

'Finally!' he exclaimed. 'I'll massacre that lily-livered bastard as soon as I get my hands on him. He'll spit blood into the dust and quiver like a goat when you've slit its throat and it's about to die. I'll throw his miserable body to the dogs like I promised. Or I'll eat his heart myself.'

'No,' I stopped him, 'not like that. King Priam will come in person to sanction the pact. Solemn sacrifices will be made to the gods of the heavens and to the divinities who rule the Underworld. The man who falls will be returned to his people, so that funeral rites can be celebrated. Then, if the victory is ours . . .'

'You can be sure of that!' broke in Menelaus.

'If victory is ours,' I repeated, 'the Trojans will have to return Helen and make rich reparations in gold, silver and bronze. If victory is theirs, we promise, instead, to raise our siege and return to Achaia. Tell me if this agreement is acceptable to you. I told Antenor that, were it up to me, I would accept these conditions.'

Menelaus nodded.

'I accept as well,' said Agamemnon. I watched as he drew a long breath and smiled. He too felt the weight of so many lives spent without obtaining any results, and he was wary of damaging the prestige he had always enjoyed. His heart still ached with the loss of Iphigenia, the loveliest and sweetest of his daughters. Iphi, he used to call her.

But now, after the first moment of enthusiasm, doubt crept in.

I was too well aware of how fate, or the will or caprices of the gods, could destroy the plans of men. I said: 'Prince Hector, the heir to the throne, will be lined up on the right and Paris with him. Aeneas at the centre will lead the Dardanian formation, and Deiphobus, Hector's dearest brother, will be on the left. Therefore you, Menelaus, will be at the front of the left wing of our army. You will make the first move, stepping forward to challenge Paris. We'll protect you, but I don't think you'll have to worry because Antenor will have the situation under control. There's no one who wants the war to end more than he does, and he'll have convinced Priam as well. Keep Achilles far away from our left wing. He's too rash; he could ruin everything.'

We walked out together and Menelaus clasped me to him: 'I swear that, if everything goes as it should, I will give you fertile lands from my kingdom, close to the sea; I will give you cities that you can settle in if you'd like to spend some time close to me for, of all the Achaian kings, you are the dearest to my heart and the one I esteem most greatly.'

'Thank you for honouring me with your friendship. But let us pray to the gods tonight, that they may favour our endeavour. Everything is possible for them, while fate governs us, and can shatter the plans we have carefully laid, or even our very lives. Sleep as much as you can, rest and build up your strength so that tomorrow your arm may be unstoppable. Remember: she is certainly watching you from high up on the walls.'

I said nothing else but hoped ardently that everything would go as noble Antenor and I had anticipated. As soon as I reached my ship, I raised a yellow banner on the forward yard. As soon as day broke, it would be seen at a distance.

The next morning, when the rays of the sun lit up the clouds from behind the mountains, we assembled the army and led them out of camp, towards the city. The gates of Troy opened, spewing forth chariots and men who surged into the field and devoured the space that separated them from us. The time to act was approaching and I scanned all that I saw before me, searching for any mysterious presence that might overturn our plans, but I found nothing. If there were gods hostile to us, they were well disguised. I soon spotted the gleam of Hector's bright helmet and there at his side was Paris. A leopard skin partially covered his chest and shoulders.

'There he is!' I shouted over to Menelaus, who was advancing on his chariot not far from my own. What a sight my friend was to behold: the bronze cladding his chest shone like gold, his every movement sent off blinding flashes. The high crest on his helmet rippled with every gust of wind.

As soon as he saw his enemy, he bellowed in a thunderous voice: 'Paris! Traitor, coward! You've lain low as long as you could, you've always avoided facing me. Show us now, finally, what you're worth. Can you only win over a woman, or do you have the courage to take on a man?' Saying thus, raising his shield and grasping his spear, he advanced with a heavy step towards his adversary. Paris tried to retreat to safety among the ranks of the Trojan warriors but Hector stopped him and shouted something I couldn't understand. Paris turned and began reluctantly to advance towards the front line.

'Trojans!' Menelaus shouted out again. The army slowed their march and ours halted as well, at a signal from Agamemnon, who raised his spear, jutting it forward crosswise. 'Trojans, I propose a pact! It is not right for all of you to suffer for the fault of one man alone. I am ready to fight Paris in single combat. It will be only the two of us risking our lives!'

The two armies were just a few paces away from each other now. The warriors on both front lines trained their weapons at the other, ready to launch an attack at the slightest movement from the other line.

Paris looked around anxiously, seemingly unable to understand what was happening. Hector, accompanied by his herald, approached Agamemnon, who beckoned for me to join them.

'We're ready to listen to Menelaus' proposal,' said Hector, the Trojan prince. My heart leapt with joy in my chest: one more decisive step towards the end of the war. The two high commanders were in agreement. Achilles was far away.

Agamemnon, our king of kings, replied: 'Prince Hector! We have suffered too greatly, we Achaians and you Trojans, for the offence of a single man. We shall allow your brother, Prince Paris, to fight my brother, *wanax* Menelaus. If Paris wins, we will leave Troy without demanding anything. We will weigh anchor in three days' time and we will never return. If Menelaus wins, you will return Helen, along with a good number of precious objects, to redress the damage we have suffered.'

Hector asked that the pact be approved and sanctioned by King Priam and we agreed to this. All the warriors of both armies sat down and placed their weapons on the ground. It was like when the wind flattens a wide field of wheat, bending all the pointed stalks to the ground. It was an extraordinary, unbelievable event in the minds of all those present except me: everything was going exactly as Antenor and I had foreseen. Certainly Hector had been informed as well, and had agreed to this. Perhaps the only one who knew nothing was Paris himself.

We waited anxiously for the king, who had been summoned by a messenger, to reach the battlefield and swear to the terms of the pact before the two drawn-up armies. We finally saw him arriving. When the chariot was close enough for me to see Antenor standing at his side, I truly began to think that it was the day we could start planning our return.

Two pairs of lambs were slaughtered, two of them white-fleeced and two black. The pact was sworn and the terms of reparation defined. My eyes happened to meet Antenor's, but only for a moment. He must have been blaming himself as the engineer of such a painful compromise; humiliating, but necessary. Could pride ever be measured against the lives of so many young men? The anguish of so many women, so much bloodshed, such grief? I realized how much he must have struggled and I admired him then, as greatly as I had ever loved and esteemed the hero Laertes my father.

And yet deep down in my heart I felt a strange anxiety, a vague uneasiness that I could not define or banish from my thoughts. I was sure we were close to the finish, because Menelaus would certainly strike down his adversary, who was all show and no guts, and the war would be over. That must be why I felt so uneasy: we were so near to the end.

The two adversaries faced off, very close to one another. They were covered with armour from head to toe, and were studying the gaps into which a spear could be thrust, thirsting for the heart or the throat or the groin of the other. Paris had first throw; he flung his spear without waiting an instant. Menelaus raised his shield swiftly. The bronze point pierced the shield and stuck there, the hanging weight of the long heavy shaft deforming the hard metal. It was Menelaus' turn, and his powerful throw ripped through the shield and breastplate of his adversary. Everyone shouted out, imagining that Paris had been struck down, but it wasn't so. No blood dripped to stain his tunic. I bit my lip in disappointment. Menelaus had to toss aside his useless shield and he lunged forward with his sword, while Paris broke the spear shaft to extract it from his shield and held it up again to protect himself.

My uneasiness mounted, surging from my heart to my throat.

Menelaus attacked him furiously, like a ravenous beast: his sword fell with such hammering violence that the great bronze shield protecting Paris rang out under his blows, as deafening as thunder. The Trojan prince was driven back and turned, as if seeking shelter among the ranks of his army but there was no shelter to be found; all of them were sitting down, only Hector was on his feet, leaning on his spear. He was scowling, and biting his lower lip. I heard a distant noise, coming closer, like wind rushing over the plain, amidst the trees. A slight haze seemed to be drifting in from the east.

With his second assault, Menelaus' sword broke into jagged splinters; smashed by the hand of a god, perhaps? I began to despair. I could not believe what I was seeing. The haze became denser, swirling, blown by the wind between the two armies. Menelaus picked up the broken shaft of his spear then and delivered such a devastating blow to Paris' right arm that he dropped his sword. Menelaus gave a mighty leap, landing on top of him, and pressed with all his weight on the prince's shield to crush Paris' chest and heart. Paris slipped sideways and avoided death, but the king of Sparta grabbed him by the crest of his helmet and dragged him over the ground towards the lines of the Achaians, who urged him on, yelling for Menelaus to strangle him. The helmet strap sank into his flesh. The haze invaded the field, shrouding the two armies, the raging combatants, everything. I could see nothing.

Then the wind shifted direction, the mist cleared and I realized that Menelaus was quite close to me. He held Paris' empty helmet in his hands: the strap was broken. Hot tears rolled down his cheeks.

The Trojan prince had disappeared. And now all the Trojans were on their feet.

A low drone, then a shrill whistle.

A clean, metallic strike.

A roar.

Menelaus had been hit by an arrow!

The arrow was stuck in his side. A trickle of blood slowly descended his thigh. Scarlet.

Do you see that Helen, the blood? Do you see it? The blood of your husband, the father of your child?

Too far away to see, too high, up on the highest tower, alongside the king, alongside Antenor. Alongside Paris, even.

It was over. The dream, our careful plans, gone. The oath pledged by two great kings violated. And I had been so sure that our departure was imminent!

But my unease had warned me. How often would I be prey again to such bitter disappointment in my life? Driven back into the unknown, when everything had seemed ready, secure, easy and visible, a victory in my hands.

The two armies clashed like black clouds in the sky storming with lightning. Hatred, rancour, dismay set men's hearts aflame.

Fury chased them into the ferocious brawl, wrapped them in blood, in screams, in the din of bronze. Horror girded their temples, hate issued from their eyes. They locked their breath tight behind their teeth and all you could hear were beastly growls. How long would it be before evening fell? Before merciful darkness covered the corpses, gave the wounded a chance to live, allowed us to weep our dead!

I let out the triple war cry of the king of Ithaca, inflecting my voice, shrill and short, calling my men to rally. Many were dead, killed by spear and by sword, others wounded, others maimed, struck in the arms, legs, face, yet others blinded, forever denied the light of the sun. I led those who remained with fury, so none of us would be cheated of our share of the massacre.

Makahon was there among us: the best of surgeons and a great warrior as well, son of Asclepius, who had defeated death. He was summoned to gauge how far the dart had penetrated Menelaus' flesh and to treat his wound. He put the blade of his dagger into the flames until it was red hot and inserted it in the path cut by the arrow until it reached the tip. The muscle had clenched so hard that it had stopped the tip from piercing Menelaus' internal organs. Makahon extracted the shaft, cauterized the wound, stitched the ragged edges and applied an ointment whose preparation had been passed down by his father; no one but he knew the ingredients. Then he gave Menelaus a potion that would calm him and allow him to rest. The king of Sparta, who had suffered so in his flesh and in his soul, fell asleep.

That night, Diomedes invited me to his tent along with Achilles. Achilles was not suffering at all; war was his element, like air for a bird and water for a fish. Diomedes was similar to him in many ways. I went. I needed to swallow my bitterness, to stop agonizing over what had happened.

'What's wrong with you?' asked Achilles. 'Menelaus will live, and he'll have plenty more opportunities to kill that bastard.'

I nodded. If I had told him how I felt he wouldn't have understood. It was late when I returned to my ship. I didn't want to sleep inside a tent; I wanted to stretch out on a rowing bench like my father used to do when he had sailed out with Jason of Iolcus to Colchis in search of the fleece.

In the middle of the night, when the Great Chariot was beginning its downwards course towards the sea, I heard a footstep in the dark. A footstep that I recognized . . . I'd been hearing it since I was a boy. I jumped onto the ground and scanned the gloom all around me, and then I saw him. Damastes!

He looked somehow bigger, but otherwise the same as the day he left us. He was wearing the same armour, his hair was streaked silver at the temples, his arms strong, his shoulders wide.

'I thought you were up in the mountains, my friend, watching for the chimeras to take off in flight between the cliffs of Mount Pelion and Mount Ossa and listening for the echoes of their shrieks. How did you get here?'

'I always follow you, king of Ithaca. I've always protected you.'

I sighed. It was hard for me not to weep. 'Then, o goddess, why did you allow Paris to slip away in the thick fog, to escape death when Menelaus was ready to strangle him? I would be preparing for departure now, I would be fitting the rowlocks and stretching the stays from the mast to the pins on the railing. My heart would be singing in my chest, impatient as I pushed my ship into the sea. And instead I'm in agony, thinking of how much more distant the day of return will be for me and my companions. Why did you do this to me? Why did you dash my hopes and why do you continue to taunt me by appearing to me in disguise?'

'Do you truly not understand? Don't you know why I look like Damastes?'

'Are you saying that Damastes never existed? It was you hitting me with that stick when I was learning to use my sword? And Mentor never existed either?'

'I suppose you can't hope to understand, as versatile and acute as your mind is. Take what you can from my benevolence and don't ask other questions. I couldn't change what happened today because it was decreed by the gods that dwell in the heavens. They don't want the war to end; they want this deadly game to continue, for their enjoyment. Some of them help the Trojans, others help the Achaians. And so the conflict will go on without respite or interruption, for a long, long time. Accept it: mortals cannot escape the will of the gods.'

'So this is why our blood has spilled, the reason so many brave souls have been crowded into Hades?'

'No, not only. What happens is a mystery for us as well. Fate is unfathomable and has neither a face nor an expression, neither a reason nor a cause.'

'What possesses you to help me then, if it's all useless anyway?'

'Fate is nothing more than the result of thousands and thousands of wills, an infinite number, divine and human, along with the force of the waves and the rush of the wind, the song of the birds and the movements of the stars. Like a great river, it is made up of thousands and thousands of streams and its power is invincible. I remain close to you because from the beginning of time all the way to the end, no one has ever been like you and no one ever will be. I love your fear and your courage, your hatred and your love, your voice and your silence, and so live your life, king of Ithaca, as long as you have breath. No god could ever be what you are, not even if he wanted to.'

She left and I listened to her steps leading away from me.

25

FOR A VERY LONG TIME, I tried to conquer my doubt, my uncertainty, my fears. What I feared most was the madness I could feel snaking its way between us, creeping into our minds, taking possession of the weakest but also the strongest of us. Living and killing were, in reality, two distinct actions, but one was the negation of the other. At its start, my life was tied to where I had grown up: an island, with its waters, its trees, its fruits, its sounds, songs and sorrows. I came from a family with parents, a wife, a son, my servants, my dog, the herds and flocks. An almost divine equilibrium.

And then everything changed. Before I went to war, I'd never killed, except for the animals I hunted. And now I was killing men, continuously, on the first try or sometimes not; sometimes I killed them after wounding or crippling or maiming them. I saw them in the throes of death, shaking, jerking. They were still alive when my men would strip off their armour. My right, the right of all kings. In this way, the victor could seize precious trophies that would sit proudly in the armoury of his palace once he returned, witness to his valour, his wealth and his prestige. When the spoils of war fell to me, my companions carried the booty to my ship and piled everything up at the prow.

In the beginning it was their eyes that tormented me. The dying kept staring at me, even after I'd fallen asleep, and they gave me no rest all night long. Sometimes, in the thick of combat, in the frenzy of screaming and blood, I thought of Damastes' words when he was teaching me hand-to-hand sword-fighting: 'This is what they call glory.'

As time passed, *how much time?*, I got used to the killing and I realized I had changed, I had become more like Diomedes. In fact, Diomedes and I had become fast friends. He too had left his beautiful young bride, Aegialia, and every night, when all you could hear was the voice of the sea that never sleeps, I would see him sitting on the shore with his head low, and I imagined he must be thinking of his distant queen. Far, far beyond his reach. He wasn't consoled by the spoils that he carried off from the field of blood either.

There was something that distinguished us, though: the chariot that he had and I didn't. I wouldn't know how to start fighting from that platform racing through the fields, mowing down men like a reaper cuts down wheat.

The chariots distinguished the great kings from the less powerful ones, like me or Ajax Oileus, who was bold and ferocious and feared nothing, not even the gods. Or like Ajax the son of Telamon, the gigantic prince of arid Salamis, an island that was perhaps even poorer than my own. Great Ajax was a fortress on his own, so massive that nothing and no one could move him when he stood there wide-legged, one foot forward and the other behind. He towered over everyone. The spear he brandished was cut from the trunk of a young ash tree and was impossible to crack, with a tip that was nearly a whole cubit long. The shield he wore covered his whole body; it was so huge that it covered Teucer as well, his half-brother, as they were born to different mothers. Teucer was a formidable archer: he would come round the edge of the shield, let fly and then duck back behind quickly to nock another arrow to his bowstring.

Nestor, the wise lord of Pylos, was perhaps the most tranquil of us all. Only once, to my immense surprise, did I see him in the midst of his warriors and servants in battle. What a bitter, anguished-filled day that was. Perhaps he wanted to feel the thrill of combat again after so many years, or maybe he'd decided that was the way he wanted to face death: headlong, sparing himself a long, sad decline. In the same way, I often saw him ordering his men to bring some pretty young woman seized in plunder into his tent and into his bed; to see if her soft thighs and smooth breasts would reawaken some desire in him.

In those clanging, ear-splitting years we fought anywhere, under any skies. Not even a sudden cloudburst, with thunder and lightning, could rend that monstrous tangle of men and horses, could make itself heard over the roaring metallic din. It was in those moments that yes, I felt different from any human being. I realized that exploring the extreme limits of what a man can feel and withstand in the course of his existence, makes that man different and incapable of going back to what he had always considered a normal, desirable life. *There is no return from the extreme confines of our world, of our mind. And when a man has understood this, he is gripped by a kind of dizziness that makes him feel similar to the gods, both those of the heavens and those of the Underworld. Accompanied, unhappily, by an infinite melancholy. What sailors feel when they are leaving the land they love, where they were born, where their wives and their children are, because they know in their heart of hearts that they will never be able to return.*

I understood why those who had taken part in certain exploits – if destiny or the gods allowed them to return – felt the need to seek each other out, to talk, to hunt, to eat, to take pleasure from beautiful women, together. Or even just to sleep under the same roof, in the same place. Together. It was only then, while banqueting, hunting, visiting, that they felt surrounded by other men like them. Alone they were only prey to anguish.

There was no point to what we found ourselves doing, except that of pushing ourselves beyond every limit and every imagining in inflicting fury and suffering, on a field where every day, when the sun rose, we could measure the width and length with our own eyes. It was as if the reapers woke up every morning, took their sickles in hand and went to the fields to cut down the blond stalks, bending their backs under the scorching sun, wearily returning to their homes at night to consume their dinners. That's what we did. Every day we went back into the field to mow down men.

And I learned how many ways there are to die, all of them infinitely painful.

I saw a young Trojan jolted out of his chariot by a spear hurled by Diomedes. The blow was so powerful that his body was flung backwards. He'd been hit square in the chest and the spear had pierced him straight through, ripping into his heart. His driver, terrified, had tried to wheel the steeds around in order to flee, but Diomedes threw another spear that entered through the nape of his neck, cut off his tongue and ended up sticking out between his teeth. As his servants were releasing the horses from their yoke so he could take them back to the ships, he let another spear fly and this one penetrated a warrior's buttocks and exited from his stomach, dripping blood and urine; it had pierced through his bladder.

Another time I saw Diomedes strike such a cleaving blow on one of the Lycian warriors who had managed to get in his way that he cut off the man's entire shoulder, detaching it from his neck and his chest, revealing the cavity within and all the organs it contained, as life escaped from that horrible gash. I saw all this as though there were another looking through my eyes, because I and my formidable Cephalonians were pressing forward against the enemy ranks and I had to use all my wits so as not to get hit myself by one of the thousands and thousands of spears flying around me, or slashed by any of those innumerable swords.

And we learned to ignore pain, if we weren't already inured to it. I myself saw Diomedes have his charioteer Sthenelus pull out an arrow stuck in his shoulder. He clenched his teeth so he wouldn't scream and was growling like a wolf as he grabbed a spear and hurled it at the man who had wounded him. Another time I saw Teucer wrenching an arrow from the thigh of his brother Ajax.

In the insane fury of battle, in the unbearable commotion of smashing bronze and snapping limbs, I could often hear, above all the rest, the song of the poet, the one I heard that night in the port of Troy. The same who led me to my meeting with Antenor, which in my mind would have ended the war. The song was a long wail, a desolate sigh . . . and yet its intense, sublime melody welled up above the other noises, so different was it from the screams of war and of death. What it was I'll never know. Perhaps my heart conserved its echo, or perhaps the poet was a god who had the power to sound such unique notes in my head: the wailing of mothers, of fathers, of wives, a music of the heart that drowned out everything else.

Many times the Trojan champions challenged our most fearsome heroes and the clashes were terrible to see. All the men would stop to watch how Prince Hector, Aeneas the commander of the Dardanians, and Deiphobus, Hector's brother, could stand against our most valorous warriors. But none of them ever dared to face up, alone, to Achilles, knowing that challenging him would mean certain death. His attackers would join in compact ranks, shield to shield and shoulder to shoulder. They surrounded him all together, but never stepped forth alone. It was the only way to prevent loss after loss. It was the same strategy shepherds used if a lion got into the sheep's pen. They would band together closely and wave pointed pikes in the air until the beast backed away or escaped from the pen with a single leap; none of them would ever press forward on his own unless he wanted to be slaughtered.

Achilles believed that he would die young; he had made his choice. He wanted his fame to make him immortal, and make immortal all he had touched: his weapons, his friends, the enemies he had killed. They would all be remembered. But if Achilles died, how would we be able to win? Wouldn't it be futile to go on? I couldn't find an answer to this question, not even when I spoke with him. 'We'll make it back,' I'd tell him. 'We'll make it back together.' He would smile, but never answer. What struck me more than anything else was that smile, and the calm, almost serene look in his eyes when we sat in my tent or his, drinking wine and talking. But when he put on his armour and got into his chariot, he was a man transformed. His eyes glittered with an evil light behind his sallet, his hand clutched the shaft of his spear like a claw, his voice sounded inside his helmet with a deep, cavernous rumble. His flesh and his bones rang like bronze.

There seemed to be an unspoken agreement between the two mightiest champions, Achilles on our side and Hector on the other, not to attack each other in combat: too much was at stake and the risk wasn't worth it. Better for each of them to earn immortal glory by annihilating scores of enemies incapable of withstanding their power.

THE WAR dragged on and on, for years, and we all changed. I don't know whether we got better or worse, but we were different. And given that the changes were more or less the same for all of us, the differences among us remained the same as they had been at the beginning of the war. The most important thing, every day, was deciding on an objective.

How I longed to talk to my father! I was certain he'd never had a similar experience, over such a long time with such a great number of men, with such forces facing each other. Not even the exploits of the Argonauts could be compared to ours.

I was a special friend for Achilles, unique, I believe, and yet he couldn't understand me.

'I don't understand why you're always so far away from me on the battlefield,' he complained.

'Maybe because I have a wife and a son?' I replied.

He smiled, as he did when he talked about death.

'Why are you smiling?' I asked.

'You know why. You saw him yourself. I have a son, too, but no wife. He must be twelve or thirteen by now.'

Twelve years old already . . .

That evening I'd come back with wine from Thrace. I'd gone out with my men, we'd crossed the sound that separated us from the coast opposite our camp, and we had loaded up two of our ships with tall jars of red wine, sweet and strong. It was keeping us company now.

'You know that my father, Peleus, had sent me to spend some time in the court of Lycomedes, the king of Scyros, to learn about their different customs and habits, and so that I might experience life in a rich, refined palace, so different from our bleak fortress up in the mountains,' Achilles reminisced. 'I was thirteen, and the king had six or seven daughters who were ten to fifteen years old. One of them, Deidamia, was very pretty and I liked being with her, playing with her. No one paid any attention to us because we were just a couple of kids, but we were not children any more. One winter's night I slipped into her bed and she welcomed me, without any reluctance. She said it made her feel protected, and that the warmth of my body comforted her and gave her pleasure. It started as a game. Our caresses became bolder, and more intimate, and when I entered her we were enveloped in the most intense heat we'd ever felt, swept away, inebriated, the way this wine is making me feel now . . .'

'And she became pregnant.'

'That's right. But no one had even been close to imagining it. I was so blond and slender, with such a gentle face, that I looked like another girl. You wouldn't have been able to pick me out.'

'Oh, I certainly would have. I would have flushed you out instantly.'

'How?'

'The way I did with your son, remember? I would have come bearing gifts! Embroidered dresses, dolls, hair bows and then, a miniature suit of armour, finely crafted, with a sword and a spear. One of those little girls would have jumped at it. You!'

'A fox is a witless creature compared to you!' exclaimed Achilles, laughing.

'Did you ever see her after the child was born, apart from that time we went to the island together?'

'No. As you can imagine, the king hates me. He was furious when it happened and he summoned my father to come and take me away, immediately! But it was winter by then, and that spring was very windy as well. Perhaps my father couldn't leave his kingdom so suddenly and risk such a storm-tossed sea. Anyway, by the time he arrived, my son had been born. With hair the colour of fire, and that's why I call him Pyrrhus. I wanted that to be his name. They gave him a different name, Neoptolemus, but for me he'll always be Pyrrhus, hair of fire. Lycomedes told my father to take us both back home, me and my little bastard, as he called him. But his mother, my sweet, sweet friend, wanted to keep him with her, and nurse him like a real woman.'

'All right, you have a son, but it's as if he didn't exist, for you. I wanted Telemachus, just like I wanted his mother Penelope.'

'You're wrong. I often think of him, try to imagine what he must be like now. He knows I'm his father and he talks about me all the time; he says he's going to come and fight here at my side. He's a real lion cub!'

'With the way this war is going, he may very well succeed. But when the time comes, no one will be left here. The two armies will have devoured each other completely.'

'No,' said Achilles. 'We'll win, and Troy will be razed to the ground, wiped off the face of the earth.'

When he said that his eyes blazed up with that grim, restless look that he got when he leapt onto the chariot with his spear in hand.

Sometimes he liked to sing. He had brought a lyre with him, the work of a skilled craftsman, inset with ivory, and he had a beautiful voice, strong and high-pitched. When he was on the field, it inspired raw green terror in the enemy, but when he sang it was harmonious and resonant, with a touch of melancholy.

Patroclus was his shadow, his lieutenant on the field, a kind of older brother off the field, privy perhaps to the secrets of his soul. He was originally from Opus, but he'd taken refuge at Peleus' palace after he'd murdered a man over a dice game; the killing had been accidental, but no less serious for that. The victim's parents did not believe his testimony and had refused the blood money that his father, Menoetius, had offered; they had sworn to go after him no matter where he tried to hide. Patroclus knew he was a dead man outside the confines of the kingdom of Achilles' father Peleus, who had simply believed his story, and this made him exceedingly loyal to the throne and ready to give up his life for the king if necessary. Patroclus and Achilles had grown up together, although Achilles was a few years younger, and they'd always trained together. No one knew Achilles' style of combat better than Patroclus: the way he struck a blow, his feints, his dodging and lightning-quick reactions, and his friend knew he could never compare. He just didn't have Achilles' brutal ferocity and devastating power, the swift pounce and amazing speed on foot that guaranteed that, even weighed down as he was by his armour, his prey would never get away.

That evening Patroclus hadn't spoken much. He had been occupied with the weapons, sharpening swords and spearheads, polishing shields, greaves and breastplates to a mirror-finish, but he'd certainly heard everything. He never missed a word.

When I got up to go back to my tent and rest for a while, Achilles walked back with me along the seashore.

'It's a beautiful night,' he said, watching the clouds pushed by the wind.

'You're right; this wind passed by our homes before coming here.'

'You want to go home, don't you?'

'Not at any cost,' I answered. 'If you start a war you have to win it, and we haven't won.'

'Not yet.'

'The sound of the sea reminds me of my island,' I said. 'You?'

'My mother,' he answered.

We walked in silence for a while, listening to the undertow.

'Your mother?' I said then. 'They say she's a goddess of the depths.'

Achilles smiled, like he did when he was thinking of death.

THAT NIGHT, I got an idea fixed in my head: I wasn't interested in counting the enemies I'd downed, or weighing the booty that had accumulated at the ship's prow. I wanted to find a way into the city.

I had to know what gave them the strength to fight with so much tenacity. And what resources they had; how were they managing to get what they needed to survive despite such a long siege? I was tired of sitting back and waiting for something to happen. I'd had no news of my land, my family, for such a long time and I couldn't understand why. Just thinking about it drove me mad.

I told myself that there were only two ways out. The first was to leave for home. I'd kept my promise, respected my oath, but things hadn't gone the way they should have. I couldn't besiege that city for all eternity. But I would be the first to leave, and probably the only one. The shame of it would forever taint my family name, and I could never allow that to happen.

The second way out was to cause the city to fall, and I had to find a way to do just that.

A few days later I summoned my comrades Euribates, Sinon and Eurylochus and laid out my plan.

'Tomorrow when we go into battle, you stay at my side and behind me. If Athena allows me, as I fervently hope, to fell an enemy, you'll snatch away his body, strip it and put his clothing and arms in a safe place. When evening comes and the Trojan warriors are going back through the city gates, I'll don the armour, soil my face and body with blood, and mix in among them. I'll look like just another warrior returning home wounded after a bitter battle.'

'What if you're discovered? They'll surely torture you,' Eurylochus said to me.

I showed him a pointed spike. 'No. If that should happen, I'll use this, and all they'll have to torture is a lifeless body.'

'Which they wouldn't bury – you'd be left to the dogs!' replied Eurylochus.

'I've decided. Nothing or no one can change my mind or convince me to do otherwise.'

We didn't go into battle again for eight long days; the Trojans never left the city for that whole time, despite our taunts as we lined up on the battlefield every day. When they finally decided to come out, the fighting was as keen and cruel as it had ever been, if not even more so. I drew up with my warriors far from the most illustrious of our combatants, who hurtled forward on chariots drawn by fiery steeds, and when the approach of night brought an end to the clash and each side hastened to carry off their fallen, I hid with my most loyal companions behind the wild fig tree, stripped off my arms and put on the garb of a Trojan warrior that I myself had downed with a spear thrust; Eurylochus finished him off with his sword. I dabbed the blood soaking through the dead man's tunic on my face as well so that I looked both horrible and pitiful. I joined a small group of enemies who were hurrying towards the main gate just as it was closing. Seeing that I was limping, they actually gave me a hand, grabbing me under the armpits and hoisting me up the crooked steps that led to the Skaian Gate.

Just a short time passed before I found myself alone and I melted away down a dark little road.

26

Every now and then I'd run into groups of warriors who were patrolling the roads or helping the wounded, but most of them were busy carrying the dead up towards the eastern hill where the pyres had been raised. An entire forest had been cut down to build them, so funeral rites could be celebrated for the heroes who had given their lives for their homeland. I could hear weeping and moaning, muted at that distance, *echoes of agony* . . . When no one could see me I was free to run and move quite swiftly from one side of the city to the other. I wanted to reach the citadel, I needed to see the walls, the gates, the palace and all the other landmarks from above. I already had some idea of how the city was laid out, since I'd been there with Menelaus, but many things had changed. Bulwarks had been added and the stone itself had been cut to eliminate any footholds which could have been used to climb to the top of the walls. There was even an earthen rampart – we didn't know it existed! – which protected the camp of the Trojan allies: the Thracians, Phrygians, Lycians and those from the other nations of Asia. Thousands and thousands of warriors who often faced us alongside Priam's army. At other times they were absent, back at home sowing seed or gathering the crops in their fields.

The citadel was close: I was high enough to see the pyres burning in our own camp, and the others blazing on the eastern hill of Troy. The harbour, once crawling with ships, was deserted now. I tried to impress every detail in my mind before darkness fell and obscured everything. I finally arrived as far as the greatest of the sanctuaries, dedicated to Athena, on the highest part of the citadel.

A mystery for me: how could the goddess turn her gaze from the city that honoured her so greatly? Surrounding the sanctuary on all sides were lines of bronze-clad warriors gripping heavy spears, casting long shadows. The torch light projected them onto the pavement.

I approached and waited for the right moment to discover the reason why so many warriors were drawn up to protect a sanctuary, a sacred enclosure that no one would dare to violate. How could I possibly get by the row of warriors on guard? I crept as close as I dared, remaining in the shadows of the portico which flanked the southern wall of the citadel, trying to spot a weak point in their defences. I decided that I'd have to distract them somehow, and I threw my helmet as far away as I could towards the opposite end of the portico. The bronze rang out loudly when it hit the wall and then again each time it bounced on the pavement. A few of the guards rushed towards the source of the noise. Others lit torches from the brazier to see what was happening and in the meantime I slipped unseen up to the entrance. The door was not completely closed, as if someone had just gone in and was planning on leaving. I entered. From outside I could hear shouting and commotion, and then the steps of the guards approaching. I looked through the crack in the doorway and I could see them closing ranks around the sanctuary again. Now my problem would be getting out.

I turned towards the interior and saw a woman standing perfectly still in front of the statue of Athena, which was very small, no more than three cubits high, representing the goddess on her feet, with a spear in hand and a helmet on her head. It wasn't made of metal or wood. It seemed to be sculpted from a stone, but one I wasn't familiar with. Rough and porous, with crystals that glittered and turned red as they reflected the light of the torches and the brazier. The statue's eyes were framed by lashes and brows and were made of mother-of-pearl, and they seemed to be staring at you no matter where you were in the sanctuary. The young woman standing in front of the image wore a richly decorated gown and a gold diadem in her hair; she was clearly a royal princess and this explained why armed guards were surrounding the sacred enclosure. One of Priam's daughters! But who could it be? Or might she be the wife of Hector the exterminator?

I kept moving, light and invisible as a ghost, until I was facing her. I could see her face and her expression and the big tears flowing from her eyes. Sad, terrified eyes. Should I abduct her, take her back to our camp? No. I would never commit such a detestable act inside a sanctuary.

The princess wet the statue's feet with her tears, saying a prayer through her sobs that I could not understand, and then she turned towards the exit. The door was bolted shut behind her and I listened to the footsteps of the warriors as they marched off, escorting her back to her home. I was alone with the goddess and I approached the image.

There was something very disturbing about it. The mother-of-pearl eyes were fixed and staring, and yet they pierced through you. The spear seemed to be vibrating in the goddess's hand. Although the strain of such an intense confrontation made my own eyes frantic to seek out a distraction, I was certain, almost certain, that as I looked away, the goddess's eyelids opened and closed. I felt it happen; the air in the sanctuary was moving in short, fast puffs. It was unnatural in the closed space I was in.

'Show me a way out!' shouted my heart, but all I heard in return was a distant grumbling of thunder. A sudden bolt of lightning lit up the sky, revealing the opening in the ceiling from which the fumes of the burning incense and torches could escape towards the heavens.

The goddess had answered me!

I climbed up a pillar all the way to the ceiling and pulled myself through an open hatch onto the rooftop. The moon was just breaking through the storm clouds and it lit up the whole city with a light blue glow.

The city was silent now. The Trojans sought respite from their daily sorrows in sleep. Their lives must have been agony. We Achaians were all warriors, accustomed to giving and receiving death, but they were a community of families, with wives, husbands, sweethearts, sons and daughters, parents: grief was multiplied beyond measure within the limits of the walls, like the echo of a shout rebounding from the cliffs of a rocky valley. I contemplated sacred Troy for long, endless moments. Splendid, with her towers and her walls, her palaces and sanctuaries, the houses built on sloping terraces all the way down to the outer rampart, the altars, the carved and painted funerary monuments, raised to remember ancient kings and heroes, the pinnacles and pillars. I thought that one day we would win, and that all of these things would be ours for the taking, but the thought gave me no joy, because I was feeling that I never wanted to be wrenched away from this enchanting vision.

I lowered myself to the ground without making a sound and as I was about to slip into the shadows under the portico, I felt a hand on my shoulder. I wheeled around with my sword out and ready to kill. The bronze stopped a hair's breadth from a throat of divine perfection, from a face that only the goddesses of Olympus could boast of: Helen! My sword trembled in my hand like my heart had trembled in my chest the day she chose a husband for herself in distant Sparta.

'Odysseus,' she said, 'I knew it had to be you. A warrior who went from limping one moment to scampering like a young ram the next, bounding from one spot on the walls to another . . .'

'What are you going to do?' I asked her. A cry from her and I was dead. But my hand had already hesitated; I'd missed my chance to kill her. That would have been another way to end the war. Why hadn't I thought of it?

She seemed to read my mind. 'Why did your hand falter? Why didn't you take the life of the bitch who gave herself to a man she'd never seen before, betraying the husband she herself had chosen? The war would have ended and you'd be on your way back to Penelope.'

I was shaking, strangled with the emotion that flooded my heart and made me unable to utter a word.

'Follow me,' she said, and walked away, turning her back to me. I followed; what else could I do? Helen, gorgeous as a crimson flower. Could an entire city be sacrificed for such beauty? The deaths of thousands of young men in the fields of blood had not seemed to disconcert her in the least. Her sinuous, sublime body swayed under a thin gown, her hair was like sea foam in the moonlight, flickering with gold every time the sky was set afire by a sudden burst of lightning.

She opened a little door set under an arch, entering a long, narrow corridor lit by a few oil lamps. Another door at its end opened onto a richly decorated room, surely part of the house she lived in.

'Come,' she said, and opened yet another door. We found ourselves in a room whose walls were covered with alabaster. Against the wall was a tub filled with scented water and jars brimming over with rare essences.

'I had it prepared for me,' she said. 'Undress, have a bath. Once the Trojan princes bathed in the sea, but now their sea is occupied by Achaian ships, and they have to bathe indoors.'

I took off my clothes, lay down my sword and stood before her naked and defenceless. Helen took a silver bowl, drew water from an urn and poured it over me, washing away the clotted blood from my hair, my shoulders, my face. She asked me: 'I've never been able to see my brothers, Castor and Pollux, when I watch you from the towers. Where are they?'

'No one knows. They left for an expedition in the north, and never came back. I've heard that each of them died to save the other. They are venerated in your city as immortal heroes.'

She sighed and hid her face as she had me enter the tub. She sat down next to me and washed my back and my chest with a sponge. Was I perhaps in the home of a god on Olympus? How could what was happening be possible? Helen's eyes gleamed with a tremulous light as contrasting emotions vied for possession of their expression, and yet, for an instant, in those gestures, in the way she was looking at me, I could see Penelope.

'Why are you doing this for me?' I asked.

'Because I've always desired this,' she replied. 'Remember the horses' pen? Remember what I said to you?'

'How could I forget it?'

Heavy footsteps could be heard on the street outside: a group of armed men, heading this way.

'Paris. Returning from the war council, where all show disdain for him. Leave now, quickly, and don't forget me. I've never betrayed you.'

She gave me a clean robe and wrapped me in an embrace that I would never forget for the rest of my days. Tears were falling from her eyes.

'Why?' I asked her again.

'Because this is what I dreamed the night before I made my choice: you and I, as husband and wife, in a beautiful place, in the intimacy of our own home. I thought it was a sign, a message about my future. It was, in fact, but not as I had imagined it then. This is how the gods have tricked me! This is the vision of that dream, and I brought it about without wanting to, I'm just realizing that now. Cursed be that god who sent me the dream, made fun of a girl in love. That was not to be my destiny. No. My destiny was this dreadful, cruel, bloody war, whose true purpose still eludes me but which the gods are taking such pleasure in . . . Go now, king of Ithaca, lest you lose your courage.'

She kissed me. A long, insane, desperate kiss.

Now I LOOKED like a Trojan again, like an aristocrat with those robes, wandering around the city at that time of night. I asked my goddess from the depths of my heart to guide my steps in the darkness. I warily made my way down the roads of Troy, giving a wide berth to patrolling warriors and sentry posts while saving all the details of the city's defences in my heart and mind. The one thing I couldn't stop thinking of was the image of the goddess Athena in her sanctuary: mysterious, enigmatic, yet tremendously powerful, with that mother-of-pearl gaze and shining crystals on her body. Where had such an ancient simulacrum come from? What power did it have?

I finally reached the walkway that led to the Skaian Gate, the only one that opened out onto the countryside. I lowered myself down the outside, clutching at any handhold on the rough stone, skinning my hands on the cracks and sharp edges of the blocks. Then I let myself tumble to the ground. I rolled, wounding my elbows, my shoulders and my back and ending up against a boulder that could have killed me. My blue-eyed goddess was certainly watching over me from her sanctuary. A dog barked a long way off and another answered with a long howl, as scattered drops of rain fell. When I reached the wild fig tree I was panting. My clothes were still there and I changed into them: dressed in those Trojan robes, any of my own men might have killed me.

Soon afterwards I entered Agamemnon's tent and a war council was immediately convened. I told them that the city had not given in to despair and that a rampart had been raised on the north side to protect the camps of the allied warriors who could not be lodged inside the city: there were Thracians, Lycians, Phrygians there, as well as other Asian nationalities. I told them that much work had been done to further isolate the Skaian Gate from the surrounding territory, making access even more difficult. And I explained how a frontal attack on the fortifications, realistically, would be impossible. All we could do was continue fighting on the open field, seeking a decisive victory: without this, there would be no way to bend the will of the Trojans.

'I saw no public manifestations of sorrow; only the grief of mothers and fathers accompanying their sons to the pyres. Surely there must be something that gives them the strength to go on despite their mourning, their maimed and wounded.'

'And what would that be, wise Odysseus?' asked Agamemnon.

I fell silent, quite uncertain, until the image of Athena in the sanctuary on the citadel came clearly to mind. Then I answered: 'The love they have for their city and their land. Because of this love, they are willing to face any danger and even to lose their lives, if necessary. All of us out here are alone, while they are surrounded by their wives and children, their parents, brothers and sisters, the people they love. This is their strength. Let's hope that the night will bring counsel and may the gods grant us peaceful sleep.'

I walked towards my ships and my tent, and when I was a short distance away I noticed a dark shadow on his feet in front of the entrance: Calchas was waiting up for me.

'I heard your words even though you did not see me.'

'And you're not content with what you heard?'

'The person you met in the sanctuary is Cassandra, Priam's daughter. She too has the gift.'

'All I could see was a lonely, sad, frightened woman.'

'Anyone who has the gift is lonely. The gift is also a curse. They say that when Paris was born, she was only a child, but she ran into the room of the queen who had just given birth. Hecuba and her handmaidens smiled to see that the little one was already so eager to meet her little brother. But Cassandra regarded the child with an icy glare and said: 'Kill him.'

'The queen burst into tears at those dreadful words, even more terrible coming from the lips of an innocent child. No one understood. They imagined that the little girl, who had been her parents' favourite, feared that the new arrival would rob her of their affection and caresses. Little Paris was sent to the house of his wet nurse, a shepherd's wife who lived on Mount Ida, because of their fear that Cassandra would try to harm him. Even today, King Priam and his wife refuse to understand the message, even while they see their other sons falling under Achilles' blows.'

'So what is the message?'

'You've understood it well: Paris would bring about the ruin of his homeland and thus it was necessary to eliminate him.'

'So Troy will fall.'

'Thus it is written. But not now.'

'Yes, I think that's true: not now.'

'Don't make fun of me: you saw the reason with your own eyes. It's not just love of their homeland, not only that: it's that stone statue covered with sparkling stars. As long as it remains where it is, the city will not fall.'

I didn't want to ask anything else. The image of the goddess with the mother-of-pearl eyes still haunted me, and Helen's kiss had poisoned my blood. I said only: 'I wish you a good night, Calchas, without nightmares.' And I left him.

MUCH TIME PASSED and much blood was drunk by the earth, and still Zeus' scale would not tip in favour of one side or the other. It sometimes happened that some of our strongest champions were wounded and could not take their places in the battle line; other times, even when our forces were superior in number, the invincible walls of Troy became a safe refuge for our enemy, and all we could do was batter ourselves against the bloodied jambs of the Skaian Gate. We tried more than once to line Achilles up against Hector, but the Trojan always succeeded in escaping the challenge by flying off on his chariot in another direction, where another part of his formation was yielding to the pressure of Agamemnon, Menelaus and Diomedes.

There was never a decisive moment. Hector was a sagacious commander: he wouldn't put his life at risk and thus deprive the army of his leadership. The lives of his people and his city came before his personal glory as a warrior.

It seemed that nothing would ever change, that the gods had used bronze nails to pin our destiny to that horrible field of agony and despair, until one day something happened that changed our fate.

That year the summer was scorching, suffocating. The heat was so unbearable that even the war was melting. Neither the Greeks nor the Trojans could fight any longer from inside armour baked in the sun, their strength fading before they had even begun. It took no time before we were all completely exhausted. But in the middle of those dog days, a sickness spread through our camp which cut down scores of victims every day and night and threw us all into the utmost consternation. A warrior can bear up under thirst, hunger, wounds, death in battle, but cannot rot away in the stink of his own sweat and vomit, cannot die such a senseless death.

The plague was almost certainly willed upon us by an irate god. It was necessary to understand which of the gods was offended, what we had done to warrant his anger and how it could be placated, with sacrifices and rites of expiation. Achilles himself demanded that the council of all the kings and princes of Achaia be called so we could consult the seer Calchas.

We assembled one evening near the seashore, standing within a circle traced in the sand surrounded by twelve lit torches. Agamemnon was vexed because the meeting had been called by Achilles and not by himself. And it was Achilles who spoke first: 'Speak up, o diviner, which god has been so greatly irritated that they send us this scourge? What is the cause of their wrath?'

Calchas seemed reluctant to answer.

'Speak up, I said! Why are you holding back?' demanded Achilles.

'What I have to say will not please our high commander.'

Achilles, without even looking at Agamemnon, replied: 'Fear nothing and no one! You are under my protection.' This was an outright challenge to the most powerful sovereign of Achaia, pronounced in front of us all.

Calchas raised his cane, shaking the bells that adorned its tip, and silence fell over the assembled kings and princes; I could hear the waves lapping at the shore and the groans of the dying. The smoke from the pyres had enveloped the setting sun in black soot. Against that atmosphere of death, the words of the seer rang out: 'Apollo is incensed at us because his priest Chryses came to our camp, as many of us saw with our own eyes, bearing riches to pay the ransom for his daughter, whom Agamemnon has taken as his war prize, but Agamemnon refused to return her. In his dismay, the priest called upon Apollo to avenge his humiliation and the god heeded his prayer, flinging his deadly arrows our way. The only way to put an end to this scourge is for Agamemnon to return Chryses' daughter to him and sacrifice a great number of victims on the altar of Apollo, in the hopes that the god will accept this act of expiation.'

Never in all those years of war had the high chief of the Achaians been humiliated in public or forced to swallow such an arrogant challenge. The Achaian king of kings reacted harshly to Calchas' words. 'You visionary of hell! Never have I had fair play in your prophecies! You have never brought me a happy portent, only trouble and misfortune fall from your lips. I don't want to deprive myself of my slave. Why should I? Chryseis, the priest's daughter, belongs to me. She is beautiful: her face, her body, her mind, and I want her here with me. It was my right to take her and my right to decide whether to accept the ransom or refuse it. The same would have been true for any one of you! But if what you say is true, Calchas, I won't have anyone thinking that I do not have the destiny of my men at heart. My only concern is the warriors who are fighting under the walls of Troy.

'I will return her to her father if this will placate the ire of Apollo, but it is not fair that I alone must do without the most precious part of my war winnings. And so you kings and princes present here will have to give me another prize of equal value and beauty. It is not just that I, your supreme commander, be deprived of my rightful due!'

I could foresee what was about to happen. Achilles was the mightiest warrior of the whole army, Agamemnon was the high chief and most powerful sovereign; their words could only become harsher and more aggressive. I could not, however, foresee the consequences of a clash, if words spilled over into actions. The end of our great enterprise, perhaps. The shame and disgrace of defeat. Although I desired to return to Ithaca more than any other thing on earth, I would rather have died than accept such a dishonourable end.

Achilles answered: 'O great – and greatly covetous – Atreides, there are no further war prizes to be split up to satisfy your demand, but if we succeed in conquering Troy, you will be the first to choose from among the most precious objects and the most beautiful women.' I felt that I could breathe again: the prince of Phthia, lord of the Myrmidons, had managed at least in part to maintain control of himself. I waited in trepidation for Agamemnon's response.

'No,' shot back the king of Mycenae. 'I want my prize now, and if you don't give it to me I will take it. From you, Achilles, or from Ajax or Odysseus.'

I had to smile at hearing my own name: he would find nothing on my ship to compare to his splendid slave and he knew that well. He also knew how hard I had worked, first to ensure peace and later to make war. He was behaving like a man of no worth. Now anything could happen. And of course, it did. Achilles insulted him ferociously, reproaching him for his greed and self-indulgence, calling him shameless and contemptible. But those words didn't really make much of an impression on me; it was what he said afterwards that broke my heart.

'I've always fought with all my strength, conquered villages and cities, flocks and herds of thousands of animals, and I always saved the richest part for you, out of respect. A respect you never deserved, Agamemnon. It's on my shoulders that the weight of the war lies. The only reason I'm here with my men is because your brother's wife was abducted: to keep faith with a promise,' and here Achilles shot me a piercing look. 'The Trojans never did me any harm; they never robbed me or invaded the kingdom of my father, and so I'm leaving. I'm going back home. I have no desire to stay here to accumulate riches for you, to fight your war!'

'Go!' shouted Agamemnon. 'I won't try to hold you back. Others no less valiant than you will stay to fight at my side and I'll have the support of the king of the gods, who protects the king of men. I won't miss you, you quarrel-seeking, hot-tempered, rebellious villain! Go, I'm happy to see the end of you, you have my permission. But since I'm the one who has to pay by sending my slave back to her father, I'll come by and take your own Briseis. Yes, I'll take her to my own tent.'

This was too much, Achilles would never allow such a thing to happen. He threw his sceptre to the ground, heaped insult upon insult on Agamemnon, and put his hand to his sword. It was the end.

But suddenly, all at once, I felt her presence: Athena. It wasn't that I saw her, no. But who else could have abruptly stayed the murderous wrath of the strongest and most impetuous warrior the world had ever seen? Induced him to sheathe his sword?

I saw Achilles speaking without a word coming out of his mouth. He was close to me, I could see him well. He turned and his eyes seemed to lock on to something just behind him, and then he lowered his gaze.

Nestor saw his chance to plead for peace, but I said nothing. He went on and on as he usually did, recalling the endeavours of his youth and the prestige he had accumulated in so many long years of experience. He tried to soothe their quarrel and remind them of their duties. Too late. Agamemnon sent his men to Achilles' tent to carry off his woman: Briseis, a radiant beauty whom he had fallen in love with, and she with him, although Achilles had killed her husband. Then Agamemnon had his mightiest warship readied, along with the biggest of his cargo ships, which would carry the animals destined to be sacrificed. He had me summoned, and I walked at his side as, pensive and downcast, he made his way back to his tent.

'I need you, Odysseus. I want you to command the ships on this journey and to sustain me when we meet the girl's father. We can't make any more mistakes; too many terrible things have already happened. I have great faith in you.'

I accepted, although he'd done nothing to deserve my help, and the next day I woke up early and had the cargo ship pushed out empty into the water; only then were the sacrificial animals put aboard, using a wooden ramp. When the ship was fully loaded, and even Chryseis, with her statuesque figure and deep, moist eyes, had come aboard my vessel, I gave the order to hoist sail and sent the men to their oars. Before we put out to sea, Agamemnon came to say goodbye.

'Why did you provoke the savage warrior?' I asked him. 'Without Achilles, we have no hope. And we cannot count on the support of the gods. They don't help fools.'

Agamemnon did not answer and I fell silent as well, my heart heavy. The sun's first rays were lighting up the towers of Troy and I boarded the ship.

27

ONCE MORE I HAD THE DESTINY of Achaia in my hands. And once again it was a woman who had set off everything. But we could no longer count on the might of Achilles: our pure, raw, implacable thunderbolt. Gone. All that was left was my heart and my mind. Could that suffice to guide the powerful brawn of Great Ajax, the fury of Diomedes, the noble prowess of Idomeneus and Menelaus? But first of all, the plague had to be stopped. If Makahon, our warrior surgeon, son of Asclepius, who overcame death, hadn't succeeded, I needed to come to terms with men and gods and redress the offence. My time had come.

I spoke with the girl during the voyage and discovered that her name was Astynome, even if everyone referred to her using her father's name: Chryseis, daughter of Chryses.

'What kind of a welcome can we expect from your father?' I asked her. 'I've decided to come without an armed guard, and have left my own weapons behind, so I can offer sacrifice to the god pure-heartedly.'

Astynome hesitated – she was accustomed to being the property of another man, and she had never spoken with him as she did with her equals and friends – but then decided to answer me. Her voice sounded very young, but was intense and slightly husky, which made her all the more intriguing. 'He'll be very happy to see me again. I am his only daughter and he was willing to pay my ransom with all the wealth in his possession. He'll want to give it to you, since you are the one returning me.'

'I'm relieved to hear that he won't receive me in anger. How were you treated by Agamemnon, our supreme leader?'

'Like a slave,' she answered.

There were no words to be said after such an answer, but I decided to continue nonetheless. 'Even slaves can be treated in different ways. Did he treat you well or badly?'

'Like a slave . . . a beautiful one.'

I was struck by her clarity of thought and sincere words.

'I possess slaves as well, in the palace and fields of my island. They all love me, and I them, as part of my family.'

'Do you have children, *wanax*?' It was the first time she'd asked me a question. I was gaining her confidence.

'Just one. Telemachus is his name, born of my wife, Penelope. When I left he hadn't even started speaking yet, although sometimes I thought I heard him say *"atta"*.'

She smiled. 'That's what all children say before they learn to talk.'

I don't know what she thought of me, but I tried to help her understand that I was a person, with a mind and heart, thoughts and hopes. Above all, hopes. I think she understood.

By the time we reached Chrysa, her city, she would speak with me easily without waiting for me to start the conversation, and that was a good thing. I put my warship and the cargo ship ashore, had Astynome disembark and started unloading the animals to be sacrificed.

I walked with the girl until we reached the sanctuary and the altar. Her father had just begun to celebrate rites in honour of Apollo and when he saw us his face lit up; joy shone in his eyes. I put her hand into his and said: 'The lord of all our peoples, Agamemnon, has sent me to you so that I may return your daughter who is so dear to you, and offer sacrifice to placate the god, if you will appeal to him on our behalf.' I heard Astynome speaking to him in their language. There was only one word I understood: my own name.

The priest invoked the god with a prayer: 'God of the silver bow who reigns sovereign over our city, you have heeded my words and you made the Achaians pay dearly for their affront. You have done me justice. Now that the wrong has been righted, a sacrifice will be offered to you and a choir will sing your glory. Turn your ire from the camp of the Achaians, I beg of you.'

When we had offered the animals we'd brought with us in sacrifice, the meat was distributed among the people, who ate it happily and celebrated with wine. My men and I spent the night sleeping on the rowing benches or on the beach. I prayed devoutly to my goddess to intercede on our behalf with Apollo, to convince him to accept the prayer of his priest. When dawn awoke us, we unfurled the sails and raised anchors. Only then did I notice the girl walking on the beach, barefooted on the fine sand. She had begun to live again.

I still think of her. Does she still exist? What happened in her life? She incarnated, for us, the hope of salvation or the threat of catastrophe, at least for that brief time in which I knew her. Did she have children? A husband? Was someone willing to take her after she had been in the bed of the king of Achaian kings? Or did she decide to dedicate herself, still a virgin in her heart, to the cult of her father? In my mind she still lives the way I saw her that last time . . .

The ire of Apollo was not soon placated. Perhaps he wanted to finish the arrows still remaining in his quiver, perhaps he was as slow in abandoning his wrath as he had been swift at kindling it. It's difficult to understand the mind and intentions of the gods. In the end, the plague ceased but the fighting began again. Achilles would not take part, although he hadn't set sail as he had threatened to do. He'd stayed put, and he was seething at not taking his place in the action. Keeping out of the war was a punishment he'd inflicted on himself, not on Agamemnon. It wasn't long before the enemy became aware of his absence. That hit us even harder. Achilles inspired terror and he was unstoppable. Every day, the number of dead that we carried back from the battlefield increased, and the men were becoming greatly discouraged. My mission had served no purpose. That didn't mean I was giving up.

I met Patroclus one day as he was returning from the hunt with a roebuck on his shoulders. He realized that I'd been waiting for him and he stopped in the shelter of a tree, where Achilles, who had left his tent, could not see us. As we spoke he began to flay the animal and gut it.

'He respects you,' Patroclus told me, 'and he can't understand how a man like you can still recognize the authority of Agamemnon. But what's really killing him is that his woman is in that tent, perhaps even in that bed. He has proved that he's much more judicious than anyone would have imagined. He could have killed Agamemnon, and he didn't.'

'Perhaps a god stayed his hand. Anyway, I haven't given up hope. He hasn't left; he's still here. Unless he's told you he has other intentions. I know he has no secrets from you.'

Patroclus sighed. He was suffering as well for our misfortunes but could do nothing. 'That same night,' he told me, 'when Agamemnon's heralds came to take Briseis away, I saw him sitting on a rock on the shore. I think he was crying. A man who will take on any pain or suffer any wound without a whimper, who would never shirk danger of any sort . . . crying. Out of anger, humiliation, despair at losing his love.

'He'd taken her from her husband, the king of Lyrnessus, after killing him in combat. His name was Mynes and he fought like a lion but he had no chance against Achilles. At first, and for a long time after, she hated him. She wouldn't speak to him or look him in the eyes. I was afraid she'd plant a dagger in his back while he was sleeping, or try to poison him. But none of this came to be. She submitted to him, like any slave with a master, forsaking pleasure or emotion. At first. Until she was swept away by him, his passion, his ardour. They fell in love. She was a queen, after all, and she had the dignity, the beauty and the bearing of a queen, although she was very young, and this turned their union into something that was noble and true. Her arms were a safe refuge for him. The hours he would spend with her in bed after the battle calmed his fury, tamed the beast that lived inside him. Now he cannot tolerate her being in the power of a man he detests. He knew that if he opposed Agamemnon, disaster beyond any imagining would result. But for him, giving her up was an immense sacrifice: Briseis was his lover, sister, mother.'

'His mother,' I mused. 'No one has ever seen her. They say she is a goddess of the sea.'

'You think that's so?' asked Patroclus. 'I've seen Achilles' blood spilled many a time and it was the blood of a man, believe me.'

'Then who might she be, if not a goddess who can hide from our eyes and show herself only to him?'

'Maybe she never existed. Maybe she died when he was born. Maybe he's talking to a ghost when he sits on the seashore in the evenings with his lyre, singing those sad songs.'

'Or she may truly be a goddess of the abyss,' I replied. 'We can't explain everything that's around us. He's the only one who knows the mystery. One so great that it contains the beginning, but also the end, of his life.'

Patroclus dropped his head and fell silent. I watched as his blade peeled back the skin and sliced through the muscles in the animal's neck. His hands plunged into the belly and pulled out the entrails.

I started talking again. 'Have you ever met another man like him, your whole life? I haven't. I was the one who convinced him to come here and that makes me suffer now. Understand?'

'Yes, I do.'

'You said that maybe he's talking to a ghost when he sits on the seashore at night. What's he asking this invisible creature for?'

Patroclus raised his eyes to mine. 'Revenge,' he said.

AND REVENGE it was.

As soon as the Trojans realized that Achilles had withdrawn – he was nowhere to be seen, nor was his sparkling silver and orichalch chariot, nor were his magnificent bronze-clad steeds, Xanthus the blond and Balius the dappled – they took heart. Our own ranks were daunted and jumpy. To the point that one day, like when a shepherd secretly sets fire to a luxuriant forest in order to have more grazing land for his sheep, a rumour spread like wildfire among the men: that the chiefs had decided to return home. Thousands of warriors surged to the beached ships and started pushing them out to sea. All the kings were gripped by panic; no one knew how to react. It was my goddess who spoke to me, placing her bronze hand on my shoulder: 'Stop them!'

I obeyed. I shouted like a madman: 'Stop, Achaians! Where are you going?' I whirled my sceptre like a club, driving away anyone who dared approach one of the ships. I hit some of them: on their backs, their shoulders, their faces. No one dared to strike back. At that point, the other kings came to my aid and we finally managed to herd all of them into a single area, where we held a huge assembly. I found myself standing next to Calchas and said to him, in a low voice: 'Give me a prophecy . . . tell me that Troy will fall within a year! I want it now!' And in an instant he was telling me a story, true or false, about a portent that had occurred in Aulis before our departure.

I shouted out: 'Listen to me!' and before I knew it the men had fallen silent. I told them of how a red-headed serpent had crawled out from under the altar at Aulis, slithered up a plane tree and devoured eight sparrow chicks, and their mother as well when she came too close, chirping in protest. Then the serpent turned into stone. We would fight for nine solid years and then Troy would fall in the tenth year.

'Don't tell me you think you can go now! Run off like a bunch of cowards! Stay here and fight! Troy will be razed to the ground. I promise you! I swear to you!' I didn't even know what I was saying but I was shouting so loud that my throat was bleeding. Everyone had to hear me.

Even the other kings were looking incredulously at me. Where on earth were my words coming from?

'And now, everyone in combat formation!' Agamemnon echoed me.

It was a memorable day. We had hit our stride and we were a formidable force again. Diomedes had become the new Achilles.

The son of Peleus and his Myrmidons may have disappeared from the battlefield, but the king of Argus had started to shine like the new star of the war. At the first opportunity he raced out on his chariot, driven by Sthenelus, the son of Capaneus, who had fought with Tydeus at seven-gated Thebes. He urged his chargers into a gallop and broke through the Trojan ranks like a boulder rolling down a steep slope, overturning and smashing everything he found in his path. He struck out with his spear and his sword, without respite, animated by an inexhaustible strength. His passage left behind a host of corpses, strewn over the bloodied ground; his servants didn't even have the time to strip the bodies to seize their armour and precious ornaments.

I found myself at another point of the front line with my Ithacans and Cephalonians and I could see the other kings fighting with a vigour I'd never seen before, as if they wanted to prove that they didn't need Achilles to defeat the Trojans, no matter how many enemy warriors they had to take on. It was said that Athena herself, as well as Ares and Apollo, took part in the battle that day and that Athena had removed from Diomedes' eyes the cloud that prevents mortals from seeing the gods. A dreadful vision that I was spared.

Once I was sucked into the whirlwind of the battle, the cries, the whinnying, the roar of the chariots, the flashing of the armour, I threw myself into the fray as well *with a violence that I would unleash only once more in my life.* I took on anyone who got in my way, slashing, thrusting, killing. The lamb grazing on the fields of Ithaca had become a huge white ram with curved horns, possessed with the awesome, unfailing strength of a bull.

All at once I saw Diomedes hurtling in his chariot towards Aeneas, who was second in strength only to Hector among all the Trojans. He charged him without hesitation. I saw his helmet glittering in the sun and the tip of his spear swaying as he weighed the shaft in his hand, preparing to hurl it. Then he plunged into the melee and I lost sight of him, as I could not let myself be distracted from the battle raging on every side of me, with its deafening din.

Upon my return I learned, and saw for myself, that Aeneas had saved himself at the last moment by leaping off his chariot but had lost his two splendid chargers, which I saw being led away by Sthenelus. They were steeds of ancient, noble lineage, a gift from the gods to one of Aeneas' ancestors. From that moment on, they followed Diomedes. Aeneas had escaped death through a true miracle and unfortunately we would have to face him again.

Hector appeared then, a powerful vision clad in bronze, fresh to the fight, and the battle began to turn in favour of the Trojans. I sent in the only man we had who had a chance of stopping him: Great Ajax. Steady as a rock, the only hero to rely solely on his own stamina and strength; it was never said that he had been helped by one of the gods. They'd already given him his incredible bulk and seemed unwilling to give him anything else. Like packs of dogs assailing a boar, the Trojan warriors swarmed around him, and he struck down a great many of them, so many he didn't have time to strip them of their arms and take home his prizes; it was all he could do to wrench his spear out of the bodies of the fallen. He'd plant his foot heavily on the body and yank it out with one hand while the other held up his enormous shield against a constant hail of arrows.

Ajax of Locris was at his side, as he had been so many times before, so his lightning swiftness was added to Great Ajax's power, but not even the two of them together could check Hector's driving force. It seemed that arrows and spears could not strike him; as if a god were deflecting them with an unseen hand. And thus we continued until nightfall, when darkness separated the combatants. It had been Diomedes' day. Like a star he had shone: a formidable warrior, fierce and flashing with his own light in the sun's rays. Aeneas would have certainly been crushed by his blows, had a god not snatched him from death that day. Although at the end we had been forced to yield ground, we had killed a great number of enemies and curbed Hector's onslaught.

As we were returning to camp, I saw Patroclus again, sitting in front of his tent. Behind him, at the end of the beach, were the powerful Myrmidons, swimming in the sea and frolicking like children. Shock overwhelmed me. Here were my men dragging themselves back to camp, wetting the ground with their blood. One comrade sat not two feet away from me with his back to a rock, groaning as another man extracted an arrow from his thigh. The hours following a battle were the most grievous. As long as you are fighting, it seems like you are in another world, in another place, you feel neither fear nor pain, you become invaded by a frenzied inebriation, like the feeling produced by wine, by fever and by love, all together. It's the nearness of death that makes you feel that way. Afterwards, you sink into a state of quiet desperation; a sort of fear. Fear of emptiness, fear of the dark.

I gestured to Patroclus, raising my chin as if to enquire if anything had changed. He shook his head. Achilles had not got his fill of revenge yet; he hadn't seen enough to appease his wrath. He wanted to watch and savour the scene: that's why he had stayed and had not weighed anchor to return to Phthia, where his old father watched the waves every day, longing to catch a glimpse of his son's ships.

The dead and wounded were counted up. Even Diomedes had been wounded, in the shoulder. Sthenelus had dragged him away from the front line to the shelter of their chariot, where the Argive warriors had closed ranks around him so that Sthenelus could extract the iron point as Diomedes never stopped shouting: 'Let me go back! I have to kill the man who hit me!' And no sooner than that, he was back in the brawl, searching for the Lycian warrior who had wounded him. The man's name was Pandarus, and when he saw Diomedes reappear he stopped dead in his tracks, as incredulous as if he had seen a ghost returning from Hades, and it was thus that he was run through by the relentless spear of Diomedes, son of Tydeus.

In the following days we fought and fought and fought. It would have been impossible not to, even if we had desired to stop. The Trojans, led by Hector, Deiphobus and Aeneas, who was miraculously on his feet again, surged out of the gates every day, and we had to stop them if we didn't want them to advance all the way to our ships. One day, Hector stepped forward and launched a challenge: he was prepared to take on any one of our champions willing to face him in single combat. It was strange, very strange behaviour indeed, and I wasn't expecting it. The Trojan prince had always avoided a one-on-one encounter because he knew his adversary would be Achilles. Now, sure of winning, he was daring us to a duel so that he could pick off another one of our bravest combatants, destroy the pride of the entire army and break their will to fight.

I remember that terrible moment. Fear froze us all. Shame did not suffice to restore our courage. Menelaus was the first to advance, shouting: 'I will face the Trojan prince. It is my duty, unless someone who can match him steps forward.' Nestor, king of Pylos, rained insults and disdain on us. He lamented his lost youth, cursed the white hair that prevented him from taking on the bold challenger. Then Agamemnon, our high commander, stood. Diomedes followed his example, as did Ajax of Locris, and Great Ajax son of Telamon, and then Idomeneus, lord of Crete and of the labyrinth, and even Merion, his shield-bearer, and Thoas, king of Calydon. At least four of them had no chance against the man-slaughtering strength of Hector.

I stood last, hoping not to be chosen. I wanted to survive. I wanted to return to Penelope, to whom I whispered my love every night when the sun sank into the purple sea, I wanted to hear Telemachus calling me '*atta*', I wanted to see sea-kissed Ithaca again. But I would have fought had I been chosen.

There were nine of us.

The lots were put into Agamemnon's helmet and he shook it. A herald picked one out and held it high so all of us could see it. Ajax, colossal Ajax! We exalted. And he – the Achaian bulwark, the walking mountain – rose to his feet. The shield made of seven bull hides, covered with bronze, was like a tower. His sallet was lowered over his face, letting only his eyes be seen, and they were glittering ominously in the darkness of the helmet. His hand gripped his massive five-cubit-long spear. His footsteps made the earth shake. Hector paled. He had perhaps never found himself face to face with the son of Telamon, and fear nipped at his heart like a dog.

They stood facing each other. Ajax shouted: 'Did you believe there was no Achaian capable of beating you? It's true that Achilles has left the fight. You no longer see him among us, otherwise you would never have dared to make such a challenge. But there are other Achaians no less powerful than he, if lacking his fame! Well now, prince of the Trojans . . . bring it on!'

Hector replied: 'Don't treat me like an ignorant child, or like a woman, Ajax. I'm an expert in war and massacre! Show me what you have!'

Hector impetuously hurled his spear: it passed through six ox-hides and stopped at the seventh. Ajax threw his own: the tip pierced Hector's shield and his breastplate and tore his tunic, but only just scratched his skin. Each ripped the spear from the other's shield and they attacked each other again like famished lions. In their hand-to-hand duel, Ajax thrust his spear at Hector's shield and its tip slit the skin on his neck. We saw blood and a roar erupted from our army. But once again, it was only a surface wound. Hector lifted a boulder and pitched it at his adversary: it thundered upon impact but the seven-hide shield was not damaged. Ajax picked up an even huger boulder and let it fly; its impact knocked Hector off his feet and Ajax ground the stone into him. It looked as if he would crush the man under his own shield. We were ready to claim victory, but incredibly the Trojan prince twisted out from under that immense weight, drew a long breath, recovered his strength and challenged Ajax again, with his sword this time.

They fought for hours without pause, with an energy that seemed unceasing although they were burning with thirst, dripping with sweat and smeared with blood. Until night fell between them. As soon as the sun disappeared under the horizon, Talthybius and Ideus, the heralds of the two armies, approached and thrust their sceptres between the two combatants. The fighting ended. The two champions exchanged words of praise and precious gifts: Ajax's brilliant purple baldric and Hector's silver-studded sword – glorious objects that would, for years, speak of such a formidable contest. *I always wondered: what would have happened had Ajax killed Hector?* What would everyone have thought then of the wrath of Achilles, who had sacrificed the lives of thousands of comrades to his wounded pride? But it was fated that the most powerful, generous and faithful of our companions would not be able to bring our endeavour to an end.

We returned to camp, to rest after a day of fatigue, fear, anxiety and mourning. The field was covered with dead bodies. I reached my tent and my ship. There was nothing I wanted more than to plunge into the sea, yearning to be born again from its clear waters and shining waves. When I emerged, I was, in fact, calmer in my heart and more lucid in my head.

28

A VOICE FROM A LONG TIME AGO called out, close to me: 'Wanax Odysseus!'

I turned: a young warrior with the marks of combat on his body and face, and in the feverish light of his eyes. 'Eumelus!'

'It's been a long time since we've spoken, wanax, but I always see what you're doing here and I admire you for it; your resourceful mind, your eloquence.'

'In a place like this, when you don't see a person for some time it's easy to think he doesn't exist any more . . . you didn't use to call me wanax.'

'You're the king of Ithaca, and I honour you.'

I sat down on a bench and had another one taken from my tent, along with two cups of wine from jars kept cool in the seawater. One of the women I'd been given as my share of the spoils after helping to conquer an Asian city brought me these things.

'You should have come sooner. We went through so much together,' I offered.

'I'm sorry. I don't know why, but I didn't dare, and the longer I waited the more I was ashamed at myself for waiting! So much time has gone by since then. And Hercules is dead . . .' said Eumelus.

'Hercules can't have died. He just disappeared from our world. He was certainly welcomed by the gods, because he lived such a bitter existence; he suffered unspeakable sorrows and in the end he simply couldn't bear to be separated from those he loved. But he always took on any task, no matter how impossible, to help those who could not defend themselves. Sometimes I think back on those days and I think of your parents, *wanax* Admetus, *wanaxa* Alcestis, your mother, an incomparable woman, beautiful and proud, more generous than any other. How did you say goodbye to her?'

Before Eumelus lowered his eyes, I could see his dismay. 'I promised them that when I returned, my ships would be laden with bronze and silver and precious fabrics,' he said.

'Nothing else?'

'Every night I think of my mother. I wonder what she's like now, whether she has overcome the memory of the fate she had agreed to suffer.'

'Is that why you came to fight this war? To escape your mother's tears? Your father's confusion?'

'Of course; in part, anyway. But I can vividly remember that night I scraped the stones near your door. The time I spent in that place was endless and terrifying for me, but just meeting Hercules was enough to make it all worthwhile. I'll never forget him.'

Time flew as we recalled times and emotions gone by, dredging them up from the bottoms of our hearts, as the air around us grew dark and the sea slowly calmed. We were sometimes silent: another way of sharing our common memories and drawing strength from those we had loved. We were startled by the voice of a herald and the heavy footfalls of a man clad in bronze. '*Wanax* Odysseus, you are summoned to the council of kings and princes, immediately. The Trojan herald, noble Ideus, is here at the camp and has asked to be received by the council and to present a request.'

The man covered in bronze was Diomedes.

'We need someone who can use words better than a sword,' he continued.

I laid a hand on Eumelus' shoulder: 'I have to go, *pai*, this may be important. But I see that you have a splendid team yoked to your chariot and I hope you'll be back soon to show me what they're worth at a gallop.'

Eumelus smiled and embraced me: 'Whenever you want, *wanax*, they'll be waiting for you!'

Almost all of the commanders had already gathered at the circle on the seashore, with torches lit all around. Others were still arriving, depending on how far their tents were from the meeting place. Then Agamemnon asked for silence and turned the floor over to the herald.

'I come on behalf of King Priam,' said Ideus. 'An assembly was held this evening. Noble Antenor proposed, first of all, that we return Helen and pay reparations, and secondly that we ask for a truce to allow us to bury our dead. Paris responded to the first request stating that he would be willing to give back all the treasure taken as booty and add more as reparation, but that he would not return Helen under any circumstances. King Priam supports the request for a truce. I have come to obtain your approval for this and return to Troy, if possible, with an agreeable response.'

Antenor had never ceased in his attempts to stop the bloody war and return Helen, but Paris was still strong and Priam was not yet ready to contradict him.

Diomedes, who was standing next to me, stepped up to speak, even before Menelaus. 'I say we refuse Paris' proposal: we simply cannot accept. What's more, if they've come forward with this request, it means that their people are tired of the war and don't want to pay for the prince's errors with more blood. They've realized that we can win, even without Achilles. On the other hand, we can accept the proposal of a truce. It is only right that each side gathers up their dead and celebrates proper funeral rites.'

Menelaus spoke next: 'Diomedes has expressed my own thoughts. A sacred right that we all swore to protect has been violated, and making amends can only mean one thing, exactly what wise Antenor has proposed: Helen's return. We cannot accept other proposals.'

The others spoke up to say things that left no room at all for negotiations. I was surprised that no one asked me to speak. The reason became clear to me when Agamemnon asked me to accompany Ideus on my own to the edge of the battlefield, after he had exchanged courteous words with the herald and asked him to thank Antenor for his judicious words to the assembly.

'Noble Ideus,' I began as soon as we had started walking, 'wanax Diomedes and wanax Menelaus could say nothing different from what they said, but now no one can hear us and we can use other words, different ones; perhaps we can seek another, less impervious path to our goal.'

'I'm listening, King Odysseus. Many in Troy remember your wise speech and believe that had we listened to you then much heartache would have been avoided.'

'There is a possible solution. What King Priam and King Menelaus cannot accept in the light of the sun can be done in the darkness of night, with a secret agreement.'

Ideus stopped and sought my eyes in the gloom. 'Speak,' he said.

'Turn Helen over to me. I'll be at the old port, in disguise, whenever it suits you. With a symbolic token of reparation. Huge quantities of bronze, gold and silver are not the likely companions of a man seeking to escape notice.'

'Would Menelaus accept?'

'No one can resist Helen, least of all Menelaus. Taking her back to Sparta would be a sufficient trophy for him.'

I had hoped that Ideus had been given the authority to negotiate; what I'd proposed would resolve everything, restore life to two peoples and allow all of us to stop thinking about death day after day. His brief silence filled me with anxiety.

'It's very unlikely they'll agree to it,' he answered, finally. 'Now it's Hector who is the biggest obstacle. Not even Andromache, his wife, who begs him not to expose himself to danger, can hold him back. He thinks he can win. He's a warrior, and the glory of defeating the greatest army of all times, of drowning it in the sea and burning its ships, would turn him into a god for the people of his city. That is a prize too big to give up. He would refuse what you're proposing and without him we can't do it. Nevertheless, I will try. If I can arrange what you suggest, in three days' time you'll see a light at the foot of the wild fig, at this time of night. Tomorrow the truce for gathering up the dead will be in force.'

I nodded. He said nothing about Achilles. He did not mention his name, nor did I. But his ghost was there between us, a mute giant whose absence made the winds of war favour our enemies.

Each of us went off on his own road.

The next day, before the sun rose, the gates of Troy opened and families streamed out over the field covered with dead bodies. The Achaians mixed with them, disentangling and separating the cadavers that were still bound together in the final spasms of combat. Both sides loaded the dead onto carts.

The pyres burned all night and every night, as long as the truce was in force. Only the commanders were given the honour of having their names shouted out ten times by the warriors drawn up in formation. Their swords were ritually bent and their remains were preserved in finely decorated, well-made urns. All the others became ashes without a name, covered up by earth or blown off on the wind. On the third day, I spent the night scanning the plain but I saw no light illuminating the trunk of the wild fig tree. No hope.

When we started fighting again, it became clear that neither our bravery or strength, nor the passion we poured into winning honour on the field of battle, was enough to keep the Trojans away from our camp. They were the ones assaulting us; it was they who launched the attacks. We had to resort to digging a deep trench and erecting a rampart with a palisade to defend our ships. If the enemy managed to burn them, our fates would be sealed. It was an enormous structure that could be seen from a great distance. We raised it in no time; a monument to our fear.

On the night that we finished the sky grew black with storm clouds and the roar of thunder made the earth shake. We were together in Agamemnon's tent, drinking wine. I saw the glimmering red liquid tremble in my cup. I watched as Menelaus grew pale. This was a terrible omen.

But the truce was over. The next day, Hector led his men into an attack. We climbed the rampart and crossed the trench and drew up our ranks. Agamemnon gave a shout and raised his arm, brandishing his spear, from on high on his chariot. We rushed forward. We ran, closely united, one alongside the other, without thinking, our minds empty, our hearts seeming to burst in our chests, our breath not finding a way out from between clenched, gnashing teeth, our feet devouring the space that still separated us from impact, from the mouth of Hades. Myriad shields clashed, raising an unearthly uproar to the skies. The ground turned red in an instant, slippery with spilt blood. The sky was black above us. Enormous, swollen, yellow-rimmed clouds sailed above us, bursting with thunderbolts, but no rain, only blood, everywhere, and we were blinded by the red as we were slashed and crushed and we shouted, shouted, shouted!

A flash of lightning struck the tip of Ajax son of Telamon's spear. The giant fell to his knees. Swarms of arrows were flying everywhere, men fell to the ground, others took shelter behind their shields. Terrified, we began to retreat: Zeus himself was fighting against us! Diomedes himself pulled back, as did both Ajaxes, and Idomeneus. Nestor, who had advanced too far on his chariot, remained isolated. An arrow struck one of his horses on top of his head between his ears, piercing into his brain. The horse collapsed to the ground and the old warrior fell over as well. He struggled to his feet and stood, alone, next to the overturned chariot. Hector was closing in on him, charging at him, unrestrained. I could see it happening but I was terror-stricken and I ran the other way, fleeing. Diomedes shouted: 'Odysseus! Where are you running to? Turn back, defend the old man, he'll never make it alone!' But I was past any understanding, I wasn't hearing, wasn't feeling, wasn't breathing, was left with nothing: no strength, no courage, no shame.

I heard Diomedes screaming again: 'You'll die with a spear in your back, you coward!' I crossed the ditch, the palisade, took shelter on my ship, and hid.

The din of the battle, crashing furiously against the wall, reached all the way to where I was but it didn't touch me, bent in two under the benches, weeping. Hiding. I could feel how cold it was and I wanted darkness to come, wanted the night black as pitch to cover me, cover the camp and the ships and the faces of the living and the dead.

Darkness, dense shadows, burning tears. And finally, silence.

How much time passed, how much pain? I finally got to my feet. The wind was blowing from the mountains and I climbed up the ship's mast, reached the top, panting, and looked out over the plain. Fires were burning in the deep gloom, hundreds, thousands, myriads of fires. There would be no truce, no way out this time. Hector besieged us, waiting for dawn, as patient as a starving wolf. He was waiting to mount the final attack and end the war. Then I saw fires being lit in the camp, on this side of the rampart. I heard shouting and the long blaring of the horn.

Time went by, silence, then a voice. The voice of the son of Tydeus, wild and indomitable.

'The old man wants to talk to you,' said Diomedes. 'Agamemnon, too. In his tent.'

'Talk to me? About what?'

'Achilles has to come back. Nothing else can save us. Everything is against us.'

He said nothing about my ignominious flight, and I was grateful to him for that. I followed him to Agamemnon's tent.

I found him sitting with Nestor, Idomeneus, both of the Ajaxes, Menelaus and his heralds. Diomedes sat down with them and I next to him.

Nestor, whose face and body still showed signs of his ruinous fall, turned to me: 'Agamemnon has recognized his error and is ready and willing to make amends, but you must convince Achilles to come back and fight at our side. The Trojans are much bolder and more aggressive now that they know that Achilles won't fight, and we do not have the strength to win without him. Agamemnon offers as reparation enormous riches in bronze, gold and silver, one of his daughters in marriage with seven villages as her dowry, fertile fields with herds and flocks, grapevines and olive trees, and seven beautiful maidens, including Briseis, whom Achilles so loved and who was unjustly taken from him. Agamemnon swears on his honour that he has not touched her; he has not taken her into his bed and she herself will confirm that. Go, Odysseus, only you can convince him. He trusts you.'

Agamemnon spoke next. His face was pale and he seemed exhausted with the strain of combat and lack of sleep. 'Take his cousin Ajax, whom he esteems greatly, with you. Convince him, Odysseus, and you will forever have my gratitude and that of my brother Menelaus.'

I saw that Diomedes was watching me as well, waiting to see what intentions I had.

I answered: 'I will go because I suffer to see my comrades, our warriors, slaughtered on that blood-soaked field. I can only hope that Athena will guide us and inspire our words.'

We left and headed towards Achilles' camp, walking along the seashore. A lamp burned inside the tent, casting a dim glow all around. Patroclus was awake and saw us coming. He came to meet us and led us inside to meet with his friend Achilles, the stubborn, vexed warrior still thirsting for revenge.

Achilles greeted us like old friends: 'Odysseus, Ajax, what brings you here in the middle of the night? Shouldn't you be in bed resting? I'm happy in any case to see you, to welcome you to join me here in my tent, to offer you a cup of wine and exchange a few words.'

'Achilles, you know well why we've come. Don't you hear the screams of our comrades? Haven't you noticed the pyres burning for days? Listen to what I have to say: Agamemnon has realized that he has wronged you and he wants to make amends. He offers you great riches, one of his daughters in marriage with seven cities as a dowry, and seven beautiful women, including your beloved Briseis. He swears that he has not touched her, that he has respected her . . .'

He was shaking his head even as I spoke and my words died in my throat.

'No, my friend. No, I don't trust him, I don't believe him, I have no respect for him. His words are air for me. And what's more, it's too late. I've decided: I'm leaving, Odysseus. Tomorrow I'll set sail and if the weather assists me we'll be home in three or four days. Home, do you understand that? We've spent years and years in this bloody, horrible place. We've forgotten everything, neglected everything else, wasted years of our lives. Life, Odysseus! Our only true treasure! One of his daughters? I'd never marry her even if she were more beautiful than Aphrodite. There are lots of pretty girls where I come from, you know? Daughters of illustrious, noble men of great lineage. I don't need his gifts. My father has a palace full of gifts. I can't even imagine how happy my old *atta* will be to see me. And what are you all worried about anyway? You've built a rampart and a palisade. That should be enough to stop Hector, shouldn't it?'

He was playing with us. But I tried again. I couldn't give up. 'Don't you care about your comrades? You've seen them coming back from the battlefield wounded and bloodied. You've seen them burning on the pyres. Won't you forgo your revenge, for them?'

'No, Odysseus. None of what happened is my fault. He treated me like nothing, took away the woman I loved, humiliated me in front of everyone. I fought for him for years and years, I conquered scores of villages and cities, I brought enormous treasure back to him. I did not deserve what he did to me. No. I could have killed him like a dog, but I spared his life so war would not break out among us and destroy the entire army. No, really, I cannot give him this satisfaction. On the contrary, tell the others they should follow my example. You too, Odysseus. You should all go back home. This damned city will never fall.'

'Don't go, Achilles!' I pleaded with him.

'Forget it,' said Ajax. 'He couldn't care less about us. We can all die as far as he's concerned and he wouldn't move a finger. And all over a woman. While we're offering him seven!'

I smiled sadly at my friend's artlessness, but I had to admit he had a point. There was nothing that would convince Achilles to take up arms again.

Patroclus hadn't opened his mouth through any of this, nor did Achilles ever ask him what he thought. Patroclus was simply his shadow, his double. I got up, ready to go back and report on the unhappy outcome of my mission . . .

'Odysseus . . .'

I turned. Was there still hope?

'Maybe . . . maybe I won't leave tomorrow.'

There was nothing else I could ask him and I knew I couldn't insist, but Achilles' words left me a glimmer of hope.

It was quite late by the time we returned. Agamemnon's tent was lit and the other kings were waiting for us.

'Well?' they asked, gathering around us.

'Nothing doing. He's adamant. He even said that the rest of us should follow his example and leave.'

'Let him go wherever the hell he wants!' said Diomedes. 'We'll fight without him. Each one of us will speak to our own men and we'll steel them to the fight. Every battle is different from the next. Today we had trouble, tomorrow victory could be ours.'

The meeting broke up, each of us going our own way.

I looked northward, at the long line of beached ships. In Achilles' tent the light was still on.

29

THE FAILURE OF MY MISSION had made it clear to all of us that we had no alternative but to fight. Turning tail and going home was unthinkable.

The one who felt this most acutely was Agamemnon. He was, after all, our high commander, king of the Achaian kings. His quarrel with Achilles had made him look bad in the men's eyes and had destroyed their fighting spirit, their willingness to take on further sacrifices. It was up to him to set the right example now. He had to be the first to lay his life on the line, prove to them that he deserved the power he exercised with his sceptre.

That was my advice to him. I urged him to concentrate the greatest number of chariots in the area of the front line from which the Trojans would least expect a swift, sudden attack; that is, as far as possible from the access to the rampart and the camp, where our ships were beached. He approved my reasoning and went to ready himself for the battle.

He appeared on his chariot wearing armour that no one had ever seen before. It was blinding, studded with enamel, silver and bronze. On his arm was a huge shield with a Gorgon at the centre, and on his head a double-crested, winged helmet. He was truly an incredible sight. Everyone understood instantly that it would be his day, if only the god who protected Hector would train his gaze elsewhere. Agamemnon's new armour and the change in his colours would make him look like a new, unknown warrior to the enemy. He would seem glorious and dreadful in their eyes and they would surely mistake him for a god or a demigod. Perhaps not even the gods would recognize him at first! His altered appearance had imbued him with overwhelming power and energy.

He charged the Trojan front flanked by our greatest champions, in an onslaught of chariots, horses and warriors that ploughed into the enemy lines with a ferocious crash. Hector, on the opposite end of the front, was easily defeating the less-seasoned warriors drawn up there. I led my men in support of the main attack, pouring into the breach that Agamemnon had created and continued the massacre.

Agamemnon fought like a lion until midday, with a fury that would have amazed even Achilles, slaying at least ten of the enemy by his own hand. For all that time it seemed that nothing and no one could stop him. The storm of unerring blows added to his momentum and inspired those fighting at his side. He was terror personified.

I myself couldn't believe what I was seeing. To our left the tomb of an ancient Trojan king, which surged like a cliff from the waves of the sea, was surrounded by warriors fleeing in every direction. At a certain moment, the Skaian Gate appeared, the city's main bulwark looming over us. As we advanced, I could see limbs and lopped-off heads littering the ground, the work of Agamemnon and the other warriors.

But when the sun rose to the centre of the sky, only then did destiny turn against us. I saw Agamemnon's chariot racing back towards our camp, his face – no longer covered by the helmet! – a mask of pain. The king had been wounded!

Hector must have realized what had happened and he turned in our direction. The sight of him struck terror into our hearts: he was travelling at tremendous speed, overturning everything he found in his way. He had surely seen Agamemnon retreating towards the rampart and imagined he could put us all to flight. Our men were indeed withdrawing towards the camp. Even indomitable Diomedes was yielding ground, and then decidedly pulling back in the face of Hector's rage. What the Trojan prince wanted was to get at our ships and burn them. Now it was my turn to call after Diomedes, and I shouted with all the wind I had in me: 'Where do you think you're going, mate! What happened to your courage? You can't expect me to stop him alone! Give me a hand, together we can do it!'

Diomedes turned towards me and focused on me with that same strange expression he'd had when he picked me out of the crowd at his father's funeral in Argus. A few moments later he was at my side and was aiming his spear. He flung it with a violent thrust at Hector, who was no more than twenty cubits away from us. The shaft flew as straight as an arrow shot from a bow and hit Hector square in the head. We saw him sway and then collapse onto the bottom of his chariot. His driver turned the chariot in the direction of the gate while Diomedes screamed any number of insults after him. He pushed his way through the enemy throng, shoving them aside with his shield and sword, desperate to get his spear back. He didn't trust any other. I didn't want to leave him alone and ran after him, catching up with him just in time: an arrow had nailed his foot to the ground.

I planted myself directly in front of him, protecting him with my shield and trying to keep the enemies flocking in from every direction at a distance.

'Don't let up!' Diomedes yelled. 'I'm going to pull out the arrow!' But as soon as I looked around me, I realized that I'd lost contact with all the others. Diomedes couldn't keep on his feet and his men lifted him onto his chariot and had his driver Sthenelus take him away.

I knew that it was all over for me.

I heard Diomedes' voice, then, as his chariot moved further and further away: 'Don't give up, Odysseus! Don't give up, we'll come back to get you!' I remembered the promise I'd made to Penelope, *that I'd come home from the war*, and I saw her eyes and her filmy gaze. I whirled my sword and spear all around me, making sure that my shield was solidly fastened to my arm. I didn't know how long I'd be able to hold out. I stopped for a moment, gasping for breath, and instantly became the target of an unknown man, *who would soon be given a name: the man who had killed cunning-minded wanax*

Odysseus. A swift, solid spear took flight from his hand as I shouted out the triple war cry of the king of Ithaca:

'He – ha – heee!

'He – ha – heee!

'He – ha – heee!'

The spear had pierced my shield and breastplate without silencing my shout.

But I was at the end of my strength. In no time at all they would have the better of me. I extracted the spear from my shield and breastplate so I could defend myself and I felt hot blood streaming down my thigh. The unknown warrior cried out in exultation, but a sharper, more vigorous cry blared out like a trumpet behind me: 'We're here, Odysseus!' And an enormous shield, a wall of bronze, was raised before me. A huge body covered me, while another bright warrior set himself firmly beside me, on my wounded side. Ajax the Great! Menelaus!

Menelaus grabbed my arm and someone else hoisted me onto a chariot. We took off swiftly, bouncing over fallen bodies and cast-off weapons, in the direction of the ditch and the palisade and then all the way to the ships.

I was eased onto a bed; my armour was taken off me and tossed onto the ground – the noise rang loudly in my ears. Pain seared through my wounded side, but I clenched my jaw shut. There were so many screams of pain all around me.

For a moment I lost the light; I could see nothing at all, but then I felt flames burning my flesh again and smelled an acrid, scorched odour. I opened my eyes to see Eurylochus, my cousin, bending over me with a red-hot dagger in his hand.

'I've stopped the bleeding,' he said. 'You'll heal.'

'What's happening?'

'The only ones still holding out are the two Ajaxes, Idomeneus and Menelaus; all the other commanders are wounded and incapable of fighting. Hector has come back out and he's flanked by his best: Aeneas, Helenus, Deiphobus, even that spineless worm Paris has somehow found some guts and is shooting off arrow after arrow and hitting his mark every time. They left their chariots on the other side of the ditch, descended on foot and climbed back up the side of the rampart. They're pressing against the palisade now with everything they've got, trying to take the gate off its hinges; the bolts look like they may give at any moment. Our men are utterly exhausted. They haven't rested all day, haven't eaten since dawn.'

I felt my heart sinking. Could it be possible that so much toil, blood and grief had all come to this? My goddess hadn't shown herself for such a long time. Perhaps she had abandoned me; even she could not defy fate. Or perhaps she simply no longer loved me. That was natural; after all, how could a being that would never die feel any real emotions?

I said to my cousin: 'Go outside, go to the top of the rampart and then come back to tell me what's happening. This uncertainty is killing me! Go, and take care!'

Eurylochus left and I dropped back down onto the bed, exhausted. My side hurt terribly; the pain was so acute that no other part of my body could relax or rest.

Time passed and then my ears were assaulted by a confused noise: thousands of shouts melting into a single shout, into a single language, into a single, immense, senseless shudder of pain.

How many of us would survive? Who would outlive the massacre and who would be cast headlong into Hades, leaving dreams, desires, hopes to the winds?

As my heart pondered these questions, I heard voices very close to my tent. One of them was familiar to me: Patroclus!

I slipped off the bed onto the floor, dragged myself to the tent entrance and looked outside. There they were, at less than five paces from me: Patroclus, helping one of our warriors who had been wounded. An arrow was sticking out of his thigh and he was bleeding copiously.

It was the wounded man he was talking to: 'I'll get this out of your leg and medicate your wound, but I can't stay long to help you. Nestor has given me an important mission. I have to talk to Achilles at once.'

Before I knew it, Patroclus was running past me.

'Patroclus!' I called out.

'Odysseus! No! You've been wounded as well.'

'So have Agamemnon, Diomedes, and so many others. Even Makahon, our surgeon himself, is down. Patroclus, there's no one at the head of the army. The only men still out there are the two Ajaxes, Menelaus and Idomeneus. I even saw Nestor, old as he is, entering the battlefield to defy death.'

'I'm so sorry,' he said, 'I have to go.'

'Go. But tell me, what mission has the old man given you? I overheard you speaking to that warrior.'

'I can't tell you. I can't tell anyone! No one must know. It's our last hope.'

He fled, swift as the wind. As I was pulling myself back towards the bed, Eurylochus burst in, sweaty and panting. 'Hector has overwhelmed our defences,' he said. 'The Trojans are pouring in from every direction. They're carrying torches!'

'Help me,' I replied. 'Bandage this wound as tightly as you can, and help me get my armour on. I won't die in a bed.'

I LEFT THE TENT, leaning on my spear, and headed to Agamemnon's tent, where I found Diomedes as well. We decided to join our men who were still in combat; our presence would give them courage, if nothing else.

The clash became even fiercer. Hector sensed that victory was very close at hand; he was convinced that Zeus himself was protecting him and he seemed animated by unrelenting energy. But our own men were emboldened to see that Diomedes and I were still alive and they regrouped compactly around Idomeneus, the two Ajaxes and Menelaus.

The battle dragged on without either side prevailing, but with heavy losses on one side and the other. Severed heads rolled on the ground under my feet, others were hurled by the Achaians towards the Trojan ranks. Men with spear shafts run through them front to back keeled over onto the ground, their fingers clawing into the sand in the spasm of death. I could see Agamemnon's face, sallow with anguish, his features tense and twisted, his hand spasmodically gripping the handle of his spear.

The howl of battle swelled in intensity until it pierced the clouds. The wind of madness had enveloped me again, whipping me into a delirium that made me feel I was outside of myself. I was no longer in my body, in my time, in that place. I was no longer perceiving what was around me, not measuring with my eyes or with my mind. It was in that kind of dimension that I could feel the presence of the gods and if Athena had removed the fog that prevents mortals from seeing them, they would have appeared to me in their true guise. If only I could have taken up arms, if only my wounded side would sustain me!

Hector's torch was getting closer and closer to our vessels. The battle was raging within sight of the ships; at certain spots even between one craft and another. The bulk of enemy forces was trying to isolate the ship of Protesilaus, the furthest from the centre of the camp, the closest to the rampart and the most exposed to the wind. If that ship was set ablaze the fire would spread to all the others.

Ajax jumped onto the beached ship that had never been put to sea since the moment of our landing. He planted himself at the prow and grabbed with both hands an enormous spear with a huge metal head built for naval warfare. Many men were normally required to handle it; they would push it with great thrusts into the keels of enemy ships below the waterline in an attempt to sink them. But Ajax brandished it with no help, mowing down his adversaries, running through two or three of them at once. Men dropped to the ground all around him as he leapt from one rowing bench to another, roaring like a lion. Arrows rained like hail on his helmet, on the shoulders covered by a double plate of bronze, but he seemed not to feel them. His heart must have been shouting in his chest: 'Hold out, do battle, rock of the Achaians, mountain that walks, do not give in to the fatigue cramping your muscles, to the pain in your chest. Hold out, friend, Great Ajax!'

It was all useless anyway. Even Ajax, surrounded on every side like a boar by a pack of dogs, would fall. It was just a question of time. Ajax never asked the gods for succour; the only help he got was from his own arms, his great heart, and his friend of the same name. All at once, I became aware that what I was seeing was changing slowly before my eyes. *I wasn't seeing what was real.* Colours were melting into one another and the racking scream of the battle, the shrill choir of thousands of men hit, pierced, slashed, was fused for me into a single strain, the same the solitary poet had sung for me at the port that night so many years before. *Could that be me, crying such a bitter cry?* I was like a man who has fallen into a swirling river who can no longer fight the force of the current. Arrows were whistling by me alongside my head, my neck, but I could do nothing to bend or dodge them. I didn't know, couldn't see, couldn't feel. And as I awaited the final blow I sought deep inside myself the strength to shout out the triple war cry of the king of Ithaca for the last time.

But the sound changed. It was a roar now, of thunder in a storm, the clash of thousands and thousands of shields beaten by thousands of swords. Something had changed the course of events; the scale of fate had sharply, swiftly tilted. The shouting I'd heard, so confused and unrecognizable at first, became clear and distinct. The shout was: 'Achilles!'

How was that possible? Ignoring my pain, I ran towards Protesilaus' ship which was already being licked by fire. Hundreds of men with buckets and urns, with their own helmets, were throwing water at the flames, extinguishing them as they were born. The Trojans were fleeing as the Myrmidons exited their tents in their black, shining armour, a warrior as luminous as the star of Orion leading them. Orion, the most magnificent of all stars, but always accompanied by grief, tears and misfortune.

It was him. Blindingly bright in his divine armour, a fury with his spear and sword. Reaper of men. He was a dazzling sight on his chariot and the Achaians were all streaming towards him. At his side were Menelaus, mighty Idomeneus, Ajax of Locris and

Ajax son of Telamon both. Great Ajax had cast off his exhaustion and had once again taken up the shield of the seven oxhides. He was advancing with the others. I could see clearly now, could see Diomedes and Agamemnon at my side, watching incredulously as the Achaians were swept up in the impetus of the unstoppable warrior and were murderously chasing the terrorized Trojans in a rout towards the Skaian Gate.

We made our way to the palisade so we could watch the flight of the Trojans as they scrambled across the ditch and sought refuge behind the gates of their city walls. Hector, back in his chariot, was among them. And there was Achilles' sparkling helmet, topped by its swaying crest, crossing over as well. Automedon, his charioteer, dashed over hastily laid planks, urging on his master's prodigious steeds, Balius and Xanthus, in hot pursuit. We lost sight of him then.

Diomedes shouted: 'Achilles is back!'

As much as I wanted to, I could not believe in his words. I turned to Agamemnon and said: 'It's not Achilles. It's Patroclus.'

'How can you say that?' asked Agamemnon.

'I overheard Patroclus talking about a mission that Nestor had given him, and I asked him about it. He was in a rush and said that he couldn't say anything, that it was a secret, but that it was the only thing that could save us from a complete rout. I'll tell you what has happened: Patroclus has donned Achilles' armour, taken his chariot and his driver. *Wanax* Agamemnon, quickly, send someone out to the field. We have to know what is going on.'

Agamemnon didn't wait to be asked twice; he dispatched one of his most trustworthy shield-bearers, Alcathous. He told him to take a chariot and two rested horses and to go after the army. And not to lose sight of Achilles. That's what he called him. And then to come back at once and report to us. The man did as he was ordered. I kept my gaze trained on him as long as I could, until he dissolved into the red dust that covered everything.

Our army continued to advance, nothing could stop them as they surged towards the Skaian Gate in waves, like the sea in a storm.

'That has to be Achilles, who else could have done this?' said Agamemnon.

'It's the terror of Achilles, not the man himself, that has turned the tide. The mere sight of his armour, his chariot, his driver, has spread sheer terror among the Trojans.'

We fell silent for a long time, unable to say a single word. Our eyes were fixed on the army as we measured the distance that separated them from the wild fig tree and then from the Skaian Gate. It was rapidly diminishing; they were truly closing in. I bit my lower lip until it bled and the pain in my side sharpened as if a spear were piercing my flesh at that very moment. Where had Alcathous, Agamemnon's shield-bearer, disappeared to? Why wasn't he back? Had he been killed?

I can't remember how much time had passed when I was shaken by the cry of Diomedes: 'Something's happening, look! Our men are retreating!'

Then a chariot streaked across the plains before us at a tremendous speed: only Achilles' horses could run so fast! A black foreboding gripped my heart but I said nothing. It wasn't long before we could make out the colours of Achilles' chariot and the figure of his charioteer, and then, almost in its wake, the chariot of Alcathous, which roared to a halt at the gate. The shield-bearer was panting hard by the time he reached us and we could see that he had participated in the fighting himself.

'What's happened? Talk!' ordered Agamemnon.

'It wasn't Achilles! It was Patroclus in Achilles' armour,' he replied. 'He was racing forward at an awesome rate at first, it seemed that no one or nothing could stop him, but then something happened. Perhaps he'd isolated himself by going too far, too fast; he must have been trying to reach the Trojan prince and kill him. When he was finally face to face with Hector, a Trojan warrior behind him thrust a spear into his back. And then Hector had an easy time finishing him off and stripping Achilles' armour from his body.'

'What about his body?' I asked. 'Patroclus' body, where is it?'

'A terrible brawl broke out over his corpse. The Trojans had managed to tie a rope to his foot and were trying to drag him over to their side, but then Menelaus and the two Ajaxes threw themselves into the fray, striking out in every direction, and won his body back. Just as I was leaving to come back and report to you, Hector himself entered into the melee and was determined to claim the body for himself. Ajax and *wanax* Menelaus managed to lift the body from the ground and hoist it up to their shoulders, so that all of our men could see that the corpse of Patroclus was still ours and would take heart. They're retreating on foot, in order to bring him back here, to deliver his body to Achilles, but I don't know if they'll succeed, the Trojans are attacking from all sides like rabid dogs.'

'Only Achilles can stop them,' I said.

'How? He has no arms or armour. The only suit that would fit him might be Ajax's, but he needs it himself, more than he ever has.'

'Take me to Achilles!' I said. 'At once!'

Alcathous helped me get into his chariot and he drove the horses wildly towards the Myrmidons' camp. Every bump we hit caused me stabbing pain and I was afraid my wound would open up again, but we never slowed down until we reached the tent of Achilles. Automedon, the charioteer, was tying the steeds to a ship's mast, which had been driven into the ground, when Achilles came out. He knew. He looked as though a lightning bolt had struck him. Pale, he was, and still. Deathly shaken. I'd never seen him that way.

'Achilles,' I said, 'no one could have imagined that he would dare so much . . . but a battle is raging now over his body. We can't leave him; they would throw him to the dogs and vultures. Ajax and Menelaus won't be able to hold out much longer and the weight of Patroclus' body is holding them up. Our enemies are close to the camp already. Stop them, Achilles! You're the only one who can do it!'

Achilles looked at me as if I were mad. Then my words struck home. He ran up the rampart, racing as swiftly as the wind, and there he stood, his legs planted wide. He brought his hands to his mouth and let out his war cry. It was as if a great bellow had erupted from the earth, like the roar of a lion that became the shrill shriek of an eagle: long, never-endingly long, and deafening.

Our men reacted as if a mysterious energy had invaded their exhausted limbs, and they all shouted out together, uniting their voices to the vehement cry of the prince of the Myrmidons. The Trojans fled in terror, their horses rearing up at the ditch and tearing off at a wild gallop in every direction.

Before the sun had set on the horizon, Ajax son of Telamon, Ajax of Locris and Menelaus, weary and spent, entered from the rampart gate, escorting the body of Patroclus, which had been hoisted onto the shoulders of four Myrmidon warriors. The rest of the army lined the way, in honour of the hero who had given his life to save them from defeat and destruction.

30

I MET ACHILLES VERY LATE that same night, after silence had long fallen over the camp. The exhaustion of such a dreadful, endless day, that had drained the men's hearts and their limbs, had plunged them into a sleep so deep it resembled death. All that could be heard was the intermittent cries of the sentries who were watching over the rampart and the ditch.

No one had asked for a truce, like we had so many times before, because there wasn't a single man either inside the walls of Troy or in the naval camp who could imagine for a moment that a truce was possible. Achilles was honour-bound by Patroclus' death to claim revenge, and it was sure to be as bloody and brutal as he could make it. There would be no escape for anyone. Blood could only call for more blood, to the most extreme limits.

Ninety-nine Myrmidon warriors, lined up in three rows on three sides, wearing their black tunics and carrying burnished arms, were the honour guard for Patroclus, who lay on a bier, a purple sheet covering his pale, naked body.

Achilles, who had routed an entire army solely by dint of a war cry, sat weeping disconsolately, his face hidden between his hands.

Briseis, who had been returned that same evening by Agamemnon, wept as well, because Patroclus had always treated her with respect and affection, from the first moment she had been taken prisoner. Even the Myrmidon warriors, still and stiff as statues in their funeral vigil, wept silently, tears coursing down their cheeks. But it wasn't only the fallen warrior they mourned, their prince's dearest and most loyal friend. They mourned Achilles:

his inevitable return to the war could only mean a headlong plunge towards his death.

Even Balius and Xanthus, relieved of their yoke and their trappings, their backs covered by gold-embroidered purple caparisons, stood unmoving, their big eyes feverish and shiny, as if they were crying. I had always had so many words at my beck and call, no matter how dire the predicament, but this time my heart suggested nothing and my lips were closed at the sight of that boundless grief.

It was Achilles who spoke: 'Had I listened to you, had I swallowed my wrath, Patroclus would not be dead now. I myself gave him permission to don my armour so he could provide relief for our routed army, and in doing so I brought about his death.'

I didn't have the heart to remind him that Nestor had been behind the plan. 'I could never have imagined it myself, Achilles,' I said. 'When such terrible misfortune strikes, our sorrow leads us to seek thousands of alternatives to the destiny we have suffered, but none of them are possible, none real. Only one, the one that has fiercely wounded us, is true. We are mortals, Achilles, we must accept death.'

'I've always sought death out. All I wanted in exchange was that my name would survive my brief existence. And if my wrath had led me to question whether there might be a different future for myself, now I have no further doubts. Whoever killed him must die. Whatever happens after that has no importance. Go to Agamemnon, tell him that I accept his reparations, but that his gifts are not necessary. What I want from him is that the army be ready for combat tomorrow morning, at the first light of dawn. I will be there with my Myrmidons.'

'Combat? How do you propose to do that? Naked, without your armour? Three of us have already been wounded, must you add grief to our grief? Do you want your own body to rest next to Patroclus' on the pyre? Wait. Tomorrow you will reconcile with Agamemnon in front of the assembled army, and we'll wait until an able craftsman, as there are still many among us, can forge a new suit of armour for you, worthy of you, Achilles. Heed me this time,

Achilles. Once before you refused to accept my counsel and it was not a wise choice you made.'

Achilles looked deeply into my eyes, and I would never forget that look – melancholy and ferocious at the same time. I lay a hand on his shoulder and then went back to my tent at the centre of the naval camp.

The next day, a ceremony of reconciliation was held inside the assembly circle on the sand. Agamemnon sacrificed an animal and solemnly swore that he had never touched Briseis and that she had never shared his bed. The promised gifts were turned over to me and I had them carried in procession to the Myrmidons' camp. Achilles announced that the next day at dawn he would attack, even alone if necessary. We all answered that we would be with him, to win or to perish at his side.

I fell into a nightmare-ridden sleep, but before dawn I saw my goddess hovering over the prow of my ship. She was looking at me intensely. Maybe I was still dreaming, or maybe Athena had wanted me to feel her presence. I pleaded with her: 'Goddess of the green-blue eyes, how will Achilles be able to fight without arms? Has he perhaps convinced giant Ajax to hand over his own?' The goddess answered me with an enigmatic smile and vanished into thin air.

I opened my eyes and felt stronger. My wound was dry and the scar was healing. It made me think of my adventure hunting the boar during that first visit to my grandfather Autolykos. I wondered where he might be. Whether he'd had news of this interminable war, of this endless massacre.

I had Eurylochus help me put on my armour and I walked to the extreme northern end of the naval camp where Achilles' tent was. A breeze laden with sea salt lapped at Patroclus' body and kept his limbs from suffering decay. Six Myrmidon warriors had watched over him all night. Achilles had ordered that his body not be put on the pyre until he had killed Hector with his own hands. The camp was silent, only the waves of the never-tiring sea let their crashing voice be heard. I walked almost all the way out to the line of the undertow to watch the sun rise. The first ray stopped me dead in amazement. In front of me, hanging on two crossed sticks, was a suit of armour of stupefying splendour: a helmet with a vermilion crest, a breastplate of blinding brilliance, embossed shin plates rimmed with gold plating and a shield completely carved in concentric circles with hundreds of figures. A wonder that would take the very best of the master craftsmen of Hephaestus' art at least a year to complete. I couldn't believe my eyes and I had to get close enough to brush the metal with my fingers to convince myself that it was real.

'See? My armour is ready. I didn't have to ask my cousin Ajax son of Telamon for anything.'

'How did you get this? Who crafted it for you?'

'I don't know. How can one explain a miracle?'

I looked at the glittering gravel all the way down the beach. The foaming waves caressed the tiny multicoloured pebbles, a thousand reflections making them shine like precious stones. I could see *the armour of Achilles carried in by the billows and deposited on the shore.* Had this happened during the salty, bitter night?

I tried to imagine what that splendid armour, jewel of a craftsman's art, would look like that same evening, after being tormented by thousands of blows, disfigured and deformed by the violence of combat.

'A real pity, isn't it?' said Achilles, reading my thoughts.

'It is. But I don't think we have another choice.'

His face suddenly turned grey as metal, his jaw clenched. 'War is the most cruel of all parties, but a party it is. We have to dress up in our best to dance with death. Tonight Hector will be biting the dust, run through by my spear.'

I watched as he approached his horses. He was speaking with them.

'What did you say to Balius and Xanthus, Achilles?' I asked.

'I said: "Bring me back safely to my tent tonight; don't abandon me in the middle of the field as you did with Patroclus."'

'And they? Did they answer you?'

'Certainly. They always answer me.'

'What did they say?'

He half closed his eyes and I saw that he – the inexorable warrior, the ruthless exterminator – was hiding tears. Why such agonizing grief? Many of our companions had died, many of them friends, and I had never seen him show such despair. I looked out towards the sea, towards Patroclus' white, dead body. What glorious deeds had he performed before the one that led to his death? Not a one. Or if he had, no one remembered them, because he was only the shadow of Achilles. All the glory was always for the son of Peleus and of the mysterious, invisible goddess of the sea. But no one can live without his shadow. A man without a shadow no longer has a life. He's only a ghost.

'They said: "We will bring you back once again to your tent safe and sound, Achilles. But, beware. After you've killed Hector, it will be your turn. Your turn to die, and we won't be able to do anything, even if we are as fast as the wind."'

I smiled: 'Maybe they're wrong. They are only horses, after all.'

'They're never wrong, my friend,' he replied. 'Never!'

He jumped onto the chariot where his driver, Automedon, was already waiting for him. The two divine horses, with a solemn step, arched their powerful necks and advanced to the point at which they would join the ranks of the Myrmidon warriors.

They were joined by a multitude of Achaians, all covered in bronze. The gates of the rampart were opened, wooden planks were thrown down over the ditch and the chariots crossed to the other side. Achilles' preceded them all, blazing like the sun. The ranks crossed over behind them on foot: a forest of beechwood spears with shining tips swayed as they moved like a field of wheat in a gentle breeze.

In the distance I could see the Skaian Gate opening at its askew angle, and the secondary gates as well. Two rivers of warriors, on foot and mounted on chariots, surged into a single mighty front. The warriors of Troy felt sure that they could stand against Achilles, they had done so for many a long year, and that day they certainly called upon all the reserves of energy remaining in their hearts and arms to face the implacable warrior. But they did not know his wrath. Or rather, they'd only heard its voice. That day they would experience it.

Neither I nor Diomedes, or even Agamemnon, should have taken part in that day of blood and delirium; we weren't even close to regaining our strength and if any of us were overrun, many others would have to lose their lives in the effort to save ours. But I could not imagine hanging back in my tent on such a day, and it struck me that there was a weapon available to me, one that I had never yet used in battle under the walls of Troy, only when I'd been hunting now and then in the forests of Mount Ida: my bow.

I regretted not having the one that grandfather Autolykos had given me, but I chose an excellent and very powerful weapon nonetheless and I made my way to the ships of the Thessalians of Pherai and the tent of Eumelus.

'Pai,' I said, 'you promised you'd let me try out your horses.'

'And I always keep my promises, wanax.'

'You had said, "whenever you want".'

Eumelus was starting to get the idea: 'As in today?'

I nodded. 'You will be my charioteer. We have no roads in Ithaca, only narrow paths, so I've never trained a team or owned a chariot myself. But my aim is true and if you can take me to where the enemy are drawn up, carry me up and down the ranks, stopping where the fray is thickest, my arrows will thin out the field for Ajax, Idomeneus, Menelaus, or any of the others.'

Eumelus' eyes smiled at my words: 'Just give me the time to yoke my beloved chargers and to pass on the command of the Thessalians to a friend I can trust and I'll come for you at your tent.'

I went back, covered my head and face with a helmet that left only my eyes exposed, put on a leather cuirass and slung my sword from my shoulder. I took my bow and a couple of quivers, filled with nail-hard, three-headed arrows, and stood thus, waiting for Eumelus. When he came I mounted the chariot as he urged on the horses and we flew, roaring, over the planks covering the ditch.

We crossed the wide plain on a slant as I drew my first arrow and notched it to the bowstring.

The day was wholly Achilles'. The two Ajaxes, Idomeneus and Menelaus fought as they always had against the Trojans and, this time, maybe against the gods as well, but in lesser corners of the battlefield. I could see where Achilles was from my chariot. I saw, or perhaps only thought I could see, what is normally hidden from mortal sight. Was it Athena passing close again? She found me wherever I was, sleeping or awake, in the forest, on the mountains, on the sea.

The peak of Mount Ida was hidden by dark clouds. A loud thunderclap greeted the onset of the carnage that day as the gods started mixing with the men: they'd never have another chance like this one to kill so many mortals on a single day.

Hector's army had drawn up in all its glory. Warriors had come from as far as distant Hatti to help, as well as Thracians from the straits, Lycians and Mysians from the south, Paphlagonians and Eneti from the shores of the Terme river.

Achilles charged the centre of the formation, hoping to find Hector, his hated enemy, there. But he found only warriors trying to stop him. The front wavered here and there, depending on who was faring better at that moment, or where a brave champion had managed to drive back the enemy with his shield and spear.

I gestured for Eumelus to race along the front; upon my command to stop, I would let fly, wait for the strike, then move on swiftly. I fired off arrow after arrow without pause. Eumelus' horses were as fleet as the wind and it only took a light touch on the reins and bit from my young charioteer to keep them flying.

The battle continued to rage that whole day, as did the storm on Mount Ida. Zeus was proclaiming his anger, but even He, who had always held out his hand to protect the city, had to bend to fate. We watched as the Scamander and Simoeis swelled up with turbid, foaming waters that looked like they would carry our warriors off, but Achilles wouldn't be stopped. He entered the Scamander, holding back the current with his shield, treading over the bodies of the dead Trojans being washed by the river away to the sea. His Myrmidons plunged in behind him and emerged to attack a flank of the Trojan army, sending them into a rout.

The great gate opened, as did the city's lower gates, to offer refuge to the warriors in flight. Where was Hector?

'Look!' shouted Eumelus. 'Down there, between the wild fig tree and the Skaian Gate! It's him and he's wearing Achilles' own armour, stripped from Patroclus' body.'

'You're right. Those arms will be the death of him if Achilles sees him and succeeds in isolating him.'

From our chariot we could see both champions, their helmet crests waving, both men much taller than the other swarming warriors. Hector, realizing the danger he was in, headed for the gate. Achilles called out to his horses and jumped on the chariot.

'He'll never get away,' I said. 'Hector is done for.'

Great numbers of our warriors were massing around the fleeing Trojans, but our men suddenly drew up short, and were left crowding, milling, pressing murderously at the Skaian Gate as it was being pulled shut against us. We were too close; if the gate remained open the Trojans knew we would surge into the city. But Hector himself had been closed out as well.

The moment had thus come for the final test. Men and women had gathered on the walls of Troy and the standards that always accompanied the king were flying at the top of the tower flanking the gate. Perhaps Andromache herself was watching in anguish as her husband faced such terrible danger.

I could not bring myself to watch the end of such a valiant, worthy hero, who had allowed himself to be blinded by the thirst for glory and defeated by his love for his homeland. Nor could I have watched his end had I wanted to: tens of thousands of warriors were thronging in front of us and it would have been impossible to make our way through the fray.

'Let's turn back,' I said to Eumelus. 'We've done what we could. Now all will be decided by fate, whom even the gods fear.'

We were the first to reach the rampart. Eumelus tied his horses to one of the palisade trunks, without removing their yoke, and we both went up to the sentry walk. The plain stretched out before us littered with lifeless bodies; already the stray dogs were creeping close. Other warriors, wounded or crippled, were struggling to make their way back to the camp. The sun was on our left, already descending towards the sea. The great black clouds crowning Mount Ida were rent by lightning bolts. The dying sun cast bloody stains on their wind-tattered edges.

All at once, the thunder hushed, the lightning ceased, even the voice of the sea vanished. In the utter silence we heard a cry, muffled by the distance. A cry of despair and delirium that rose like a dart into the impassive sky and finally died there in a long, agonizing lament.

'Hector is dead,' I said. Then we saw the army split and draw back into two wings to allow the passage of . . . the chariot of Achilles, which crossed the plain and then the ditch and then the rampart. Dragging behind it, in the dust, the broken body of Hector, stripped of his arms: the Trojan prince, untiring defender of sacred Troy.

31

ACHILLES PROCLAIMED SOLEMN funeral games in Patroclus' honour, so that his friend's shade might find peace. It was said that Patroclus had appeared to his friend in a dream, to ask for the sacred rites to be held as soon as possible. All the kings and princes were to participate.

In the meantime, Merion, the shield-bearer of *wanax* Idomeneus, had led a party of men armed with axes to cut down a great number of oaks on Mount Ida. The logs were dragged back by mules, trimmed using hatchets and piled up to build a funeral pyre. When the pyre had been completed the funeral procession moved out. In front were the war chariots with heroes and drivers decked in their best armour. Then a great number of warriors on foot. At the centre was the bier, borne by six men, with Achilles at its end cradling the dead man's head in his hands. As the procession passed, the Myrmidons cut off locks of their hair and let them fall onto the corpse. Last of all, Achilles sheared off the long plait he always wore because he had vowed to the god of the Spercheios river that he would loosen it only upon his return home. But there would be no return, and his hair would honour his fallen friend instead. The squared-off pile of wood, one hundred feet long on every side, was ready and Patroclus' body was laid on top with his sword at his side.

Then the games began. A part of the camp had been cleared for the races, which Achilles himself would judge. In addition to the chariot race, there were contests in archery, wrestling, running and sword duels. I took part in them as well, and I won the running race, but only because Ajax Oileus slipped on the dung of the sacrificed bulls. And I wrestled honourably with Great Ajax; whoever would have believed it! Ajax also took part in a sword duel against Diomedes; the king of Argus was first to wound his opponent, only grazing Ajax's skin, but Achilles stopped the fight immediately, assigning the victory to both in equal measure.

The time came for the final honours over the hero's body: first fire, then blood.

All the kings and princes were present in the front row: the two Atreides, Agamemnon and Menelaus, at the centre; to their right Diomedes, Thoas, Sthenelus, Nestor and Antilochus; to their left Great Ajax, myself, Ajax Oileus, Idomeneus, Makahon and Menestheus of Athens. Behind us the whole army thronged, each man dressed in his best armour. Four Myrmidons of the honour guard set fire to the four corners of the enormous pyre.

The flames were whipped up by the wind coming from the sea. They rose high, seething and roaring and turned from red to white as the entire pile of timber sizzled and burned. Even the sea seemed to take flame as the reflections of the blaze spread out. Then blood. The Trojan prisoners were dragged to the site of the funeral rite, their hands tied behind their backs with willow shoots. Like beasts to be sacrificed, they were pushed to their knees and slain with a single sword's blow between the shoulder blade and collarbone. When the tip sank into the heart, a fountain of blood spurted upwards and the victim collapsed as life fled.

One after another, the bodies of the sacrificed Trojans were thrown onto the pyre, offered to the lord of Hades, so they could serve the dead man in the afterlife.

I had long become accustomed to any and all atrocities in so many years of war and I realized that such a brutal act did not touch me. My heart was not horrified. But it was this very lack of horror that wounded me as if an arrow had been plunged into my chest.

The name of the dead man was shouted out ten times by the Myrmidons lined up in formal order, and then by the kings and by the whole army, who beat their spears against their shields with a thunderous roar.

When the pyre was consumed, the priests gathered the bones of the dead man and bent the incandescent sword with pincers so that it could be buried with his urn. Achilles looked like a man gone insane. His eyes were dry, and he stood straight and motionless in front of the blaze that sent off its last sparks. I think he could see himself reduced to ashes in the crumbling firebrands of the pyre. They had burned his shadow and now the ministers of Death were gathering, howling like starving dogs, around him. Outside his tent lay Hector's body unburied, his spirit still hovering restless over the muddy banks of the Acheron, futilely seeking a place on the boat of hell's own ferryman. Patroclus' ghost would pass him by at a run, sprinting to cross the black waters.

I looked at Hector's body for a moment. Swollen, bruised, covered with clotted blood, unrecognizable. Nothing remained of the glorious warrior, splendid as a star, who had attacked our vacillating defences with his fierce battle cry. *For an instant I thought I saw my own body abandoned on a deserted beach in a remote, unknown land. I saw myself, someone, No One. There's no escaping fate.* Would I suffer the same destiny?

I waited until everyone had gone, waiting in the shadows until the moon set. I had a premonition. The Great Bear had descended towards the mountains, at the lowest point of the sky, when a hooded figure appeared out of nowhere and entered Achilles' tent furtively. He made no noise at all, almost as if he were not touching the ground. The guards did not move – were they sleeping? Was it perhaps a god moving in the dark, in human guise? I didn't take a single step, but remained where I was, hidden in the shadows. After a short time, the hooded man left Achilles' tent, and a cart appeared pulled by a horse. Four Myrmidon warriors lifted the corpse of Hector and placed it upon it. The hooded figure, whoever it was, covered the body with a black cloth, got into the cart, took the reins and moved off slowly without making a sound.

A voice at my right: 'Achilles showed pity.'

My knees trembled. Only a god could have known so much. 'Who are you?' I asked.

'Ideus, the king's herald.'

'Priam? He came here?'

'Yes. Someone more powerful than we are guided us through the darkness. Priam knelt at Achilles' feet and kissed the hand of the man who killed his son. He begged him. An old man humbled by his grief. He touched Achilles' heart. Hector will be honoured by tears . . . those of his mother, of his grief-stricken wife, of his comrades, of the entire city. This is true glory, *wanax* Odysseus: the tears of those we love when we leave this world. Who will cry for Achilles?'

'Who? His father, so far away. And Priam will cry for him, because he took pity on his suffering. And because when war is rampant, a single man's sorrow is every man's sorrow; every father is the father of every son, every son is the son of every father.'

I turned my back to him and walked back to my own ship.

In the days that followed nothing happened. It seemed that the two armies, and the two peoples, had been devastated by grief and prostrated by exhaustion. Now that Patroclus was dead, and Hector dead, Achilles had nothing to dedicate his life to, if not combat for combat's sake: the pursuit of a glorious death. And when the war flared up again, he began to challenge and strike out at the two Trojan warriors who had taken Hector's place after his death: Deiphobus and Aeneas. We all imagined that fate would now be on our side. After all, Achilles was back in the fight, while they had lost their mightiest warrior. But the tide of war didn't turn as we expected: the Trojans became more cautious and they lined up all their best warriors against our champion. More than once, Achilles succeeded in overwhelming them and routing them, and they were once again forced to seek shelter behind the walls of their city, but those walls were unbreachable.

Then one day at the beginning of the autumn, it finally seemed that the Trojans had been put to flight. Achilles turned to his men and was urging them to follow him and block the doors of the gate before they could be closed, when a poisoned arrow soared through the air and pierced Achilles in the leg, near his heel. He stopped and tried to pull out the arrow in his fury to continue the assault, but his vehemence suddenly faltered and he collapsed to the ground before the cursed, unconquerable Skaian Gate.

Paris' hoot of triumph, as he raised his bow in his right hand so all could see, made us realize that it was he who claimed victory over the greatest warrior who had ever set foot upon the earth. What a cruel twist of fate! But his exultation was short-lived. I had been at the rear lines, close to the wild fig tree, because every now and then my wound would make itself felt and I'd have to break off fighting to catch my breath. But from where I was I could see Paris distinctly. I nocked an arrow to my bowstring. I could not shoot directly because there were too many obstacles between us so I aimed slightly upwards; a curved shot, very difficult if not wholly impossible. But my goddess had to heed my prayer this time. 'Listen,' I said, 'no one will ever know where this arrow came from. You can dedicate the victory to Hercules, because it is he who I am thinking of in this moment.' For an instant Damastes took shape next to me and I could hear his voice in my heart: 'Keep in mind the wind!' The heavy, well-balanced arrow followed its arched path, soaring up and then gaining force and speed as it began to descend. It struck the target fully, plunging into Paris' throat. He died instantly. All those around him were astonished, as if the fatal shaft had been cast from the top of Mount Ida, or from Olympus itself.

A fierce battle immediately erupted over the corpse of Achilles, and I pushed my way through the crowded warriors to lend a hand. The Trojans wanted the body of the man who had tied their beloved Hector to his chariot and dragged him through the dust. Their prince, so generous as to give his very life for his city, begged for revenge. We knew we had to prevent this at any cost because losing the body of Achilles to the enemy would have meant our definitive defeat. And so many of our best warriors, in the bloom of youth, lost their lives that day to gain possession of a dead body. I had become accustomed, after so many years of war without quarter, to any sight, even the most horrendous, the most macabre, but seeing the corpse of Achilles, which just moments before had been bursting with invincible vitality, now reduced to an inanimate thing, dragged, yanked, trodden upon by those who until now would not have dared to look him in the eye, left me with a sense of infinite bitterness and despair.

And fury.

I fought shouting, weeping, howling like a wolf. The only remedy for such desolation was to fight, to pour out energy, sweat, fiery passion. I watched as Great Ajax's arm came down like a maul on his enemies, as Diomedes' spear sprang to life in his hand, and I understood that killing, at that moment, was the only way we could feel alive.

The brutal brawl lasted until nightfall. I had taken position between Menelaus, who had drawn incredible energy out of Paris' death, and the two Ajaxes, who fought like a pair of lions. In the end, we were joined by Diomedes with his deadly spear and we managed to get the better of the Trojans. Great Ajax heaved Achilles' body over his shoulder and made his way out of the melee after throwing his huge shield onto his back as protection.

When evening fell, Achilles' body was laid on the bier that had borne Patroclus only four months earlier. We were all oppressed by the blackest humour, even though all the prophecies had always predicted that this would happen. But our sorrows were not over. I felt inside that an even more bitter and harrowing misfortune was in store for us.

Achilles' funeral rites were celebrated three days later, at dusk. Thousands and thousands of torches illuminated the clearing on the beach, where an enormous pyre of pine and oak trunks had been erected. Our warriors had donned their brightest, most precious armour and high horsehair-crested helmets, and were drawn up kingdom by kingdom, city by city, with their princes, kings and commanders. The sea was rough and the big foam-tipped waves crashed deafeningly against the cliffs at the edges of the bay. A storm was coming in. Big black clouds raced across the livid sky as thunder rumbled in the distance. The whole world, sky, sea and earth, was readying to give its last farewell to the divine and wild warrior: Achilles, son of Peleus, prince of Phthia.

One thousand Myrmidon warriors escorted the bier, followed by the hero's empty chariot, pulled by Balius and Xanthus, who strode forward matching their step to the sound of the flutes and horns.

Four Myrmidons hoisted the bier with Achilles' body, wrapped in a rich purple cloth, to their shoulders. They carried it up the ramp that led to the top of the pyre and laid him on a wooden platform covered with gold leaf. He was not dressed in his armour and his sword was not resting next to his left thigh. They were hanging from two crossed spears standing in front of the pyre and, even empty as they were, they inspired fear. Someone – I was never to know who – had decided that they must be preserved. Too great was their value to burn them. And perhaps they were still imbued with the force of the man who had worn them: his heart had vibrated behind the breastplate only a few short days before, his hand had fastened the sword's sheathe to his side. Everyone remembered how the suit of armour had appeared just when Achilles needed it, although no one in the camp, as far as we knew, had crafted it. I had been the first to see it after Achilles himself.

The moment had arrived. The four Myrmidons who had carried Achilles' body to the top of the pyre set fire to the four corners. The greatest warrior who had ever been born on our earth would soon become ash, would leave the living and enter forever more into the world of legend. Alive only in the songs and laments of the poets. Briseis huddled in a dark corner, half-hidden, weeping for her lover and her master, the flames that were devouring his body now and then reddening her cheeks. I never heard what happened to her and I never saw her in the camp again. *I still wonder about her and what fate befell her.*

There were some who said that a sigh was heard coming from the depths of the sea as the flames licked the hero's body, but that night a great many sounds, cries and laments were borne on the wind.

When the corpse of Achilles had received the funeral honours due him and other Trojan prisoners had been sacrificed to his restless shade, the camp was plunged into silence. Agamemnon approached me. 'You will look after Achilles' arms,' he said.

'Why?'

'Because I trust you. Until we decide what must be done with them.'

'It would have been best to burn them on the pyre with Achilles. Now they can only lead to discord.'

Agamemnon looked at me for a few moments in silence as if weighing my words, and then said: 'I believe we'll have much more difficult matters to face tomorrow than who might deserve Achilles' armour. The Trojans will have taken heart. They killed the best of us and, on the same day, they lost the worst of their own.'

I said nothing.

Two men collected Achilles' armour and weapons, wrapped them in coarse woollen cloth and loaded them onto a horse-drawn cart. They were taken to my tent and mounted on a hanger. I was reminded of the armour I'd seen displayed in Mycenae, in the armoury, when I had visited as a boy. They'd looked to me like the ghosts of fallen warriors. I fell asleep late, under the empty gaze of Achilles' helmet, and woke up early. There was someone in my tent.

'Ajax!'

'I've come to take what is mine, Odysseus.'

I turned my head towards the armour. 'That?' I asked.

'Yes. Achilles was my cousin and his armour is rightfully mine as his next of kin. And now that he is dead I am the strongest warrior in this army, the only one who can wear his armour. What's more, I earned this honour on the battlefield. It was I who carried him back to the ships, on my shoulders!'

'*Wanax* Agamemnon turned them over to me and here they will remain until a decision is taken as to what is to be done with them.'

'Don't get mixed up in this. You are my friend and I respect you, but I won't let anyone take what is mine.'

'And if I say no, what will you do? Kill me?'

The look in Ajax's eyes was strange. I thought perhaps it was the uncertain light of the early morning that had created the expression on his face, but I was wrong. The madness that shone in the eyes of the gentle giant was real.

And it froze my heart.

'Don't interfere. Don't take sides with Agamemnon or I'll have to resort to physical force. Now you step aside and let me take that armour.'

I unsheathed my sword. 'Now you'll draw yours and soon one of us will be dead,' I said.

'You,' he replied, as he unsheathed his own, which Hector had bequeathed him.

The words that Penelope had said the day we met came into my mind: 'Do you know how big Ajax, the son of Telamon, is?' And I had to smile, even though his expression was so menacing.

'And if it were me? Does that really seem like such a good thing?' I challenged him. 'Killing a friend who has fought by your side for years? And who's to say you'll succeed? I won our wrestling match, didn't I?'

'By tricking me.'

'No, not by trickery. By skill. I think before I act. That's only one of the reasons I don't deserve your scorn.' He was letting me talk. Maybe I could still stem the violence in him. 'Listen to me. Achilles' armour will almost certainly fall to you. Who could have a better claim to it? No one. Each of us knows how valuable you've been, how many feats of bravery and strength you've accomplished. Many of us owe you our lives. And so, if Achilles' armour is designated for one of the princes or kings, it will certainly be you. Why take it by force and dishonour yourself? All of us swore to a pact many years ago and you've fulfilled your obligations with constancy and with great generosity. If you respect those who command the army you'll have the honour you deserve.'

His gaze was going dim again: 'I don't like the way you're talking. I don't like it when words are stronger than the sword. It's not right.'

'My friend, even animals have horns, claws and fangs and will happily fight each other to the death. We have more than that, Ajax, we have our hearts and our minds. I beg of you, wait and you'll see.'

Ajax remained silent, while his Trojan sword found its way back into its sheath.

'I've never had glory,' he said. 'I've never had a real victory; no one has ever recognized my worth. I'm like that patient ox, or that obstinate ass that is never praised for what he does. In the end, the ox's heart bursts under the yoke, the ass collapses crushed by the weight of the stones he is hauling, but no one notices. That's how it's been for me. I've never asked anything of the gods. The gods have never given me a thing. Do you understand me, Odysseus?'

I did understand him, and he was right. Ajax had never lost his temper, had never abandoned the field and left his comrades to die overrun by the enemy. No one had ever implored or begged him to get back in the fight. Ajax was a mountain and mountains don't lose control. Ajax had saved the ships because he was the cliff against which the waves of destruction could break. And cliffs don't complain. They go on being cliffs and being mountains, day after day, year after year.

But now the cliff, the mountain, had discovered he had a heart, had feelings: of friendship, of melancholy, of pain and resentment, like every mortal man.

And despair.

He wanted us to know. To recognize that there was a heart beating under his breastplate, behind the shield made of seven bull hides. How this had happened and why, I could not understand. Not then.

He turned before leaving my tent: 'Don't betray me, Odysseus.'

I HAD ACHILLES' suit of armour transported to the centre of the assembly and displayed there. Agamemnon had decided that the arms would go to whoever most greatly deserved them and thus had asked each one of the members of the council to declare his opinion. The end result was a tie.

He turned to me: 'You have not voted, while Ajax has. Express your vote and the decision will be made.'

I should have done it, should have spoken in favour of Ajax. I knew that he was the one who deserved the armour and I remembered his last words to me: 'Do not betray me, Odysseus.'

I did not do it.

And it still weighs heavily on me . . . acute remorse.

I betrayed Great Ajax, bulwark of the Achaians, when I could have saved him and saved myself by pronouncing that short, sweet-sounding name, as I had so many times in battle when I had needed him.

I said instead: 'We will repeat the voting and this time it will be secret. That way each of us will be freer.'

Agamemnon agreed. 'Each of you will have two knuckle bones, one black and one white. When your name is called by the herald, you will walk to the centre of the assembly and put your vote into Antilochus' helmet. Black for Odysseus, white for Ajax. Then we will count the knuckle bones.'

We began our voting. Agamemnon was first, and after him his herald Euribates called up the kings and princes one by one. As the voters approached the helmet placed on a little table at the centre of the assembly and deposited their knuckle bones inside, I asked myself why so many of them had voted for me when it was evident that Ajax had saved the naval camp, had faced up to Hector, had wrenched the body of Achilles from the Trojans and carried it out of the fray. But in the end I knew, even though I didn't want to admit it to myself: the others may have aspired to owning that armour for any number of reasons, but by voting for me, none of them would feel the sting of defeat. What was more, they'd ensured that the weapons would not be going to the only man who could truly defeat all of them.

In the end, I was declared the winner and everyone applauded. Bar one. Ajax left the assembly in a rage and soon disappeared from sight. The armour was taken back to my tent.

I COULDN'T FALL ASLEEP that night, not even for brief moments. But even if I had been sleeping, I would have been shocked awake by Ajax's shouting. 'Come out, you traitor! Come and see the fate that will befall those who have denied me my rights! I'll kill them all, here, right here in front of your tent *and you last of all!*'

In my drowsy confusion, I couldn't understand at first what was happening, what Ajax was doing. I ran out, unarmed, and saw something I never could have imagined: Ajax had dashed to the ground the men who were guarding the cattle and sheep that served as our foodstock; they showed no signs of life. And there he was, as blood-spattered as a butcher, massacring the animals one after another, a torch held high in his other hand to illuminate his deed. The crazed animals were crowding together, bleating and lowing in terror, powerless to escape their fate. The stench was unbearable as we were immersed in a fog of madness and nightmare. Eurylochus ran up next to me, panting: 'He thinks they're the men who voted against him. He's lost his mind! I'm going to sound the alarm.'

'No,' I replied. 'Don't do anything. He's only killing animals.'

The pen was only about fifty feet from my tent, and my tent was at the centre of the naval camp, equidistant from the Myrmidons on one end and Ajax's men on the other. Although I had stopped Eurylochus, in no time a speechless crowd of hundreds and then thousands of men were thronging to catch sight of that wretched spectacle: princes and kings, warriors, servants, slaves and concubines. I saw Ajax's slave and lover, Tecmessa, among them; she was sobbing. Everyone understood what was happening because the news had flown through the camp and many stood there numbly, tears flowing down their faces. Others had lit torches to get a better look. Last to arrive was Teucer, who looked at his brother dumbfounded, as if he could not believe his eyes.

In the end, Ajax, hoarse from all his yelling, panting, exhausted and covered with blood from head to foot, slipped and lay there among the bowels, blood and excrement of sheep and cows.

None of us moved. No one took a step or tried to approach him. Even Agamemnon, Menelaus and Diomedes watched wordlessly. Nestor and Idomeneus looked at one another and then at me, searching for an answer that no one was capable of giving. No one in all those years of war had ever seen such a thing, no one could bear to see the giant of one hundred battles weltering in the middle of that abomination. The red, flickering torchlight could only give us shredded glimpses of reality, all tinged with the saturated tones of violence. But when the cold, colourless light of the hour preceding the morning rendered the shapes and shades equal and inert, our anguish mounted until it became unbearable. I wanted to scream, to tear out my hair, to claw at my cheeks like the mourning women who follow funeral processions in countryside villages. Instead, I stood there motionless like a statue of salt.

Then came the moment of extreme horror. Ajax awakened, struggled to his feet, looked around at the friends and comrades of so many battles and then at himself. As the moments passed, his mind started to eke a bit of light from that pale sky and that still, grey sea, and he came to his senses. Disgust slowly twisted his face as shame filled his eyes with burning tears and seeped into that great heart of his. Ajax gave a scream like the cry of one hundred men, a howl of horror and utter despair. He still gripped the sword that Hector had given him after their long duel and, stumbling over the mangled carcasses, he made his way straight towards me.

I did not move. I deserved to be killed by him. He stopped a step away from me and, without saying a word, he stared into my eyes and raised his sword . . . I knew my time had come. Mine would be the death of a contemptible man.

Instead my punishment was a hundred times more bitter. Ajax turned the sword at the last moment towards himself and he stuck it right under his diaphragm. Since deathly exhaustion had deprived him of the energy necessary to thrust it into his heart, he calmly placed the hilt end upright on the earth and threw himself on the point with all the weight of his huge body. Hector's blade cleaved his great heart in two and came out of his back. The giant collapsed. And the earth trembled under our feet.

32

THE TWO MEN GUARDING THE PEN who had been struck down by Ajax did not survive the attack. This made Ajax's act even more repugnant in the eyes of those who had stood there watching and judging, without bothering to ask themselves why he had done such a thing. Agamemnon wanted him buried like carrion, but I fought to have him given the honours of a pyre: a hero's funeral. My standing up for him reflected no particular merit on my part, but it did help to assuage my remorse.

'He took his own life with his sword. What more could he do to redeem his shame? He had always fought, all these long years, like a lion. Isn't that enough to earn him flames instead of worms?'

'He thought he was killing us as he was slaughtering those poor animals.'

'Well, he must have had a good reason, don't you think? It was clear that he'd lost his mind. If he hadn't gone mad he wouldn't have been killing sheep, goats and cows, he would have been killing us, the kings of the Achaians, the comrades of a thousand battles. Because we betrayed him. But then a god made him come to his senses in time for him to experience unbearable shame and the worst pain of his whole life. Now he's dead and we've lost our greatest combatant, one of the last of his kind.'

I had my way. And thus we celebrated funeral rites for Ajax, son of Telamon, prince of Salamis, as we had celebrated those of Patroclus and Achilles. Only then did we realize how much we had loved him. We each recollected a certain moment spent together, each one of us added something of our own onto the pyre. It was I who ritually bent Ajax's sword, the cruel blade that had belonged to his enemy. He succeeded where his enemy had not, in driving it into his heart.

We chose a spot on the Rhoetean promontory to bury his ashes, then raised a high tumulus there so he would be forever remembered.

We had never felt so alone as we did after his death, we had never felt so sad. But we knew we had to react and regain control of the situation. Our army had to believe that we were still certain of victory. Ajax had descended from Zeus himself, and we needed to replace him with another warrior of his same stock. A fighter as strong and passionate as he had been.

'The son of Achilles!'

'But he's only a boy,' said Agamemnon.

'He's seventeen years old,' I replied. 'He's perfect. He has no children, no wife and no homeland. He grew up on an island far away from the land of his ancestors, whom he has never seen. He never met his grandfather Peleus; he only saw his father once when he was too young to remember. All he knows about Achilles is what he has heard, and his only goal is to surpass him in fame. He has been raised for one single thing: combat. He has no loved ones, no roots, no feeling or memories to share with another. He's an animal of war.'

'How do you know all these things?'

'When we left Aulis to cross the sea, Achilles and I stopped at Scyros to take on food and water, but mostly because he wanted to see his son. It was I who gave King Lycomedes instructions on how he was to be educated. We put him in the charge of two of Achilles' own Lapiths to be trained in the art of war. I suppose I foresaw that this day might come.'

'If that is so, leave immediately to fetch him and be back as soon as you can.'

'I will, *wanax*. I'll leave tomorrow.'

I fitted out my ship, chose my most trusted men, including Eurylochus and Elpenor, and set sail at dawn. In all those years, I had only taken my ship out for brief stretches, usually along the

Thracian coast to buy wine for the army. The sea greeted me like an old friend who hadn't shown his face in a long time. My ship ploughed the waves like it had on its maiden voyage. There was a light breeze from the north that we had to compensate for at times with the helm and at times with the oars. The smell and taste of the salty air made me remember home. Time after time, I realized that, without meaning to, I was calculating how many days it would take me, sailing at that speed, to reach Ithaca.

Scyros was in the middle of the sea, at an equal distance from Troy and Euboea.

It took me only two days to get there and I easily guided my ship into the main port. I had myself announced, and King Lycomedes greeted me with all due honours. The fame of our interminable assault had reached lands far and wide, been distorted, expanded, broken into a thousand different stories that the minstrels had seized upon and happily related, travelling from one palace to the next, one village to another. The king had a huge banquet prepared, inviting the notables of his island and the ones nearby. I was asked many questions, which I answered in part and avoided in part. Finally, after all the guests had gone home and the servants had begun to clear the tables, the king drew close and said: 'What is the reason behind such an unexpected visit?'

'Achilles is dead. I've come to get the boy.'

'I knew that,' said the king, without adding anything else.

'Does he know?'

Lycomedes nodded. 'He wants to avenge him, and to surpass the fame and valour of his father.'

'When can I see him?'

'Better tomorrow. He'll be with his concubines now. When I heard you'd arrived, I was hoping you'd come to take him away. He has become impossible to live with. It's like having a wild animal roaming your home. If he weren't my daughter's son and if I hadn't been prevented from doing so by the bonds of blood, I would have got rid of him long ago. He's indomitable, irascible, violent. I can barely manage to hold him back.'

'Sleep easy, *wanax*, tomorrow I'm taking him away with me.'

I saw the boy at dawn. He had dived into the sea and was swimming like a dolphin, slapping his chest on the strong surf that the night wind was still heaving against the cliffs guarding the port. Then he returned to the shore and began to run down the beach, faster and faster, until I could barely distinguish the movement of his feet, so swift were they. He looked as if he were racing against an invisible adversary.

His father.

I waited until he stopped. I could feel the energy that he gave off, as if I were standing before a big raging fire. His shoulder-length hair was the colour of flames while his eyes were the colour of ice. His arms were powerful, much more massive than on any boy of his age. But his hands, strangely enough, were long and tapered, with big blue veins showing under the thin skin.

'I'm Odysseus, king of Ithaca.'

'A man who uses his tongue rather than his sword, from what I hear tell.'

I drew my sharp bronze blade and pointed it at his throat before he could blink an eye. When he pulled back I kept up the pressure until it drew blood.

'Next time I'll cut the tendon in your neck so you'll keep your head down for the rest of your life, in front of men who are worth much more than you, and in front of men who are worth much less as well. I'm the man your father respected most in the whole army. He begat you but I'm the person who made you what you are. It was I who established how you were to be educated, trained and punished whenever it was necessary and even when it was not. Where are your instructors?'

'Both of them wanted to test what I'd learned from them. They're both dead.'

I didn't let the slightest emotion show on my face at hearing that news. I didn't so much as blink. I said: 'Prepare your things, we'll set sail in an hour.'

*

WE EXCHANGED very few words during the whole voyage. He never asked me anything about his father, showed no desire to visit his tomb or to sacrifice to his shade. When we arrived within sight of our destination and the city appeared on the hill, he pointed at it. 'Is that Troy?'

I nodded.

'And in ten years, with one thousand ships and fifty thousand warriors, you haven't succeeded in conquering it?'

'No. As you can see. That's why I came to get you. You'll have your father's chariot and his horses, you'll wear the armour that your father lent to Patroclus and that he himself stripped from Hector after he'd killed him.'

'He had another set,' replied the boy. 'The one he was wearing when they killed him. Where is it?'

I could never have imagined that he would know so much.

'In my tent.' And when I answered I looked him straight in the eye. He didn't say anything more.

The same evening that we arrived he was presented to the assembled army wearing his father's first suit of armour, on a podium illuminated by eight large braziers and by tens of lit torches. The warriors honoured him by shouting out his name seven times and pounding their spears against their shields twenty times, creating a deafening din.

When he passed in front of me I said: 'Tomorrow you'll be in the front line at the head of your Myrmidons.'

HE FOUGHT the whole day, until nightfall, on the chariot driven by his father's charioteer, Automedon, or on foot. He never rested, took no food or drink. His appearance served, as we had hoped, to strike terror into Trojan hearts. They thought it was Achilles himself they faced, brought back to life, and they knew they could not withstand his assault. Aeneas himself risked losing his life in a clash with him.

The boy pushed all the way to the perfidious Skaian Gate and he nearly succeeded in forcing open the doors, which had been drawn shut but not yet bolted. The enthusiasm of our army was immeasurable. But the Trojans reacted by multiplying their defences and attacking less frequently on open ground. When they did attack, they immediately honed in on Pyrrhus' position and kept him in the sights of one hundred archers, forcing him to adopt a defensive strategy.

We were at a stand-off once again. The rumour started to circulate that Troy would never fall because the gods did not want the war to ever finish.

If the men began to believe this, it would be the end of everything we had struggled for. But the days passed and if on the one hand Pyrrhus' presence had given the army the strength and desire to stay in the fight and bring the war to a close, on the other hand our lack of success was reinforcing their fear that not even the formidable energy of the son of Achilles could win the war.

What was worse, Pyrrhus was impossible to control. He tolerated no discipline, and would often attack alone at the head of his Myrmidons, who would have followed him straight to the Underworld, had he ordered them to. One night, he even decided to scale the walls of Troy alone and bare-handed, risking a fall that would have shattered all his bones. He came close to succeeding. But if there was one thing he couldn't bear it was failure; he became hateful and aggressive with all of us, even his closest comrades. I began to ask myself whether the idea that I'd had all those years ago when I'd sailed to Scyros at the head of my men and my ships, still shy of Troy, had been the right one.

I became convinced that somehow I had to find a solution. Athena had given me the strength to fight on the front line alongside the greatest warriors, but above all she had given me a mind capable of meditating, reflecting and generating new ideas. What idea could I possibly come up with? Even at night, when I was sleeping, my mind sought a solution. Very often when I woke in the morning, I felt convinced that I'd found a way. My heart filled with joy until the plan vanished along with the fog of sleep.

Time passed.

One evening at the beginning of autumn, weary from a long day of combat and disgusted at the senseless ferocity of Pyrrhus and the macabre trophies he insisted on carrying back from the battlefield, sad over Ajax's death, the thought of which never abandoned me, I found a place on the seashore where I could sit and listen to the timeless voice of the waves coming in. It lulled me, calmed the chaos in my heart and allowed me to think clearly. I was waiting for the moon to appear for my daily appointment with Penelope. I knew in that moment she would think of me and I would think of her.

I heard a voice: '*Wanax* Odysseus . . .'

'Eumelus.'

He sat down next to me. He hadn't even taken off his armour yet; I could smell his sweat and hear his heart beating in its daily struggle against death. He seemed hard to me, as if he were carved in wood, and the grey evening light made him look very pale.

'Do you still think of your parents?' he asked me.

'Always.'

'Mentor? Do you think of him sometimes?'

'As if I'd just seen him yesterday.'

As he was talking I noticed that he'd slipped his hand into the belt at his waist. He pulled something out.

'This? Do you remember this?'

I smiled incredulously: he was turning in his hand the little horse I'd sculpted in wood so many years before and given to him so he'd know he could trust me.

'You still have that! I can't believe it,' I said.

'It's one of the most precious things I have. It's my good luck charm.'

'It's only a wooden trinket.'

'Yes, but inside this wooden horse is the heart of the king of Ithaca, Odysseus, the thinker of many thoughts. My friend. What were you thinking about, *wanax*?'

I took the little horse from his hands and turned it over in my own.

'I was thinking . . .' I said, 'I was thinking it's time to go home.'

Eumelus gave me a perplexed look. 'Yes, of course. But not before we've accomplished what we set out to do,' he said.

'Not before then,' I said.

Eumelus' horses, unyoked, had come looking for him.

'They're used to me feeding them from my hands,' he said, and went off after them.

I was overcome by a strange anxiety and I felt a chill. It wasn't the wind. It was the same feeling I'd had the night I'd slept at my grandfather Autolykos' hunting cottage. I knew what it meant.

'Where are you?' I said, looking around to see her.

'Here,' said a voice inside of me. 'Here, in your heart.'

That same night I let Agamemnon know that I needed to talk to him, and that he should convene a restricted council with Nestor and, afterwards, with the camp's master blacksmith and craftsman, a Locrian named Epeius.

'What I'm telling you here tonight,' I began, 'must remain secret. I am about to reveal to you how we can win the war in a short time.' Agamemnon and Nestor started. 'How much time depends on what Epeius will tell us. The real plan will only be known to the three of us; we'll ask Epeius if he is capable of making what we require, but we won't let him know the real reason we need it.

'Listen, then. We will build a gigantic horse of wood, so big that it will have an internal cavity large enough to hold thirty men, whom I will choose personally, one by one. They will only be informed on the night we execute the plan.

'First, we will spread the rumour that we're going home because the city of Troy is unassailable and because the gods are against us, and that we are building a votive gift, a horse, an animal sacred to Poseidon, to propitiate the blue god and win his favour for our sea crossing. When Epeius' horse is ready, we will weigh anchor, but not to return home. The fleet will hide behind the island of Tenedos, where a few of our men will climb to the highest peak and wait for a signal.

337

'We will leave the horse on the beach, along with a man whose hands are tied behind his back: one of my men, a trusted, very clever friend. His name is Sinon. When the Trojans come out from behind their walls and find him there, he'll say that he's a fugitive; that he ran from us because we wanted to sacrifice him to the marine gods, and he'll ask them for exile and protection. In exchange, he will tell them about the horse, explaining that it is a powerful votive gift for Poseidon, built to guarantee our safe return. He will tell them that our plan is to cross the sea, to join up with another, even bigger army, which is already waiting for us, and then to return to Troy in the spring.

'Nothing will be left to fortune. Every moment of the plan will be carefully thought out and executed. Nothing of what we are about to do can fail. From now on, I, and only I, will do all the thinking; you two must cast thoughts of this plan from your heads so that the gods who oppose us cannot see them. At this moment, I am sure that none of them are listening to us . . . and so I'll succeed in tricking them as well. All of them, except one.'

A long silence followed. More of amazement, it seemed to me, than disbelief. Things had to proceed at once, and so I called in Epeius, telling him about our plan for a votive gift and exhorting him to speak with no one about it, although I knew that after the first two or three queries, at most, he would give in. That evening in the council of the three kings he swore repeatedly that for no reason in the world would he let slip the merest suggestion of what he was being asked to do. I explained the characteristics of the gigantic gift to Poseidon that he would have the honour of building. A horse thirty feet tall, thirty-seven feet long, twelve feet wide. The tail and mane would be in real horsehair, artfully intertwined, and the horse would be set upon a platform.

'I think you are the only man capable of building such an object,' I flattered him. 'Am I wrong?'

'No, *wanax*, you are not wrong. I will build it exactly as you have described it to me.'

'How long will it take?'

'A month, *wanax*.'

'I can give you ten days. Not one more. And all the men you need.'

He hesitated an instant, then replied: 'Ten days, *wanax* Odysseus.'

33

BEFORE SUNSET ON THE TENTH DAY, Epeius appeared in front of my tent and gestured for me to follow him. I had been careful until then not to show too much interest in the work in progress, so no one could attribute the building of the colossal horse to me and thus suspect a trick. The Trojans had also been watching closely, albeit from afar. We could see them crowding the tops of the walls, swelling in number as the figure took shape. The dimensions of the horse were growing day by day, as scaffolding made of ash poles and boards sawn from poplars was added to support its bulk. It had to look like we were racing against time. And the onset of bad weather.

It was late in the autumn by then and Orion had already started to decline in the night sky. The air was already getting cooler and more humid.

During the entire time that the works were proceeding, we never went out in battle order and the Trojans did not challenge us. They never came out of the city armed, although we noticed them creeping close at times to get a better look at what was going on. They were careful to stay beyond the reach of our archers, although our men had been instructed not to strike out in any way. In the meantime, Epeius had, as I had predicted, let slip that we would be returning to Achaia for the winter and a certain air of joy had spread through the camp, subtle and secret, as though no one dared to believe it.

Halfway through the job I had told Epeius that an offering for Poseidon, a hidden tribute, would be placed inside the horse and that I would be giving him details just before the work was completed. The opening in the horse's belly would be prepared by him alone; he would have to work at night with no help from his men. One day, I mixed in with the crowd and made my way as far as the scaffolding that still covered the construction. After checking to make sure I was alone, I slipped underneath. There was no clue to any opening, no interruption in the intertwined beams, boards, branches and ropes which held it together. The horse's secret was invisible and undetectable. A perfect job.

I looked into Epeius' eyes without saying a word. A slight nod of my head was enough for him to understand that I approved. He responded in the same way.

During the entire time that the horse was being built, not one of the kings or princes came to visit me, except for Eumelus.

'You've always liked horses,' he observed, 'but you are the only one of the kings who doesn't have a war chariot. Why is that?'

'There are no roads in Ithaca, you know that; only the trails that the goats use. Our chariots are our ships: on the sea we're the best.'

'In such a short time,' he went on, 'a horse so small that it fits inside my hand has generated an enormous one that could contain many men. Am I right, Odysseus?'

I didn't answer.

'So I am right. You have to include me then, because I'm the only one who has understood what you are thinking.'

'No. I want you to get back safe and sound to your parents in Pherai. You'll enter the city with the others when it comes time to attack. Until that moment, speak with no one, not even the air. A god who is hostile to us might hear you.'

'He couldn't hear us here?'

'Here, in my tent, there's a constant noise that human ears cannot hear, that covers our voices and even our thoughts.'

'When?'

'The day after tomorrow. On the night of the new moon.'

He nodded and returned to his tent, walking along the seashore. Before leaving he opened his hand, smiled, and showed me the little horse I'd given him as a boy.

That same night I had Agamemnon convene a very unusual council of the kings. One by one they were to come to my tent, unescorted, without arms, armour or insignia, with their heads covered and wrapped in a cloak up to their eyes. Some before sunset, others after, the rest in the middle of the night. I was dubious up to the last moment as to whether I should include Pyrrhus; after much thought, I decided that he, too, should be summoned to my tent.

When everyone had arrived, Agamemnon spoke, admitting that the rumours about our returning to Achaia for the winter in order to recruit new warriors had been spread deliberately. The truth was entirely different, and I would be the one to reveal it to them. He then nodded to me.

'Friends, courageous comrades, for years and years Zeus has held his hand over the city of Troy so that it would not fall, despite the strength, prowess and sacrifice of great heroes like Patroclus, Achilles, Ajax son of Telamon and many, many others who now lie under the soil of this land. The city still does not seem on the verge of falling, even now. Every attempt we make is frustrated and not even the valour of the son of Achilles has been enough to breach the Skaian Gate. The time has come to put an end to this endless war before it destroys us. The only way is to conquer Troy. And that is just what we'll do . . .

'Now!'

My listeners, except for Agamemnon and Nestor, looked at each other in disbelief. Some of them uttered cutting comments, others laughed in scorn.

'Tomorrow, as soon as evening falls, our entire fleet will put to sea. Our ships will move away from the coast and then, under cover of darkness, will drop anchor behind the nearby island of Tenedos and remain there, hidden. As the ships go out, I will stay here, in this tent, along with those whose names I will now call . . .

'Menelaus Atreides, for you this war has been fought, for you the moment so long awaited has come: you will win Troy and avenge your honour! Ajax of Locris, bronze lightning bolt, you who are the swiftest after Achilles: you will be the first to reach the highest point of the city. Diomedes of Argus, it is said that in battle you wounded Ares himself, the god of war, and I believe that, for no one can better you in hurling your mighty, massive spear, always thirsting for blood, straight at your target. Idomeneus, powerful sovereign of Crete, lord of the labyrinth, you will not lose your way even if the roads of Troy are dark and winding; you will emerge victorious and set the city ablaze. Eurymachus, your sight is as penetrating as a nocturnal predator's, and I've never seen you tremble: your eyes will rend the darkness for all of us. Makahon, pupil of Asclepius, warrior surgeon, you who know so well how to restore life will inflict death! Menestheus of Athens, lord of the city which belonged to Theseus, you will show us that you are worthy of sitting on his throne. Merion . . . Sthenelus . . .'

As I called out their names, I looked intensely at their faces: they were tense, drawn, some of them seemed daunted; they had no idea yet of what they were being called upon to do. '. . . Thoas of Calydon, you were Achilles' best ally; Podalirius, inseparable companion of Makahon, we'll sorely need your arts . . . Teucer! With you the spirit of Great Ajax, your brother, will surely be present to win this war with us. Neoptolemus, known as Pyrrhus, son of Achilles: the fire that will devour the city will be redder than your flaming locks! You will attain what your father would have achieved had not a god stood in his way, for nothing less than a god could have stopped Achilles.

'All of you will enter Troy with me, inside the horse. The horse will be transported into the city by the Trojans themselves; I can assure you that this will happen. When the horse is in place, one of our men will signal from the shore to our comrades on Tenedos. The fleet will head back again, without masts or sails, moving solely by the force of their oars. Invisible, our ships will return to Troy. We will wait for the middle of the night, when the city has finished celebrating the end of the war, and is enveloped in silence and darkness. Only then will we leave the horse, and take control of the Skaian Gate. We'll signal from high up on the towers and we will open from the inside the doors that we've never been able to force from the outside. Our men will rush in and take the city by storm. And that will be the end of Troy.

'I will have complete command over the entire operation. We will take Epeius, the builder of the horse, with us. Only he knows how to unlatch the belly of the monster. He is still unaware of this plan, but he will soon be informed. I've chosen you because you are the best. Your names will be remembered for centuries to come . . .

'Who is with me, then? If you are ready to join me, stand up now!'

Pyrrhus was the first to speak, with his usual arrogance. 'You're talking to us as if we were about to accomplish some glorious feat, and instead it is with deceit that you propose we take the city. We'll enter Troy in hiding, closed up in the dark like rats, and surprise the Trojans in their sleep. Is this the glory you offer us?'

'Yes, it is,' I replied. 'A man is not made only of muscles and tendons. A man's mind is his highest, most noble part: it is what makes us similar to the gods. And it is our most powerful weapon. You've been given the chance to conquer the city by fighting on the open field, Pyrrhus: it doesn't appear to me that you've succeeded. I may not have the brawn of Great Ajax and I certainly don't have the vigour of your years and the force of Achilles that lives on in your limbs.

'You know what they call me: I'm Odysseus of the labyrinthine mind. This is my greatest strength: where your father's arm failed my mind will succeed! But you are free to make a choice. You can enter Troy with me using this trick, because I need the best of you, and no cowards. Or you can stay with *wanax* Agamemnon, or even here in your own tent.'

A moment laden with uncertainty followed, until, one after another, all of those summoned got to their feet and agreed to submit to my command with immediate effect, until the moment in which the great Atreides, *wanax* Agamemnon himself, would stride across the crooked Skaian Gate.

★

We didn't meet again until dusk of the next evening. From outside we could hear the shouts of the warriors who were pushing the ships off the beach, one after another, until they filled up the whole bay. They put to sea, wrapped in darkness.

At that point Sinon, with his hands bound behind his back, bruises covering his face and body, was already in the hiding place where the Trojans would find him the next day. We left my tent to find Epeius, who, finally informed of the true plan, was waiting for us. The hatch in the horse's belly was open, and a rope ladder was hanging from one side of the opening. One by one we climbed in, me first and then all the others. Epeius got in with us and closed the hatch, pulling up the ladder after himself. The lamp he carried created a small globe of flickering light that allowed us to exist. I took it from Epeius' hands and inspected my men. Pyrrhus was with us: I counted him first, then all the others. For each one of them I had a word, a touch on the shoulder, a look. Then, all at once, as I got to the end, I swiftly drew my sword and put it to the throat of a man whose face was covered – he was not one of the men I had summoned. I challenged him: 'Who are you, friend? Speak up or prepare to die!'

He lowered his hood and smiled.

'Eumelus!'

'I held out for two years in Eurystheus' palace, you don't think I can spend a night in here? You can't imagine that I'm afraid of the dark.'

Epeius spoke up: 'I can't open the hatch up and then close it again; it might become damaged in a visible way.'

I had to surrender. I sighed: 'And your horses? Who will care for them?' I asked Eumelus.

'They're hidden in a safe place. I'll see them again soon.'

We spent the first part of the night speaking in whispers. About the expedition, about friendly and hostile gods, about our fears, about the friends we'd lost and those remaining.

'What if they realize we're in here? What will we do then?' asked Thoas.

345

'I'll think about that when it happens,' I said. 'But I don't think it will.'

'If we succeed,' asked Diomedes, 'what will we do? Who will we spare and who will we kill? Who will be sold as a slave or liberated? Who will decide how to distribute the spoils?'

I did not answer and a long silence ensued. Each of us remained alone with his own thoughts until the dawn.

THE LIGHT OF morning filtered through the gaps between one board and another and striped our faces black and grey. We were tense and restless. Some of us had fallen asleep during the night, in particular Pyrrhus – *boys are such heavy sleepers.*

'Listen!' hissed Ajax Oileus. 'There's someone out there.'

'This is it!' I answered. 'From this moment on, silent and completely still. One mistake and we're all dead.'

We could hear people running, scampering, all around us. Shouts, and then cries of joy. 'They've gone! We've won! We've won!' And then again: 'The king! King Priam is on his way here!'

Epeius caught my eye and gestured towards several slits in the wall that were wide enough to see out of. They were invisible from the outside because they were too high from the ground and embedded in the horse's rough outer surface. I could see a stream of people pouring out of the Skaian Gate and from the other gate in the lower part of the city: men, women, the old and the young as well, children who had known nothing but war. They were looking around them as if they couldn't believe their eyes. They examined the deep furrows left by the ships' keels as they had been pushed into the water, the traces of the hastily disassembled tents, the hearths where so many years of blazing fires had blackened and hardened the ground until it seemed made of stone. And the forges where our swords and the cruel heads of bitter darts and spears had been fashioned. Many of them were weeping with joy and my heart shuddered, because I was plotting the last night of their life on earth, their last day of freedom.

Then the crowd parted and Priam's chariot passed. I hadn't seen him since that time so long before when I'd gone with Menelaus to Troy to ask him to return Helen. He looked haggard: a wrinkle as deep as a wound crossed his forehead and his cheeks were gaunt. How many sons, born of wife or concubines, had he lost on the battlefield? But among those sons, and above all the rest, it was the loss of his greatly beloved Hector, bulwark of his kingdom and his city, that had broken his heart.

He got out of the chariot and walked all the way under the horse's belly. I moved to the centre, at the cavity's lowest point, without making the slightest noise. I could see his white hair, the amber brooch pinned to his left shoulder. It felt like I would be able to touch him if I held out my hand.

Then, a confused murmur of voices started to sound all around, a question, floating in the air: 'What is that?' No one answered. I was trembling. If Sinon wasn't found, our adventure would end up in the most humiliating and ignominious way. A shout: 'One of the enemy! They've captured him!'

The buzz of voices became much louder.

'Sinon,' I whispered to my comrades. 'They found him.' Another step towards completing my plan.

I could finally see him myself. Bound, his clothes in tatters, his hair tangled, clots of blood on his left arm. He threw himself at the king's feet, imploring his mercy. I couldn't hear his words but I could see the expressions on their faces, the gestures of his king and the attitude of his men, which were all just as I had expected. I was heartened and I nodded to my men so they would be encouraged as well. They were accustomed to moving freely on an open field and facing off against the enemy, and this had to be a deeply uneasy moment for them: they were impotent prisoners, surrounded by a great crowd of people, including many armed men.

The wind changed direction and I could hear Priam's and Sinon's voices. 'Why did they make it of such enormous dimensions?' the king was asking.

'So it cannot be taken up to the citadel. It is written that, if that were to happen, one day all of Asia would rise up in vengeance over these many years of slaughter and their vast armies would tear down the walls of Mycenae and Argus.'

A sudden shout that all of us heard distinctly: 'Burn it! That's no votive gift; it's certainly a threat. Anything that comes from our enemies is a danger to us and must be destroyed!' The head of a spear suddenly came up through the horse's belly, penetrating a full hand's width into our midst. The loud thud of impact and the prolonged vibration of the shaft invaded our dark cavern.

Thoas grabbed hold of the bolt on the hatch, growling: 'I don't want to die in this damned trap!'

Menelaus and I stopped him and held him still until he had calmed down. I moved back to my observation point: there was complete silence outside and everyone seemed to be looking straight up at me . . . then I heard Priam say: 'If this is a gift to Poseidon, only a god can tell us what we must do. Laocoön, you will immolate a sacrifice on the sea to the blue god who built our city. He will surely give us a response.'

So the man who had thrust his spear into the horse was a priest. A bull was dragged into the sea and this Laocoön, assisted by two adolescents, his sons I suppose, lowered an axe onto the neck of the animal, which was felled on the first stroke. A wide pool of blood formed on the surface of the sea. From my high vantage point, I could see the blue waters being stained vermilion red. Then, all at once, the surface of the sea started to boil. Two tails sprang out of the water and high fins slashed through the waves. In an instant, the priest and the two boys were dragged down under the water and devoured, their blood mixing with that of the sacrificed bull.

As a sailor, I've always known that blood can attract predators from the depths. But given those circumstances, the response had to be read as favourable to us: the blue god was obviously not pleased that a votive gift meant to win his protection be profaned by the thrust of a spear, or threatened with destruction by fire. He had sent two of his creatures from the abyss to punish the priest's sacrilege.

Priam gave orders that the horse be towed all the way up to the citadel, so due honours could be paid to the votive offering, which would be dedicated, in a solemn ceremony, to Poseidon. It was necessary to demolish the lintel at the top of the lower gate, in order to let the horse pass through.

My comrades regarded me with an admiration that I'd never seen in their eyes before. Everything I had predicted was coming true. Eumelus approached me and said in a whisper: 'Do you still think I should have stayed with my horses?'

'It's not over yet, Eumelus. You're already thinking of the moment of victory and glory. The triumphant cry of war and Troy in flames. But the worst is yet to come. I can promise you, if everything does go according to my plan, what you will see and do tonight will leave a deep wound in your heart, an unhealable wound, because every time that you kill – defenceless people fleeing from you or adversaries that are already scattered, defeated, humiliated – a part of you will die as well.'

I don't know whether Eumelus understood what I was trying to tell him and I was never able to ask him what he felt. I lost sight of him that terrible night and I never saw him again.

As we were being pulled into the city, we could hear the cries of exultation outside, sounds of feasting and celebration, rivers of wine being poured. We were cramped inside, the muscles in our limbs painfully contracted, our stomachs knotted with anxiety. Only one last act stood between us and completion of the endeavour, and yet so many dangers still lay in wait. Even if the gods had turned their gaze from the city, they emanated a dreadful energy that I could feel all around us.

When silence finally fell over the city and the revellers had all moved on, I heard a light step outside, near the horse. I asked the others in a whisper: 'Did you hear that?'

'Yes, a footstep,' replied Diomedes.

'A footstep,' confirmed Menelaus.

'I heard it too, a footstep,' said Sthenelus.

'A footstep,' I murmured to myself. Who could be out there, roaming around so late at night, ready to expose our scheme?

'It's me, Penelope!' said a voice.

'Penelope? Is that you?' asked my heart and I held my breath. I couldn't believe it.

'Aegialia, my love,' called out Diomedes, the implacable warrior.

'Tecmessa!' exclaimed the cavernous voice of Ajax from the otherworld. Teucer wept to hear it.

'Arete!' shouted Sthenelus and he leaned foward to open the hatch, but I stopped him, putting my hand over his mouth so that I was nearly suffocating him.

'Helen,' said Menelaus finally. 'Only Helen.'

She, I thought, she is all women . . . In her voice each one of us had recognized that of his bride, his beloved, forever longed for, forever desired. Her footsteps faded away into the distance.

34

Helen.

Had she come to tempt us? Had she come to trick us into revealing ourselves? Or had she, perhaps, come to tell us that she was aware of our deception but would not reveal us?

That was a night of blood and deceit.

When it was very late and everything was peaceful and silent around us, I gave Epeius the order to open the hatch and one by one we lowered ourselves down to the ground on the rope ladder. I looked at the constellations in the sky: 'By this time the fleet will be coming ashore. Go to the towers and launch the signal.' Each one of us knew what we had to do. Diomedes, Pyrrhus and Ajax Oileus were to eliminate the guards and take their places on the towers on either side of the Skaian Gate. Eumelus would signal using a torch that we had been successful. The others, including me, would provide cover for our comrades and, if necessary, defend our positions until reinforcements arrived.

Everything had gone perfectly up to that moment. I saw Eumelus' torch moving to the right and then to the left three times; he stopped and then repeated the signal. What followed was the longest time of our lives. We could still fail: a delay, a misunderstanding, an accident . . . finally another light blinked on and off from the beach. The fleet had landed. At that point I was certain that Troy's destiny was in our hands. But I refused to exult in the idea of victory until I'd seen our army charging through the Skaian Gate, finally agape.

The pounding of thousands of heavy footsteps, the clatter of weapons . . .

'It's them!' exclaimed Diomedes.

'Open the gate!' I shouted with all the breath I had in my lungs. The moment that I'd awaited for years.

The hinges creaked mightily and then the heavy bronze-plated doors swung open. The army poured into the city like a river in flood.

Troy, from that moment on, was completely at the mercy of the invading forces. The alarm wasn't sounded until it was too late. Many of the defenders, awakened by the fracas and by the cries of terror of the population, threw on their armour and rushed into the streets, prepared to fight to the last drop of blood. Others took position in front of the doors to their own homes, to defend their wives and children, but were cut down where they stood by a vastly superior force. We were drunk on the slaughter now, furious at the years spent in endless combat, dying to stamp out the per-severing, insuperable resistance of proud Troy.

The entire city was plunged into a vortex of horror. There was no way, nor was there the will, to check the endless violence of our warriors who raged on and on, killing, destroying, raping and sacking. Fights broke out between our own men, turning into bloody brawls as they quarrelled over their prey: precious objects, fabrics, weapons, women. After a short time, fires started to burn in various parts of the city: in the lower quarters first and then, as the hours went by, the flames began to lick at the citadel. The blaze spread swiftly, roaring from one point to another of the high city.

It was there that the final defence was concentrated. There were the king and the queen, their sons and wives. There were the last valiant defenders of the city and the kingdom: Aeneas and Deiphobus, Hector's brother. There was Andromache, his widow, with their infant son, Astyanax.

There was Helen.

I tried to imagine what she was doing, how she was feeling at the sight of the holocaust of the city that had welcomed her as a daughter. How she felt about the inevitable arrival of Menelaus, her betrayed husband.

There the frenzy of the fight – the roaring flames and the din of clashing weapons – had reached its apex.

That was where I was headed, running, because I still had one last task to fulfil. I'd already entered the walls of Troy twice before, once by the light of day and once under the cover of night, and the image of the roads and squares, the monuments and palaces, was still vivid in my mind.

I was looking for the house of Antenor, the man who had foreseen this ruin and who had come to me in an attempt to avoid it. I had been his guest and was beholden to him. I owed him the only possible gift I could offer him now: his life and that of his family.

I found the road, and the house, besieged by hundreds of infuriated warriors. They recognized me and I was able to push my way through to the main door. I shouted to the men milling around me, exhorting them to rush immediately to the ramp leading up to the sanctuaries and the citadel, where Aeneas was leading a counterattack and reinforcements were needed. It was difficult to get them to obey me, but when they had finally gone, I entered, struggling to find my way down the corridors and through the rooms, crossing walls of flames, until I finally found him. He was grasping a spear and he aimed it at me.

'It's Odysseus!' I shouted. 'Follow me, take your family! Show me a way to leave the city from the north.'

He understood. I returned outside and he immediately joined me, followed by a number of weeping children and women. We ran as fast as we could down dark, twisting roads, through quarters already destroyed by fire, until we got to a side gate.

He stopped for an instant and gave me a long look of infinite pain. His eyes were full of tears.

'This was our destiny,' he said. 'It was written that it would end this way, but may the gods reward you for showing us mercy.'

'Run,' I answered him. 'Don't stop until you get to a place

where you can find help, on the sea or in the mountains. No one will follow you.'

I kept my eyes on them for as long as I could make them out in the reflection of the fires, until they were swallowed up into the night.

Then I turned back towards the citadel. The end was near: Pyrrhus, flanked by two enormous warriors, was brandishing an axe and pounding it into the palace door, which finally exploded into a thousand splinters. He rushed in, followed by his Myrmidons. He came out again onto the high gallery, not long after he'd entered, letting out a bloodcurdling cry and holding aloft his horrifying trophy: Priam's head. The most powerful city of Asia, and her king, were decapitated. Weeping and moaning pierced the autumn night, flocks of birds wheeled over Troy in wide circles, like the spirits of the dead, their purple wings reflected in the flames.

Little by little, as the last pockets of resistance were eliminated, a long line of prisoners began to form: mostly women and children, but even some men, to be sold off as slaves. The Achaian kings and princes gathered to divide up the spoils. Pyrrhus saw Andromache with her crying child in her arms; perhaps someone had pointed her out to him. He immediately claimed Hector's widow for himself. He pulled her out of the line, exclaiming: 'This one is mine!' But then, irritated by the baby's frightened bawling, he tore the child from his mother's arms, strode over to the walls and flung him over the side onto the cliffs below.

I did nothing to stop him because it was me who had created that monster. He was obeying the law of war: the war isn't over until the last descendant of the enemy is dead. The crushing of those tiny limbs thus extinguished the bloodline of glorious Hector, tamer of horses, the man who had come to set fire to our ships, who had incessantly defended Troy for ten long years and who, in the end, had succumbed only to Achilles' spear. Andromache let out a scream that didn't sound human, the agonized shriek of a wounded eagle. She collapsed to the ground as if dead.

But Pyrrhus wasn't finished. He went back to the line of prisoners and yanked out the youngest of Priam's daughters, lovely Polyxena. He seized her by the hair and proceeded to drag her all the way to the tomb of Achilles, and there he sacrificed her to his father's angry shade, opening her throat with his sword.

I hadn't finished either. I had to reach the sanctuary of the citadel, where the image of Athena was preserved, the one I had seen that night long ago. As I was making my way, I met Diomedes and together we continued to the apex of the high city. We weren't the first to arrive. As we approached, we saw Ajax Oileus leaving the sanctuary and running off swiftly. We entered and saw Athena's priestess and protectress, Priam's daughter Cassandra, the princess I had seen weeping the night I had furtively entered the temple. Cassandra, sad prophet of Troy's end, was splayed on the ground half naked, and her bruised and bloodied body showed the signs of the rape she'd suffered.

She looked at me and in a faint voice said: 'He is cursed . . . he will die.' I glanced up at the image of the goddess and it seemed to me that her eyes were closed, loath to witness such horror. As I was staring at that stone face, Calchas' voice rang out in my mind: this was the most powerful idol of the entire world, the sacred image that made the city that possessed her invincible against any human or divine force, except one: the hand of Fate!

I prayed in my heart that my goddess would not abandon me and would continue to hold her hand on my head . . . We took Cassandra back with us, to the ruins of palace where all the prisoners were being held. Agamemnon, our supreme leader, claimed her for himself. Thunder rumbled in the distance, and in the flickering light of the conflagration I saw a figure at the top of the ramp: *wanax* Menelaus. His hair red as fire, his armour bloodied, he was leading proud Helen by her hand, her breasts bared. He had possessed her, they say, in the bedroom spattered with the blood of Deiphobus, her last husband after Paris. When the palace had fallen, the Trojan prince had rushed to defend his own home and there, at Helen's feet, he had been slain.

*

VALERIO MASSIMO MANFREDI

THE DAWN of the following day illuminated a desolate expanse. A grey desert streaked with whispers of stagnant smoke. Mount Ida hulked against the leaden sky, her peak hidden, encircled by ashen fog. The Scamander and Simoeis flowed sluggishly, thick with slime and mud. There was no strip of land that had not been slashed or wounded, not a single building in glorious Troy that stood where it once had. No forest had survived the years of axes chopping down trunks for the pyres of the dead. Victory had the bitter tang of blind violence and the wailing of women and children was as keen as a sacrificial blade, shrill and incessant. Only the three black-veiled Moirai rejoiced, dancing over the field of death, appearing and vanishing in the dull morning air.

Our great endeavour had drowned in a sea of tears.

The spoils distributed, the women and the weapons divided, *wanax* Agamemnon, grey-faced, convened the council of kings and princes. He proposed that we offer solemn sacrifice to the gods to appease the shades of the dead and to make the outcome of our return voyages favourable. Nestor, lord of Pylos, dissented, saying that we must all leave immediately, before the harsh winter weather set in. Once we were safely back in our homelands, we could offer sacred hecatombs. Many agreed with him. After much dispute, it was decided that each of us should be free to remain or leave at once.

I joined the latter, so eager was I to begin my return voyage, to forget these ten long years of life lost, of weeping and burning, of solitary vigils steeped in aching nostalgia, of friends lost, of spent ashes that the wind had carried off over the sea.

Of the twelve ships I had set off with, only seven returned with me now. We burned the others, because the men who had left Ithaca with me and had sat at those long oars were gone. They were dead. They now lie beneath the deserted fields of Troy. Weeping, we shouted out the name of each one of them ten times, so the wind would carry him all the way to the home of his distant parents, still waiting for news, choked with dread.

We thus set sail and rapidly reached Tenedos, as the sun, finally free of the black shroud of smoke, came out and lit up the sea. I took a deep breath and it felt like a return to life. For an instant I caught a glimpse of a fabulous glittering of bronze, silver and orichalch: my precious treasure, my share of the spoils, hidden under the planks at the prow. But the moment was fleeting. Black clouds soon gathered at the centre of the sky and a cold wind started to blow.

I felt a sharp pain piercing my heart then, heard a voice and a bolt of thunder echoing from the mountains. Who was calling me? I found out instantly, when I turned to look at the shore we had just left.

I shouted out: 'Strike the sails! Dismast! Return to your oars, we're going back!'

My men obeyed my command. The ships turned, lining up one behind the other. The prows furrowed waves that boiled higher and higher, tipped with foam. The shore was slowly getting closer; the mound on the Rhoetean promontory guided me in. My ship gained the shore and the men dropped anchor. I think they understood. I took the armour of Achilles from the bow and bound it all together with a thick rope: his storied shield, the embossed greaves, the shining breastplate, the crested helmet and the invincible sword. I jumped off the ship and my feet touched the gravel on the sea bottom. It took enormous effort for me to move forward and the weight of the bronze dragged me back every time a breaking wave pulled away powerfully from the shore.

I bent my back like an ox under the yoke, breathing hard, forcing one foot in front of the other until I finally made it to the beach. My brow and my face and my hair were dripping with seawater, huge drops that clouded my sight.

There before me rose the immense burial mound of Great Ajax, bulwark of the Achaians. I laid the shining armour of Achilles on the altar that covered his ashes. Ten times I shouted his name, raising my voice higher than the howling wind. Zeus thundered. My tears mixed with those of the sky.

Author's Note

This novel and its sequel are inspired by the Trojan Epic Cycle and tell the story of Odysseus, son of Laertes, king of Ithaca, from his birth to his last journey.

Odysseus is the absolute protagonist of the *Iliad* as well as the *Odyssey*, which is completely dedicated to him, but he is also central to the other poems in the cycle, which were oral poems at their origin and were perhaps put into writing around the 8th century BC. These have been completely lost, except for a few surviving fragments. This collection of ancient Greek epic poems still existed in Roman times and narrated the events preceding the Trojan War, the nine-year siege, the fall of Troy at Odysseus' hand thanks to the strategy of the horse, and the epilogue of the war, when the main heroes of the *Iliad* attempt to return to their homelands. Nearly all of these return journeys end in tragedy, and are remembered in part in Book 3 of the *Odyssey*, and also in Book 11, when Odysseus, like a shaman, calls up the shades of the dead from Hades.

Through the poems of this cycle, the figure of Odysseus was recovered by a poet of Cyrene named Eugammon in the 7th century BC, became known to 5th-century BC Greek dramatists like Aeschylus, Sophocles and above all Euripides, and was picked up again in Hellenistic times (3rd century BC) by Lycophron. Time and time again, over the centuries, great poets and writers, including Virgil, Dante, Shakespeare, Tennyson, Pascoli, Joyce and Cavafy, have brought him to life.

Clearly, each of these authors and poets, writing in very different ages and separated by great spans of time, have interpreted the figure of the hero in a wholly personal way, reflecting the writer's own historical period and creating a mirror for the men of his age, bringing Odysseus alive as a paradigm of humanity.

We therefore cannot – although this is often exactly what has been done – attribute specific qualities, vices and virtues to the figure of Odysseus that actually are a more accurate reflection of the epoch of the writer himself, who interprets our wandering hero according to the mores and mentality of his own time.

For this reason, I've tried to abide by the figure of Odysseus as reported by Homer, as he appears in the *Iliad* and the *Odyssey* and not in any later works. The way I see him is, of course, another interpretation, but this is, after all, the greatest characteristic of the 'classics', that they speak to men of all ages, maintaining their value and their vitality intact.

The language I've used is meant to transport the reader back to the ambience of the Homeric tradition. As far as possible, the syntax is simple and refrains from using complex sentence structures and concepts which are too abstract. Odysseus' story is narrated in a realistic key, not yet filtered or processed by the rich formulas of oral poetry in later centuries.

I've written this story with deep respect for the very ancient sources from which it takes inspiration, but I've decided to narrate Odysseus' tale using the voice of the protagonist in the first person, and thus in a very personal, 'realistic' form. In other words, I've tried to describe the facts and the events that might actually have generated the epic and mythological tales. The description that I give of Troy is largely based on the hypotheses of the late Manfred Korfmann, the German archaeologist who identified the ruins and walls on the hill of Hisarlik in Turkey as the citadel of Troy, at the foot of which an extensive 'lower city' lay, surrounded by a mud-brick wall and a ditch.

As far as the names of the characters are concerned, for the English-language version I've preferred the Latin spellings, with a few exceptions which remain in Greek: Odysseus instead of Ulysses, Autolykos instead of Autolycus, Skaian instead of Scaean Gates, Achaia and Achaians instead of Achaea and Achaeans.

As for the historical veracity of the Trojan War, it's difficult to say whether it was really ever fought and why it became the subject of such a vast epic cycle of literature. Today, most scholars believe that the Homeric poems reflect the distant echo of an event that actually occurred, perhaps the last common endeavour of a world that was already in its death throes. We cannot exclude the hypothesis that the war itself, as long and difficult as it was and with such massive loss of life, and the resulting extended absence of kings and aristocrats, was the cause of the decline of the peoples and civilizations that fought it. Perhaps, then, a handful of Mycenaean barons assaulting a stronghold on the Hellespont straits were transformed by Homer into a gathering of giants, their endeavours remembered in an epic tale that lies at the very roots of the history of Western culture.

Characters and Places

Amphithea – queen of Acarnania, wife to Autolykos, mother of
   Anticlea, grandmother of Odysseus

Anticlea – queen mother of Ithaca, wife to Laertes, mother of
   Odysseus

Arcesius – father of Laertes, husband to Chalcomedusa, grandfather
   of Odysseus

Autolykos – king of Acarnania, husband to Amphithea, father of
   Anticlea, grandfather of Odysseus

Chalcomedusa – mother of Laertes, wife to Arcesius, grandmother of
   Odysseus

Laertes – king of Ithaca before Odysseus, only son of Arcesius,
   husband to Anticlea, father of Odysseus. Argonaut.

Odysseus – king of Ithaca and of the Ionian islands, only son of
   Laertes and Anticlea, husband to Penelope, father of Telemachus.
   Inventor of the stratagem of the Trojan Horse, he thus became
   known as *ptoliethros*, 'destroyer of cities'. Homer's *Iliad* also calls
   him 'divine', 'very patient' and 'of cunning intelligence'. His
   adventures during his long and dramatic journey back to Ithaca
   give rise to the second Homeric poem, the *Odyssey*.

Penelope – queen of Ithaca, daughter of Icarius and Polycaste of
   Sparta, wife to Odysseus, mother of Telemachus

Telemachus – prince of Ithaca, only son of Odysseus and Penelope

GODS, GODDESSES AND SUPERNATURAL BEINGS

Aphrodite – goddess of love; she convinces Paris to name her the fairest of three goddesses (Athena, Aphrodite and Hera). In exchange she promises him he will possess the most beautiful woman in the world.

Apollo – god of sun and light, an archer. God of prophecy. Sides with Troy in the Trojan War.

Ares – god of war. On the side of the Trojans in the war.

Athena – daughter of Zeus, from whose brain she sprang directly, fully armed. Goddess of wisdom and protectress of Odysseus.

Boreas – the north wind

Cerberus – three-headed dog of Hades

Chaera – personification of Death

Hephaestus – the blacksmith of the gods. Forges the armour of Achilles.

Hera – sister and wife of Zeus. Protectress of the family and pregnant women. In the Trojan War, she was on the Achaians' side.

Moirai – the three Fates, who control the thread of life of every mortal from birth to death

Persephone – daughter of Demeter, goddess of nature and the earth. Kidnapped by Hades, she lives six months in the Underworld with her husband and six months on the earth with her mother. Symbol of the seasons.

Poseidon – brother of Zeus, son of Kronos. God of the sea and the ocean.

Thanatos – personification of Death

Zeus – father of all the gods, husband to Hera, son of Kronos. Personification of thunder and lightning.

CHARACTERS

Achilles – prince of Phthia, son of Peleus and the sea goddess Thetis. The greatest hero of the Achaian army. A prophecy foretold that he would have to choose either a long but obscure life or a short but glorious one.

Admetus – king of Pherai in Thessaly, husband to Alcestis, father of Eumelus. Argonaut.

Adrastus – king of Argus, father-in-law of Tydeus, grandfather of Diomedes

Aeetes – king of Colchis, father of Medea

Aegialia – wife to Diomedes

Aeneas – prince of Dardania, son of Anchises and goddess Aphrodite, cousin to Hector. Ally of Troy.

Agamemnon – king of Mycenae, high king of the Achaians, son of Atreus, brother of Menelaus, husband to Clytaemnestra, father of Iphigenia

Ajax Oileus – prince of Locris, close friend of Great Ajax

Ajax son of Telamon (Great Ajax) – prince of Salamis, half-brother of Teucer, cousin of Achilles. The strongest hero of the Achaians after Achilles.

Alcestis – queen of Pherai, wife to Admetus, mother of Eumelus. She agrees to die in her husband's place and is saved by Hercules.

Amphiaraus – seer, from Argus. One of the 'Seven Against Thebes'. Argonaut.

Anaxibia – queen of Phocis, daughter of Atreus, sister of Agamemnon and Menelaus

Anchises – king of Dardania, father of Aeneas

Andromache – princess of Hypoplacian Thebes, daughter of Eetion, wife of Hector, mother of Astyanax

Antenor – Trojan nobleman, adviser to King Priam. Mediator between the Trojans and the Achaians.

Antilochus – prince of Pylos, son of Nestor, friend to Odysseus

Antiphus – comrade of Odysseus

Argonauts – Achaian heroes who took part in the expedition of the
Argo, led by Jason of Iolcus, to win the Golden Fleece in Colchis.
The sons of many Argonauts would go on to fight the Trojan
War.

Asclepius – legendary practitioner of the medical arts

Astyanax – infant son of Hector and Andromache

Atreidae – the house of Atreus

Atreides – one of the sons of Atreus, Agamemnon or Menelaus

Atreus – king of Mycenae, father of Agamemnon and Menelaus

Automedon – charioteer to Achilles and to Pyrrhus after Achilles'
death

Balius – one of Achilles' divine horses, 'the dappled'

Briseis – beloved concubine of Achilles, claimed by Agamemnon

Calchas – priest and seer, adviser to Agamemnon

Cassandra – princess of Troy, daughter of Priam and Hecuba, sister of
Hector, Paris and Deiphobus. She was given the gift of prophecy
by Apollo, who loved her but was spurned by her; he thus cursed
her so that her predictions would never be believed.

Castor – prince of Sparta, son of Tyndareus and Leda, twin of Pollux,
brother of Helen and Clytaemnestra. Argonaut, with his brother
Pollux. According to a legend, Castor's real father was Zeus, who
appeared to his mother in the form of a swan.

Chryseis – daughter of high priest Chryses, taken as a concubine by
Agamemnon. His refusal to return her to her father set off a great
plague and much strife in the Achaian camp.

Clytaemnestra – daughter of Tyndareus and Leda, sister of Castor,
Pollux and Helen, wife to Agamemnon. According to a legend,
her real father was Zeus, who appeared to her mother in the form
of a swan.

Damastes – trainer of Odysseus, a native of Thessaly

Deiphobus – prince of Troy, son of Priam and Hecuba, brother of
Hector and Paris, husband to Helen after Paris' death

Diomedes – king of Argus, son of Tydeus, husband to Aegialia, close
friend of Odysseus. One of the strongest heroes of Achaia.

Eetion – king of Hypoplacian Thebes, father of Andromache

Epeius – builder of the horse of Troy

Eumelus – prince of Pherai, son of Admetus and Alcestis

Eumeus – swineherd of Laertes

Euribates – comrade of Odysseus

Euriclea – nurse to Odysseus, affectionately called '*mai*' (grandmother) by him

Eurydice – queen of Pylos, wife to Nestor

Eurylochus – cousin of Odysseus and his most trusted comrade

Eurymachus – one of Odysseus' comrades in the horse of Troy

Eurystheus – king of Mycenae, cousin of Hercules

Hector – prince of Troy, eldest son of Priam and Hecuba, brother of Paris and Deiphobus, husband to Andromache, father of Astyanax. Killed in a duel with Achilles.

Hecuba – queen of Troy, wife of Priam, mother of Hector, Deiphobus, Paris, Cassandra, Polyxena

Helen – queen of Sparta, daughter of Tyndareus and Leda of Sparta, sister of Clytaemnestra, Castor and Pollux, wife to Menelaus, Paris and Deiphobus. According to a legend, Helen's real father was Zeus, who appeared to her mother in the form of a swan.

Hercules - son of Zeus and the mortal Alcmene, cousin of Eurystheus, who condemned him to perform the twelve labours. Argonaut.

Hermione – daughter of Menelaus and Helen

Icarius – brother of Tyndareus of Sparta, husband to Polycaste, father of Penelope

Ideus – herald of Priam

Idomeneus – king of Crete. Part of the Trojan expedition.

Iphigenia – daughter of Agamemnon and Clytaemnestra

Iphitus – brother of Eurystheus, king of Mycenae. Argonaut.

Jason – prince of Iolcus, leader of the Argonauts, husband to Medea

Laocoön – Trojan priest

Lapiths – a tribe of Thessaly, renowned for their physical size and prowess

Leda – queen of Sparta, wife of Tyndareus, mother of Castor, Pollux, Helen and Clytaemnestra. Legendary lover of Zeus.

Lycomedes – king of Scyros, grandfather of Neoptolemus (Pyrrhus)

Makahon – surgeon and warrior of Achaian army, pupil of Asclepius

Medea – princess of Colchis, daughter of Aeetes, wife to Jason. Enchantress.

Megara – queen of Mycenae, wife to Eurystheus

Melanippus – defender of Thebes, killed by Tydeus

Meleager – king of Aetolia, father-in-law of Protesilaus. Argonaut.

Menelaus – king of Sparta, son of Atreus, brother of Agamemnon, husband to Helen. He demands that all the Achaian kings and princes honour their oath to defend his reputation when Helen is abducted by Paris, provoking the Trojan War.

Menestheus – king of Athens, member of the Trojan expedition

Mentor – tutor of Odysseus, adviser to King Laertes

Myrmidons – warriors of Phthia in Thessaly, commanded by Achilles

Neoptolemus (Pyrrhus) – son of Achilles and Princess Deidamia of Scyros. After his father's death, he enters the Trojan War. Famed for his ferocity and ruthlessness.

Nestor – wise king of Pylos, husband to Eurydice, father of Antilochus and Pisistratus. Also known as the Knight of Gerene. The great adviser of the Achaian heroes.

Oedipus – king of Thebes. Killed his father and married his mother. His two sons, Eteocles and Polynices, killed each other in a duel over the throne.

Oileus - king of Locris, father of Ajax Oileus. Argonaut.

Paris – prince of Troy, son of Priam and Hecuba, brother of Hector, Deiphobus and Cassandra, husband of Helen after Menelaus. His abduction of Helen sets off the Trojan War.

Patroclus – cousin and trusted companion of Achilles. Killed in battle by Hector.

Peirithous – king of the Lapiths, a Thessalian tribe. Argonaut.

Peleus – king of Phthia, husband to Thetis, brother of Telamon, father of Achilles. Argonaut.

Pelias – king of Iolcus, father of Alcestis. Usurped the throne of Aeson and sent Jason in search of the golden fleece.

Perimedes – trusted comrade of Odysseus

Phemius – court poet of Laertes

Philoctetes – king of Malis, famed as an archer. Part of the Trojan expedition.

Pisistratus – prince of Pylos, youngest son of Nestor and Eurydice

Polites – comrade of Odysseus

Pollux – prince of Sparta, son of Tyndareus and Leda, twin of Castor, brother of Helen and Clytaemnestra. Argonaut, with his brother Castor. According to a legend, their real father was Zeus, who appeared to his mother in the form of a swan.

Polycaste – wife of Icarius, mother of Penelope

Polyxena – princess of Troy, youngest daughter of Priam and Hecuba. Sacrificed by Pyrrhus on tomb of Achilles.

Priam – king of Troy, husband to Hecuba, father of Hector, Paris, Deiphobus, Cassandra, Polyxena and many other sons and daughters. Killed and decapitated by Pyrrhus on the night of the fall of Troy.

Protesilaus – Thessalian king, the first Achaian to die in the Trojan War

Pyrrhus (Neoptolemus) – son of Achilles and Princess Deidamia of Scyros. After his father's death, he enters the Trojan War. Famed for his ferocity and ruthlessness.

Sinon – friend and comrade of Odysseus, persuades Trojans to pull the horse into the city

Sthenelus – Argive prince, charioteer of Diomedes

Telamon – king of Salamis, brother of Peleus, father of Great Ajax and Teucer. Argonaut.

Teucer – son of Telamon and Hesione (sister of Priam), half-brother of Great Ajax. Famous archer, part of the Trojan expedition.

Theseus – king of Athens, killer of the Minotaur

Thetis – wife to Peleus, mother of Achilles. Said to be a sea goddess or nymph.

Thoas – king of Calydon, killer of the boar of Calydon. Odysseus' comrade in the horse.

Thyestes – twin brother of Atreus

Characters and Places

Tydeus – Argive prince, father of Diomedes. Ruthless warrior, killed in battle at Thebes after slaying Melanippus. Argonaut.

Tyndareus – king of Sparta, husband to Leda, father of Castor and Pollux, Helen and Clytaemnestra, although according to a legend, their real father was Zeus, who appeared to their mother Leda in the form of a swan.

Xanthus – one of Achilles' divine horses, 'the blond'

Zetes and Calais – the Boreads, sons of the wind. Argonauts.

GEOGRAPHY

Acarnania – region of south-western Greece, facing Ithaca, ruled by Autolykos, Odysseus' grandfather

Achaia – an area generally corresponding to Greece

Acheron – river in Ephyra, said to be a gateway to Hades

Aetolia – region in western Greece ruled by Meleager

Arcadia – mountainous region in the central Peloponnese where the Sanctuary of the Wolf King is located

Argolis – region of Argus in the eastern Peloponnese

Argus – city in Argolis ruled by Diomedes, after Adrastus. 'Argus' means 'shining' city.

Arne – city of eastern Greece

Athens – main city of Attica, ruled by Theseus and Aegeus before him

Attica – region of central eastern Achaia that includes Athens

Aulis – bay and port in Boeotia where the Achaian army assembles for the assault on Troy

Boeotia – region of Thebes, where Aulis is located

Calydon – city of Aetolia, famous for the hunt of the Calydonian boar, in which all the major Achaian heroes of the Argonaut generation took part

Caucasus, Mount – mountain in Colchis

Chalcis – city of Euboea

370

Colchis – region between Caucasus and Pontus Euxinus (the Black
  Sea), ruled by king Aeetes. Place where the golden fleece was
  guarded by a dragon.
Corinth – city on the isthmus that connects the Peloponnese to
  mainland Greece, between the Gulf of Corinth and the Saronic
  Gulf
Crete – island ruled by Idomeneus
Dardania – region of north-western Anatolia, near Troy, kingdom of
  Anchises, ally of Troy
Dulichium – island, part of the kingdom of Odysseus
Elis – region of the north-western Peloponnese
Ephyra – place in Aetolia where an entrance to Hades was located
Euboea – the biggest island of Greece, after Crete
Eurotas - the river of Sparta
Gythium – port of Sparta on the Laconian Gulf
Hypoplacian Thebes – city south of the Troad, ruled by Eetion, ally
  of Troy
Iberia – modern Spain
Ida, Mount – mountain south of Troy
Ilium – the ancient name of Troy
Iolcus – city of Thessaly, ruled by Pelias, port of the Argonauts
Ithaca – island in the Ionian Sea, ruled by Odysseus, and Laertes
  before him
Knossos – capital of Crete
Laconian Gulf – the gulf between Cape Malea and Cape Tainaron
Leucas – island, part of the kingdom of Odysseus
Locris – region in western Greece, homeland of Ajax Oileus
Malea – cape in the central peninsula of the Peloponnese, notoriously
  difficult and dangerous to navigate
Messenia – kingdom of Nestor in the south-western Peloponnese
Mycenae – city of Argolis, ruled by Agamemnon, after Eurystheus
  and Atreus
Nemea – city of Argolis where Hercules killed the Nemean lion
Neritus, Mount – the tallest mountain of Ithaca

Olympus, Mount – mountain in northern Thessaly, said to be the abode of the gods

Ossa, Mount – mountain in Thessaly, said to be the abode of the centaurs

Othrys, Mount – mountain in Thessaly near Phthia, the city of Achilles

Parnassus, Mount – mountain in Phocis, believed to be the abode of Apollo and the Muses

Pelion, Mount – mountain in Thessaly where the pine tree used to build the keel of the *Argo* was cut down

Peloponnesus – the Peloponnese, the southern peninsula of Greece

Phasis – river in Colchis

Pherai – city in Thessaly, ruled by Admetus

Phocis – region in south central Greece

Phthia – city of Thessaly, ruled by Peleus, father of Achilles, famous for its valorous warriors, the Myrmidons

Pylos – main city of Messenia, ruled by Nestor

Rhoetean – promontory of the Troad, where the tomb of Great Ajax was located

Salamis – small island near Attica, ruled by Telamon, Great Ajax's father

Same – island, part of the kingdom of Odysseus, probably modern Cephalonia

Scamander – one of the two rivers of Troy

Scyros – island ruled by Lycomedes

Simoeis – one of the two rivers of Troy

Skaian Gate – gate of the Trojan citadel, built to be unassailable

Sounion – southern cape of Attica

Sparta – city of Laconia, also called Lacedaemon, ruled by Menelaus

Stygia – swamp in Hades

Tainaron – cape of the eastern Peloponnese

Taygetus, Mount – mountain in Laconia, west of Sparta

Tenedos – small island near Troy where the Achaian fleet hides while awaiting the signal for the assault on Troy

Characters and Places

Thebes – city of Boeotia, ruled by Oedipus
Thermodon – river in northern Anatolia, bordering the territory of
the Amazons
Thessaly – region of north-eastern Greece
Thrace – region of eastern Greece, north-west of Troy
Tiryns – city of Argolis, near Mycenae
Troad – region of Troy
Troy – city of the Troad which controlled access to the Dardanelles,
capital of the powerful kingdom of Priam, also known as 'Ilion'
('Ilium' in Latin) and 'Vilusa' in Hittite texts. Identified by
Schliemann and Blegen with the ruins on the hill of Hisarlik in
Turkey, recently confirmed by the excavations of the late Manfred
Korfmann. Ruled by Priam, it was besieged for nine years by the
Achaians and finally fell thanks to the stratagem of the Trojan
Horse
Zacynthus – island, part of the kingdom of Odysseus